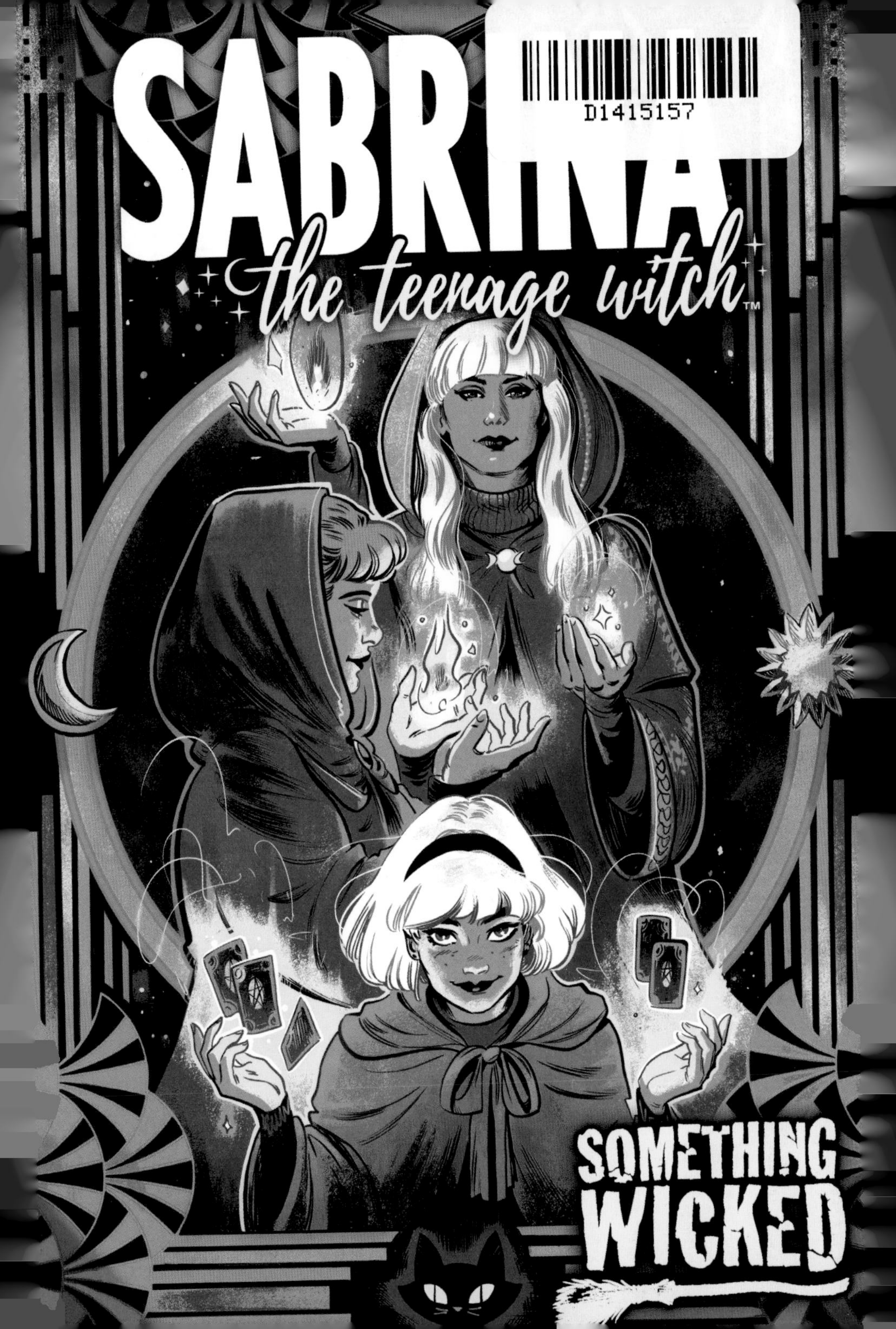
SABRINA
the teenage witch™
SOMETHING
WICKED

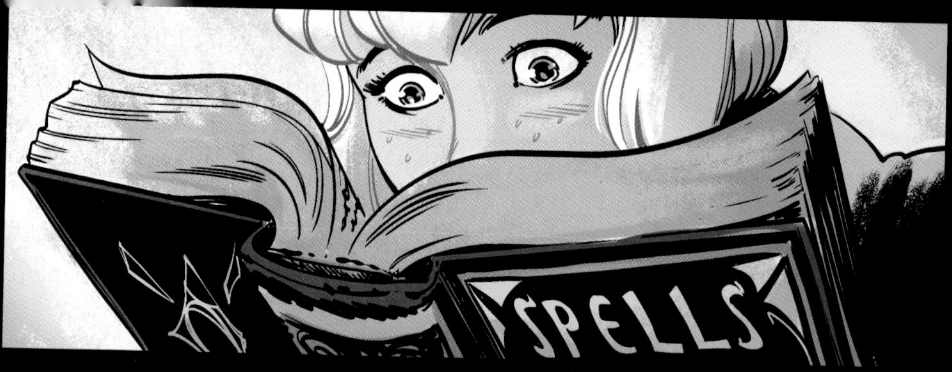
SPELLS

STORY BY
KELLY THOMPSON

EDITORS
ALEX SEGURA
AND **JAMIE LEE ROTANTE**

ASSOCIATE EDITOR
STEPHEN OSWALD

ASSISTANT EDITOR
VINCENT LOVALLO

EDITOR-IN-CHIEF
VICTOR GORELICK

PUBLISHER
JON GOLDWATER

ART BY
VERONICA FISH
AND **ANDY FISH**

LETTERING BY
JACK MORELLI

GRAPHIC DESIGN
KARI MCLACHLAN

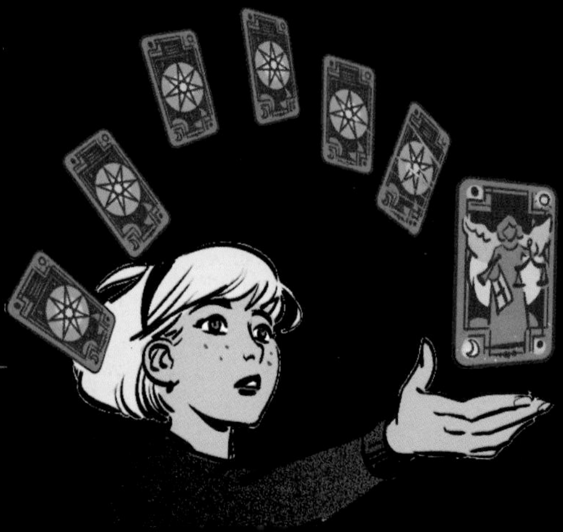

PREVIOUSLY IN...

SABRINA the teenage witch™

Sabrina Spellman is a witch—a teenage, half-mortal, half-magic witch, to be exact. And her first few days at her all-mortal high school, Greendale High, were... eventful to say the least. We're talking budding romances, spells gone awry, and magical beasts running amok *eventful*!

After thinking the worst of it was discovering that resident mean girl Radka Ransom was set on making her and her new BFF Jessa's life miserable, Sabrina soon learned that things were about to get a lot more complicated when she quickly caught feelings for handsome jock Harvey Kinkle. Followed quickly thereafter by catching feelings for mysterious bad boy Ren Ransom (yes, you guessed it: mean girl supreme Radka's brother!).

But those were just her mortal problems.

On the magical side, things were getting much, much worse. It turns out Radka and Ren weren't just obstacles in the hallways at school, outside they were also a shape-shifting wendigo. They weren't the only people targeted by dark magic, though, as Allen, a shy classmate, was also turned into a demon dragon beast. Upon hearing of Sabrina's encounters with these beings, her witch aunts Hilda and Zelda ventured into the woods to handle some unspoken magical business—and never returned! That is, until Sabrina and her former-warlock-turned-cat Salem came to their rescue, fighting off all the humans-turned-beasts and catching the eye of head witch Della in the process.

Unfortunately, she also caught the eye of Radka, who now knows her magical secret.

What's a teen witch to do?

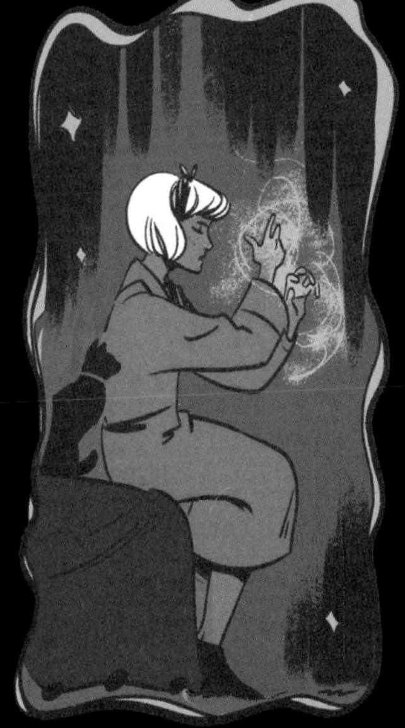

01

STORY BY
KELLY THOMPSON

ART BY
VERONICA FISH
AND ANDY FISH

LETTERING BY
JACK MORELLI

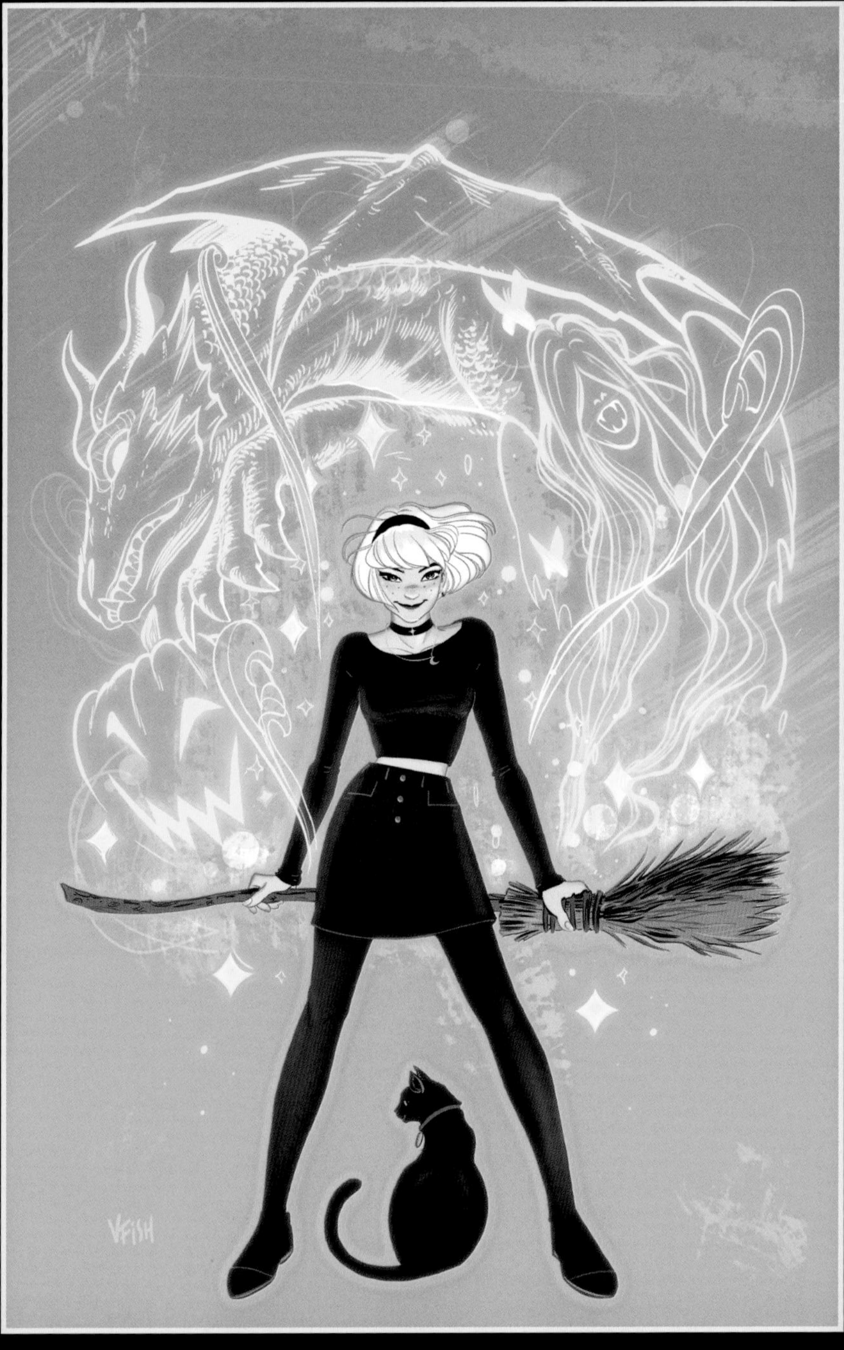
VFISH

COVER ART: VERONICA FISH

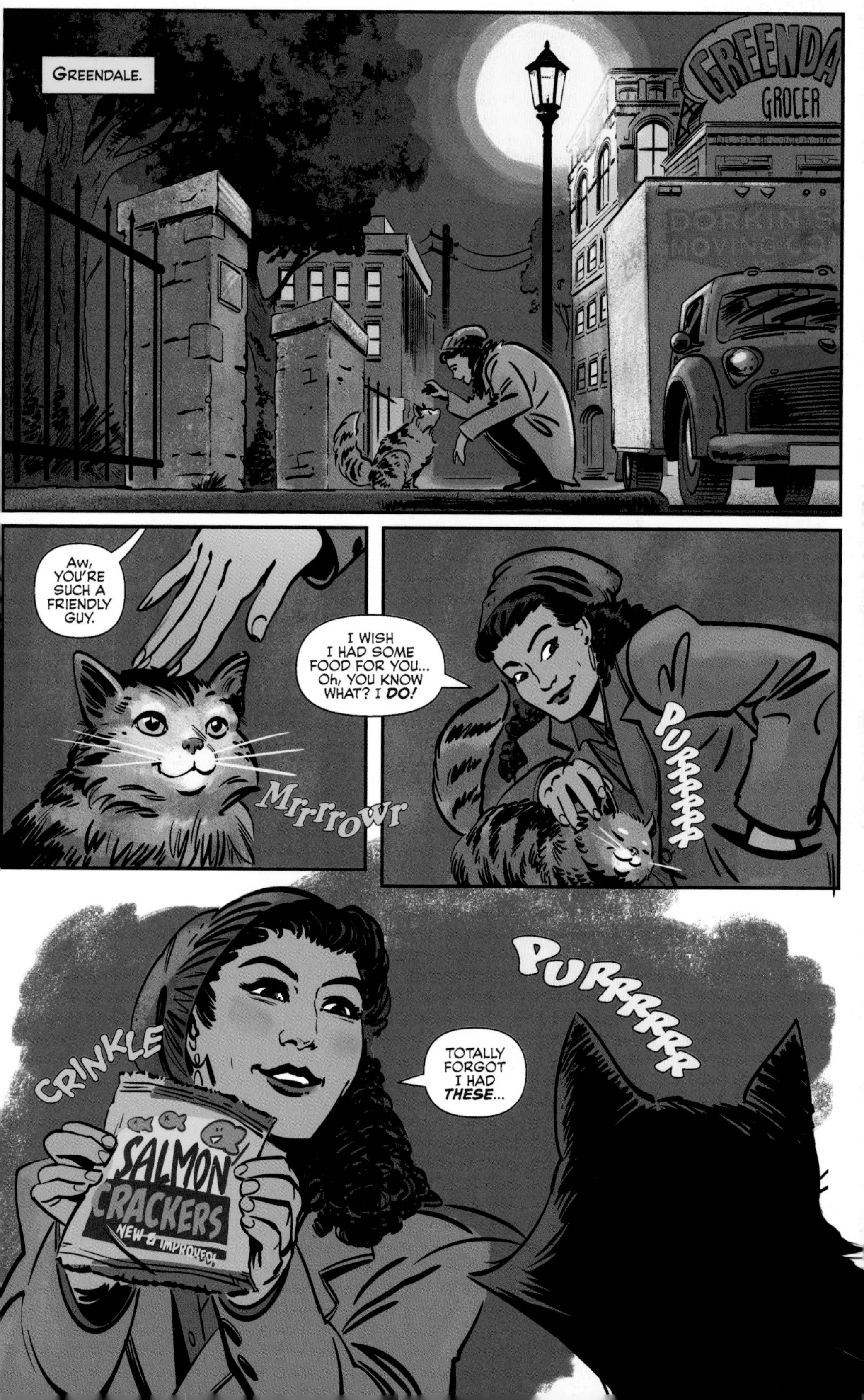
GREENDALE.
GREENDA
GROCER
DORKIN'S
MOVING CO
AW, YOU'RE SUCH A FRIENDLY GUY.
Mrrrrowr
I WISH I HAD SOME FOOD FOR YOU... Oh, YOU KNOW WHAT? I **DO!**
PURRRRR
CRINKLE
TOTALLY FORGOT I HAD ***THESE***...
PURRRRRR
SALMON CRACKERS
NEW & IMPROVED!

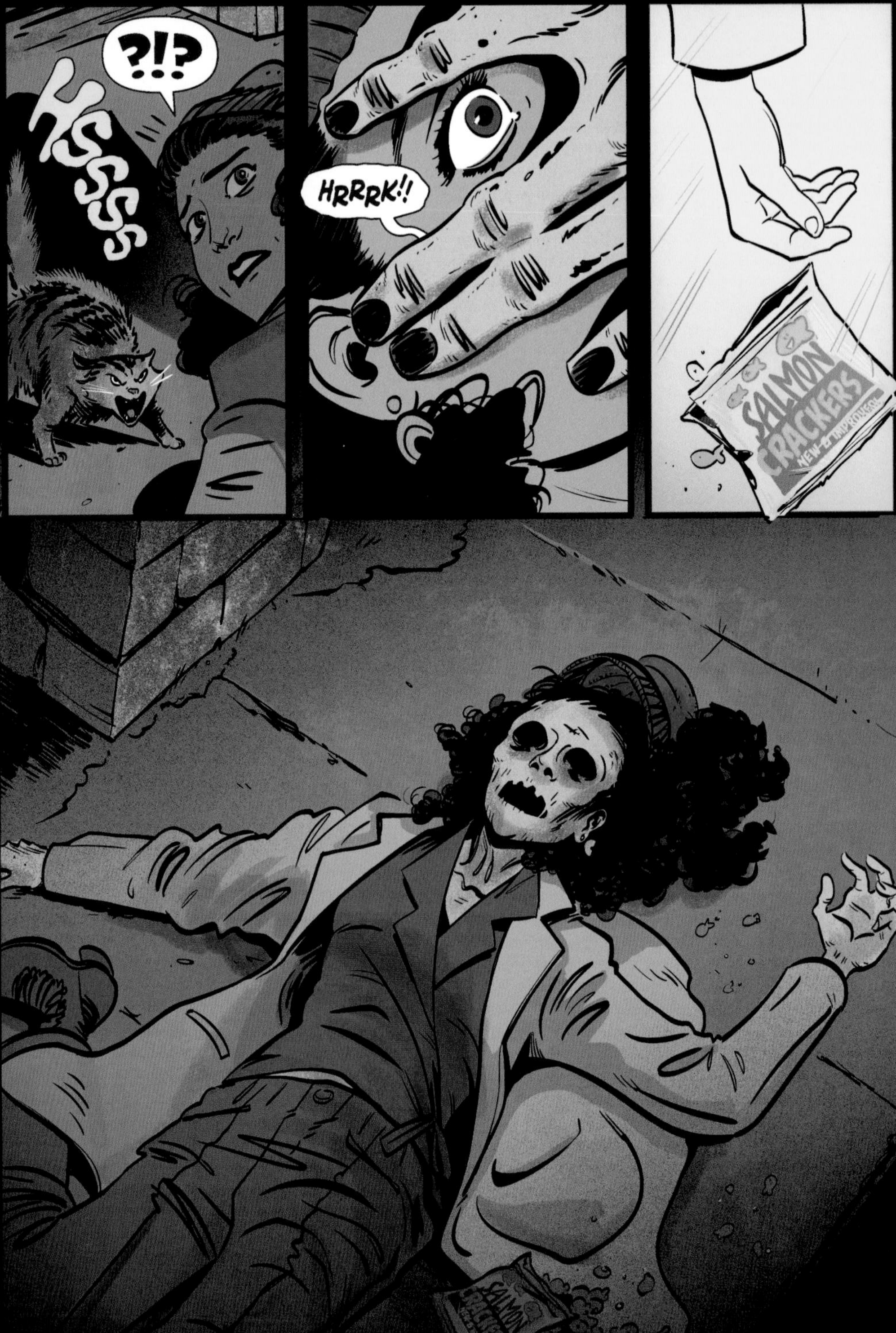
HSSSS
?!?
HRRRK!!
SALMON CRACKERS
NEW & IMPROVED!

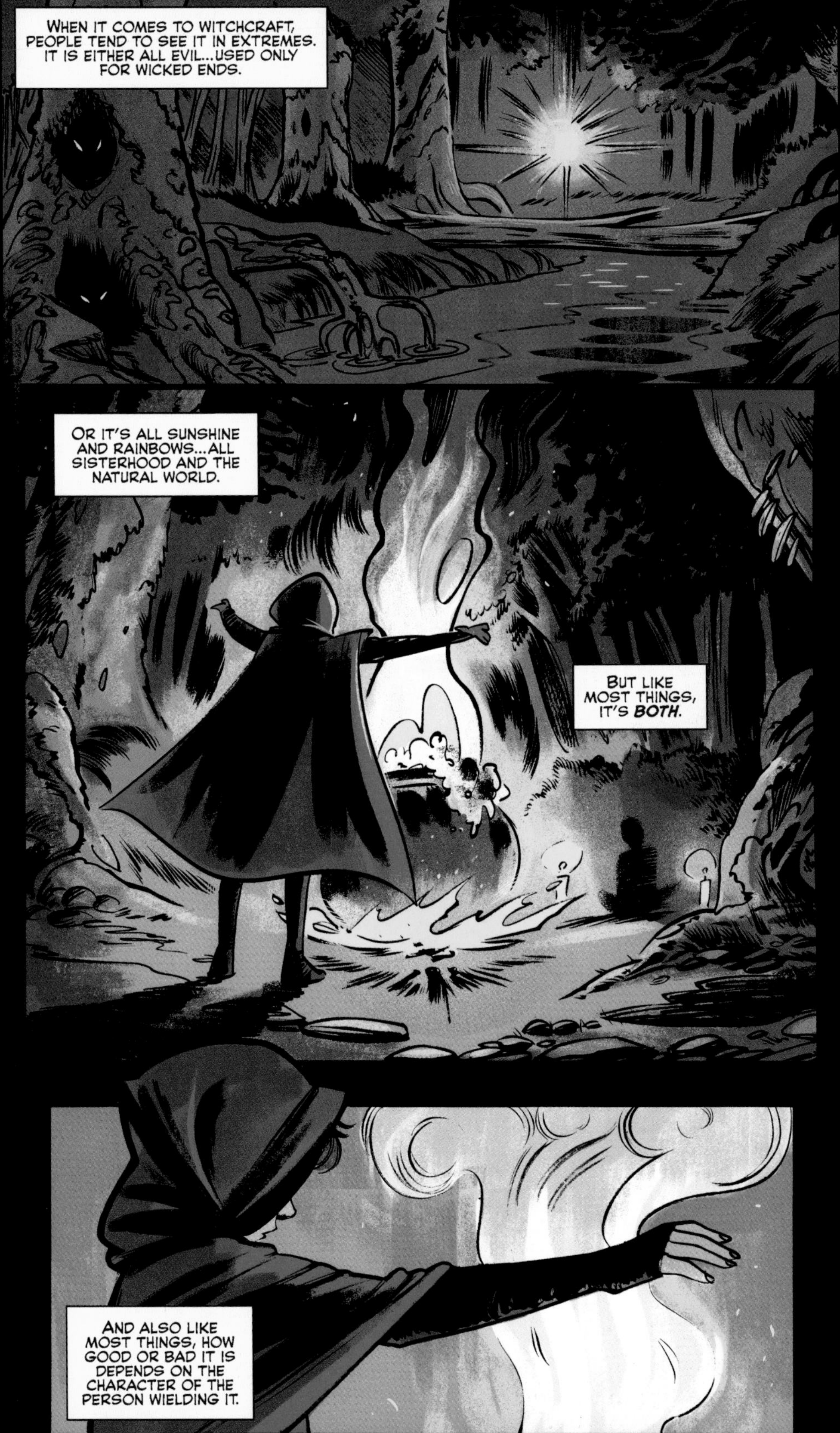
WHEN IT COMES TO WITCHCRAFT, PEOPLE TEND TO SEE IT IN EXTREMES. IT IS EITHER ALL EVIL...USED ONLY FOR WICKED ENDS.
OR IT'S ALL SUNSHINE AND RAINBOWS...ALL SISTERHOOD AND THE NATURAL WORLD.
BUT LIKE MOST THINGS, IT'S BOTH.
AND ALSO LIKE MOST THINGS, HOW GOOD OR BAD IT IS DEPENDS ON THE CHARACTER OF THE PERSON WIELDING IT.

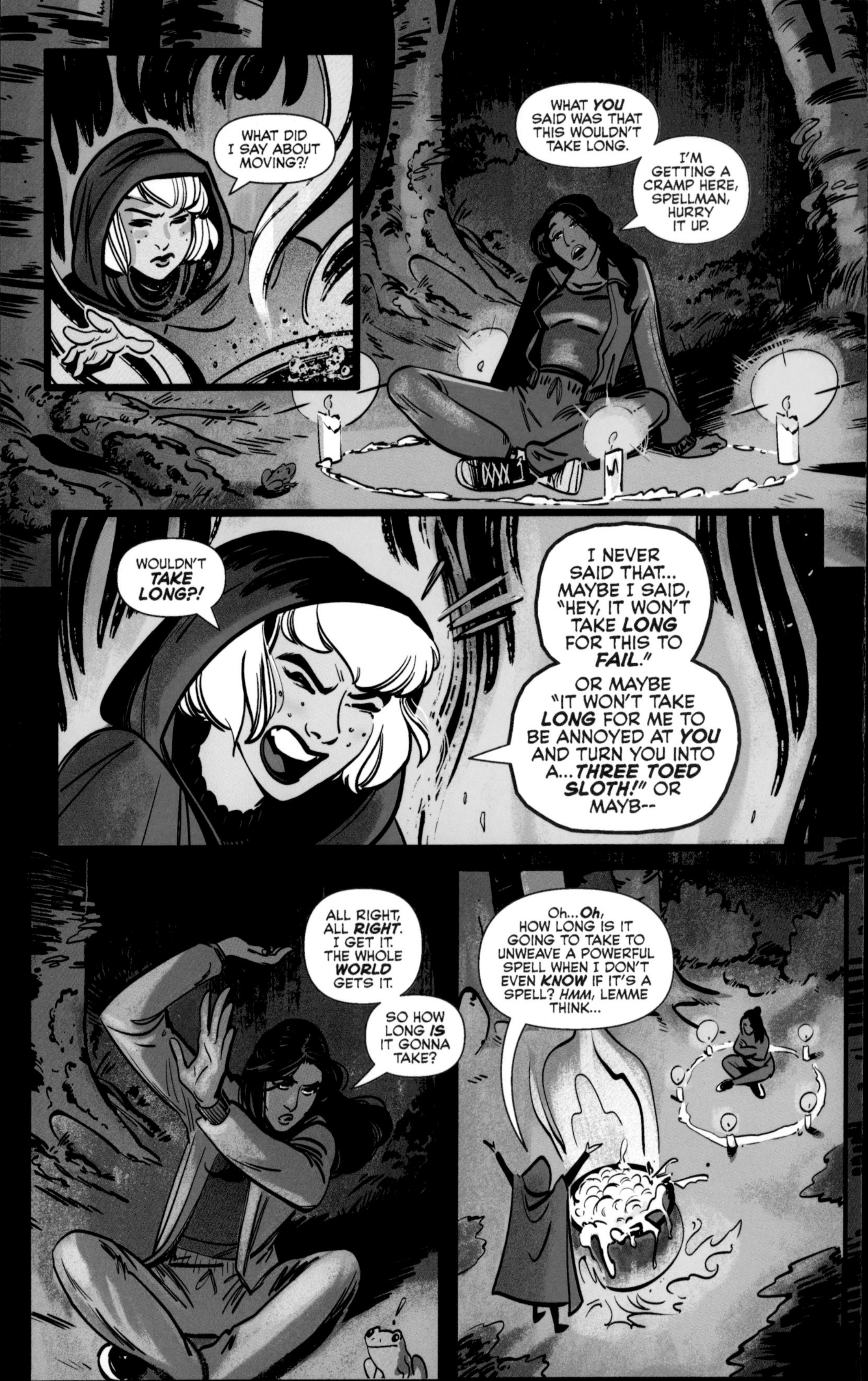
WHAT DID I SAY ABOUT MOVING?!
WHAT YOU SAID WAS THAT THIS WOULDN'T TAKE LONG.
I'M GETTING A CRAMP HERE, SPELLMAN, HURRY IT UP.
WOULDN'T TAKE LONG?!
I NEVER SAID THAT... MAYBE I SAID, "HEY, IT WON'T TAKE LONG FOR THIS TO FAIL."
OR MAYBE "IT WON'T TAKE LONG FOR ME TO BE ANNOYED AT YOU AND TURN YOU INTO A...THREE TOED SLOTH!" OR MAYB--
ALL RIGHT, ALL RIGHT. I GET IT. THE WHOLE WORLD GETS IT.
SO HOW LONG IS IT GONNA TAKE?
Oh...Oh, HOW LONG IS IT GOING TO TAKE TO UNWEAVE A POWERFUL SPELL WHEN I DON'T EVEN KNOW IF IT'S A SPELL? HMM, LEMME THINK...

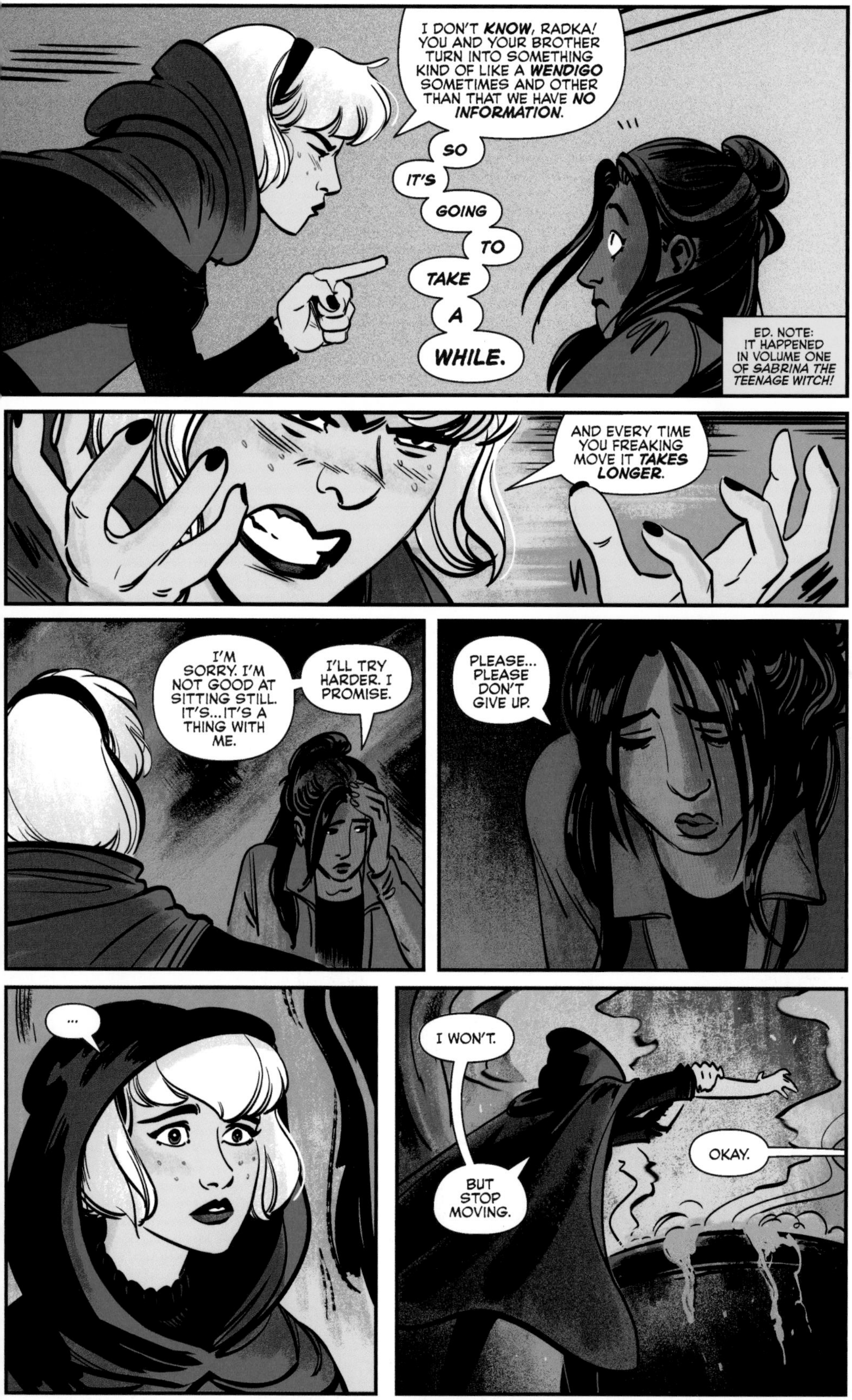
I DON'T KNOW, RADKA! YOU AND YOUR BROTHER TURN INTO SOMETHING KIND OF LIKE A WENDIGO SOMETIMES AND OTHER THAN THAT WE HAVE NO INFORMATION.
SO
IT'S
GOING
TO
TAKE
A
WHILE.
ED. NOTE: IT HAPPENED IN VOLUME ONE OF SABRINA THE TEENAGE WITCH!
AND EVERY TIME YOU FREAKING MOVE IT TAKES LONGER.
I'M SORRY. I'M NOT GOOD AT SITTING STILL. IT'S...IT'S A THING WITH ME.
I'LL TRY HARDER. I PROMISE.
PLEASE... PLEASE DON'T GIVE UP.
...
I WON'T.
BUT STOP MOVING.
OKAY.

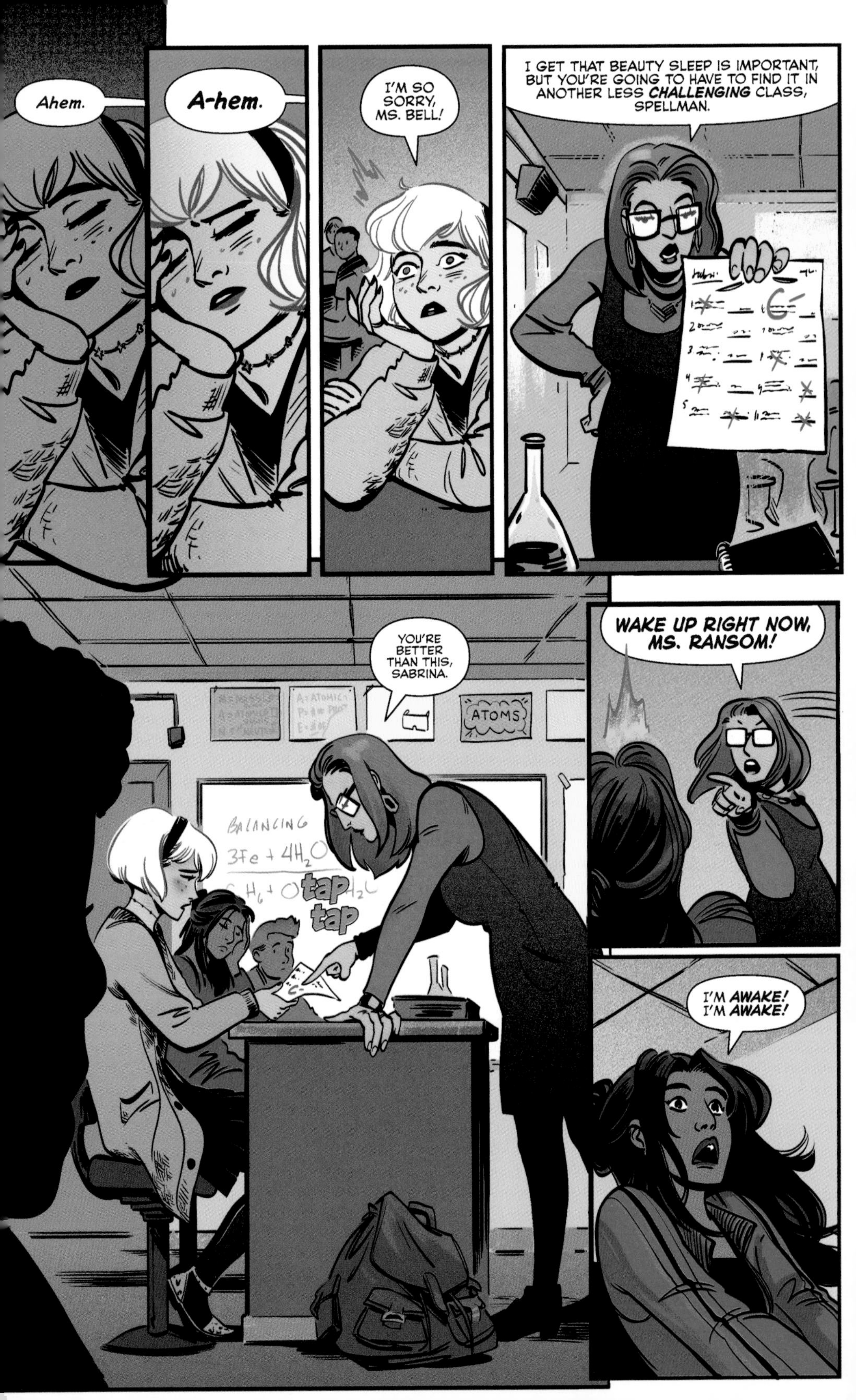
Ahem.
A-hem.
I'M SO SORRY, MS. BELL!
I GET THAT BEAUTY SLEEP IS IMPORTANT, BUT YOU'RE GOING TO HAVE TO FIND IT IN ANOTHER LESS CHALLENGING CLASS, SPELLMAN.
YOU'RE BETTER THAN THIS, SABRINA.
ATOMS
BALANCING
3Fe + 4H2O
tap tap
WAKE UP RIGHT NOW, MS. RANSOM!
I'M AWAKE! I'M AWAKE!

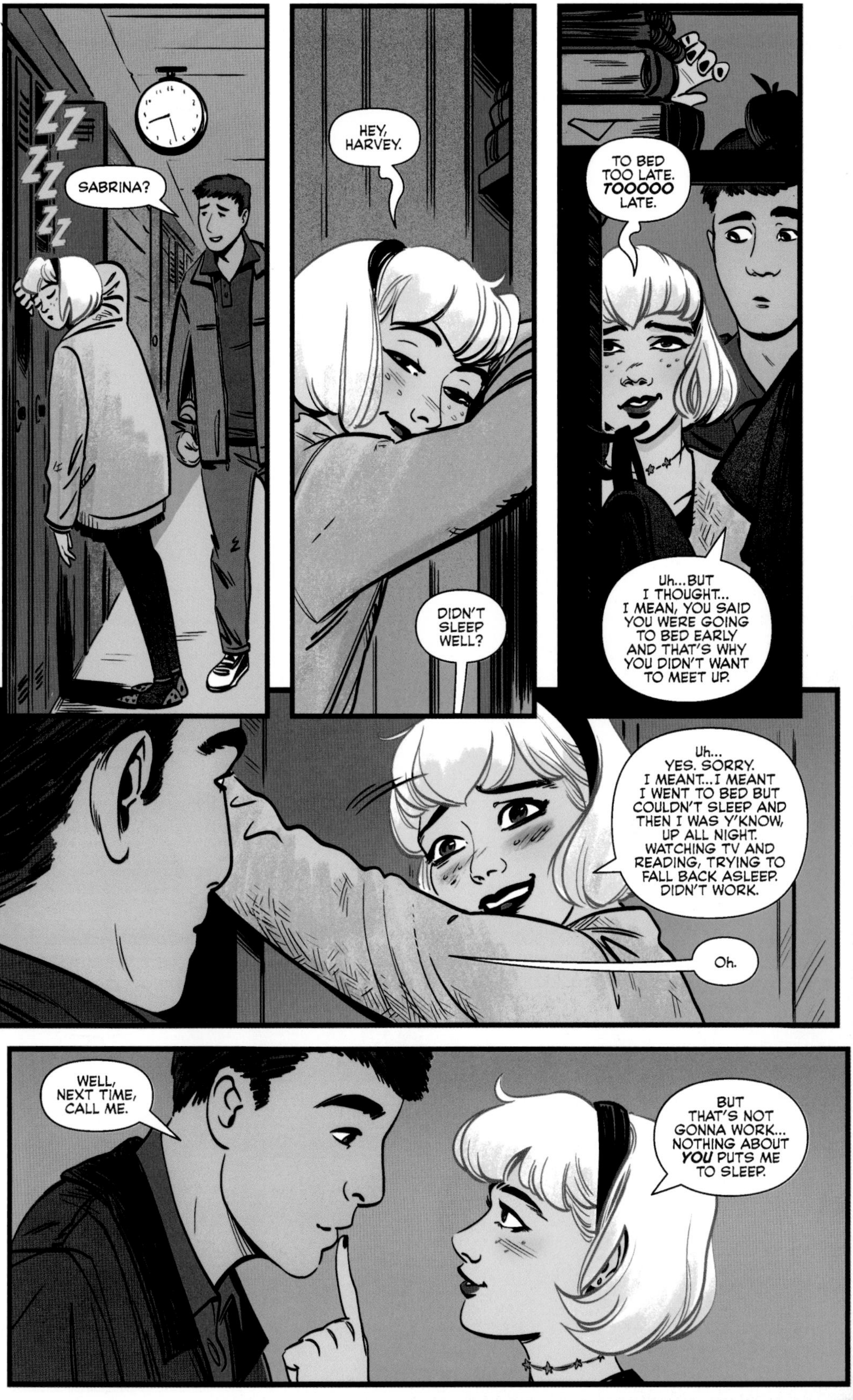

ZZZZZ
SABRINA?
HEY, HARVEY.
DIDN'T SLEEP WELL?
TO BED TOO LATE. TOOOOO LATE.
Uh...BUT I THOUGHT... I MEAN, YOU SAID YOU WERE GOING TO BED EARLY AND THAT'S WHY YOU DIDN'T WANT TO MEET UP.
Uh... YES. SORRY. I MEANT...I MEANT I WENT TO BED BUT COULDN'T SLEEP AND THEN I WAS Y'KNOW, UP ALL NIGHT. WATCHING TV AND READING, TRYING TO FALL BACK ASLEEP. DIDN'T WORK.
Oh.
WELL, NEXT TIME, CALL ME.
BUT THAT'S NOT GONNA WORK... NOTHING ABOUT YOU PUTS ME TO SLEEP.

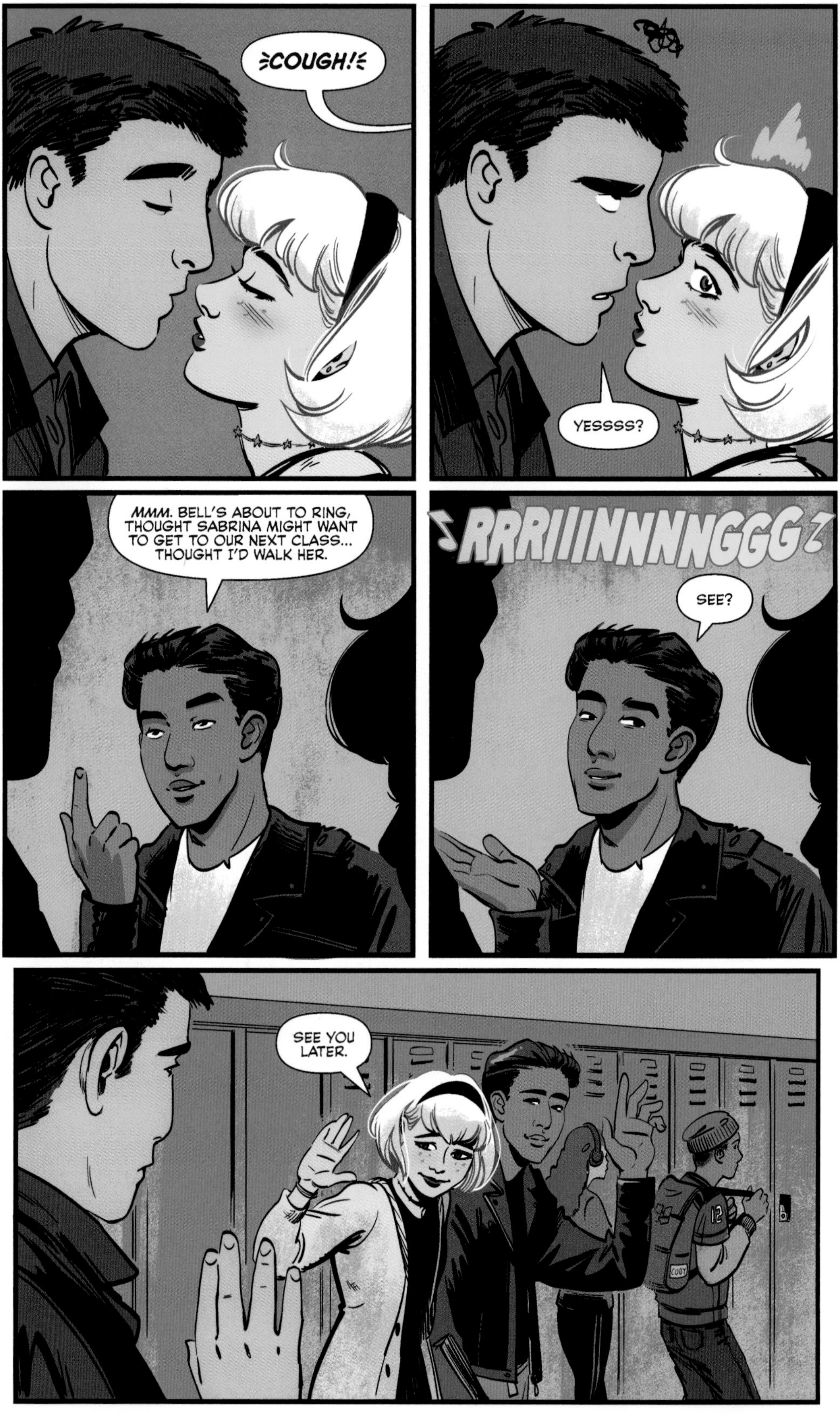
COUGH!
YESSSS?
MMM. BELL'S ABOUT TO RING, THOUGHT SABRINA MIGHT WANT TO GET TO OUR NEXT CLASS... THOUGHT I'D WALK HER.
RRRIIIINNNNNGGG
SEE?
SEE YOU LATER.
12
CODY

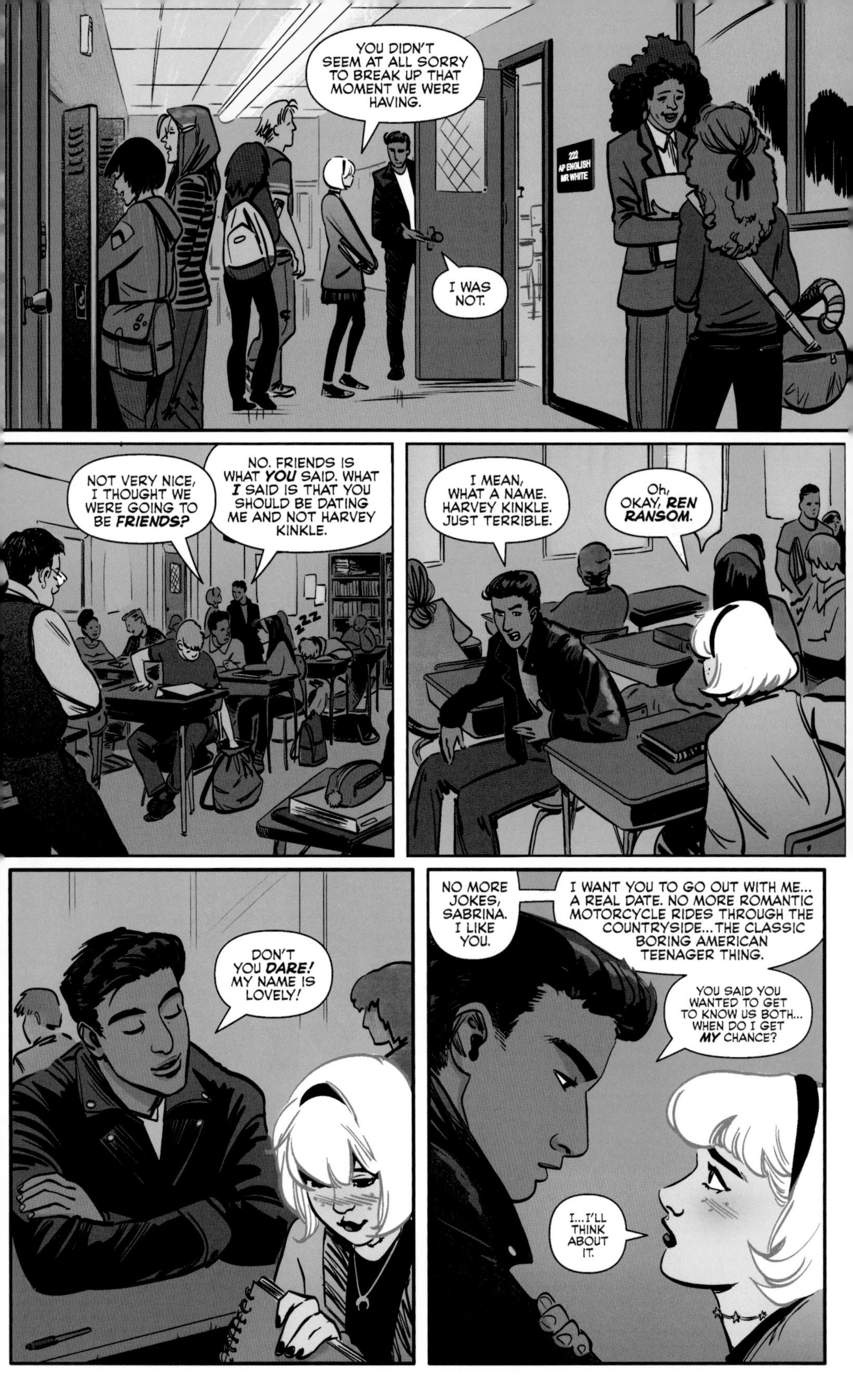

YOU DIDN'T SEEM AT ALL SORRY TO BREAK UP THAT MOMENT WE WERE HAVING.
I WAS NOT.
222 AP ENGLISH MR WHITE
NOT VERY NICE, I THOUGHT WE WERE GOING TO BE FRIENDS?
NO. FRIENDS IS WHAT YOU SAID. WHAT I SAID IS THAT YOU SHOULD BE DATING ME AND NOT HARVEY KINKLE.
ZZZ
I MEAN, WHAT A NAME. HARVEY KINKLE. JUST TERRIBLE.
Oh, OKAY, REN RANSOM.
DON'T YOU DARE! MY NAME IS LOVELY!
NO MORE JOKES, SABRINA. I LIKE YOU.
I WANT YOU TO GO OUT WITH ME... A REAL DATE. NO MORE ROMANTIC MOTORCYCLE RIDES THROUGH THE COUNTRYSIDE...THE CLASSIC BORING AMERICAN TEENAGER THING.
YOU SAID YOU WANTED TO GET TO KNOW US BOTH... WHEN DO I GET MY CHANCE?
I...I'LL THINK ABOUT IT.

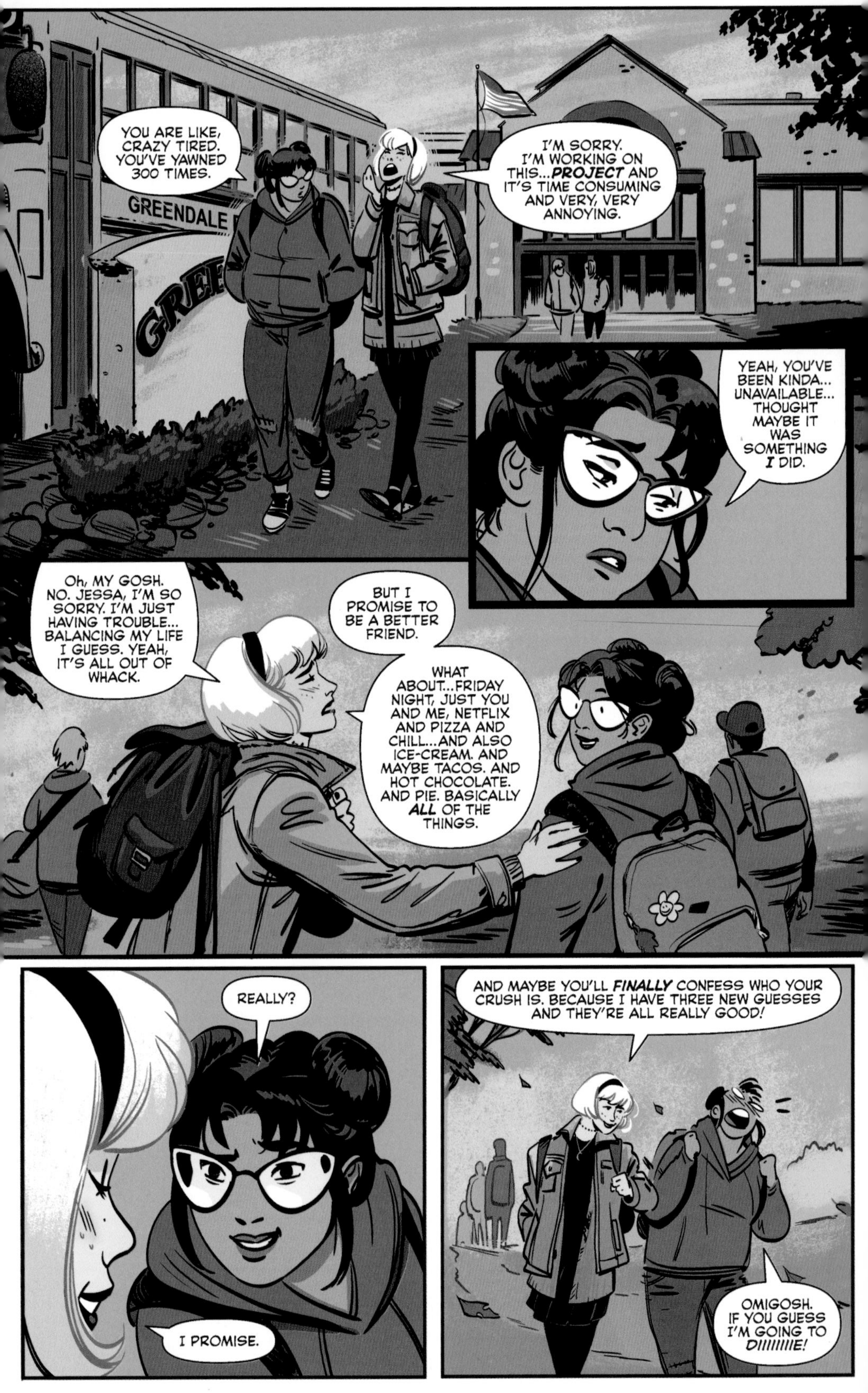
YOU ARE LIKE, CRAZY TIRED. YOU'VE YAWNED 300 TIMES.
I'M SORRY. I'M WORKING ON THIS...PROJECT AND IT'S TIME CONSUMING AND VERY, VERY ANNOYING.
GREENDALE
YEAH, YOU'VE BEEN KINDA... UNAVAILABLE... THOUGHT MAYBE IT WAS SOMETHING I DID.
Oh, MY GOSH. NO. JESSA, I'M SO SORRY. I'M JUST HAVING TROUBLE... BALANCING MY LIFE I GUESS. YEAH, IT'S ALL OUT OF WHACK.
BUT I PROMISE TO BE A BETTER FRIEND.
WHAT ABOUT...FRIDAY NIGHT, JUST YOU AND ME, NETFLIX AND PIZZA AND CHILL...AND ALSO ICE-CREAM. AND MAYBE TACOS. AND HOT CHOCOLATE. AND PIE. BASICALLY ALL OF THE THINGS.
REALLY?
I PROMISE.
AND MAYBE YOU'LL FINALLY CONFESS WHO YOUR CRUSH IS. BECAUSE I HAVE THREE NEW GUESSES AND THEY'RE ALL REALLY GOOD!
OMIGOSH. IF YOU GUESS I'M GOING TO DIIIIIIIE!

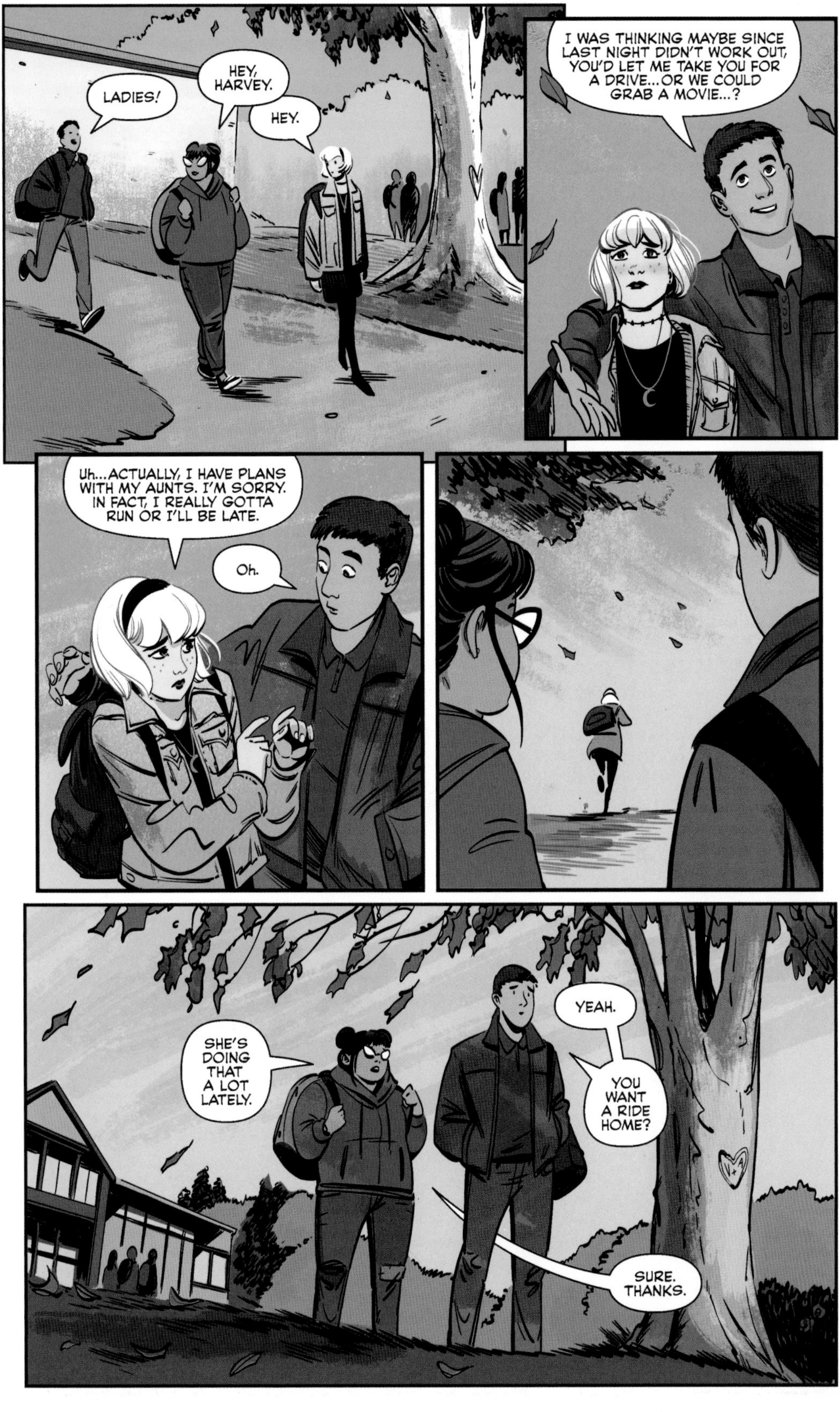
LADIES!
HEY, HARVEY.
HEY.
I WAS THINKING MAYBE SINCE LAST NIGHT DIDN'T WORK OUT, YOU'D LET ME TAKE YOU FOR A DRIVE...OR WE COULD GRAB A MOVIE...?
Uh...ACTUALLY, I HAVE PLANS WITH MY AUNTS. I'M SORRY. IN FACT, I REALLY GOTTA RUN OR I'LL BE LATE.
Oh.
SHE'S DOING THAT A LOT LATELY.
YEAH.
YOU WANT A RIDE HOME?
SURE. THANKS.

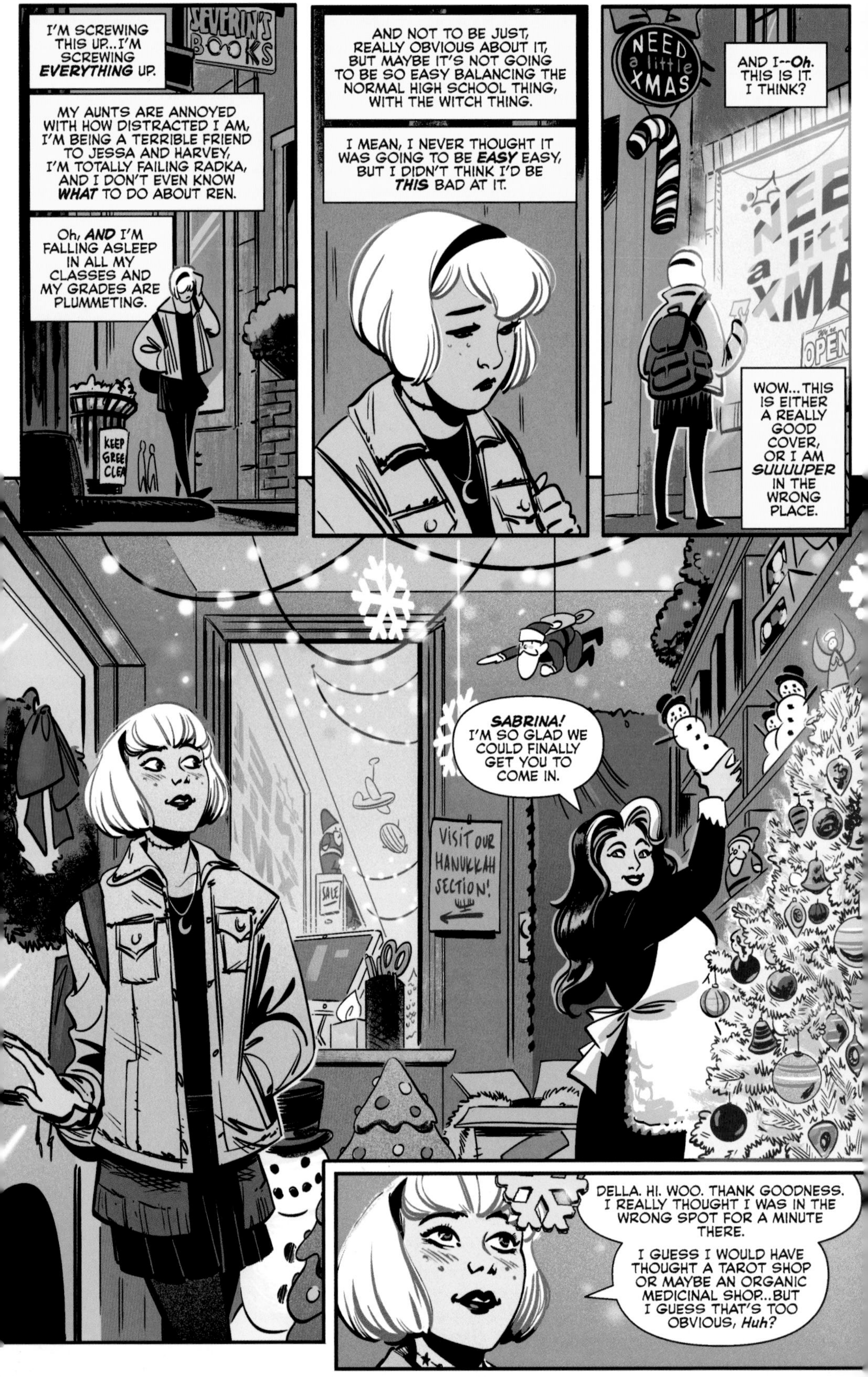

SEVERIN'S BOOKS
I'M SCREWING THIS UP...I'M SCREWING EVERYTHING UP.
MY AUNTS ARE ANNOYED WITH HOW DISTRACTED I AM, I'M BEING A TERRIBLE FRIEND TO JESSA AND HARVEY, I'M TOTALLY FAILING RADKA, AND I DON'T EVEN KNOW WHAT TO DO ABOUT REN.
Oh, AND I'M FALLING ASLEEP IN ALL MY CLASSES AND MY GRADES ARE PLUMMETING.
AND NOT TO BE JUST, REALLY OBVIOUS ABOUT IT, BUT MAYBE IT'S NOT GOING TO BE SO EASY BALANCING THE NORMAL HIGH SCHOOL THING, WITH THE WITCH THING.
I MEAN, I NEVER THOUGHT IT WAS GOING TO BE EASY EASY, BUT I DIDN'T THINK I'D BE THIS BAD AT IT.
NEED a little XMAS
AND I--Oh. THIS IS IT. I THINK?
WOW...THIS IS EITHER A REALLY GOOD COVER, OR I AM SUUUUPER IN THE WRONG PLACE.
SABRINA! I'M SO GLAD WE COULD FINALLY GET YOU TO COME IN.
VISIT OUR HANUKKAH SECTION!
SALE
DELLA. HI. WOO. THANK GOODNESS. I REALLY THOUGHT I WAS IN THE WRONG SPOT FOR A MINUTE THERE.
I GUESS I WOULD HAVE THOUGHT A TAROT SHOP OR MAYBE AN ORGANIC MEDICINAL SHOP...BUT I GUESS THAT'S TOO OBVIOUS, Huh?

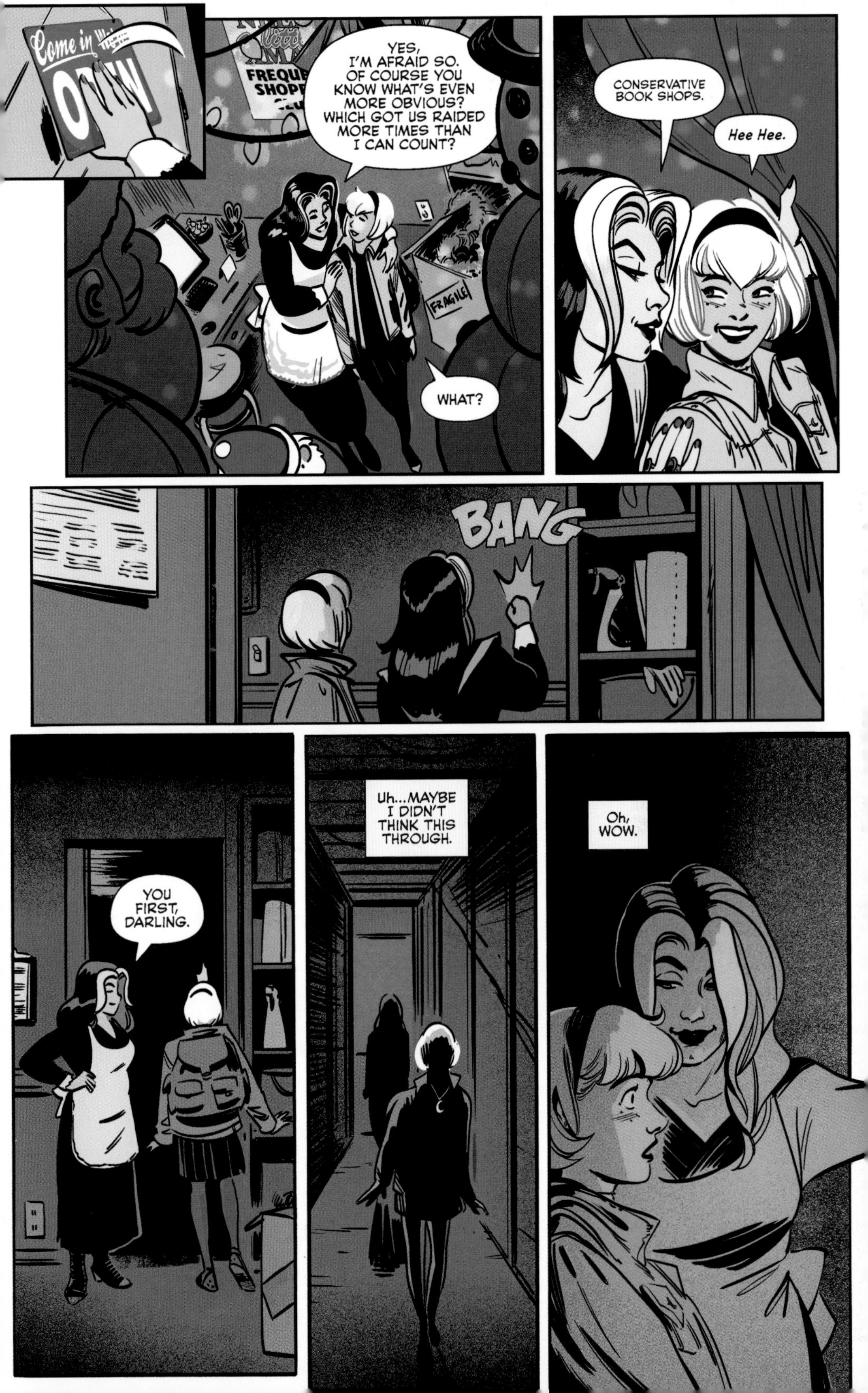
Come in
OPEN
YES, I'M AFRAID SO. OF COURSE YOU KNOW WHAT'S EVEN MORE OBVIOUS? WHICH GOT US RAIDED MORE TIMES THAN I CAN COUNT?
FRAGILE
WHAT?
CONSERVATIVE BOOK SHOPS.
Hee Hee.
BANG
YOU FIRST, DARLING.
Uh...MAYBE I DIDN'T THINK THIS THROUGH.
Oh, WOW.

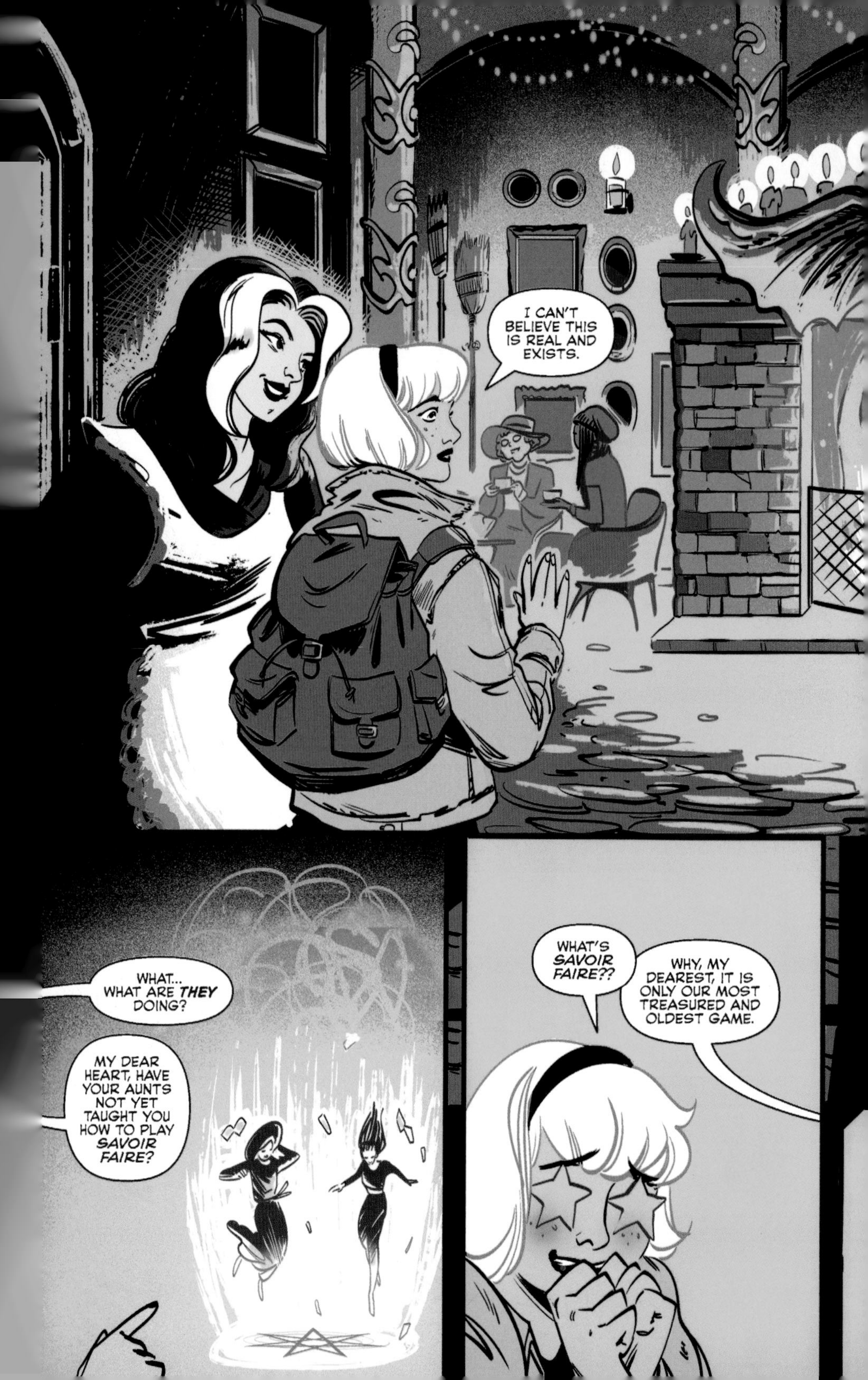
I CAN'T BELIEVE THIS IS REAL AND EXISTS.
WHAT... WHAT ARE *THEY* DOING?
MY DEAR HEART, HAVE YOUR AUNTS NOT YET TAUGHT YOU HOW TO PLAY *SAVOIR FAIRE?*
WHAT'S *SAVOIR FAIRE??*
WHY, MY DEAREST, IT IS ONLY OUR MOST TREASURED AND OLDEST GAME.

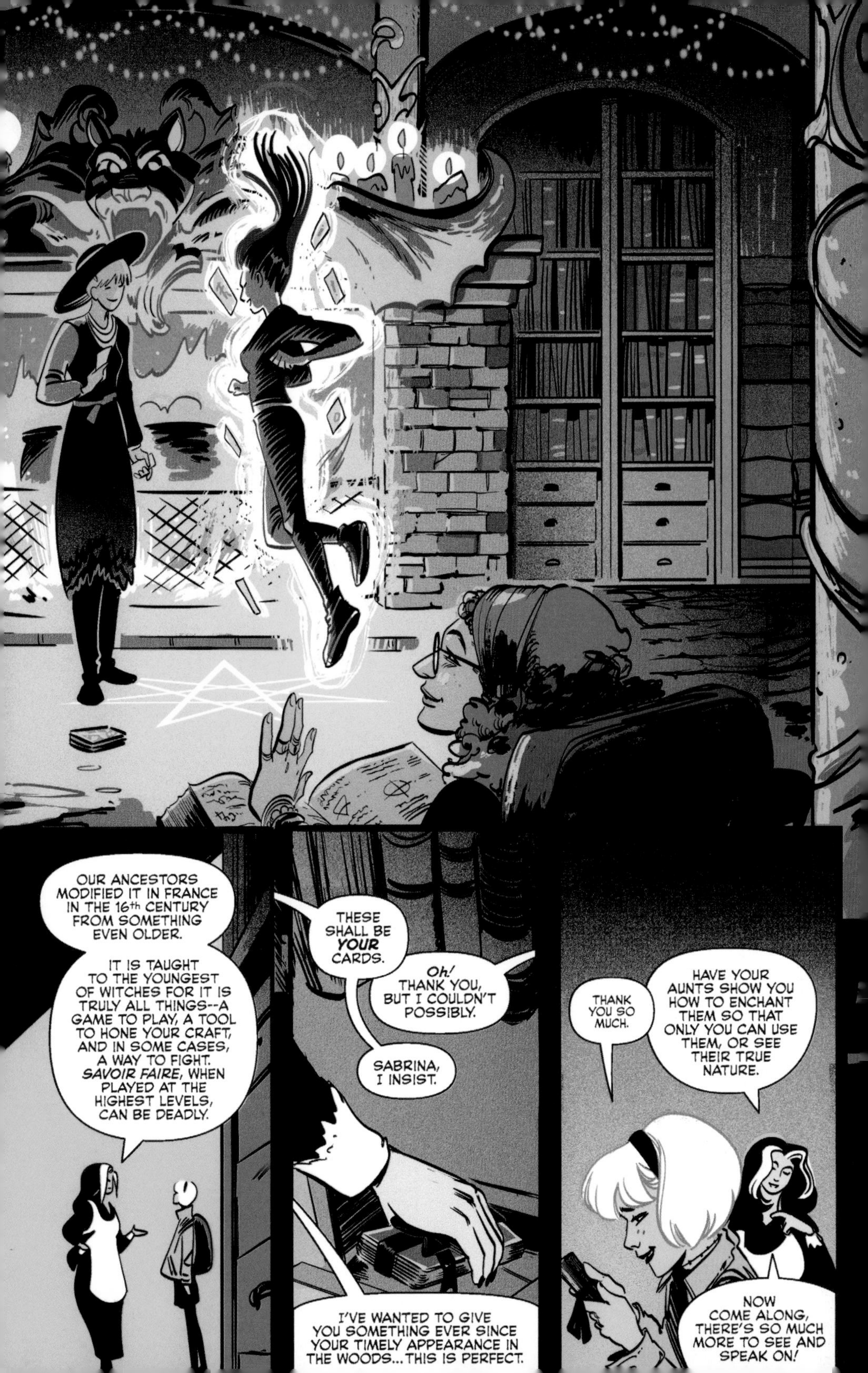
OUR ANCESTORS MODIFIED IT IN FRANCE IN THE 16th CENTURY FROM SOMETHING EVEN OLDER.
IT IS TAUGHT TO THE YOUNGEST OF WITCHES FOR IT IS TRULY ALL THINGS--A GAME TO PLAY, A TOOL TO HONE YOUR CRAFT, AND IN SOME CASES, A WAY TO FIGHT. SAVOIR FAIRE, WHEN PLAYED AT THE HIGHEST LEVELS, CAN BE DEADLY.
THESE SHALL BE YOUR CARDS.
Oh! THANK YOU, BUT I COULDN'T POSSIBLY.
SABRINA, I INSIST.
I'VE WANTED TO GIVE YOU SOMETHING EVER SINCE YOUR TIMELY APPEARANCE IN THE WOODS... THIS IS PERFECT.
THANK YOU SO MUCH.
HAVE YOUR AUNTS SHOW YOU HOW TO ENCHANT THEM SO THAT ONLY YOU CAN USE THEM, OR SEE THEIR TRUE NATURE.
NOW COME ALONG, THERE'S SO MUCH MORE TO SEE AND SPEAK ON!

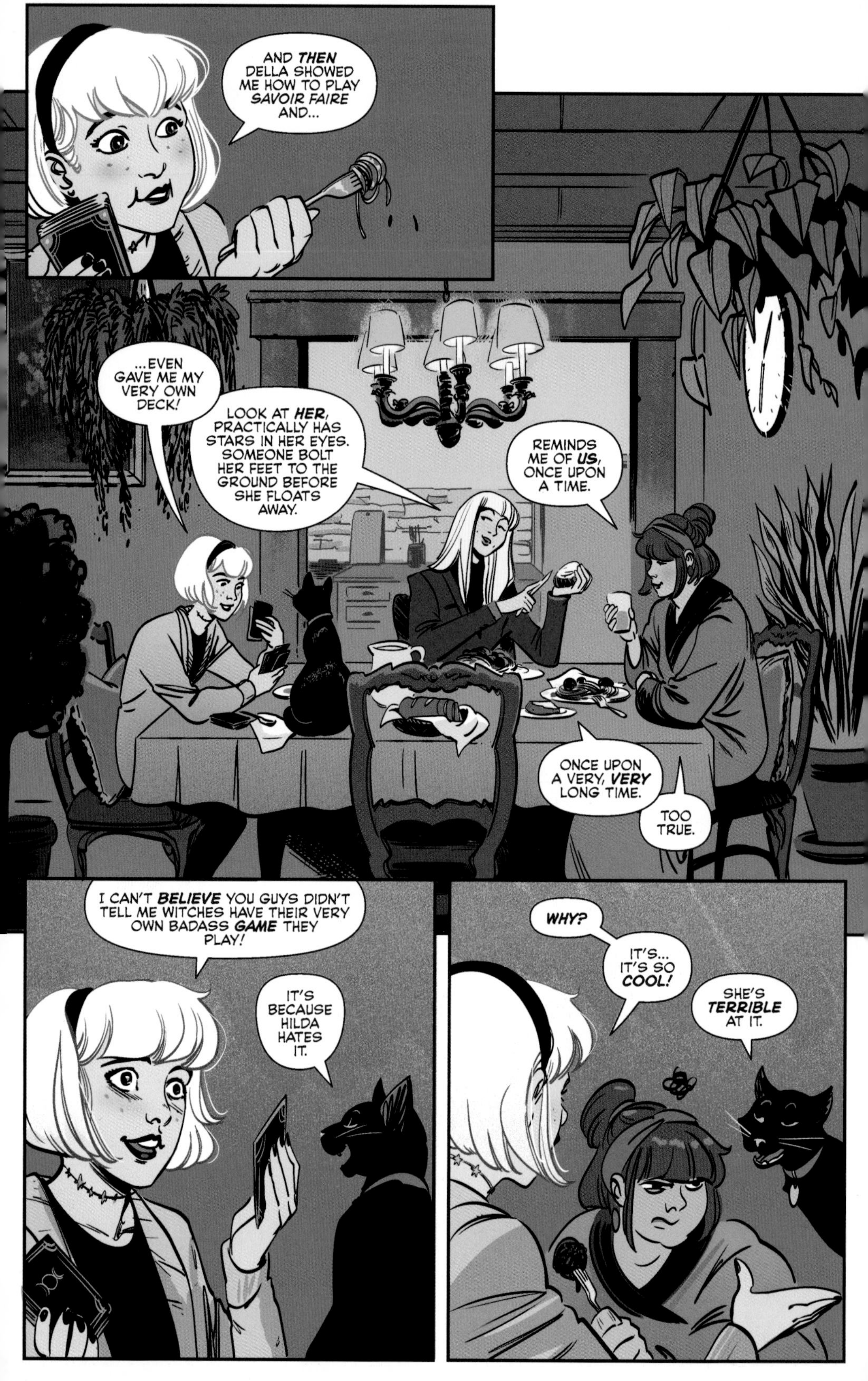
AND *THEN* DELLA SHOWED ME HOW TO PLAY *SAVOIR FAIRE* AND...
...EVEN GAVE ME MY VERY OWN DECK!
LOOK AT *HER*, PRACTICALLY HAS STARS IN HER EYES. SOMEONE BOLT HER FEET TO THE GROUND BEFORE SHE FLOATS AWAY.
REMINDS ME OF *US*, ONCE UPON A TIME.
ONCE UPON A VERY, *VERY* LONG TIME.
TOO TRUE.
I CAN'T *BELIEVE* YOU GUYS DIDN'T TELL ME WITCHES HAVE THEIR VERY OWN BADASS *GAME* THEY PLAY!
IT'S BECAUSE HILDA HATES IT.
WHY?
IT'S... IT'S SO *COOL!*
SHE'S *TERRIBLE* AT IT.

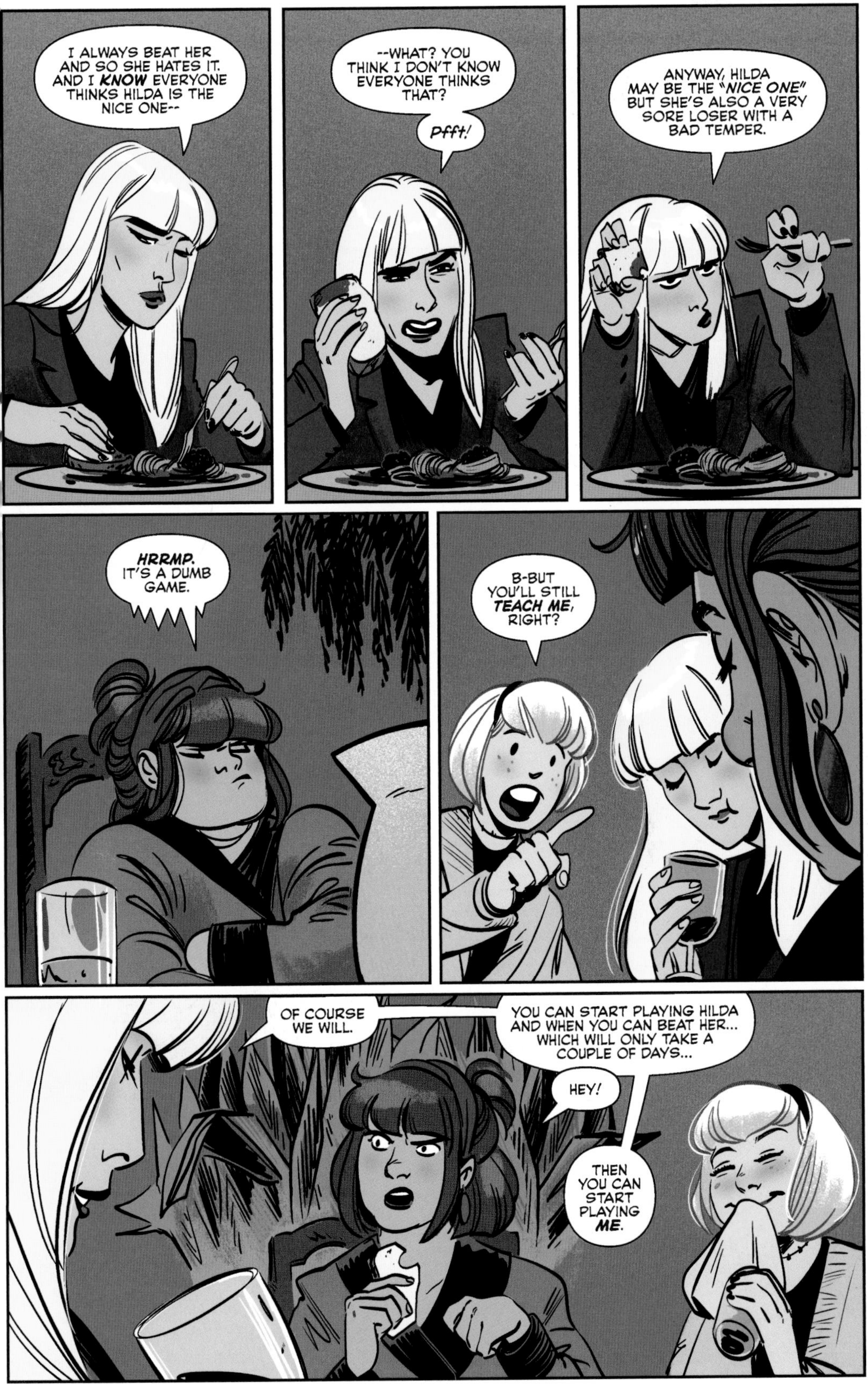
I ALWAYS BEAT HER AND SO SHE HATES IT. AND I KNOW EVERYONE THINKS HILDA IS THE NICE ONE--
--WHAT? YOU THINK I DON'T KNOW EVERYONE THINKS THAT?
Pfft!
ANYWAY, HILDA MAY BE THE "NICE ONE" BUT SHE'S ALSO A VERY SORE LOSER WITH A BAD TEMPER.
HRRMP. IT'S A DUMB GAME.
B-BUT YOU'LL STILL TEACH ME, RIGHT?
OF COURSE WE WILL.
YOU CAN START PLAYING HILDA AND WHEN YOU CAN BEAT HER... WHICH WILL ONLY TAKE A COUPLE OF DAYS...
HEY!
THEN YOU CAN START PLAYING ME.

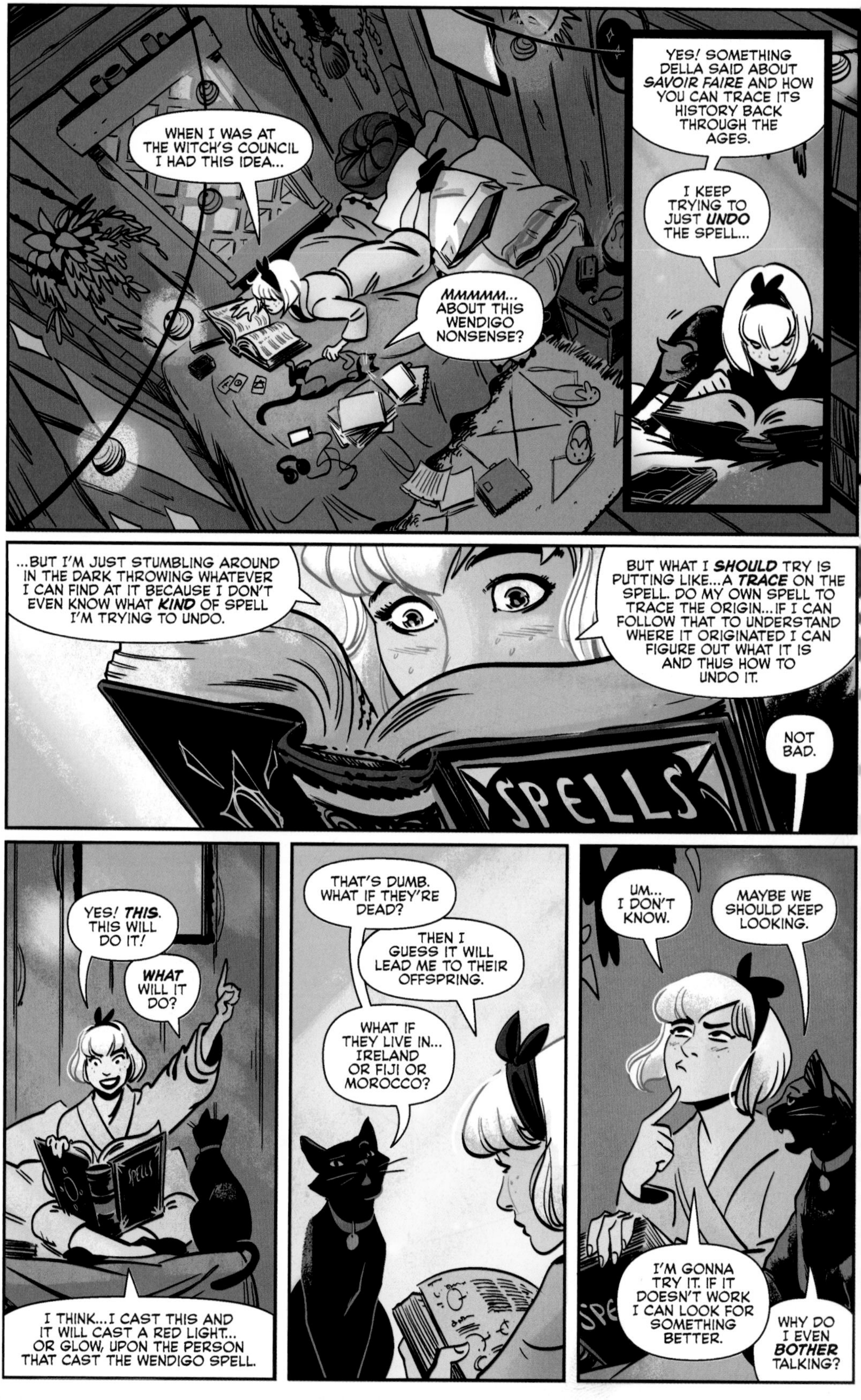
WHEN I WAS AT THE WITCH'S COUNCIL I HAD THIS IDEA...
MMMMM... ABOUT THIS WENDIGO NONSENSE?
YES! SOMETHING DELLA SAID ABOUT SAVOIR FAIRE AND HOW YOU CAN TRACE ITS HISTORY BACK THROUGH THE AGES.
I KEEP TRYING TO JUST UNDO THE SPELL...
...BUT I'M JUST STUMBLING AROUND IN THE DARK THROWING WHATEVER I CAN FIND AT IT BECAUSE I DON'T EVEN KNOW WHAT KIND OF SPELL I'M TRYING TO UNDO.
BUT WHAT I SHOULD TRY IS PUTTING LIKE...A TRACE ON THE SPELL. DO MY OWN SPELL TO TRACE THE ORIGIN...IF I CAN FOLLOW THAT TO UNDERSTAND WHERE IT ORIGINATED I CAN FIGURE OUT WHAT IT IS AND THUS HOW TO UNDO IT.
NOT BAD.
SPELLS
YES! THIS. THIS WILL DO IT!
WHAT WILL IT DO?
I THINK...I CAST THIS AND IT WILL CAST A RED LIGHT... OR GLOW, UPON THE PERSON THAT CAST THE WENDIGO SPELL.
THAT'S DUMB. WHAT IF THEY'RE DEAD?
THEN I GUESS IT WILL LEAD ME TO THEIR OFFSPRING.
WHAT IF THEY LIVE IN... IRELAND OR FIJI OR MOROCCO?
UM... I DON'T KNOW.
MAYBE WE SHOULD KEEP LOOKING.
I'M GONNA TRY IT. IF IT DOESN'T WORK I CAN LOOK FOR SOMETHING BETTER.
WHY DO I EVEN BOTHER TALKING?

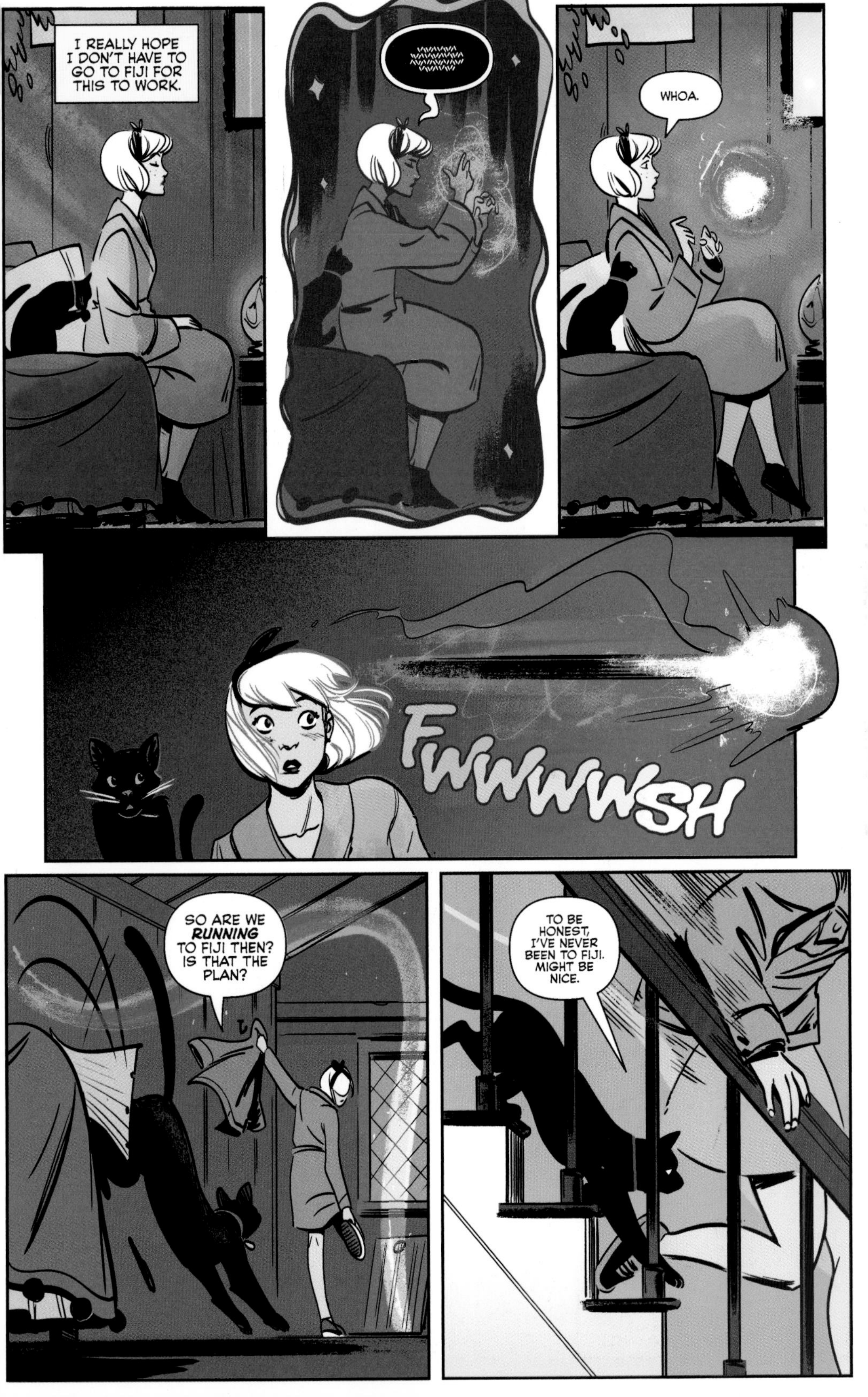
I REALLY HOPE I DON'T HAVE TO GO TO FIJI FOR THIS TO WORK.
WHOA.
FWWWWSH
SO ARE WE RUNNING TO FIJI THEN? IS THAT THE PLAN?
TO BE HONEST, I'VE NEVER BEEN TO FIJI. MIGHT BE NICE.

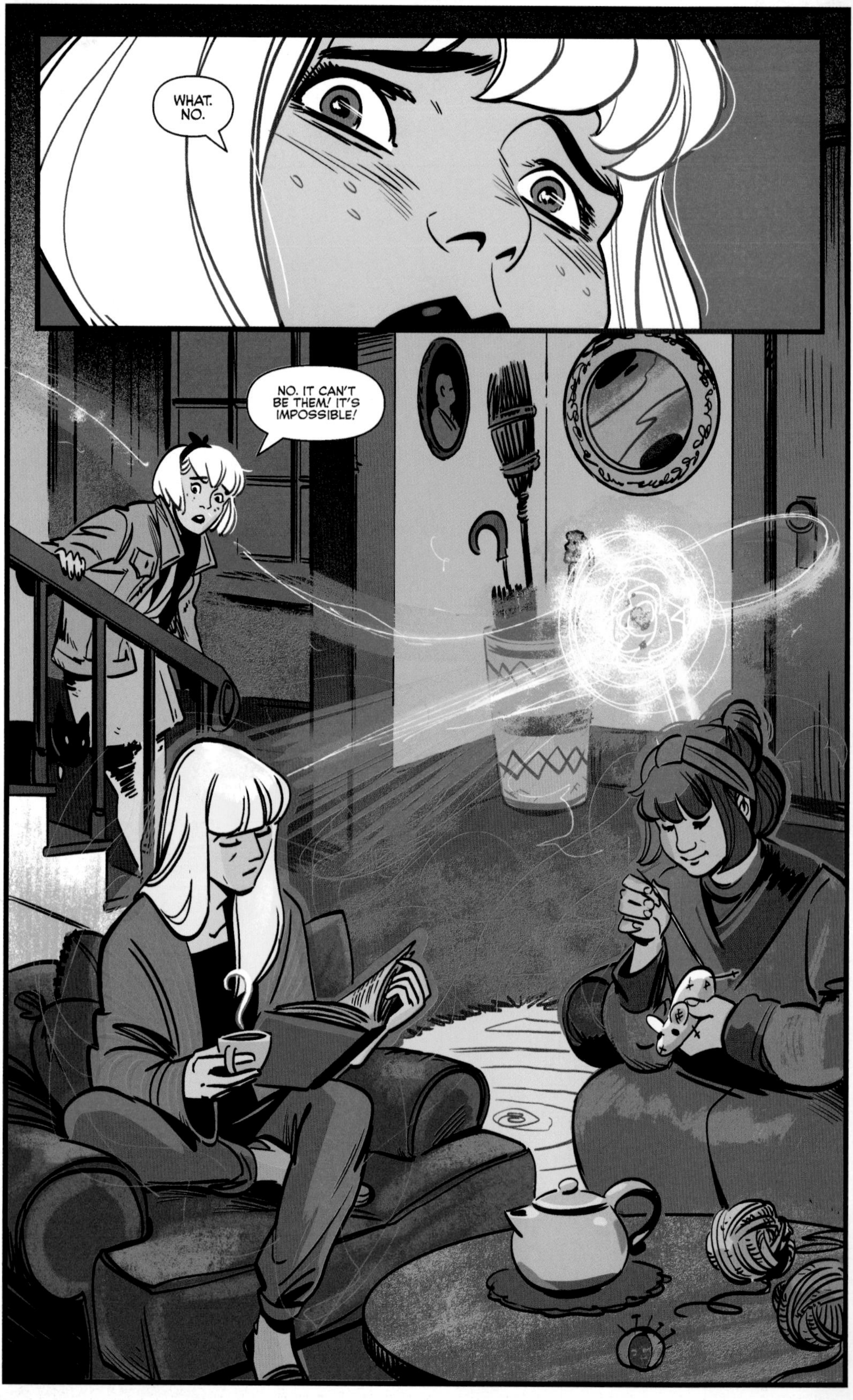
WHAT. NO.
NO. IT CAN'T BE THEM! IT'S IMPOSSIBLE!

CONTINUED...

02

STORY BY
KELLY THOMPSON

ART BY
VERONICA FISH
AND **ANDY FISH**

LETTERING BY
JACK MORELLI

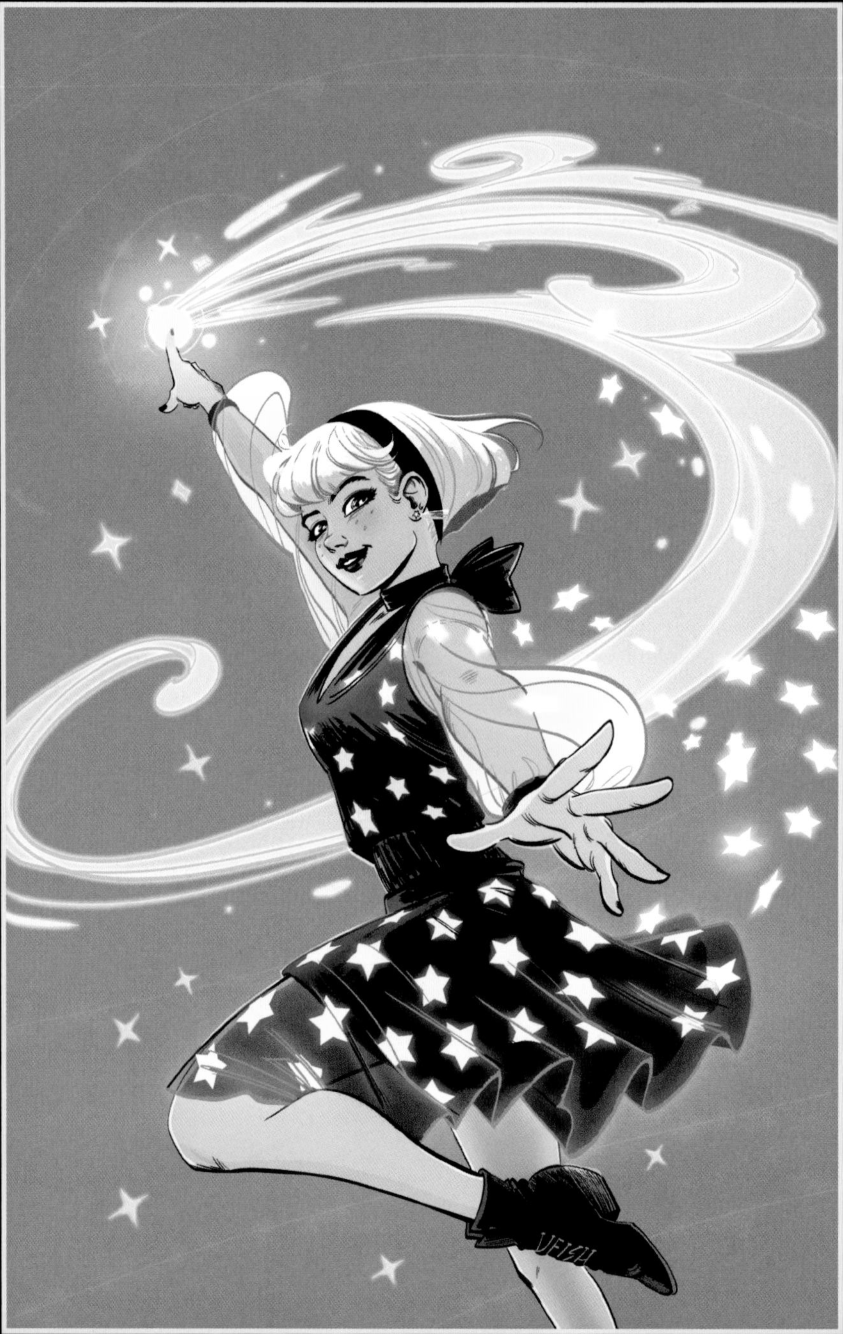
VFISH

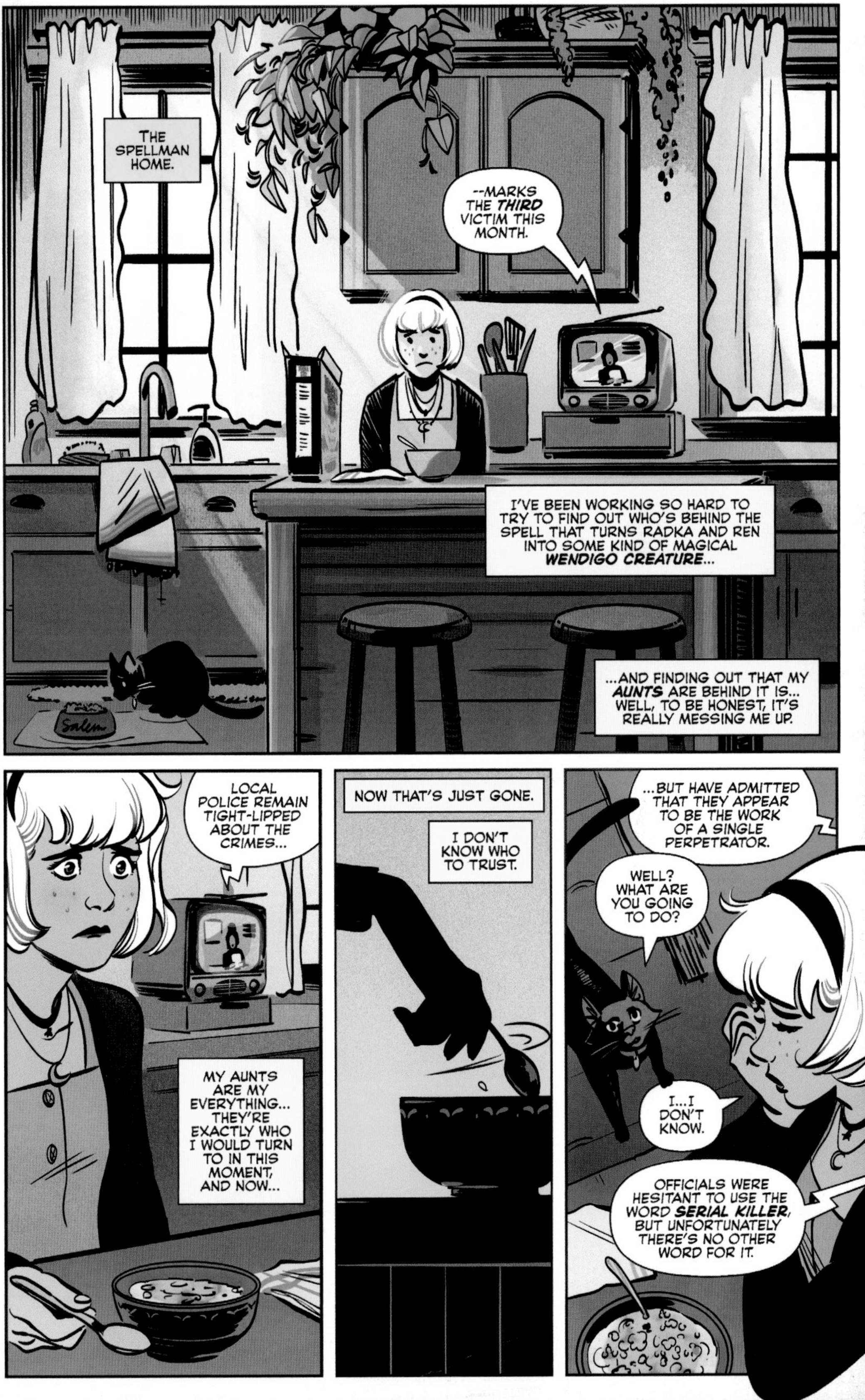
THE SPELLMAN HOME.
--MARKS THE THIRD VICTIM THIS MONTH.
I'VE BEEN WORKING SO HARD TO TRY TO FIND OUT WHO'S BEHIND THE SPELL THAT TURNS RADKA AND REN INTO SOME KIND OF MAGICAL WENDIGO CREATURE...
...AND FINDING OUT THAT MY AUNTS ARE BEHIND IT IS... WELL, TO BE HONEST, IT'S REALLY MESSING ME UP.
Salem
LOCAL POLICE REMAIN TIGHT-LIPPED ABOUT THE CRIMES...
MY AUNTS ARE MY EVERYTHING... THEY'RE EXACTLY WHO I WOULD TURN TO IN THIS MOMENT, AND NOW...
NOW THAT'S JUST GONE.
I DON'T KNOW WHO TO TRUST.
...BUT HAVE ADMITTED THAT THEY APPEAR TO BE THE WORK OF A SINGLE PERPETRATOR.
WELL? WHAT ARE YOU GOING TO DO?
I...I DON'T KNOW.
OFFICIALS WERE HESITANT TO USE THE WORD SERIAL KILLER, BUT UNFORTUNATELY THERE'S NO OTHER WORD FOR IT.

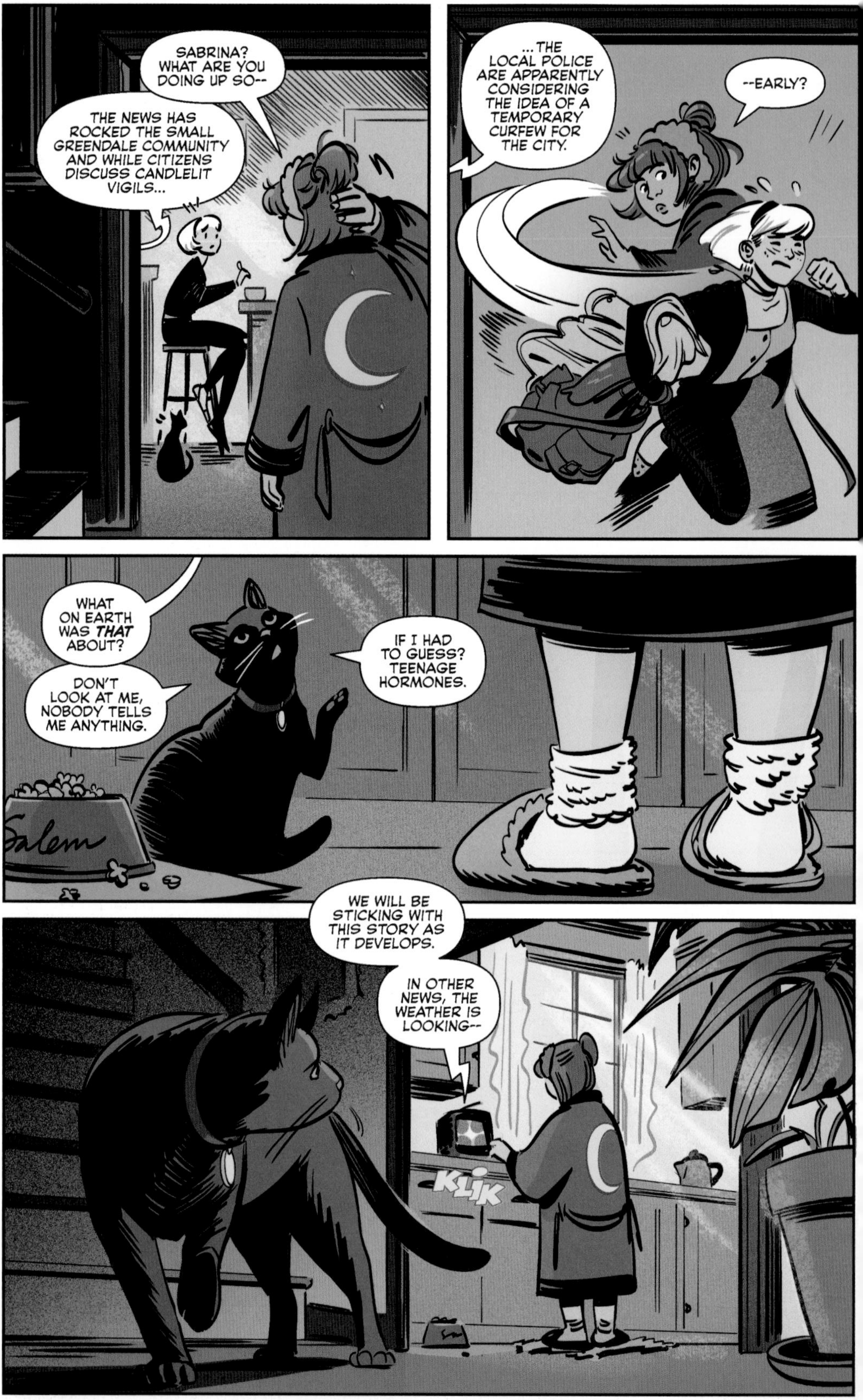
SABRINA? WHAT ARE YOU DOING UP SO--
THE NEWS HAS ROCKED THE SMALL GREENDALE COMMUNITY AND WHILE CITIZENS DISCUSS CANDLELIT VIGILS...
...THE LOCAL POLICE ARE APPARENTLY CONSIDERING THE IDEA OF A TEMPORARY CURFEW FOR THE CITY.
--EARLY?
WHAT ON EARTH WAS THAT ABOUT?
DON'T LOOK AT ME, NOBODY TELLS ME ANYTHING.
IF I HAD TO GUESS? TEENAGE HORMONES.
Salem
WE WILL BE STICKING WITH THIS STORY AS IT DEVELOPS.
IN OTHER NEWS, THE WEATHER IS LOOKING--
KLIK

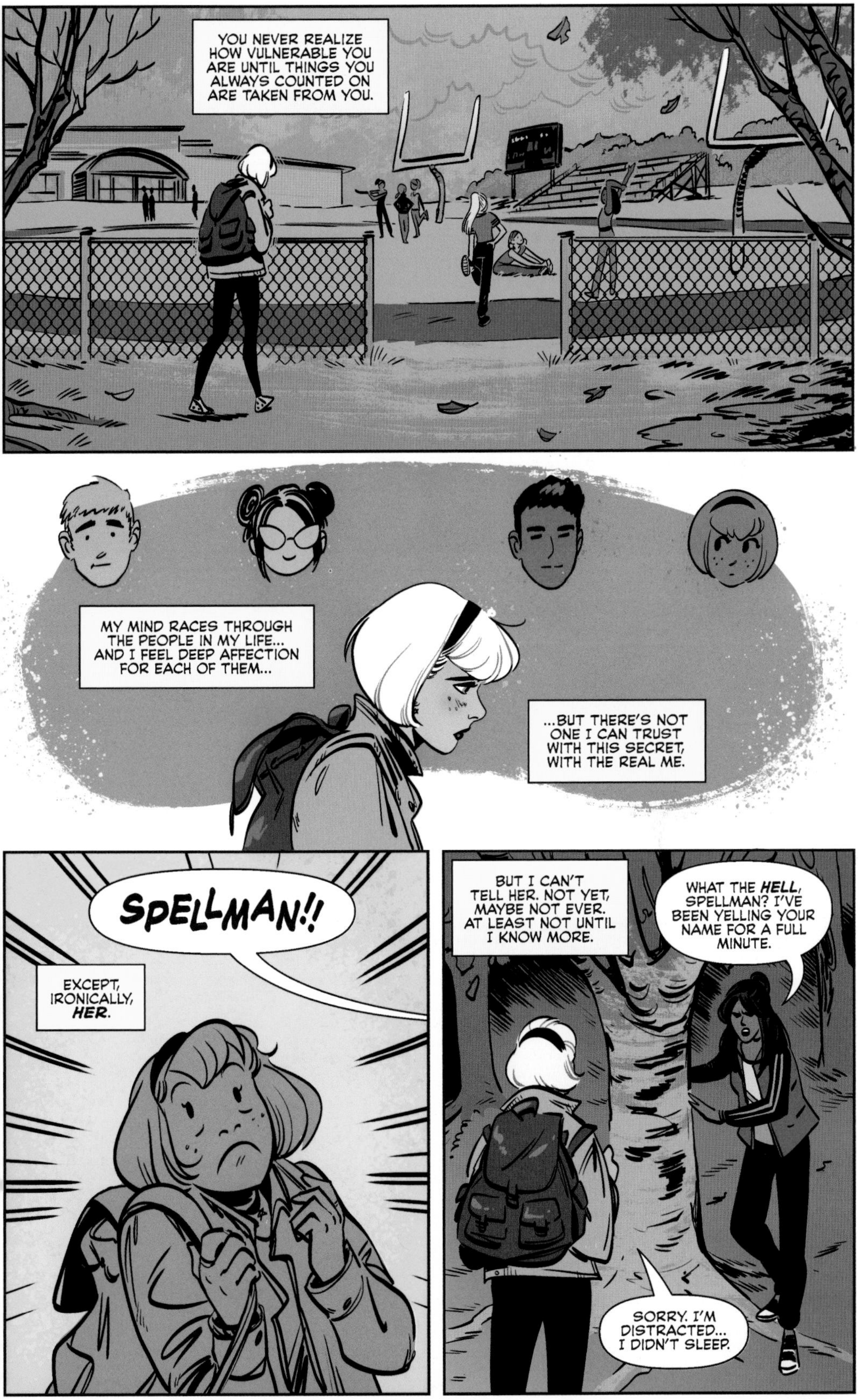
YOU NEVER REALIZE HOW VULNERABLE YOU ARE UNTIL THINGS YOU ALWAYS COUNTED ON ARE TAKEN FROM YOU.
MY MIND RACES THROUGH THE PEOPLE IN MY LIFE... AND I FEEL DEEP AFFECTION FOR EACH OF THEM...
...BUT THERE'S NOT ONE I CAN TRUST WITH THIS SECRET, WITH THE REAL ME.
SPELLMAN!!
EXCEPT, IRONICALLY, *HER*.
BUT I CAN'T TELL HER. NOT YET, MAYBE NOT EVER. AT LEAST NOT UNTIL I KNOW MORE.
WHAT THE *HELL*, SPELLMAN? I'VE BEEN YELLING YOUR NAME FOR A FULL MINUTE.
SORRY. I'M DISTRACTED... I DIDN'T SLEEP.

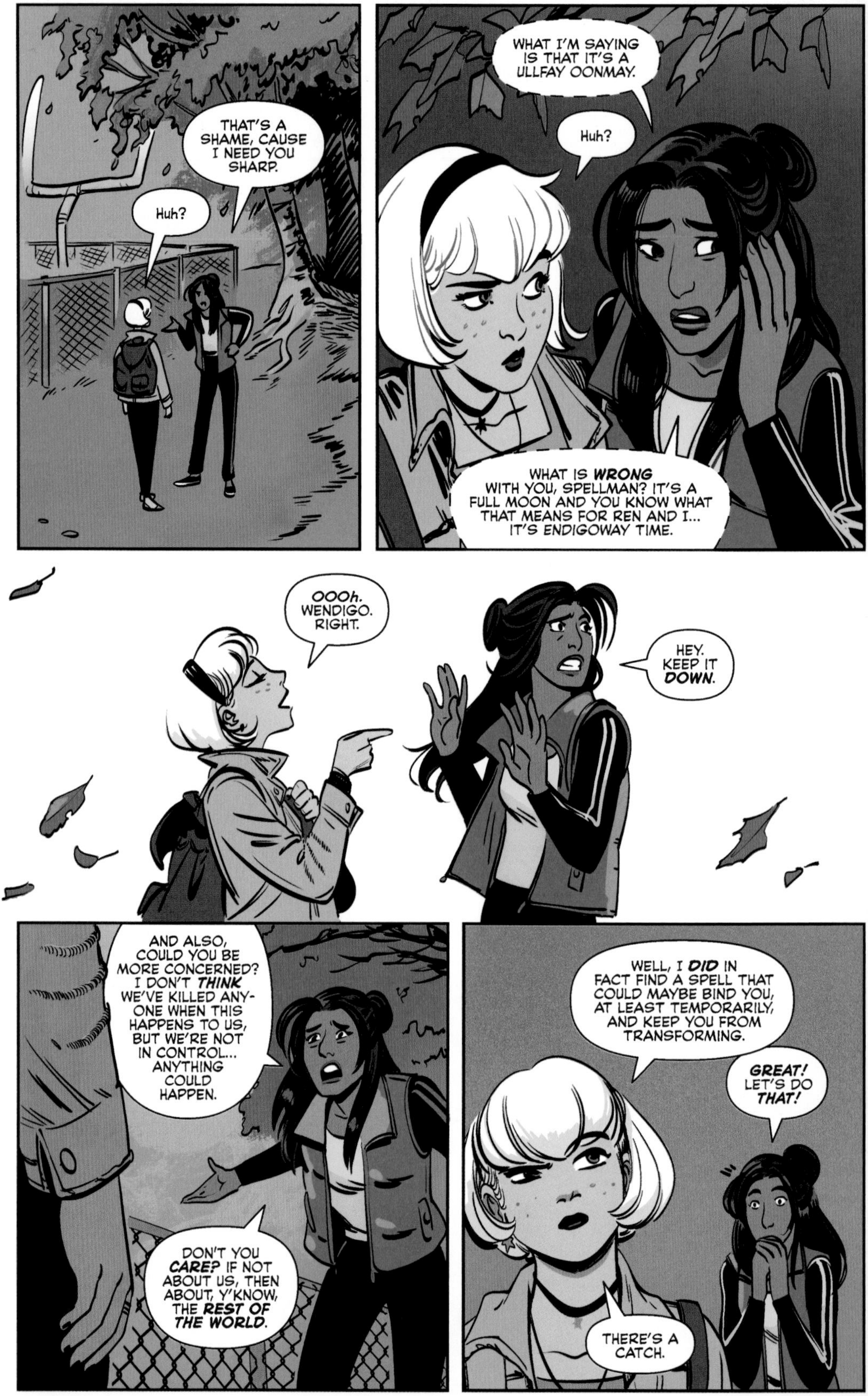
THAT'S A SHAME, CAUSE I NEED YOU SHARP.
Huh?
WHAT I'M SAYING IS THAT IT'S A ULLFAY OONMAY.
Huh?
WHAT IS WRONG WITH YOU, SPELLMAN? IT'S A FULL MOON AND YOU KNOW WHAT THAT MEANS FOR REN AND I... IT'S ENDIGOWAY TIME.
OOOh. WENDIGO. RIGHT.
HEY. KEEP IT DOWN.
AND ALSO, COULD YOU BE MORE CONCERNED? I DON'T THINK WE'VE KILLED ANY-ONE WHEN THIS HAPPENS TO US, BUT WE'RE NOT IN CONTROL... ANYTHING COULD HAPPEN.
DON'T YOU CARE? IF NOT ABOUT US, THEN ABOUT, Y'KNOW, THE REST OF THE WORLD.
WELL, I DID IN FACT FIND A SPELL THAT COULD MAYBE BIND YOU, AT LEAST TEMPORARILY, AND KEEP YOU FROM TRANSFORMING.
GREAT! LET'S DO THAT!
THERE'S A CATCH.

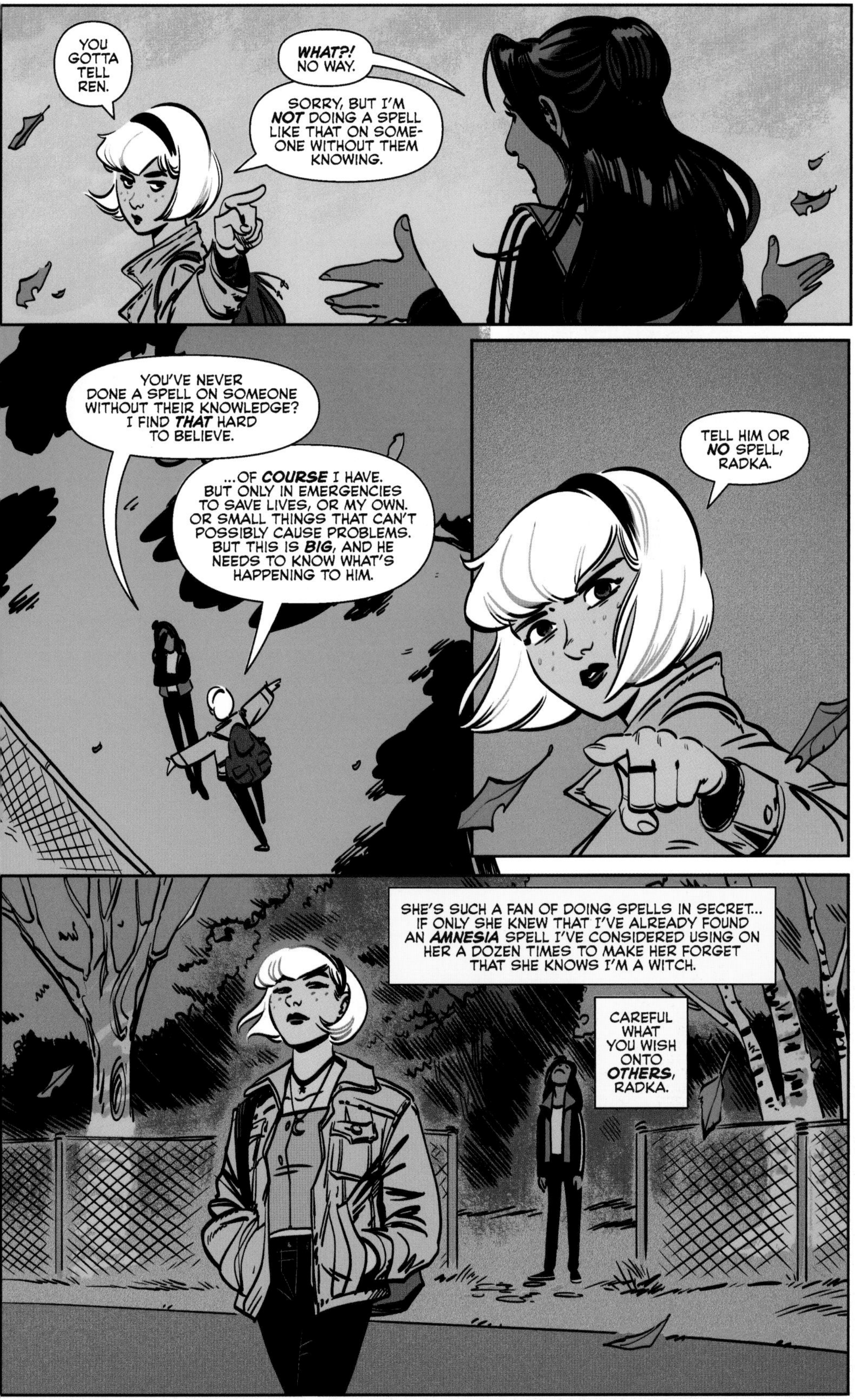
YOU GOTTA TELL REN.
WHAT?! NO WAY.
SORRY, BUT I'M NOT DOING A SPELL LIKE THAT ON SOME-ONE WITHOUT THEM KNOWING.
YOU'VE NEVER DONE A SPELL ON SOMEONE WITHOUT THEIR KNOWLEDGE? I FIND THAT HARD TO BELIEVE.
...OF COURSE I HAVE. BUT ONLY IN EMERGENCIES TO SAVE LIVES, OR MY OWN. OR SMALL THINGS THAT CAN'T POSSIBLY CAUSE PROBLEMS. BUT THIS IS BIG, AND HE NEEDS TO KNOW WHAT'S HAPPENING TO HIM.
TELL HIM OR NO SPELL, RADKA.
SHE'S SUCH A FAN OF DOING SPELLS IN SECRET... IF ONLY SHE KNEW THAT I'VE ALREADY FOUND AN AMNESIA SPELL I'VE CONSIDERED USING ON HER A DOZEN TIMES TO MAKE HER FORGET THAT SHE KNOWS I'M A WITCH.
CAREFUL WHAT YOU WISH ONTO OTHERS, RADKA.

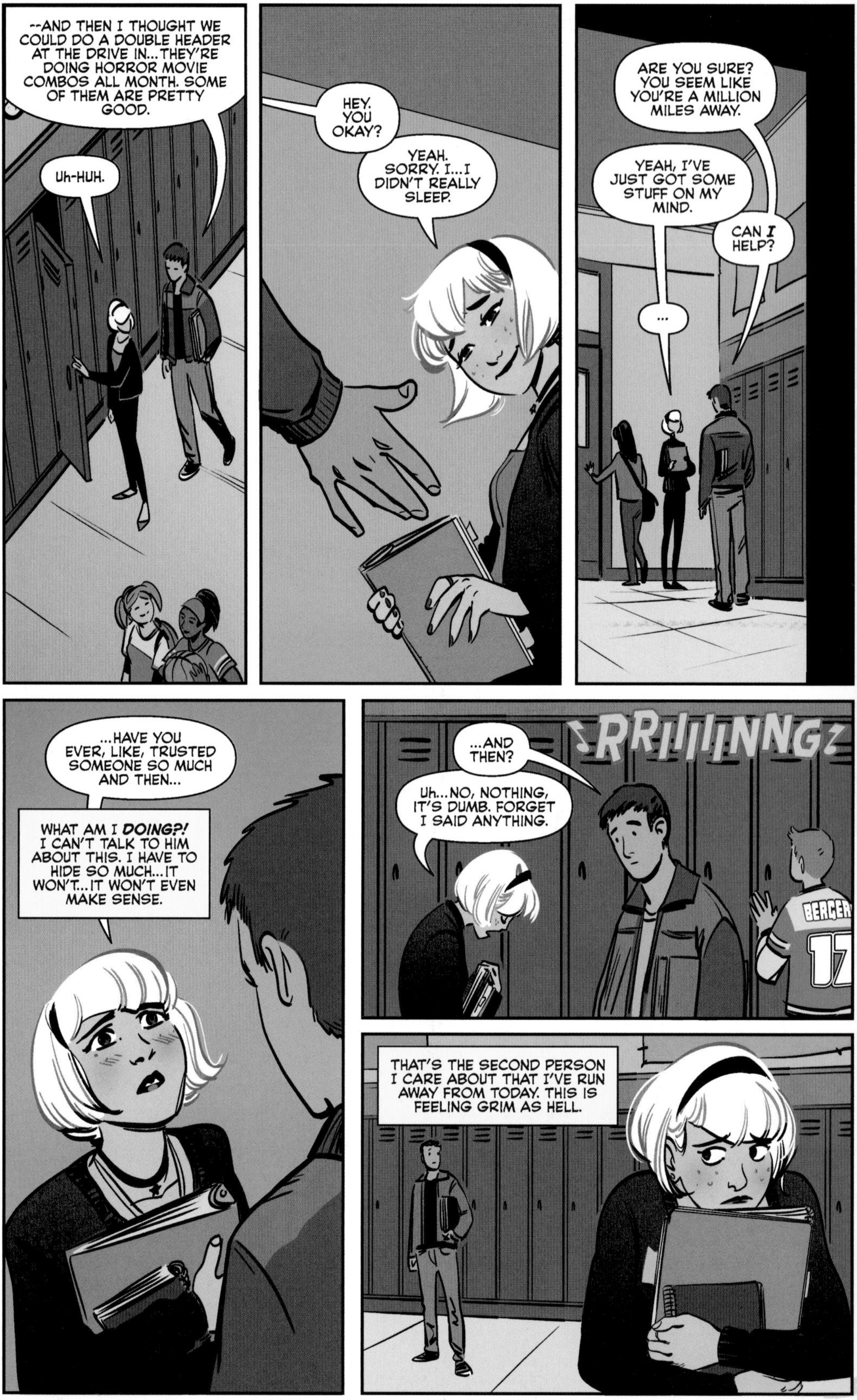
--AND THEN I THOUGHT WE COULD DO A DOUBLE HEADER AT THE DRIVE IN...THEY'RE DOING HORROR MOVIE COMBOS ALL MONTH. SOME OF THEM ARE PRETTY GOOD.
Uh-HUH.
HEY. YOU OKAY?
YEAH. SORRY. I...I DIDN'T REALLY SLEEP.
ARE YOU SURE? YOU SEEM LIKE YOU'RE A MILLION MILES AWAY.
YEAH, I'VE JUST GOT SOME STUFF ON MY MIND.
CAN *I* HELP?
...
...HAVE YOU EVER, LIKE, TRUSTED SOMEONE SO MUCH AND THEN...
WHAT AM I *DOING?!* I CAN'T TALK TO HIM ABOUT THIS. I HAVE TO HIDE SO MUCH...IT WON'T...IT WON'T EVEN MAKE SENSE.
...AND THEN?
Uh...NO, NOTHING, IT'S DUMB. FORGET I SAID ANYTHING.
RRIIIIINNG
BERGER
17
THAT'S THE SECOND PERSON I CARE ABOUT THAT I'VE RUN AWAY FROM TODAY. THIS IS FEELING GRIM AS HELL.

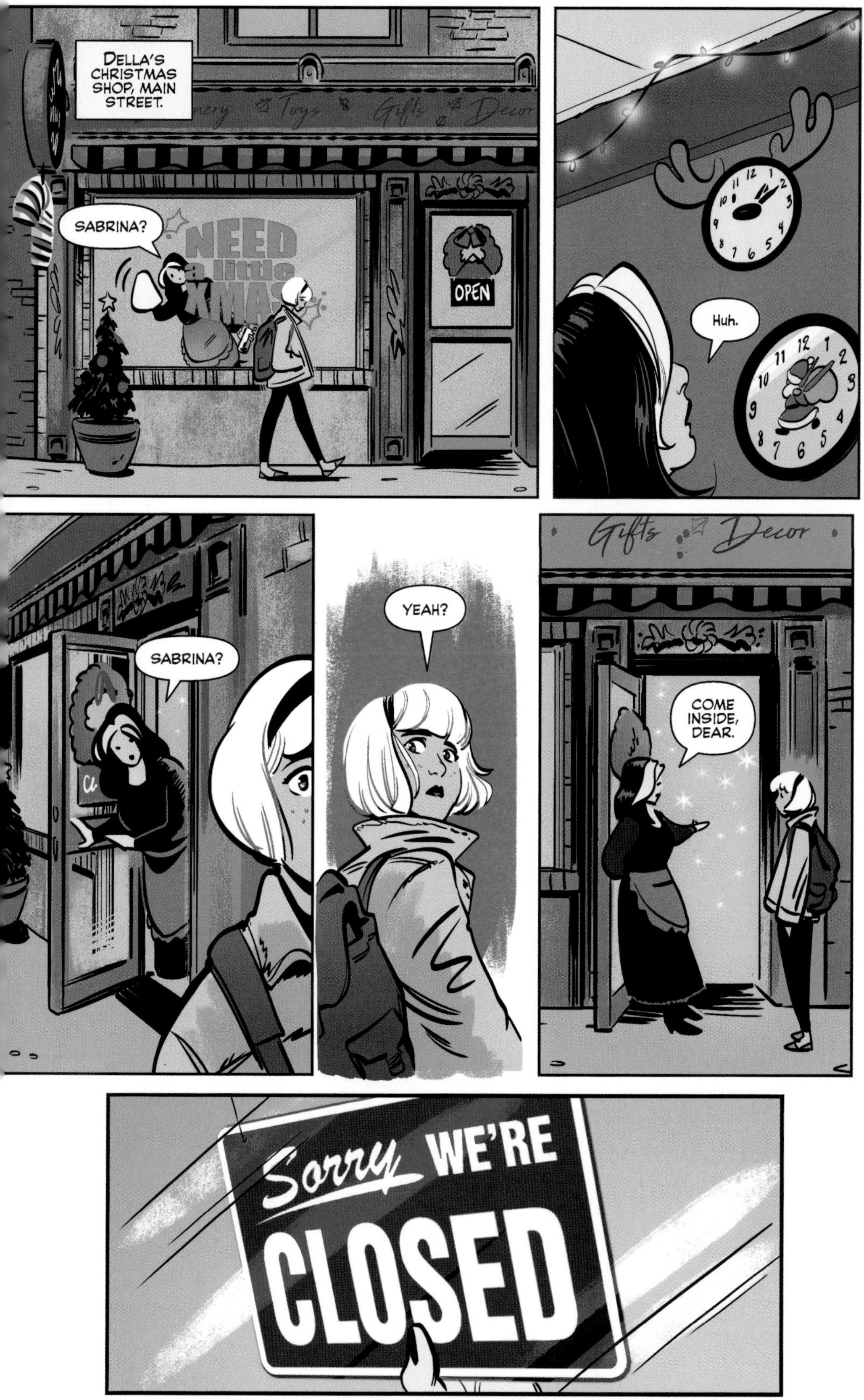
DELLA'S CHRISTMAS SHOP, MAIN STREET.
Toys
Gifts
Decor
NEED a little XMAS
OPEN
SABRINA?
Huh.
SABRINA?
YEAH?
Gifts
Decor
COME INSIDE, DEAR.
Sorry WE'RE CLOSED

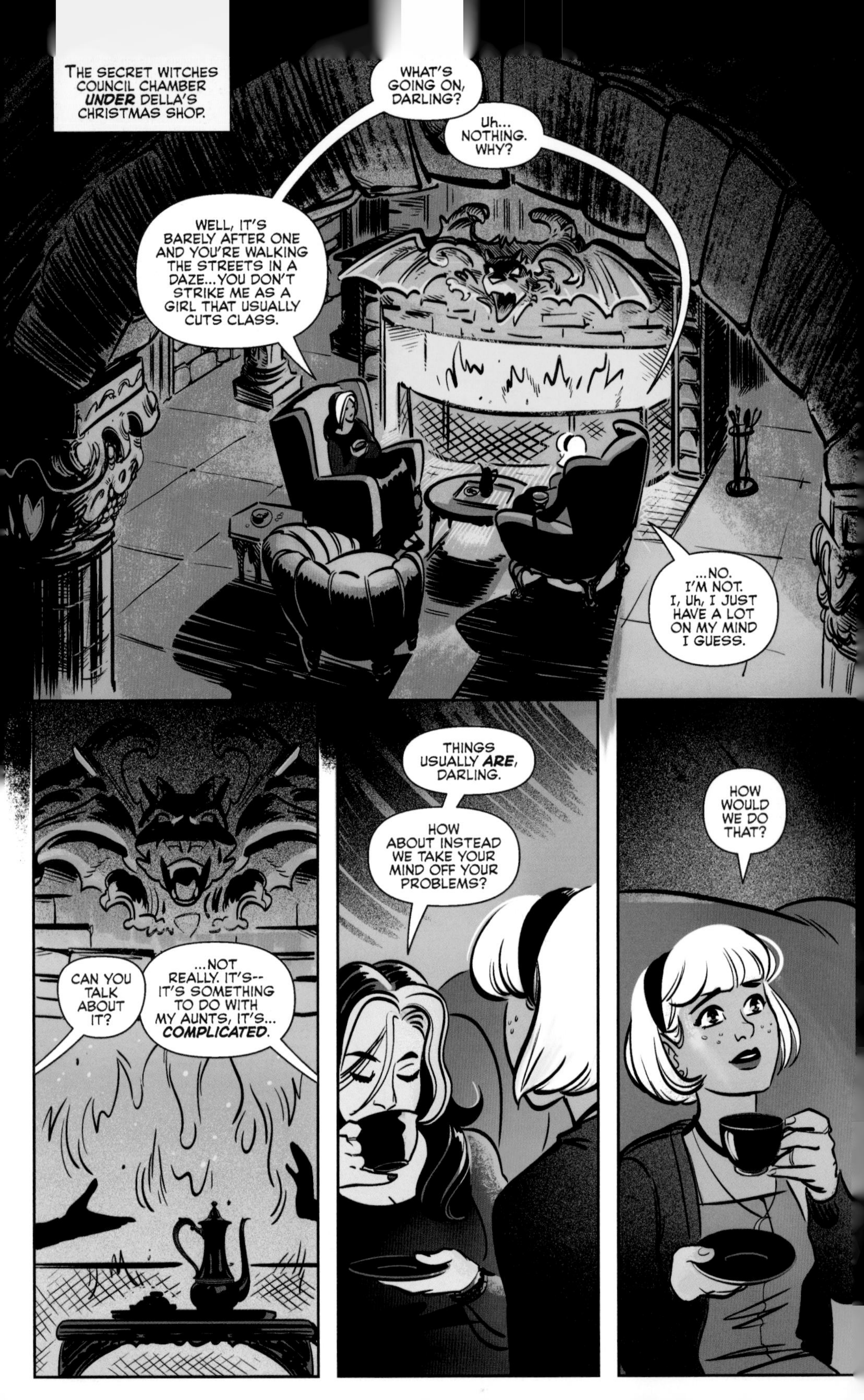
THE SECRET WITCHES COUNCIL CHAMBER UNDER DELLA'S CHRISTMAS SHOP.
WHAT'S GOING ON, DARLING?
Uh... NOTHING. WHY?
WELL, IT'S BARELY AFTER ONE AND YOU'RE WALKING THE STREETS IN A DAZE...YOU DON'T STRIKE ME AS A GIRL THAT USUALLY CUTS CLASS.
...NO. I'M NOT. I, Uh, I JUST HAVE A LOT ON MY MIND I GUESS.
CAN YOU TALK ABOUT IT?
...NOT REALLY. IT'S-- IT'S SOMETHING TO DO WITH MY AUNTS, IT'S... COMPLICATED.
THINGS USUALLY ARE, DARLING.
HOW ABOUT INSTEAD WE TAKE YOUR MIND OFF YOUR PROBLEMS?
HOW WOULD WE DO THAT?

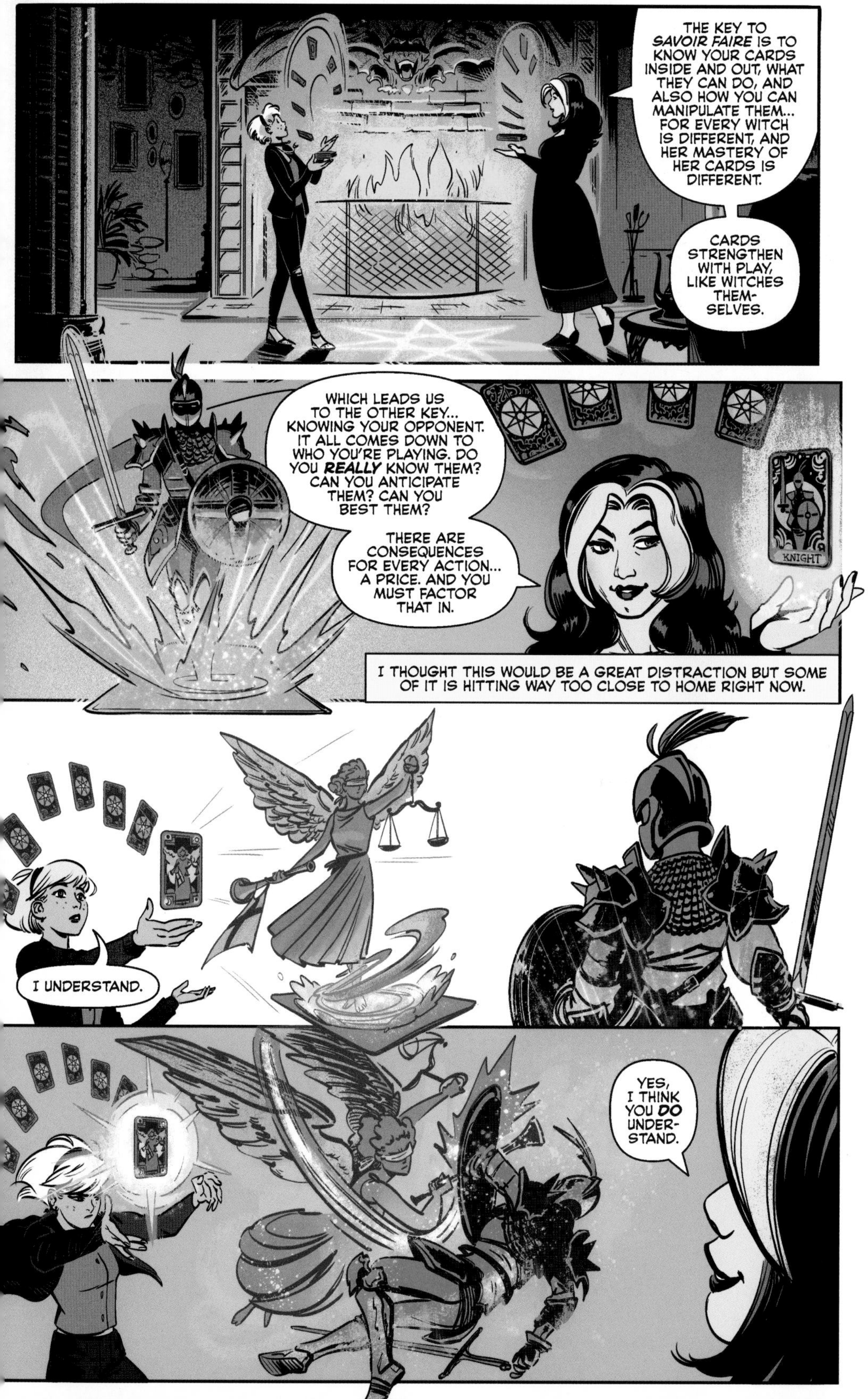
THE KEY TO *SAVOIR FAIRE* IS TO KNOW YOUR CARDS INSIDE AND OUT, WHAT THEY CAN DO, AND ALSO HOW YOU CAN MANIPULATE THEM... FOR EVERY WITCH IS DIFFERENT, AND HER MASTERY OF HER CARDS IS DIFFERENT.
CARDS STRENGTHEN WITH PLAY, LIKE WITCHES THEM-SELVES.
WHICH LEADS US TO THE OTHER KEY... KNOWING YOUR OPPONENT. IT ALL COMES DOWN TO WHO YOU'RE PLAYING. DO YOU ***REALLY*** KNOW THEM? CAN YOU ANTICIPATE THEM? CAN YOU BEST THEM?
THERE ARE CONSEQUENCES FOR EVERY ACTION... A PRICE. AND YOU MUST FACTOR THAT IN.
KNIGHT
I THOUGHT THIS WOULD BE A GREAT DISTRACTION BUT SOME OF IT IS HITTING WAY TOO CLOSE TO HOME RIGHT NOW.
I UNDERSTAND.
YES, I THINK YOU ***DO*** UNDER-STAND.

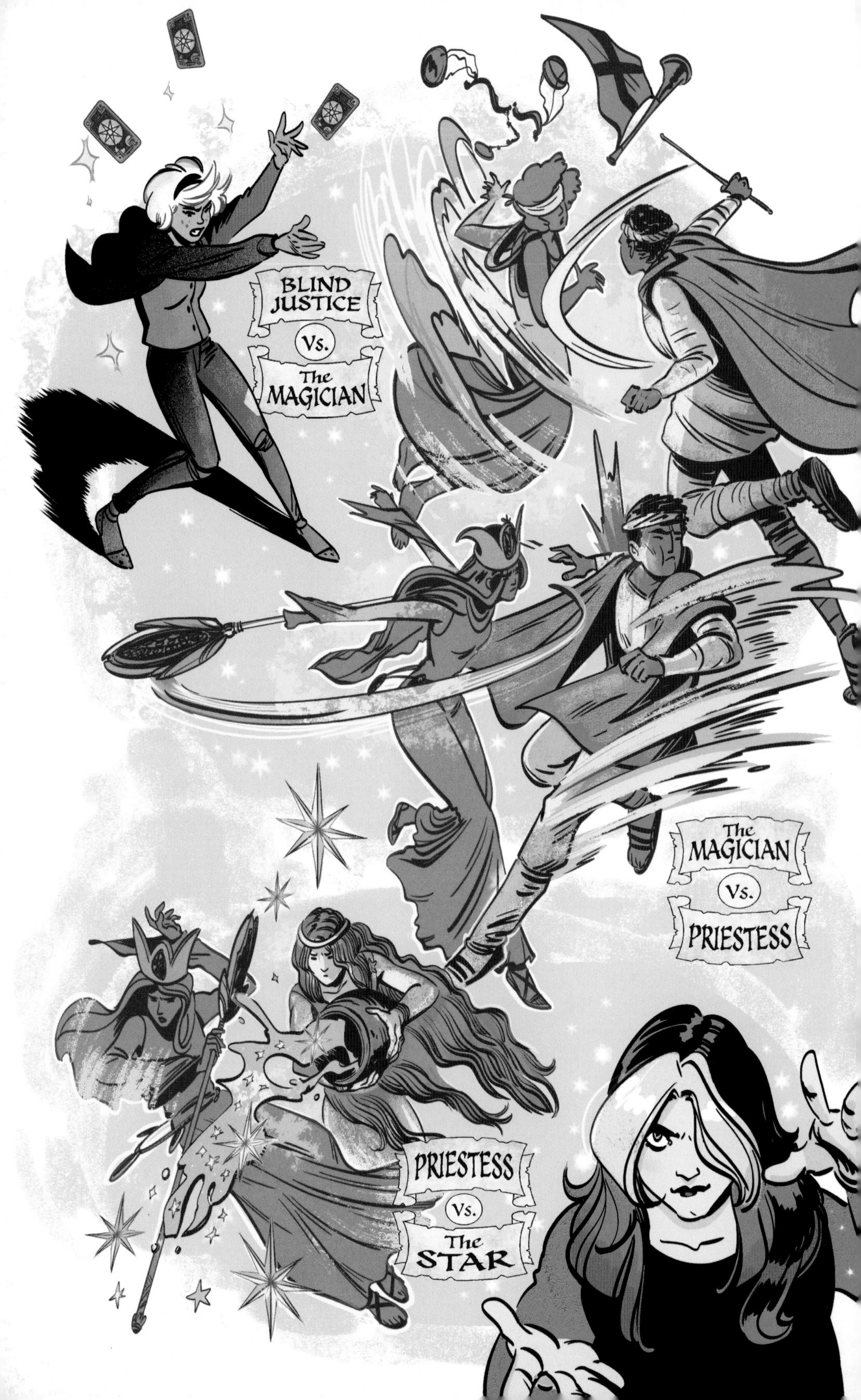
BLIND JUSTICE
Vs.
The MAGICIAN
The MAGICIAN
Vs.
PRIESTESS
PRIESTESS
Vs.
The STAR

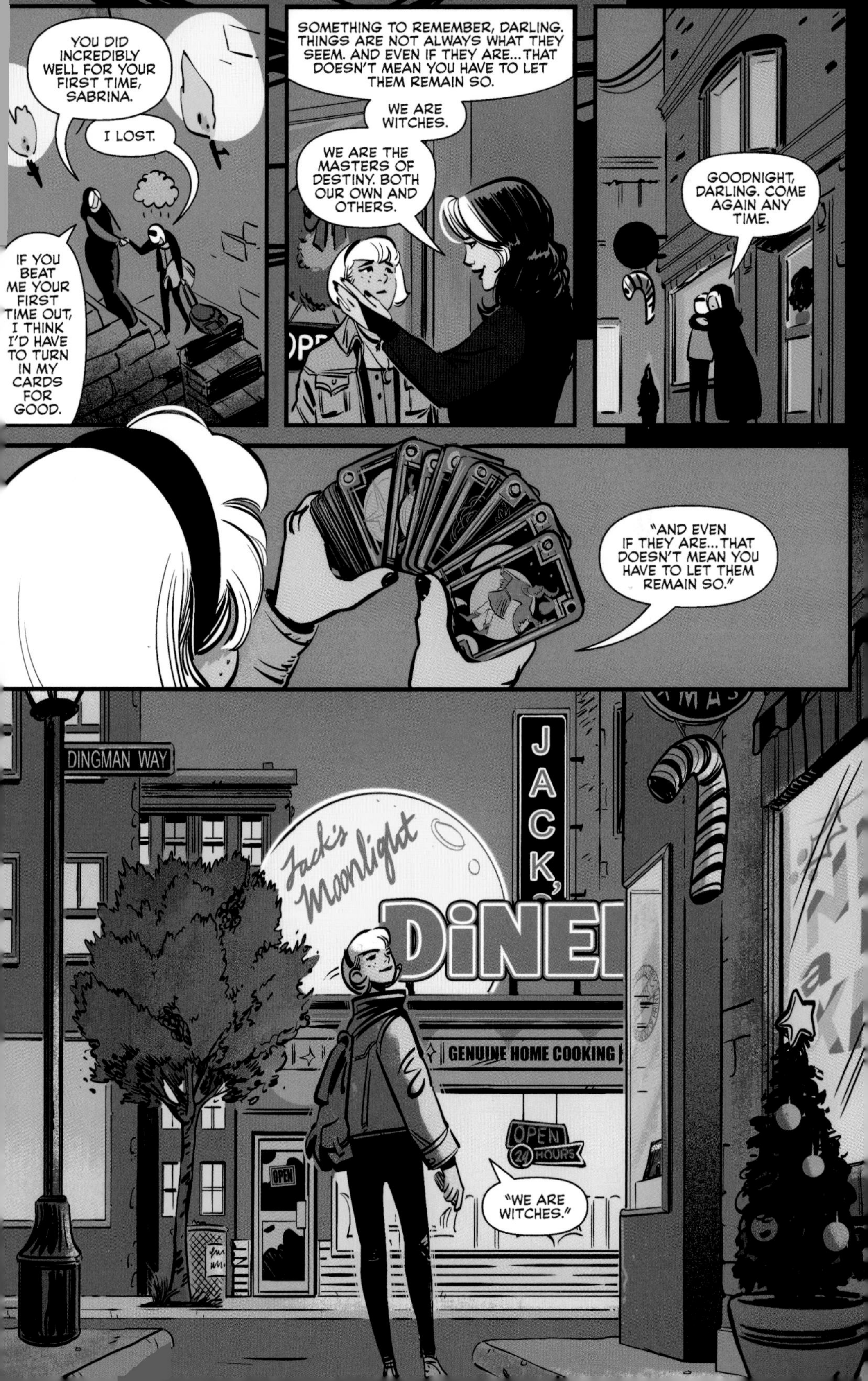
YOU DID INCREDIBLY WELL FOR YOUR FIRST TIME, SABRINA.
I LOST.
IF YOU BEAT ME YOUR FIRST TIME OUT, I THINK I'D HAVE TO TURN IN MY CARDS FOR GOOD.
SOMETHING TO REMEMBER, DARLING. THINGS ARE NOT ALWAYS WHAT THEY SEEM. AND EVEN IF THEY ARE...THAT DOESN'T MEAN YOU HAVE TO LET THEM REMAIN SO.
WE ARE WITCHES.
WE ARE THE MASTERS OF DESTINY. BOTH OUR OWN AND OTHERS.
GOODNIGHT, DARLING. COME AGAIN ANY TIME.
"AND EVEN IF THEY ARE...THAT DOESN'T MEAN YOU HAVE TO LET THEM REMAIN SO."
DINGMAN WAY
JACK'S
Jack's Moonlight
DiNE
GENUINE HOME COOKING
OPEN 24 HOURS
OPEN
"WE ARE WITCHES."

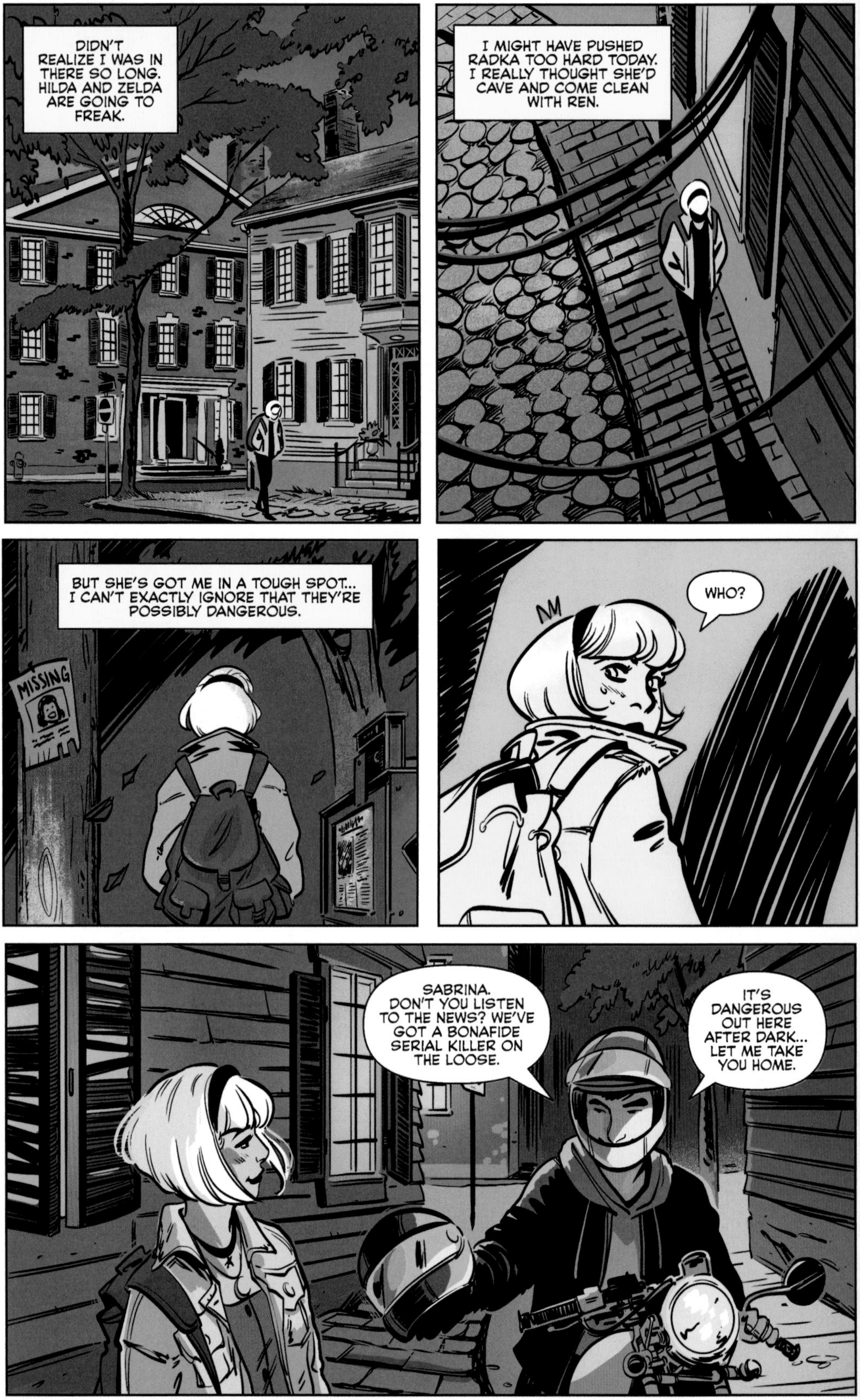
DIDN'T REALIZE I WAS IN THERE SO LONG. HILDA AND ZELDA ARE GOING TO FREAK.
I MIGHT HAVE PUSHED RADKA TOO HARD TODAY. I REALLY THOUGHT SHE'D CAVE AND COME CLEAN WITH REN.
BUT SHE'S GOT ME IN A TOUGH SPOT... I CAN'T EXACTLY IGNORE THAT THEY'RE POSSIBLY DANGEROUS.
MISSING
WHO?
SABRINA. DON'T YOU LISTEN TO THE NEWS? WE'VE GOT A BONAFIDE SERIAL KILLER ON THE LOOSE.
IT'S DANGEROUS OUT HERE AFTER DARK... LET ME TAKE YOU HOME.

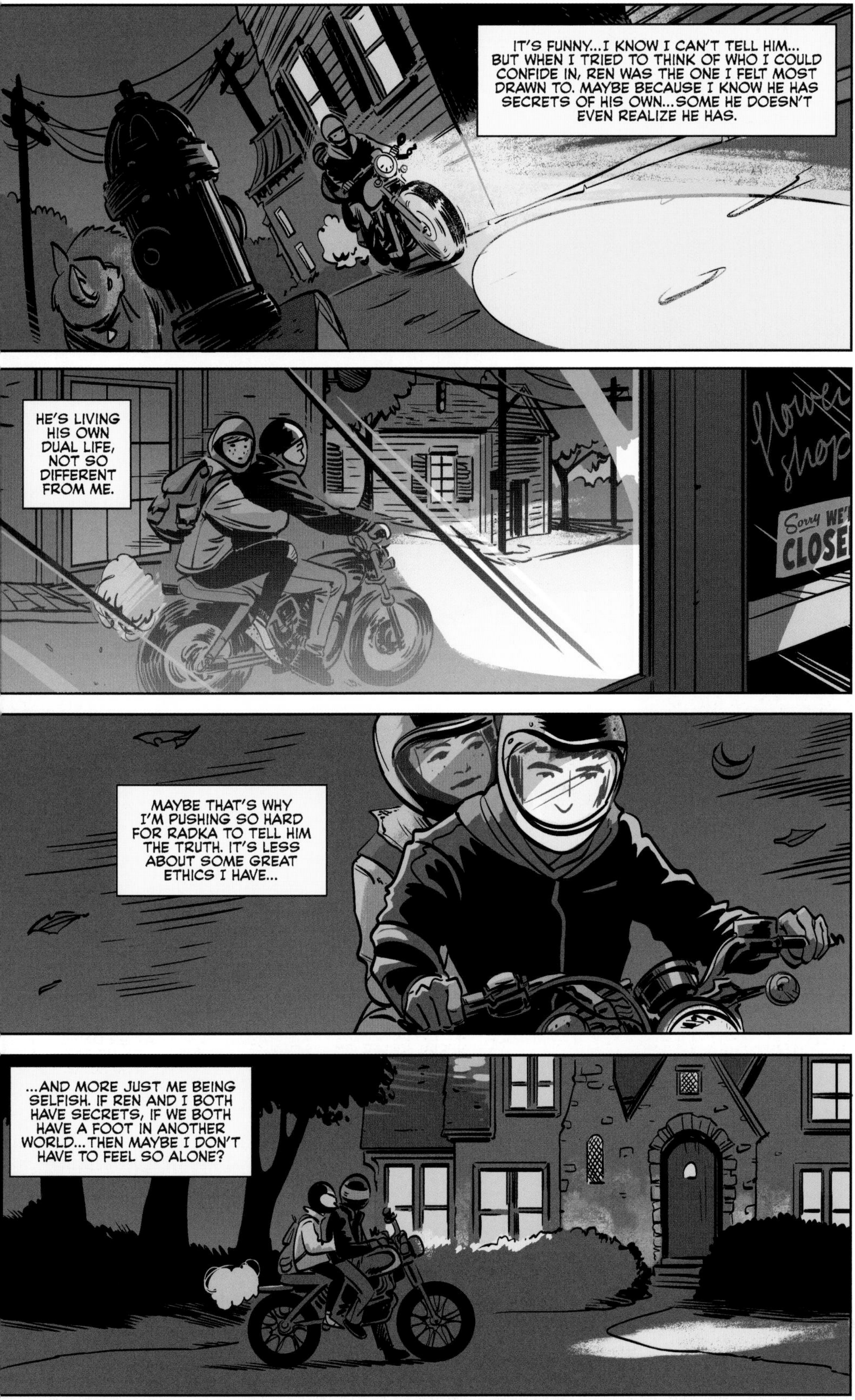
IT'S FUNNY...I KNOW I CAN'T TELL HIM... BUT WHEN I TRIED TO THINK OF WHO I COULD CONFIDE IN, REN WAS THE ONE I FELT MOST DRAWN TO. MAYBE BECAUSE I KNOW HE HAS SECRETS OF HIS OWN...SOME HE DOESN'T EVEN REALIZE HE HAS.
HE'S LIVING HIS OWN DUAL LIFE, NOT SO DIFFERENT FROM ME.
flower shop
Sorry WE'
CLOSE
MAYBE THAT'S WHY I'M PUSHING SO HARD FOR RADKA TO TELL HIM THE TRUTH. IT'S LESS ABOUT SOME GREAT ETHICS I HAVE...
...AND MORE JUST ME BEING SELFISH. IF REN AND I BOTH HAVE SECRETS, IF WE BOTH HAVE A FOOT IN ANOTHER WORLD...THEN MAYBE I DON'T HAVE TO FEEL SO ALONE?

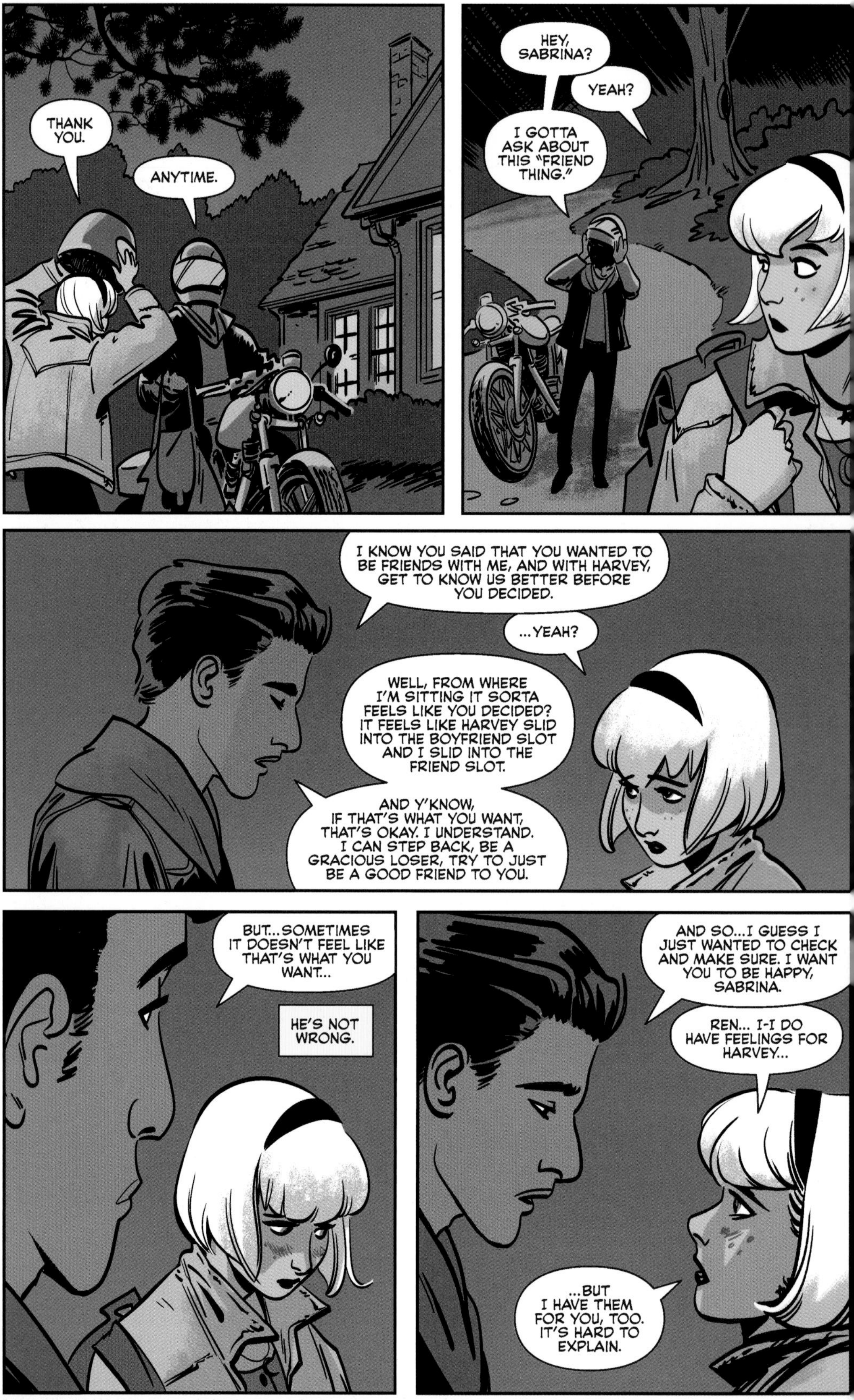
THANK YOU.
ANYTIME.
HEY, SABRINA?
YEAH?
I GOTTA ASK ABOUT THIS "FRIEND THING."
I KNOW YOU SAID THAT YOU WANTED TO BE FRIENDS WITH ME, AND WITH HARVEY, GET TO KNOW US BETTER BEFORE YOU DECIDED.
...YEAH?
WELL, FROM WHERE I'M SITTING IT SORTA FEELS LIKE YOU DECIDED? IT FEELS LIKE HARVEY SLID INTO THE BOYFRIEND SLOT AND I SLID INTO THE FRIEND SLOT.
AND Y'KNOW, IF THAT'S WHAT YOU WANT, THAT'S OKAY. I UNDERSTAND. I CAN STEP BACK, BE A GRACIOUS LOSER, TRY TO JUST BE A GOOD FRIEND TO YOU.
BUT...SOMETIMES IT DOESN'T FEEL LIKE THAT'S WHAT YOU WANT...
HE'S NOT WRONG.
AND SO...I GUESS I JUST WANTED TO CHECK AND MAKE SURE. I WANT YOU TO BE HAPPY, SABRINA.
REN... I-I DO HAVE FEELINGS FOR HARVEY...
...BUT I HAVE THEM FOR YOU, TOO. IT'S HARD TO EXPLAIN.

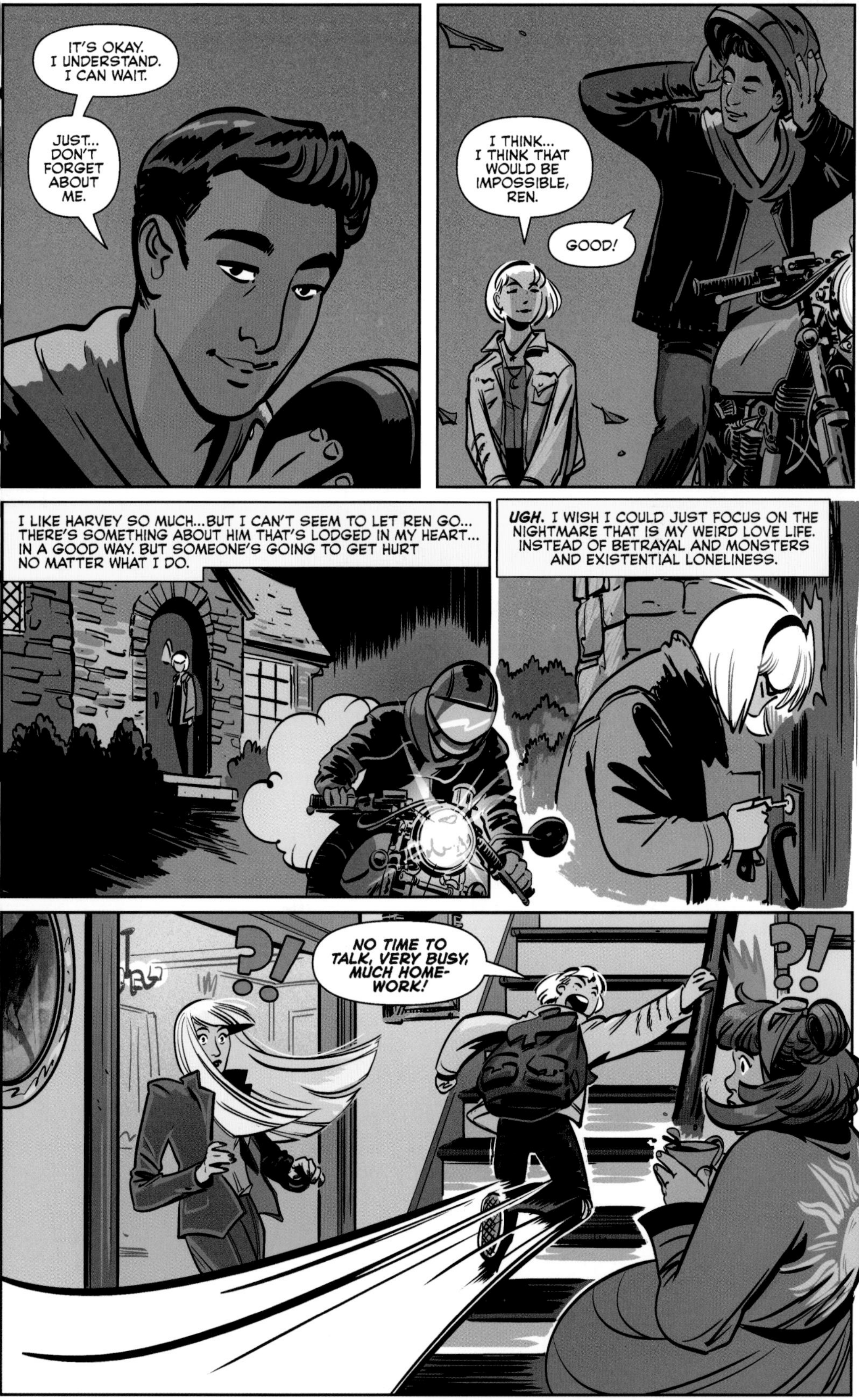
IT'S OKAY. I UNDERSTAND. I CAN WAIT.
JUST... DON'T FORGET ABOUT ME.
I THINK... I THINK THAT WOULD BE IMPOSSIBLE, REN.
GOOD!
I LIKE HARVEY SO MUCH...BUT I CAN'T SEEM TO LET REN GO... THERE'S SOMETHING ABOUT HIM THAT'S LODGED IN MY HEART... IN A GOOD WAY. BUT SOMEONE'S GOING TO GET HURT NO MATTER WHAT I DO.
UGH. I WISH I COULD JUST FOCUS ON THE NIGHTMARE THAT IS MY WEIRD LOVE LIFE. INSTEAD OF BETRAYAL AND MONSTERS AND EXISTENTIAL LONELINESS.
?!
NO TIME TO TALK, VERY BUSY, MUCH HOME-WORK!
?!

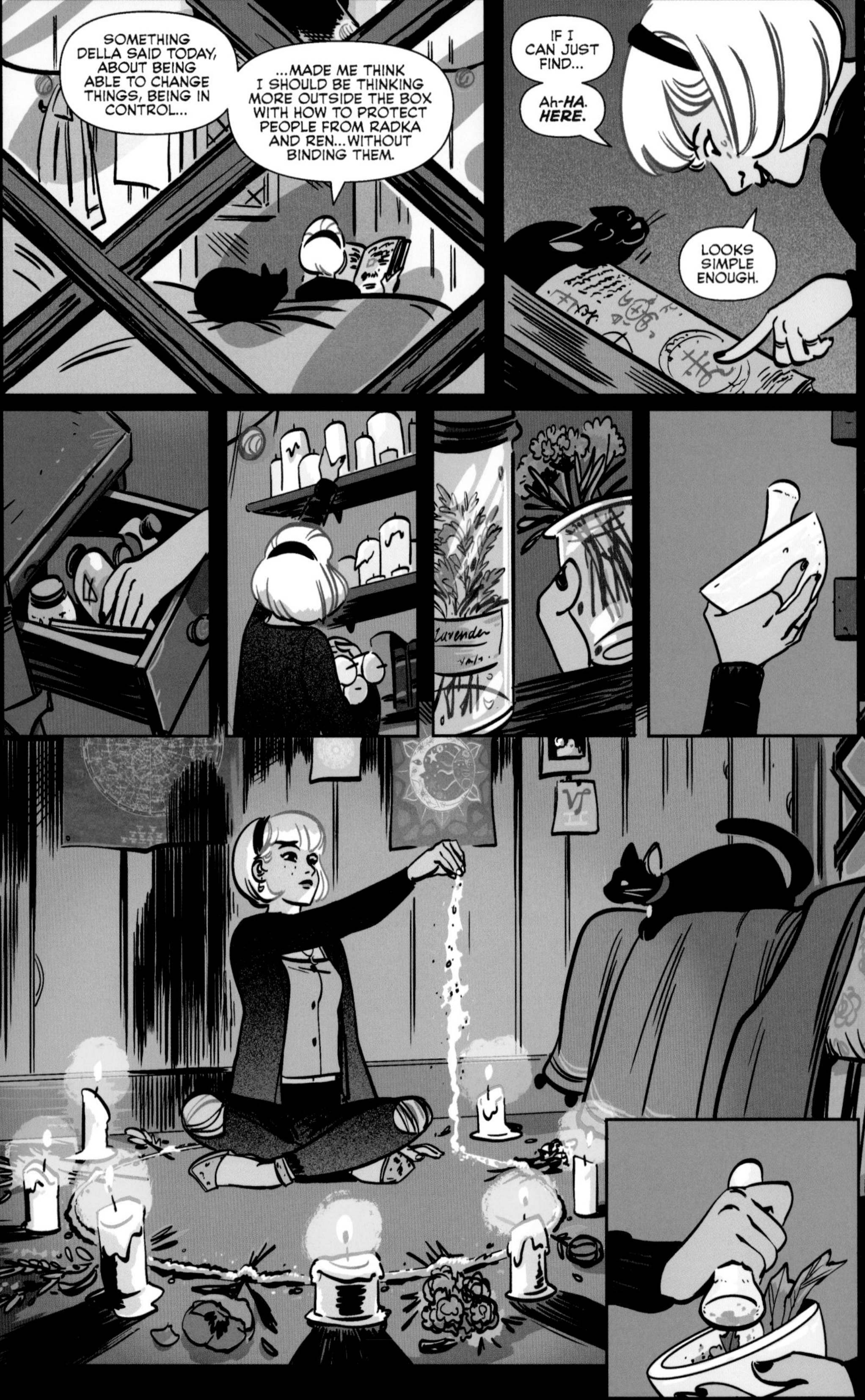
SOMETHING DELLA SAID TODAY, ABOUT BEING ABLE TO CHANGE THINGS, BEING IN CONTROL...
...MADE ME THINK I SHOULD BE THINKING MORE OUTSIDE THE BOX WITH HOW TO PROTECT PEOPLE FROM RADKA AND REN...WITHOUT BINDING THEM.
IF I CAN JUST FIND...
Ah-HA. HERE.
LOOKS SIMPLE ENOUGH.
Lavender

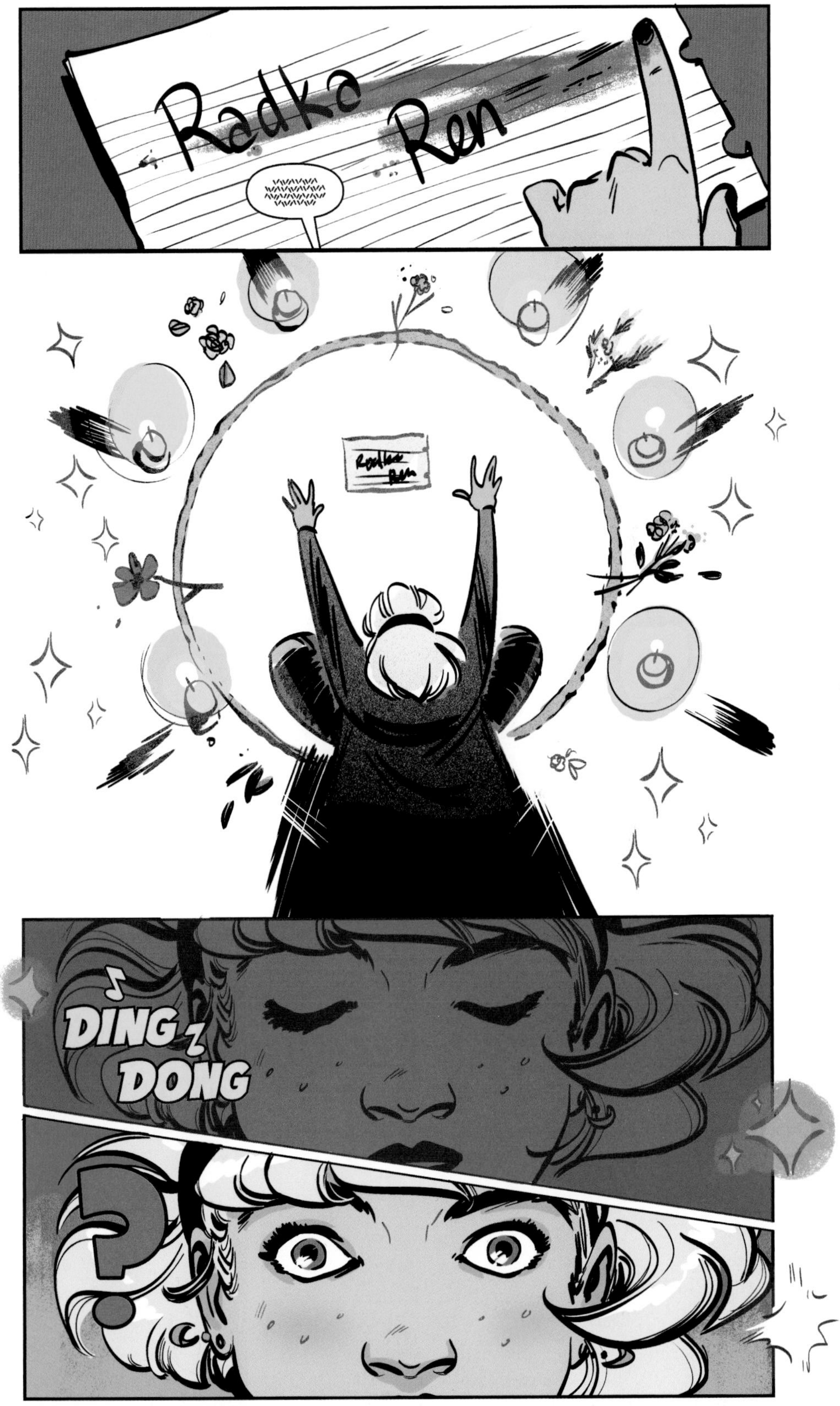
Radka Ren
DING
DONG
?

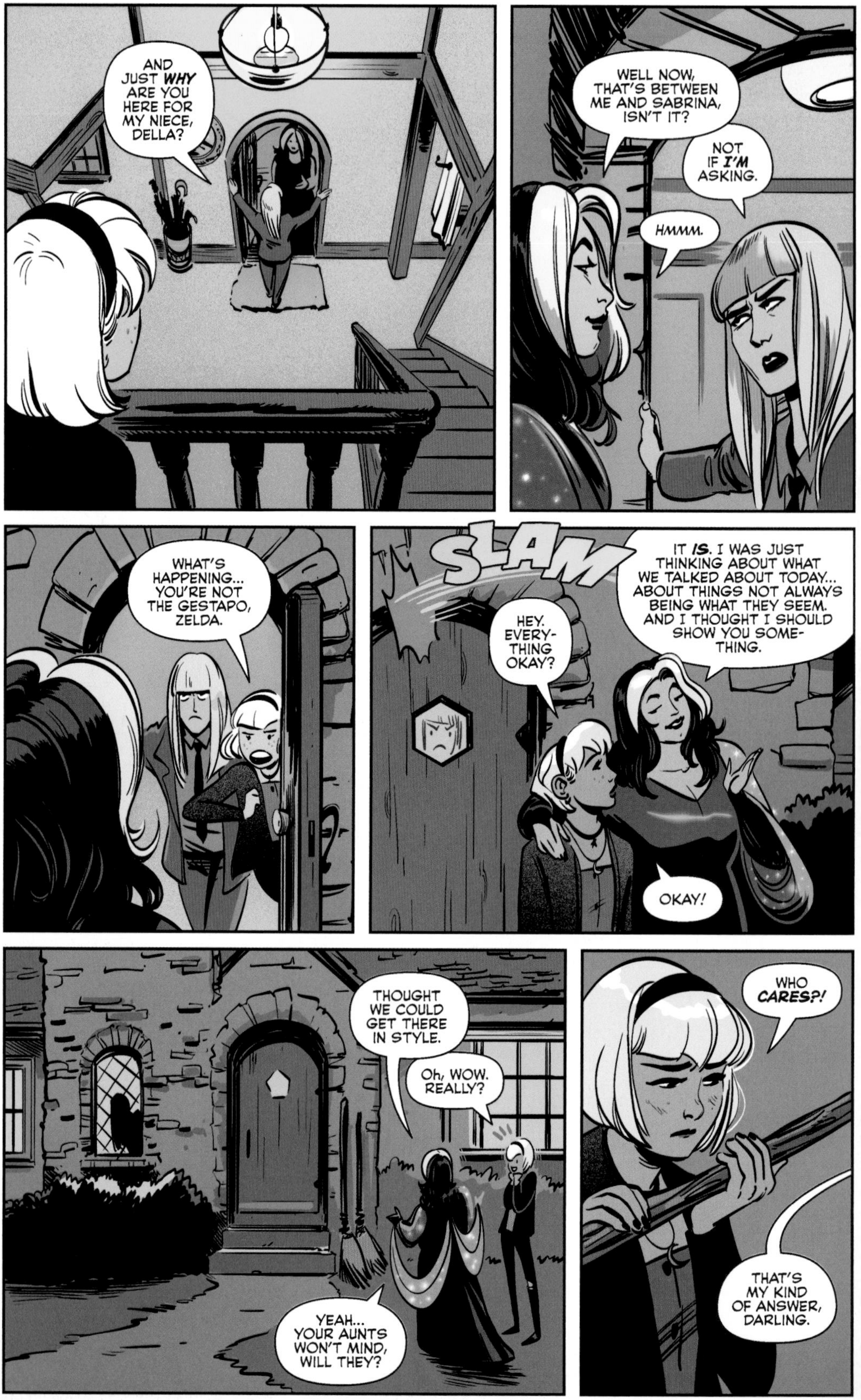
AND JUST WHY ARE YOU HERE FOR MY NIECE, DELLA?
WELL NOW, THAT'S BETWEEN ME AND SABRINA, ISN'T IT?
NOT IF I'M ASKING.
HMMM.
WHAT'S HAPPENING... YOU'RE NOT THE GESTAPO, ZELDA.
SLAM
HEY. EVERY-THING OKAY?
IT IS. I WAS JUST THINKING ABOUT WHAT WE TALKED ABOUT TODAY... ABOUT THINGS NOT ALWAYS BEING WHAT THEY SEEM. AND I THOUGHT I SHOULD SHOW YOU SOME-THING.
OKAY!
THOUGHT WE COULD GET THERE IN STYLE.
Oh, WOW. REALLY?
YEAH... YOUR AUNTS WON'T MIND, WILL THEY?
WHO CARES?!
THAT'S MY KIND OF ANSWER, DARLING.

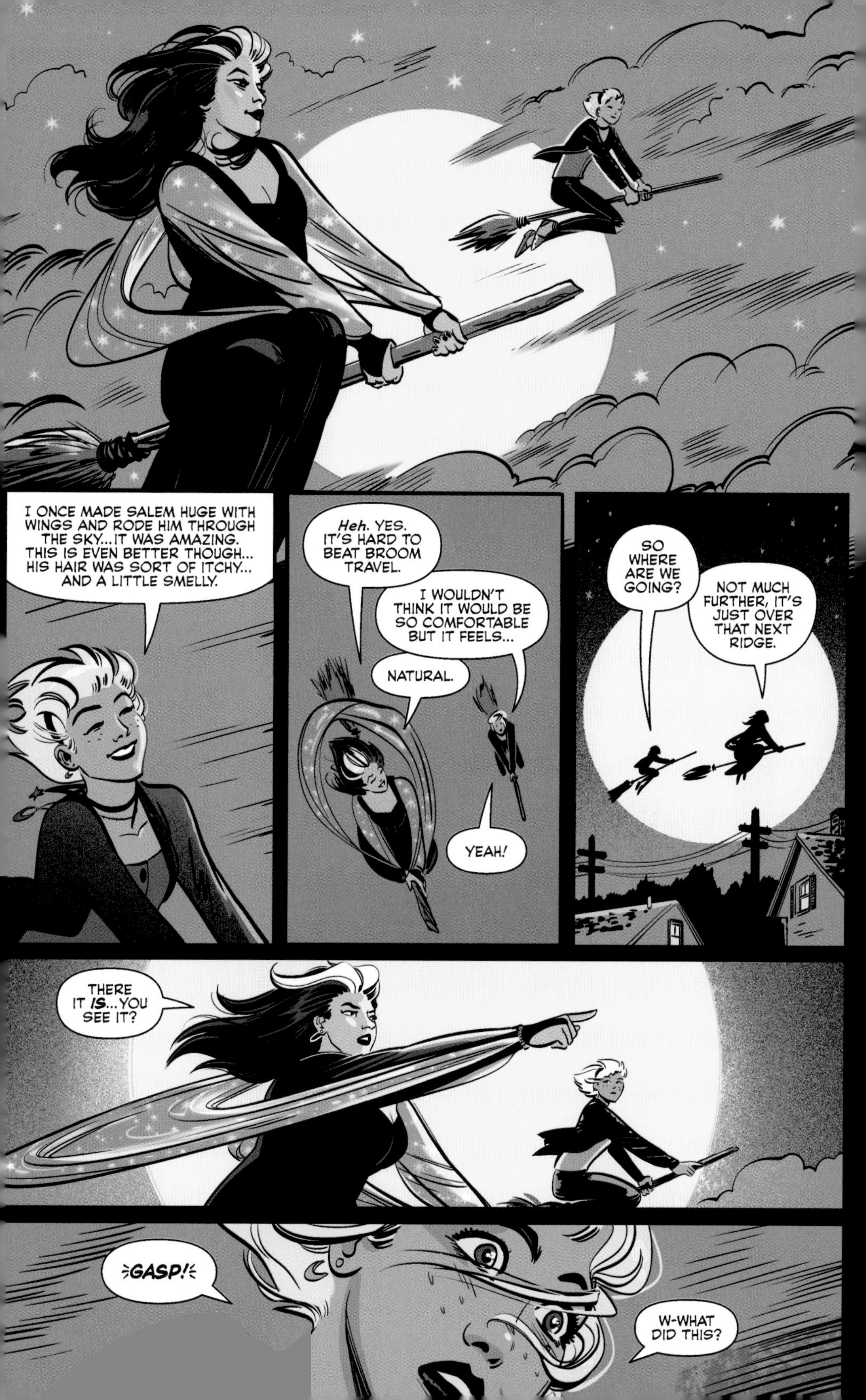
I ONCE MADE SALEM HUGE WITH WINGS AND RODE HIM THROUGH THE SKY...IT WAS AMAZING. THIS IS EVEN BETTER THOUGH... HIS HAIR WAS SORT OF ITCHY... AND A LITTLE SMELLY.
Heh. YES. IT'S HARD TO BEAT BROOM TRAVEL.
I WOULDN'T THINK IT WOULD BE SO COMFORTABLE BUT IT FEELS...
NATURAL.
YEAH!
SO WHERE ARE WE GOING?
NOT MUCH FURTHER, IT'S JUST OVER THAT NEXT RIDGE.
THERE IT *IS*...YOU SEE IT?
GASP!
W-WHAT DID THIS?

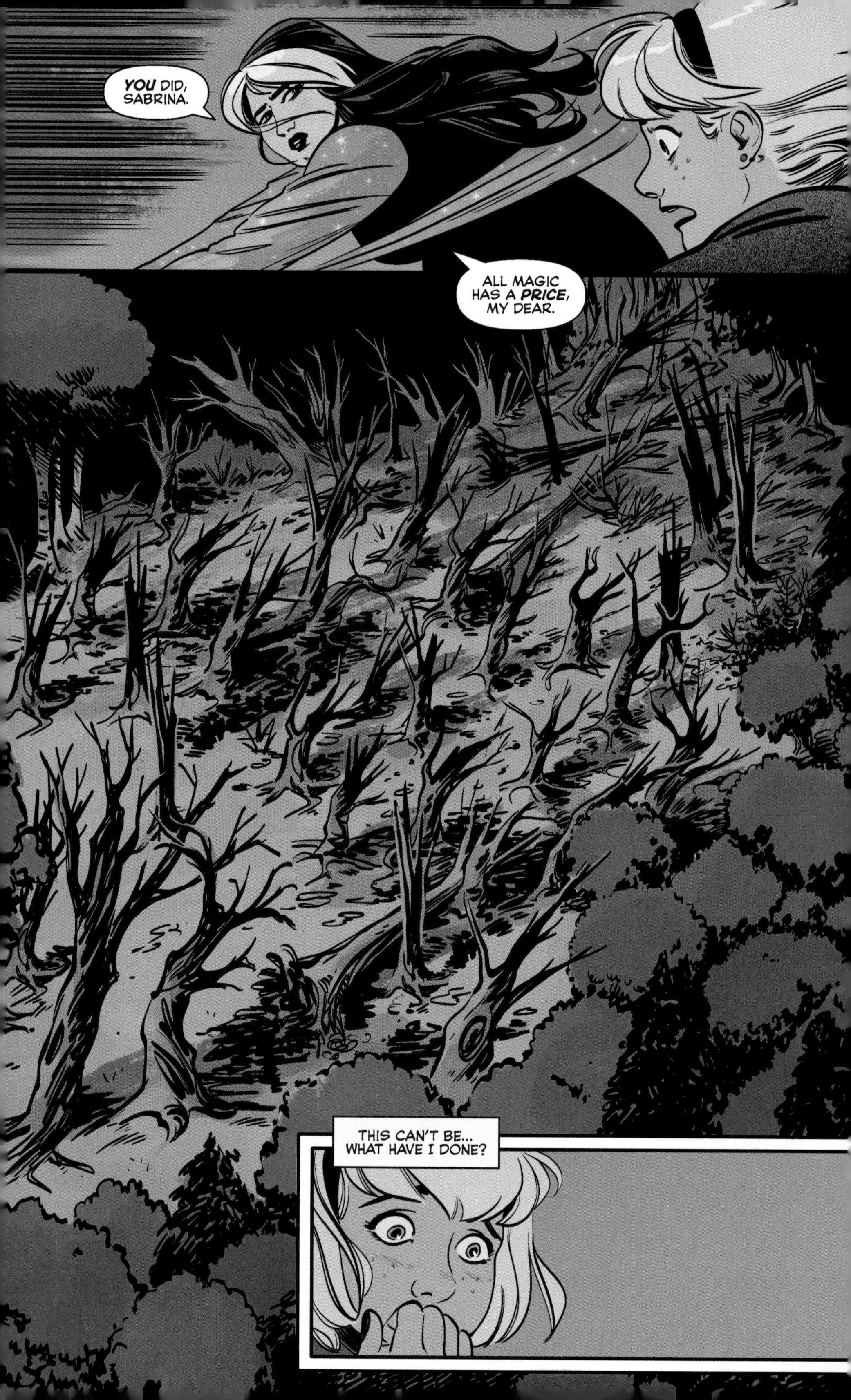
YOU DID, SABRINA.
ALL MAGIC HAS A PRICE, MY DEAR.
THIS CAN'T BE... WHAT HAVE I DONE?

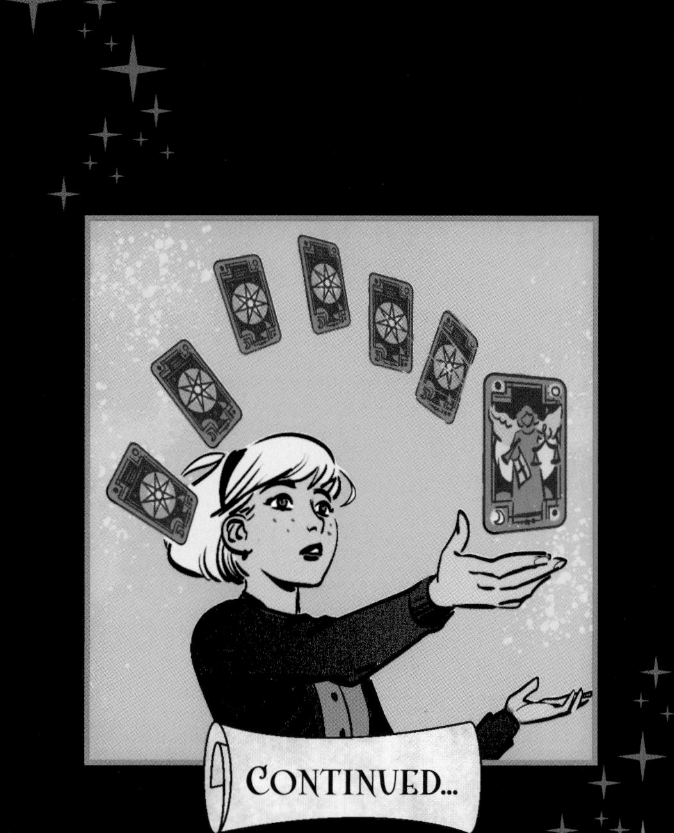
CONTINUED...

03

STORY BY
KELLY THOMPSON

ART BY
VERONICA FISH
AND **ANDY FISH**

LETTERING BY
JACK MORELLI

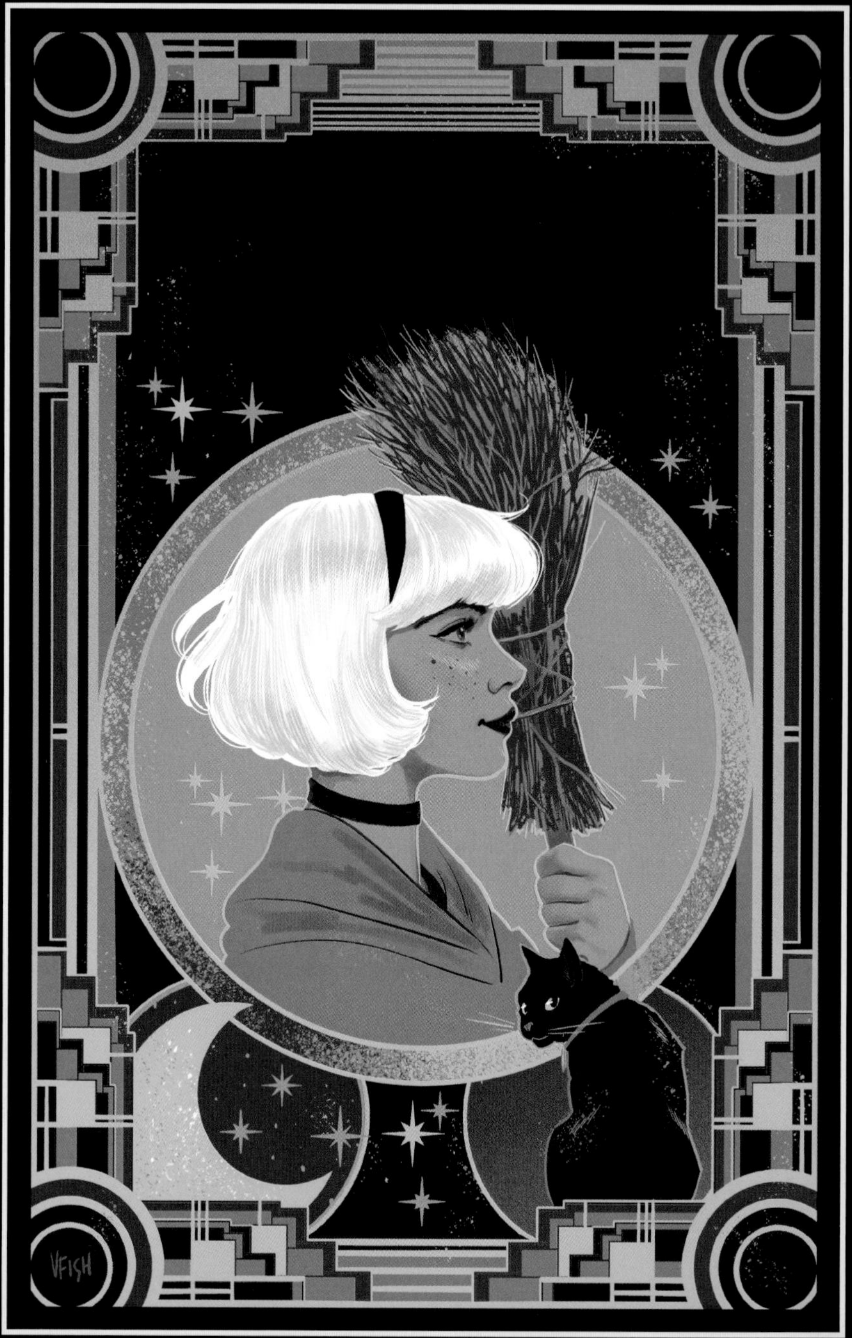

VFISH

COVER ART: **VERONICA FISH**

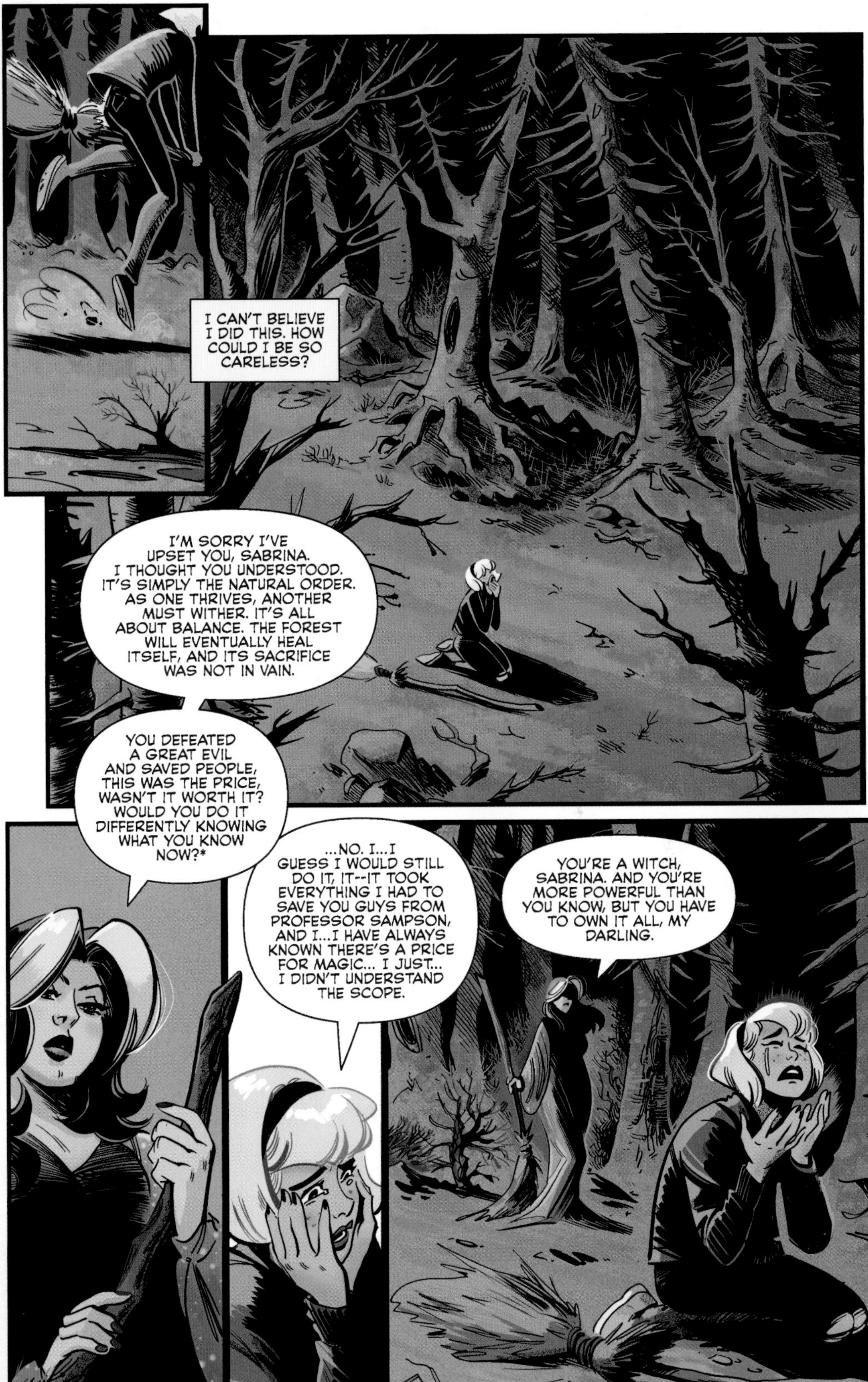

I CAN'T BELIEVE I DID THIS. HOW COULD I BE SO CARELESS?
I'M SORRY I'VE UPSET YOU, SABRINA. I THOUGHT YOU UNDERSTOOD. IT'S SIMPLY THE NATURAL ORDER. AS ONE THRIVES, ANOTHER MUST WITHER. IT'S ALL ABOUT BALANCE. THE FOREST WILL EVENTUALLY HEAL ITSELF, AND ITS SACRIFICE WAS NOT IN VAIN.
YOU DEFEATED A GREAT EVIL AND SAVED PEOPLE, THIS WAS THE PRICE, WASN'T IT WORTH IT? WOULD YOU DO IT DIFFERENTLY KNOWING WHAT YOU KNOW NOW?*
...NO. I...I GUESS I WOULD STILL DO IT, IT--IT TOOK EVERYTHING I HAD TO SAVE YOU GUYS FROM PROFESSOR SAMPSON, AND I...I HAVE ALWAYS KNOWN THERE'S A PRICE FOR MAGIC... I JUST... I DIDN'T UNDERSTAND THE SCOPE.
YOU'RE A WITCH, SABRINA. AND YOU'RE MORE POWERFUL THAN YOU KNOW, BUT YOU HAVE TO OWN IT ALL, MY DARLING.
*IT HAPPENED IN SABRINA VOL 1!

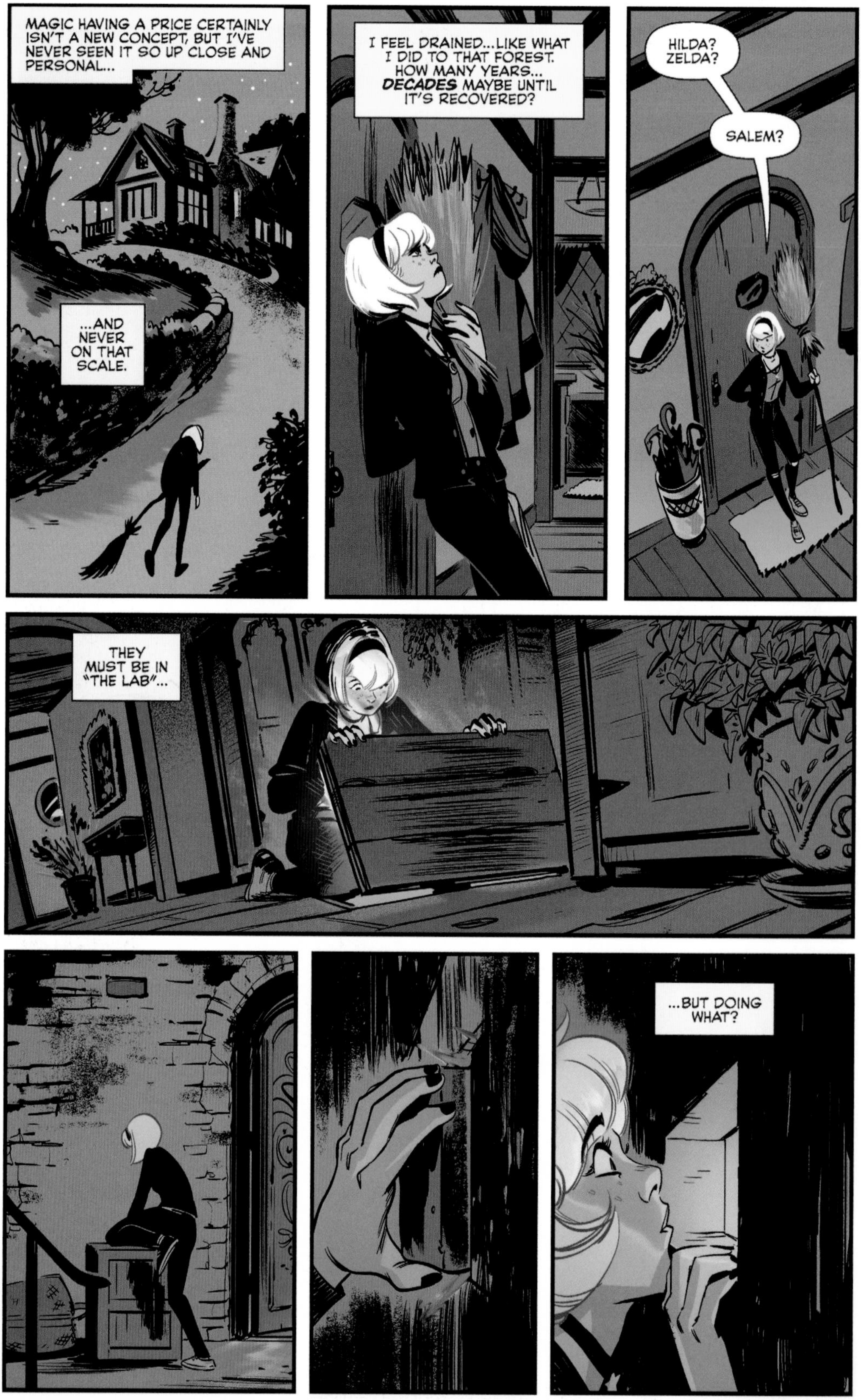
MAGIC HAVING A PRICE CERTAINLY ISN'T A NEW CONCEPT, BUT I'VE NEVER SEEN IT SO UP CLOSE AND PERSONAL...
...AND NEVER ON THAT SCALE.
I FEEL DRAINED...LIKE WHAT I DID TO THAT FOREST. HOW MANY YEARS... DECADES MAYBE UNTIL IT'S RECOVERED?
HILDA? ZELDA?
SALEM?
THEY MUST BE IN "THE LAB"...
...BUT DOING WHAT?

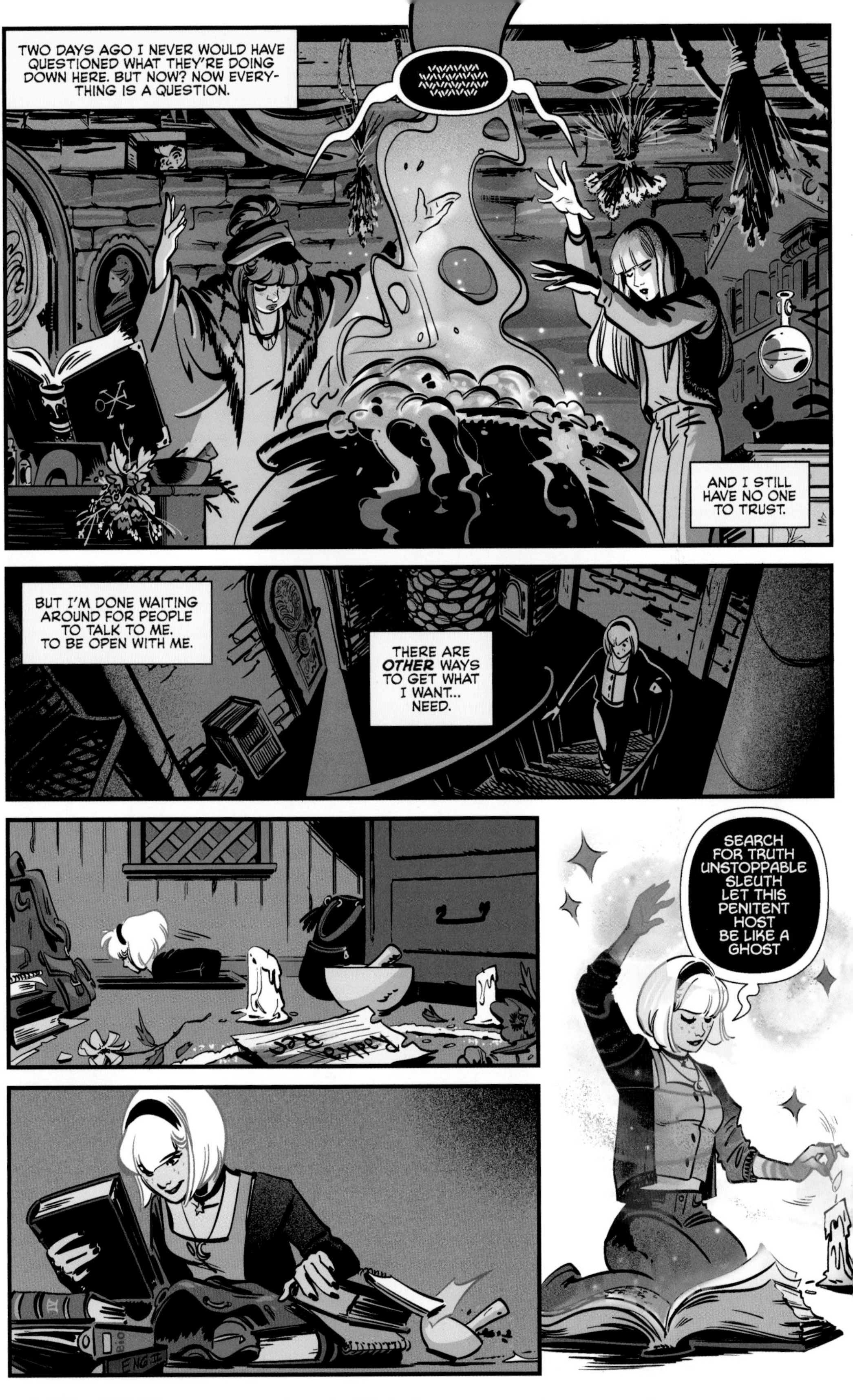
TWO DAYS AGO I NEVER WOULD HAVE QUESTIONED WHAT THEY'RE DOING DOWN HERE. BUT NOW? NOW EVERY-THING IS A QUESTION.
AND I STILL HAVE NO ONE TO TRUST.
BUT I'M DONE WAITING AROUND FOR PEOPLE TO TALK TO ME. TO BE OPEN WITH ME.
THERE ARE *OTHER* WAYS TO GET WHAT I WANT... NEED.
SEARCH FOR TRUTH UNSTOPPABLE SLEUTH LET THIS PENITENT HOST BE LIKE A GHOST

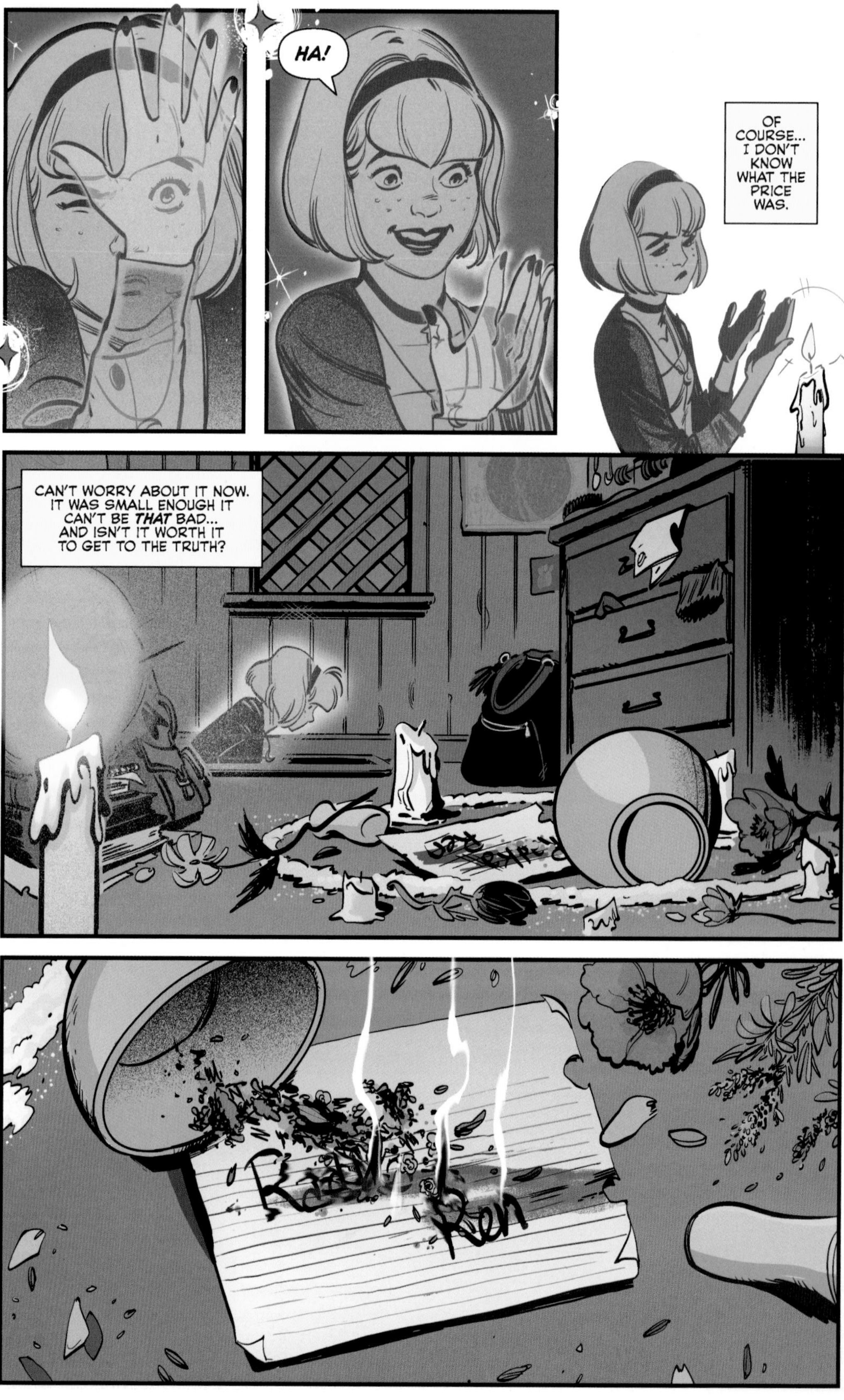
HA!
OF COURSE... I DON'T KNOW WHAT THE PRICE WAS.
CAN'T WORRY ABOUT IT NOW. IT WAS SMALL ENOUGH IT CAN'T BE **THAT** BAD... AND ISN'T IT WORTH IT TO GET TO THE TRUTH?
Ken

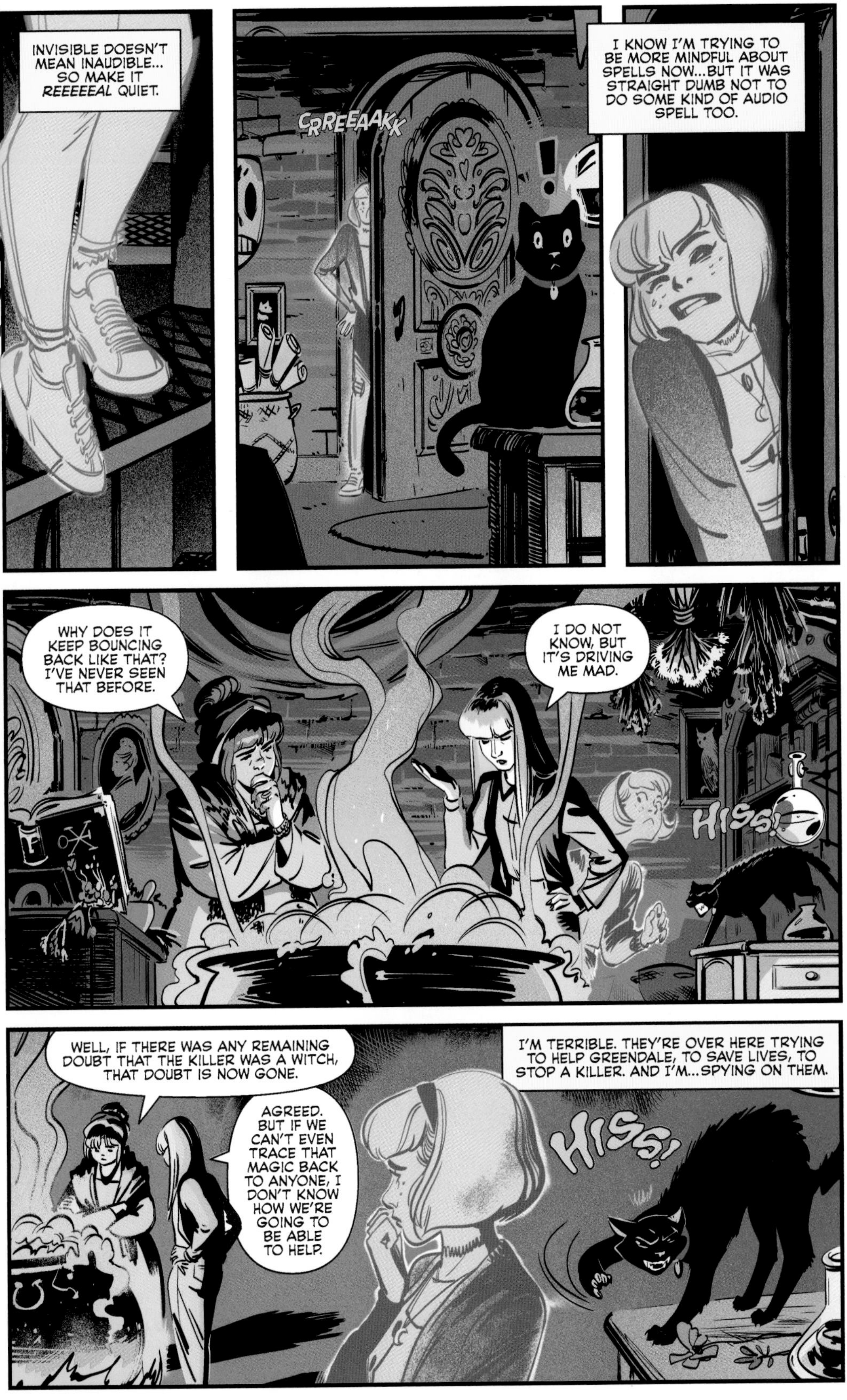
INVISIBLE DOESN'T MEAN INAUDIBLE... SO MAKE IT *REEEEEAL* QUIET.
CRREEAAKK
!
I KNOW I'M TRYING TO BE MORE MINDFUL ABOUT SPELLS NOW...BUT IT WAS STRAIGHT DUMB NOT TO DO SOME KIND OF AUDIO SPELL TOO.
WHY DOES IT KEEP BOUNCING BACK LIKE THAT? I'VE NEVER SEEN THAT BEFORE.
I DO NOT KNOW, BUT IT'S DRIVING ME MAD.
HISS!
WELL, IF THERE WAS ANY REMAINING DOUBT THAT THE KILLER WAS A WITCH, THAT DOUBT IS NOW GONE.
I'M TERRIBLE. THEY'RE OVER HERE TRYING TO HELP GREENDALE, TO SAVE LIVES, TO STOP A KILLER. AND I'M...SPYING ON THEM.
AGREED. BUT IF WE CAN'T EVEN TRACE THAT MAGIC BACK TO ANYONE, I DON'T KNOW HOW WE'RE GOING TO BE ABLE TO HELP.
HISS!

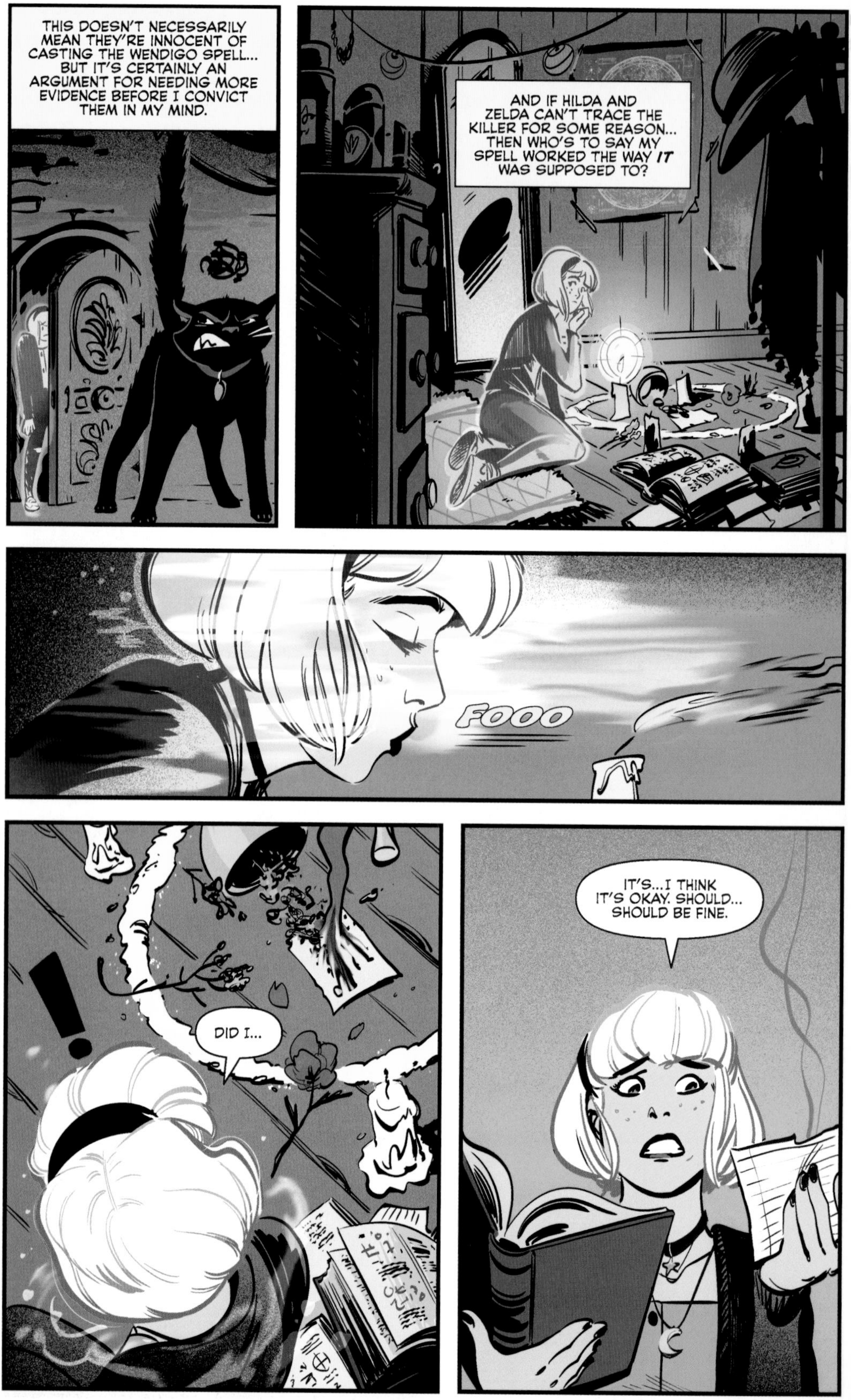
THIS DOESN'T NECESSARILY MEAN THEY'RE INNOCENT OF CASTING THE WENDIGO SPELL... BUT IT'S CERTAINLY AN ARGUMENT FOR NEEDING MORE EVIDENCE BEFORE I CONVICT THEM IN MY MIND.
AND IF HILDA AND ZELDA CAN'T TRACE THE KILLER FOR SOME REASON... THEN WHO'S TO SAY MY SPELL WORKED THE WAY *IT* WAS SUPPOSED TO?
FOOO
!
DID I...
IT'S...I THINK IT'S OKAY. SHOULD... SHOULD BE FINE.

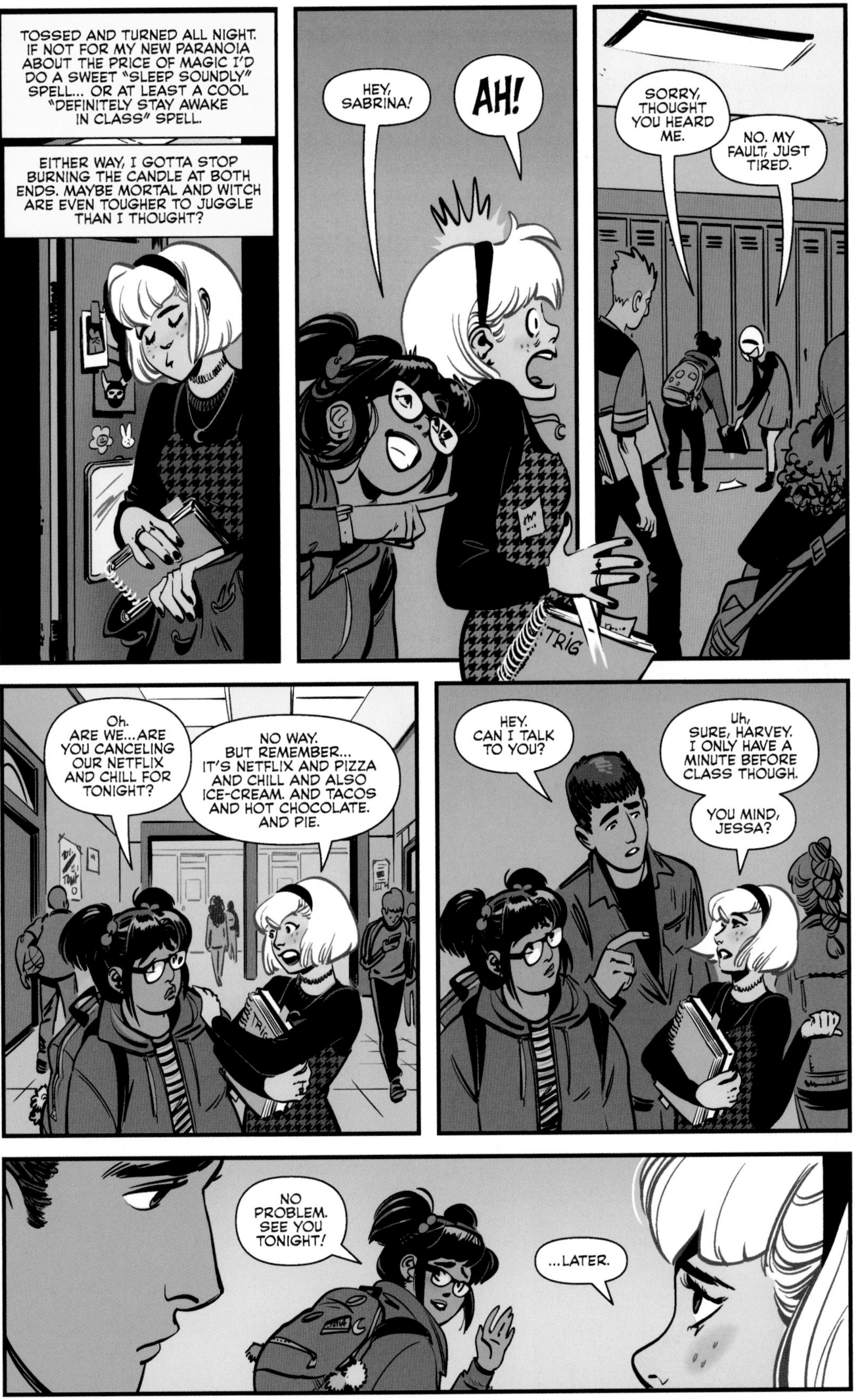
TOSSED AND TURNED ALL NIGHT. IF NOT FOR MY NEW PARANOIA ABOUT THE PRICE OF MAGIC I'D DO A SWEET "SLEEP SOUNDLY" SPELL... OR AT LEAST A COOL "DEFINITELY STAY AWAKE IN CLASS" SPELL.
EITHER WAY, I GOTTA STOP BURNING THE CANDLE AT BOTH ENDS. MAYBE MORTAL AND WITCH ARE EVEN TOUGHER TO JUGGLE THAN I THOUGHT?
HEY, SABRINA!
AH!
TRIG
SORRY, THOUGHT YOU HEARD ME.
NO. MY FAULT, JUST TIRED.
Oh. ARE WE...ARE YOU CANCELING OUR NETFLIX AND CHILL FOR TONIGHT?
NO WAY. BUT REMEMBER... IT'S NETFLIX AND PIZZA AND CHILL AND ALSO ICE-CREAM. AND TACOS AND HOT CHOCOLATE. AND PIE.
HEY. CAN I TALK TO YOU?
Uh, SURE, HARVEY. I ONLY HAVE A MINUTE BEFORE CLASS THOUGH.
YOU MIND, JESSA?
NO PROBLEM. SEE YOU TONIGHT!
...LATER.

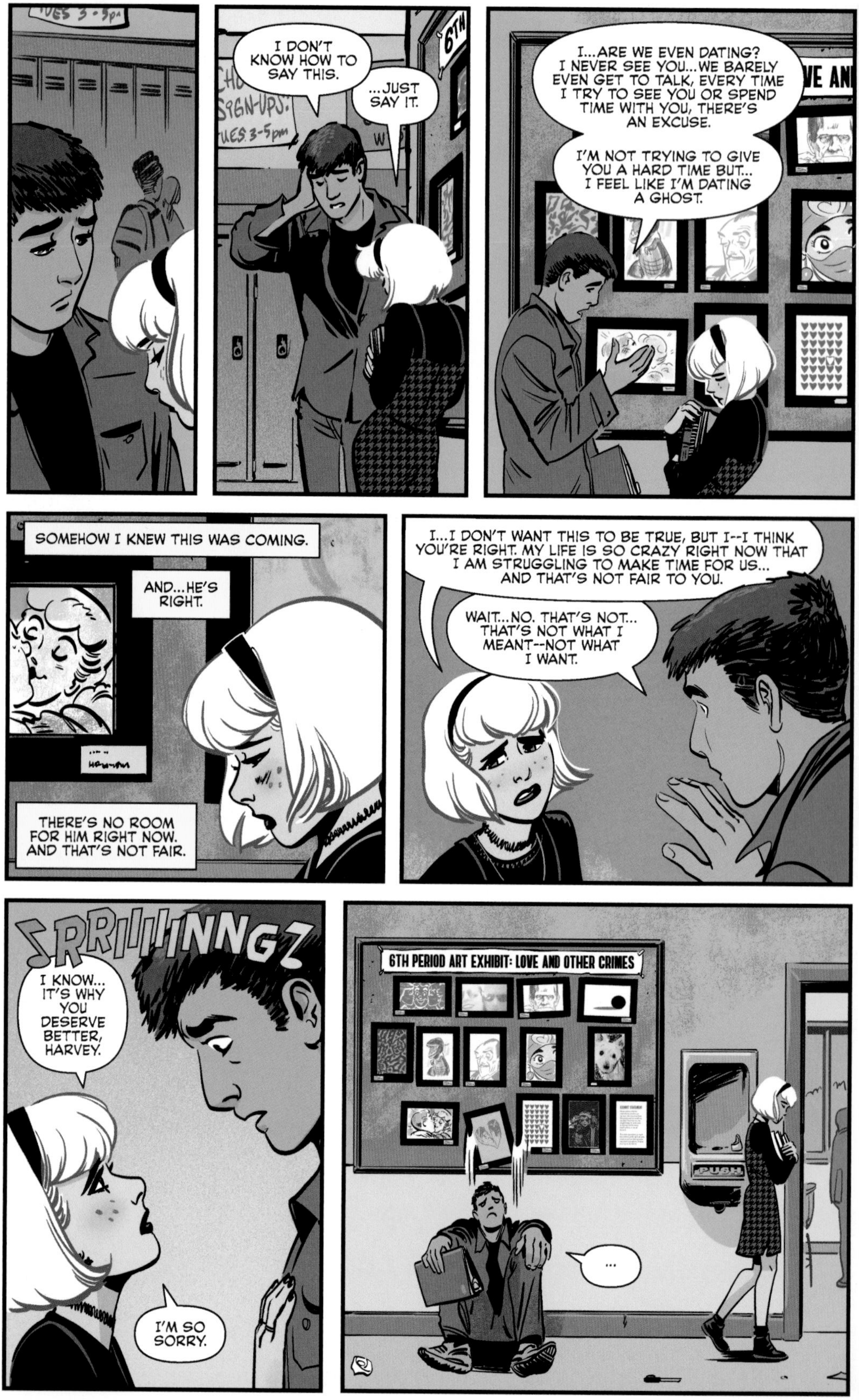
I DON'T KNOW HOW TO SAY THIS.
...JUST SAY IT.
I...ARE WE EVEN DATING? I NEVER SEE YOU...WE BARELY EVEN GET TO TALK, EVERY TIME I TRY TO SEE YOU OR SPEND TIME WITH YOU, THERE'S AN EXCUSE.
I'M NOT TRYING TO GIVE YOU A HARD TIME BUT... I FEEL LIKE I'M DATING A GHOST.
SOMEHOW I KNEW THIS WAS COMING.
AND...HE'S RIGHT.
THERE'S NO ROOM FOR HIM RIGHT NOW. AND THAT'S NOT FAIR.
I...I DON'T WANT THIS TO BE TRUE, BUT I--I THINK YOU'RE RIGHT. MY LIFE IS SO CRAZY RIGHT NOW THAT I AM STRUGGLING TO MAKE TIME FOR US... AND THAT'S NOT FAIR TO YOU.
WAIT...NO. THAT'S NOT... THAT'S NOT WHAT I MEANT--NOT WHAT I WANT.
SRRIIIIINNGZ
I KNOW... IT'S WHY YOU DESERVE BETTER, HARVEY.
I'M SO SORRY.
6TH PERIOD ART EXHIBIT: LOVE AND OTHER CRIMES
PUSH
...

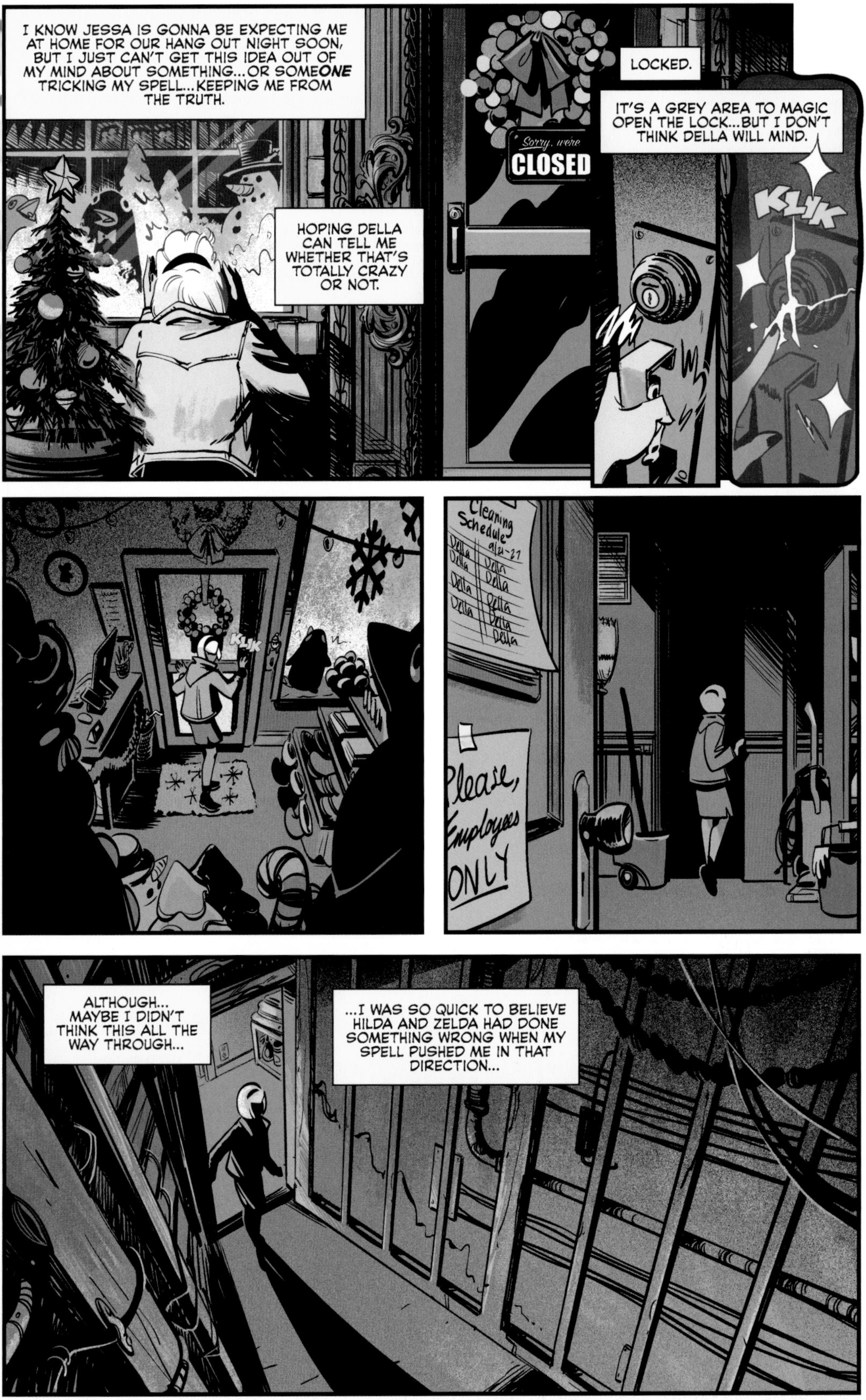

I KNOW JESSA IS GONNA BE EXPECTING ME AT HOME FOR OUR HANG OUT NIGHT SOON, BUT I JUST CAN'T GET THIS IDEA OUT OF MY MIND ABOUT SOMETHING...OR SOME*ONE* TRICKING MY SPELL...KEEPING ME FROM THE TRUTH.
HOPING DELLA CAN TELL ME WHETHER THAT'S TOTALLY CRAZY OR NOT.
Sorry, we're
CLOSED
LOCKED.
IT'S A GREY AREA TO MAGIC OPEN THE LOCK...BUT I DON'T THINK DELLA WILL MIND.
KLYK
KLYK
Cleaning Schedule
Please, Employees ONLY
ALTHOUGH... MAYBE I DIDN'T THINK THIS ALL THE WAY THROUGH...
...I WAS SO QUICK TO BELIEVE HILDA AND ZELDA HAD DONE SOMETHING WRONG WHEN MY SPELL PUSHED ME IN THAT DIRECTION...

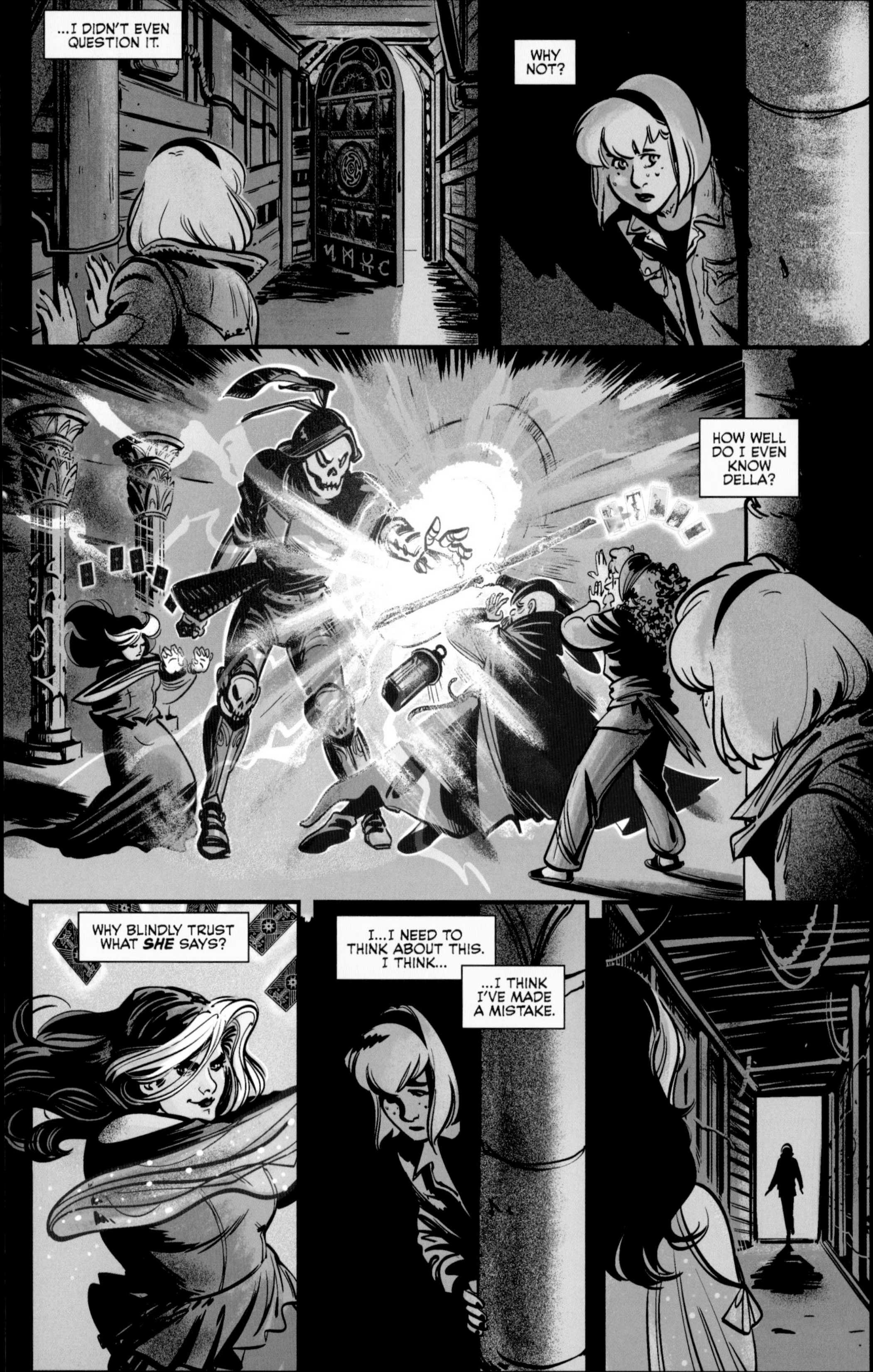

...I DIDN'T EVEN QUESTION IT.
WHY NOT?
HOW WELL DO I EVEN KNOW DELLA?
WHY BLINDLY TRUST WHAT SHE SAYS?
I...I NEED TO THINK ABOUT THIS. I THINK...
...I THINK I'VE MADE A MISTAKE.

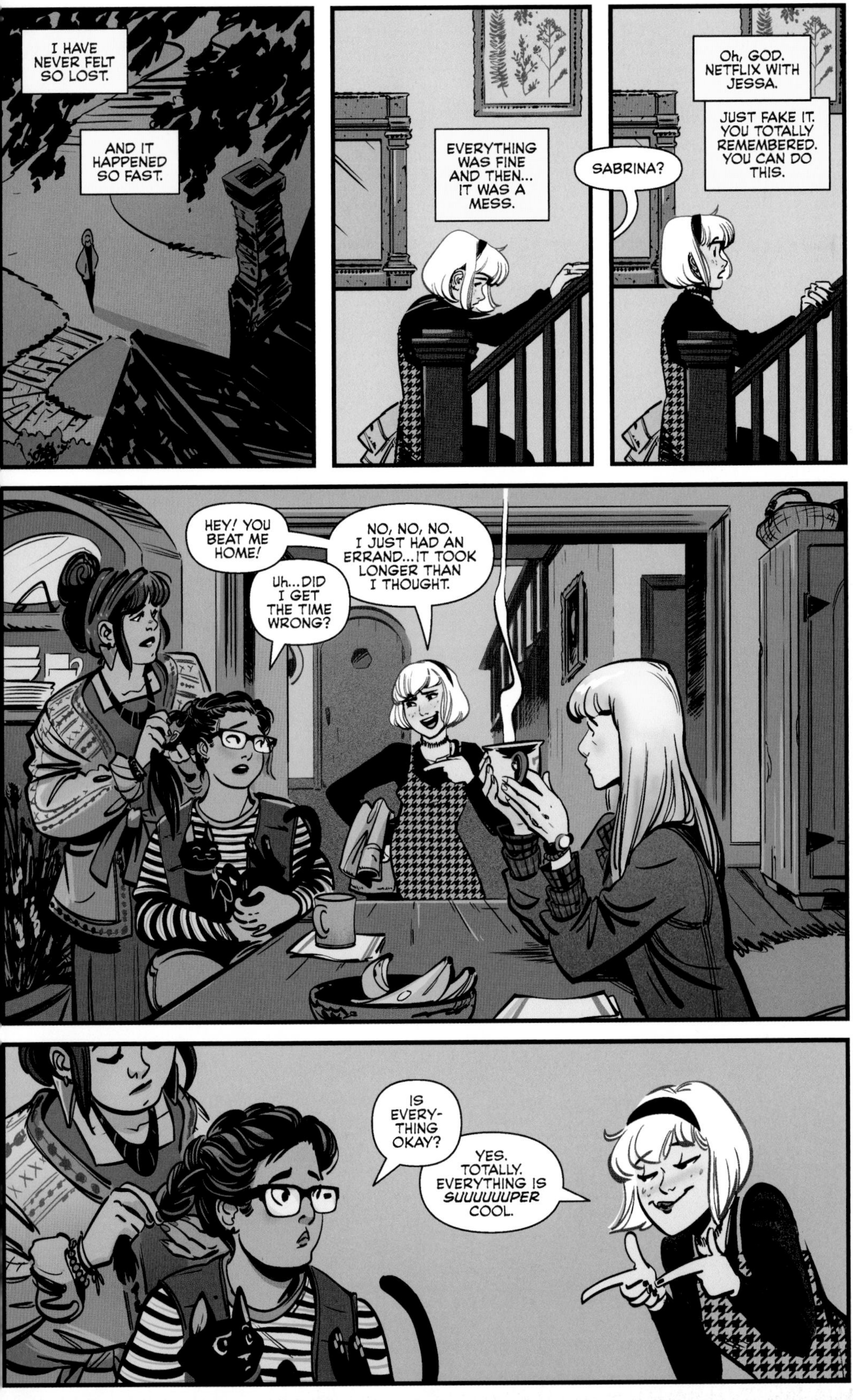
I HAVE NEVER FELT SO LOST.
AND IT HAPPENED SO FAST.
EVERYTHING WAS FINE AND THEN... IT WAS A MESS.
SABRINA?
Oh, GOD. NETFLIX WITH JESSA.
JUST FAKE IT. YOU TOTALLY REMEMBERED. YOU CAN DO THIS.
HEY! YOU BEAT ME HOME!
Uh...DID I GET THE TIME WRONG?
NO, NO, NO. I JUST HAD AN ERRAND...IT TOOK LONGER THAN I THOUGHT.
IS EVERY-THING OKAY?
YES. TOTALLY. EVERYTHING IS *SUUUUUUPER* COOL.

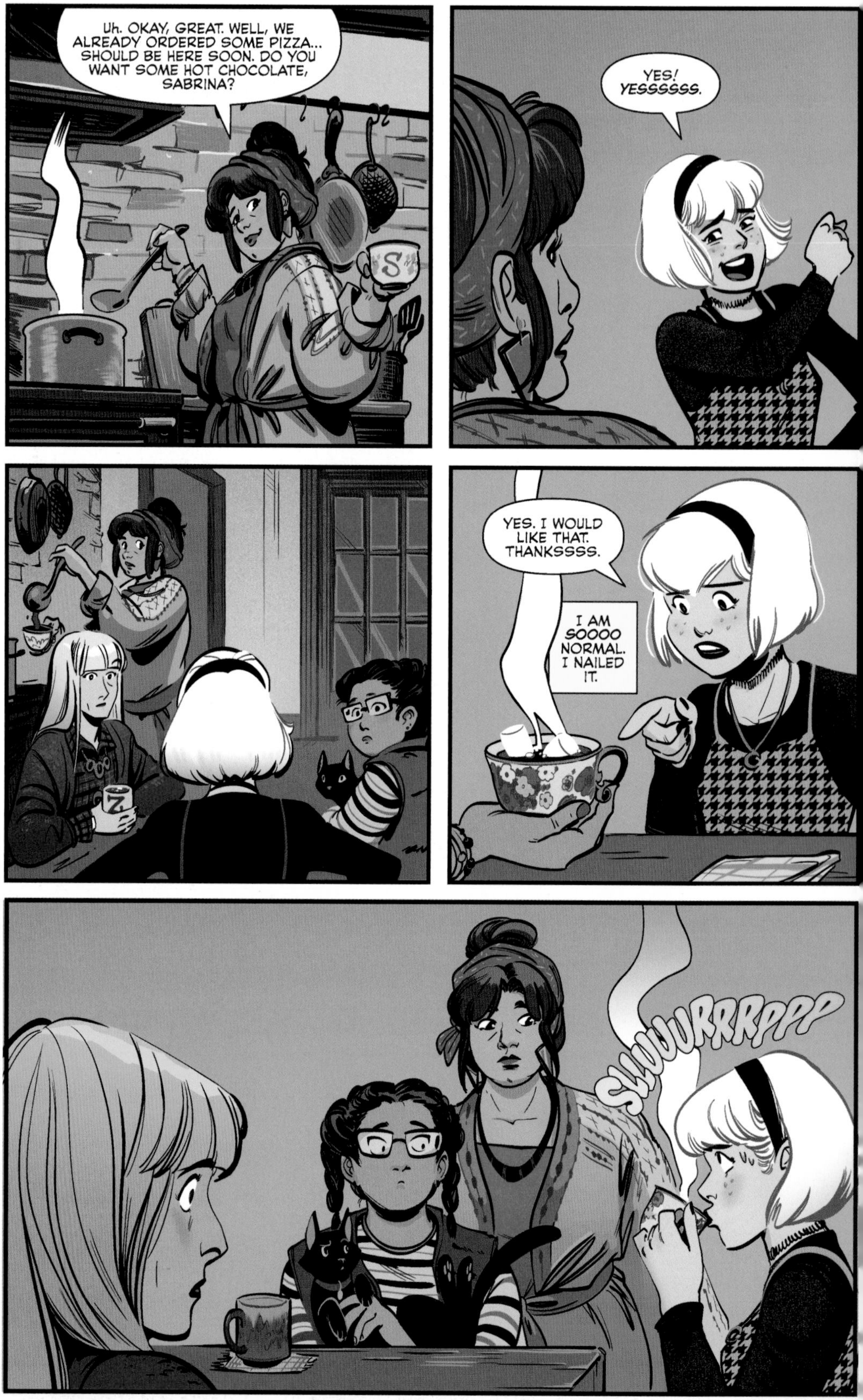
Uh. OKAY, GREAT. WELL, WE ALREADY ORDERED SOME PIZZA... SHOULD BE HERE SOON. DO YOU WANT SOME HOT CHOCOLATE, SABRINA?
YES! YESSSSSS.
YES. I WOULD LIKE THAT. THANKSSSS.
I AM SOOOO NORMAL. I NAILED IT.
SLUUURRRPPP

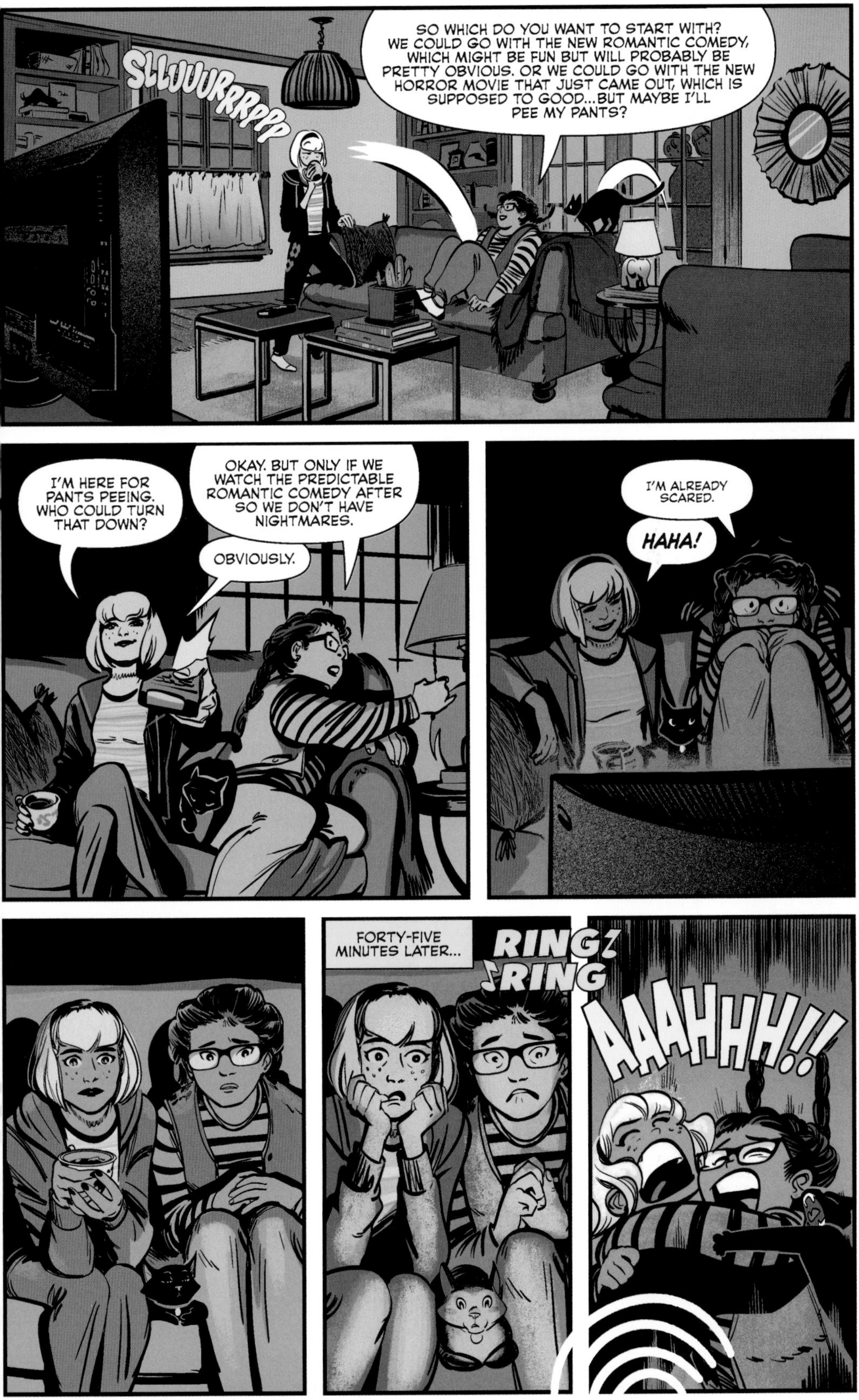
SLLUUURRRPPP
SO WHICH DO YOU WANT TO START WITH? WE COULD GO WITH THE NEW ROMANTIC COMEDY, WHICH MIGHT BE FUN BUT WILL PROBABLY BE PRETTY OBVIOUS. OR WE COULD GO WITH THE NEW HORROR MOVIE THAT JUST CAME OUT, WHICH IS SUPPOSED TO GOOD...BUT MAYBE I'LL PEE MY PANTS?
I'M HERE FOR PANTS PEEING. WHO COULD TURN THAT DOWN?
OKAY. BUT ONLY IF WE WATCH THE PREDICTABLE ROMANTIC COMEDY AFTER SO WE DON'T HAVE NIGHTMARES.
OBVIOUSLY.
I'M ALREADY SCARED.
HAHA!
FORTY-FIVE MINUTES LATER...
RING
RING
AAAHHH!!

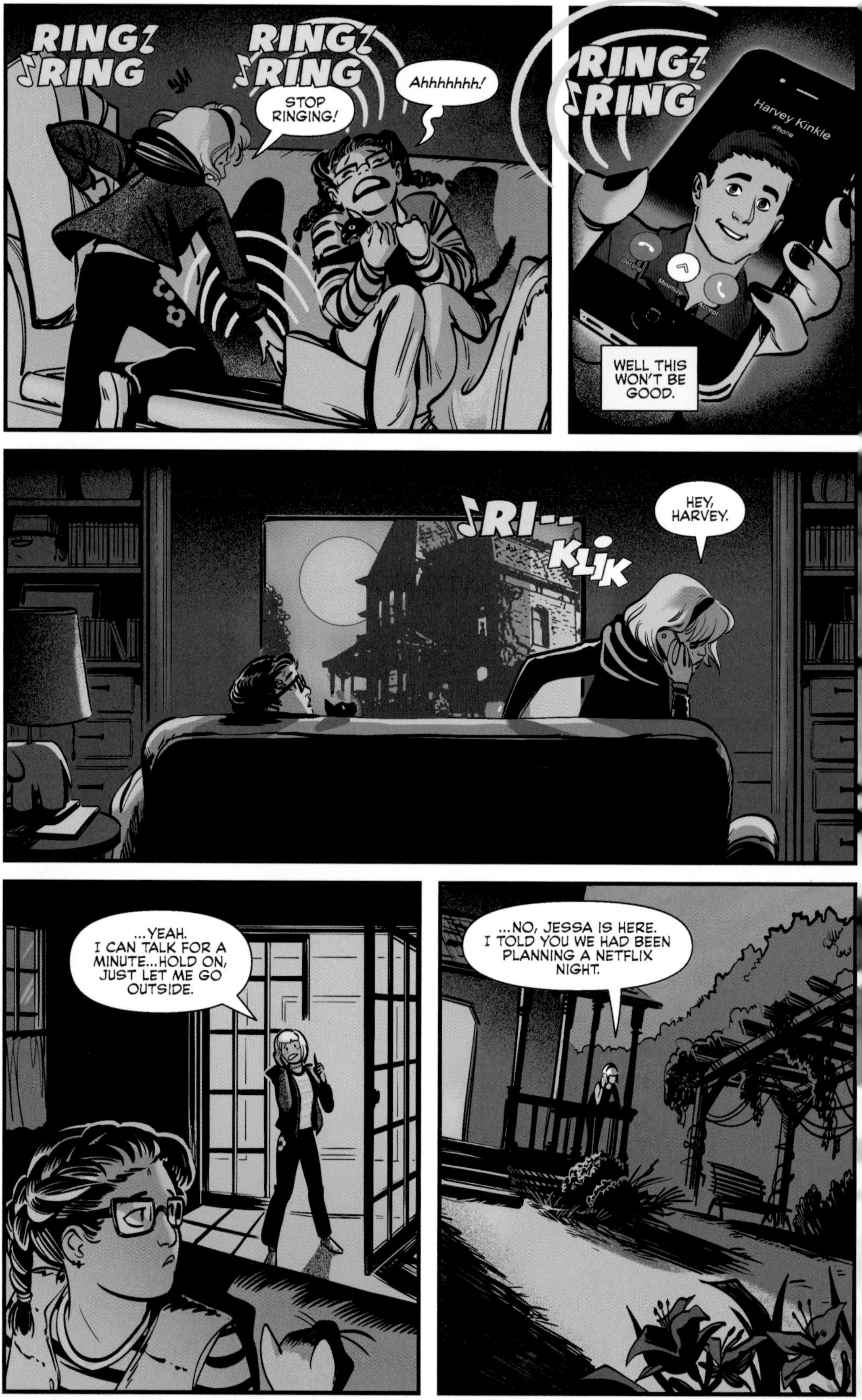
RING RING
RING RING
STOP RINGING!
Ahhhhhhh!
RING RING
Harvey Kinkle
iPhone
Decline
Minimize
Accept
WELL THIS WON'T BE GOOD.
RI--
KLIK
HEY, HARVEY.
...YEAH. I CAN TALK FOR A MINUTE...HOLD ON, JUST LET ME GO OUTSIDE.
...NO, JESSA IS HERE. I TOLD YOU WE HAD BEEN PLANNING A NETFLIX NIGHT.

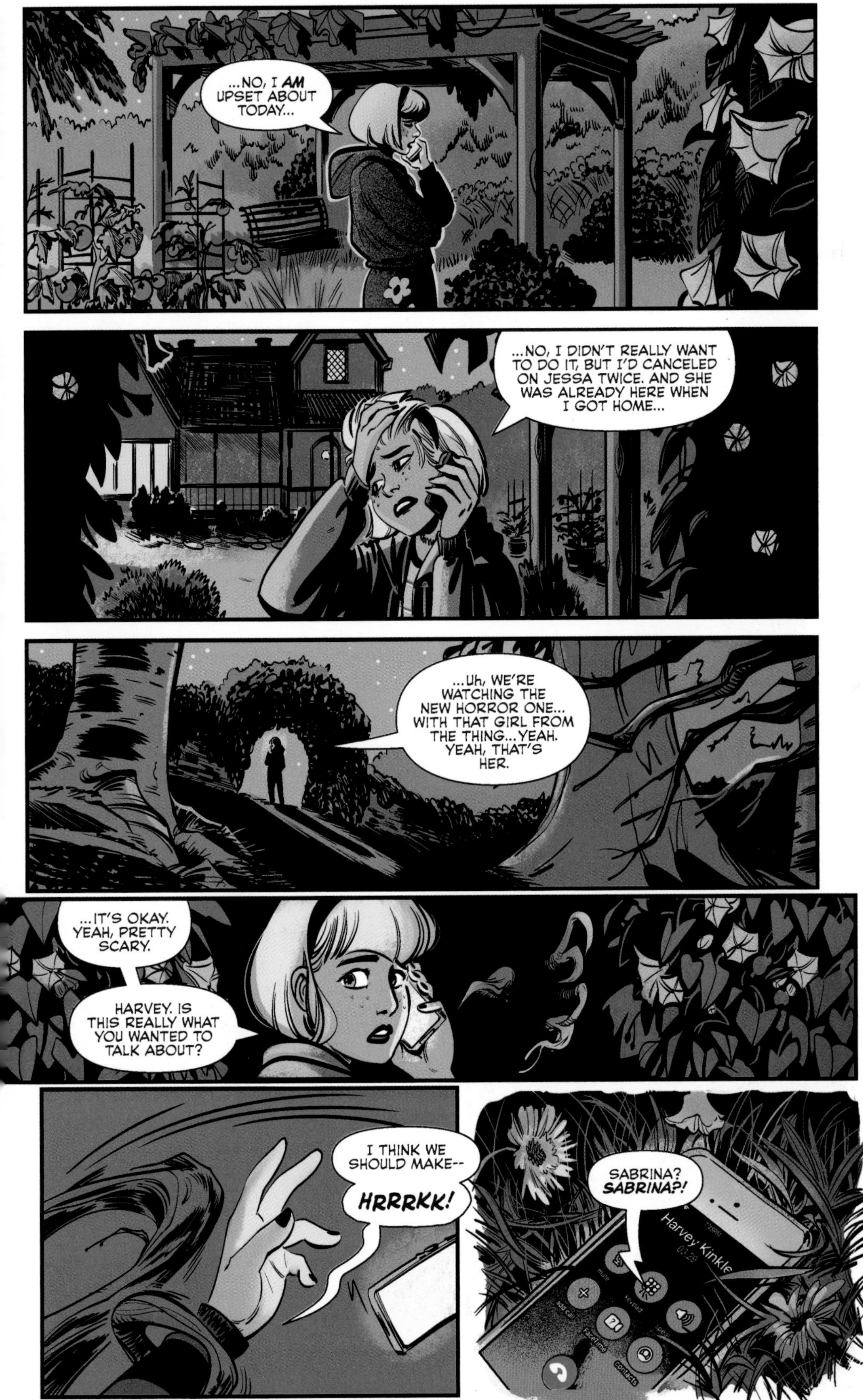
...NO, I *AM* UPSET ABOUT TODAY...
...NO, I DIDN'T REALLY WANT TO DO IT, BUT I'D CANCELED ON JESSA TWICE. AND SHE WAS ALREADY HERE WHEN I GOT HOME...
...UH, WE'RE WATCHING THE NEW HORROR ONE... WITH THAT GIRL FROM THE THING... YEAH. YEAH, THAT'S HER.
...IT'S OKAY. YEAH, PRETTY SCARY.
HARVEY. IS THIS REALLY WHAT YOU WANTED TO TALK ABOUT?
I THINK WE SHOULD MAKE--
HRRRKK!
SABRINA? SABRINA?!
Harvey Kinkle

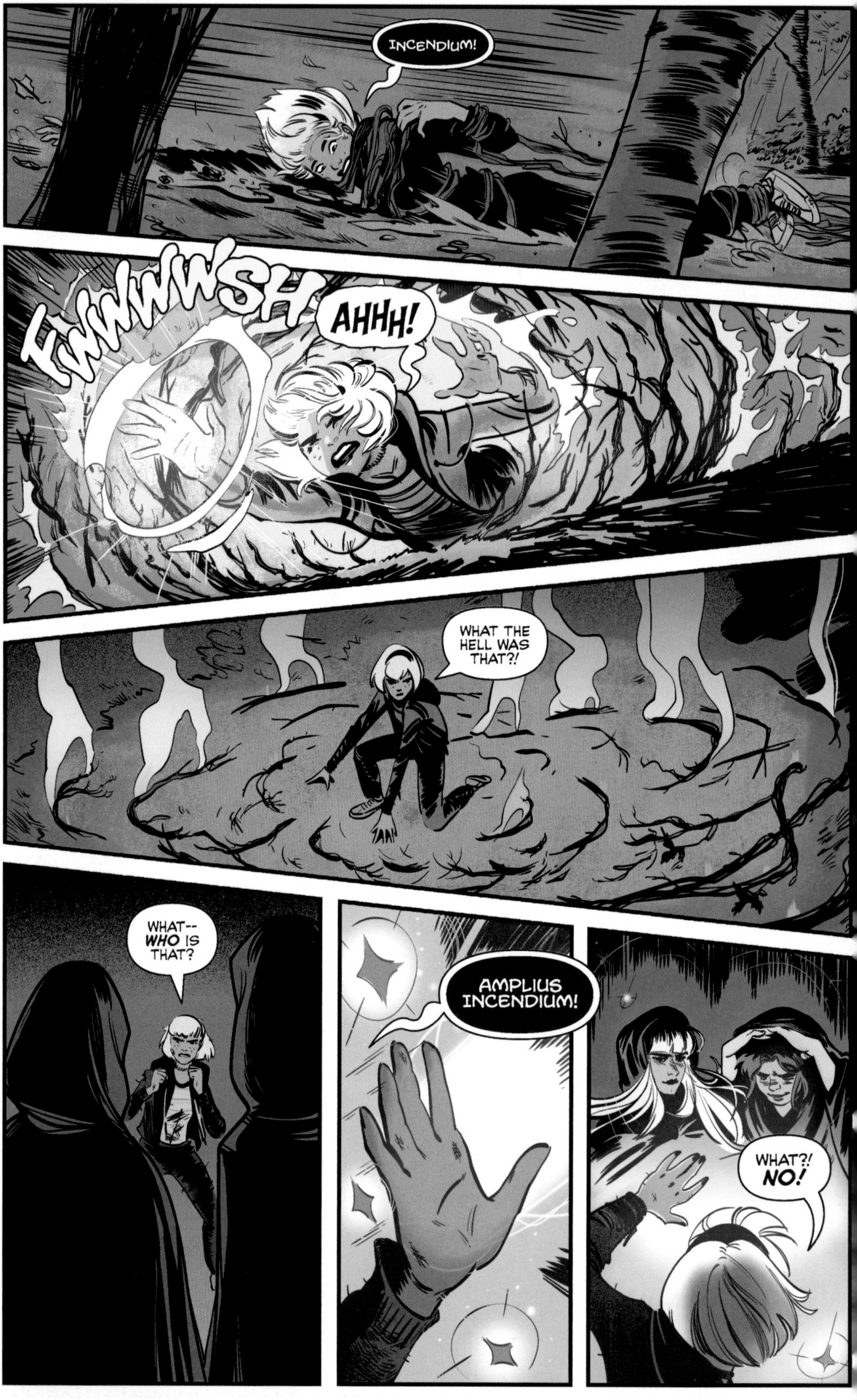
INCENDIUM!
FWWWWSH
AHHH!
WHAT THE HELL WAS THAT?!
WHAT-- WHO IS THAT?
AMPLIUS INCENDIUM!
WHAT?! NO!

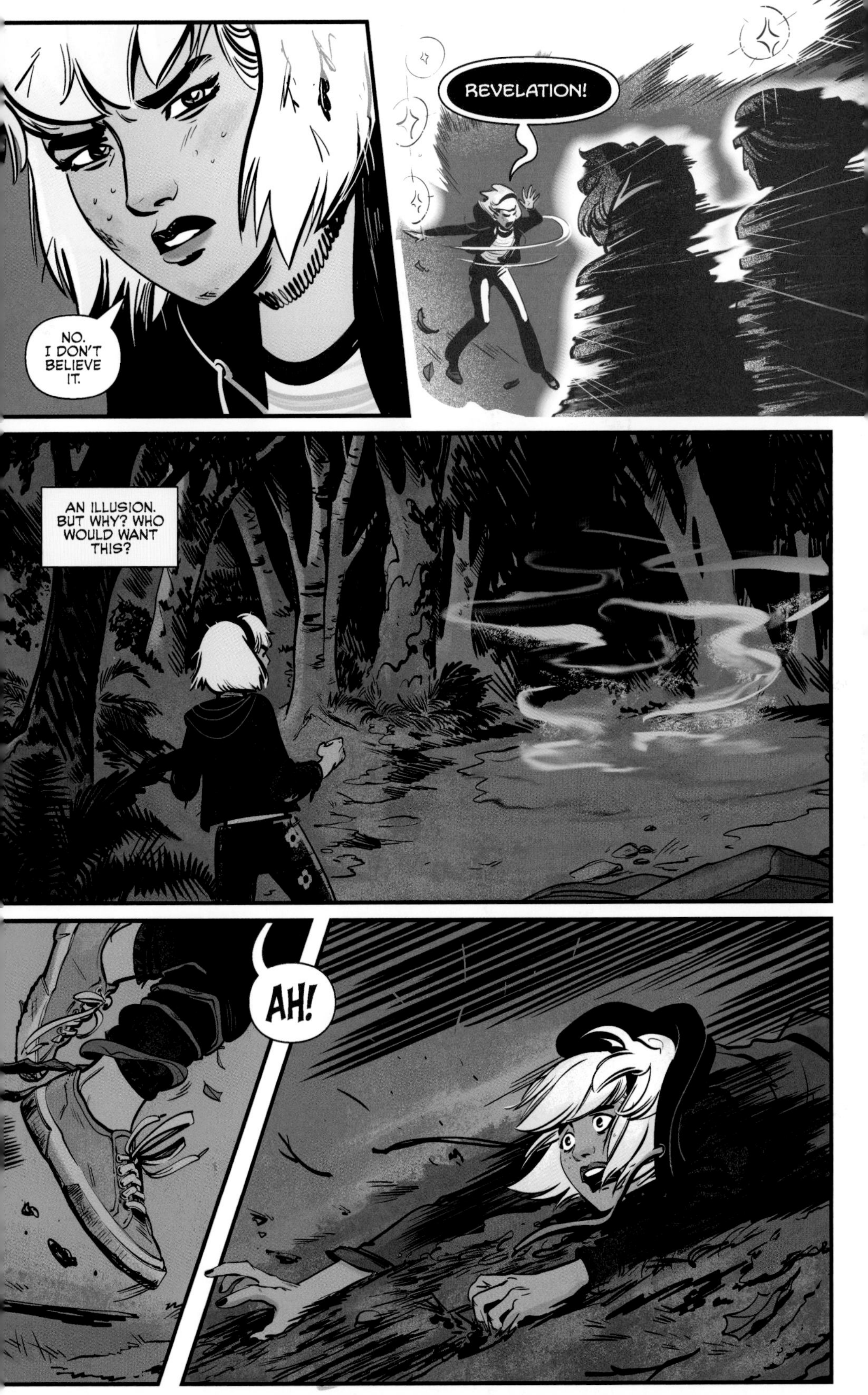
NO. I DON'T BELIEVE IT.
REVELATION!
AN ILLUSION. BUT WHY? WHO WOULD WANT THIS?
AH!

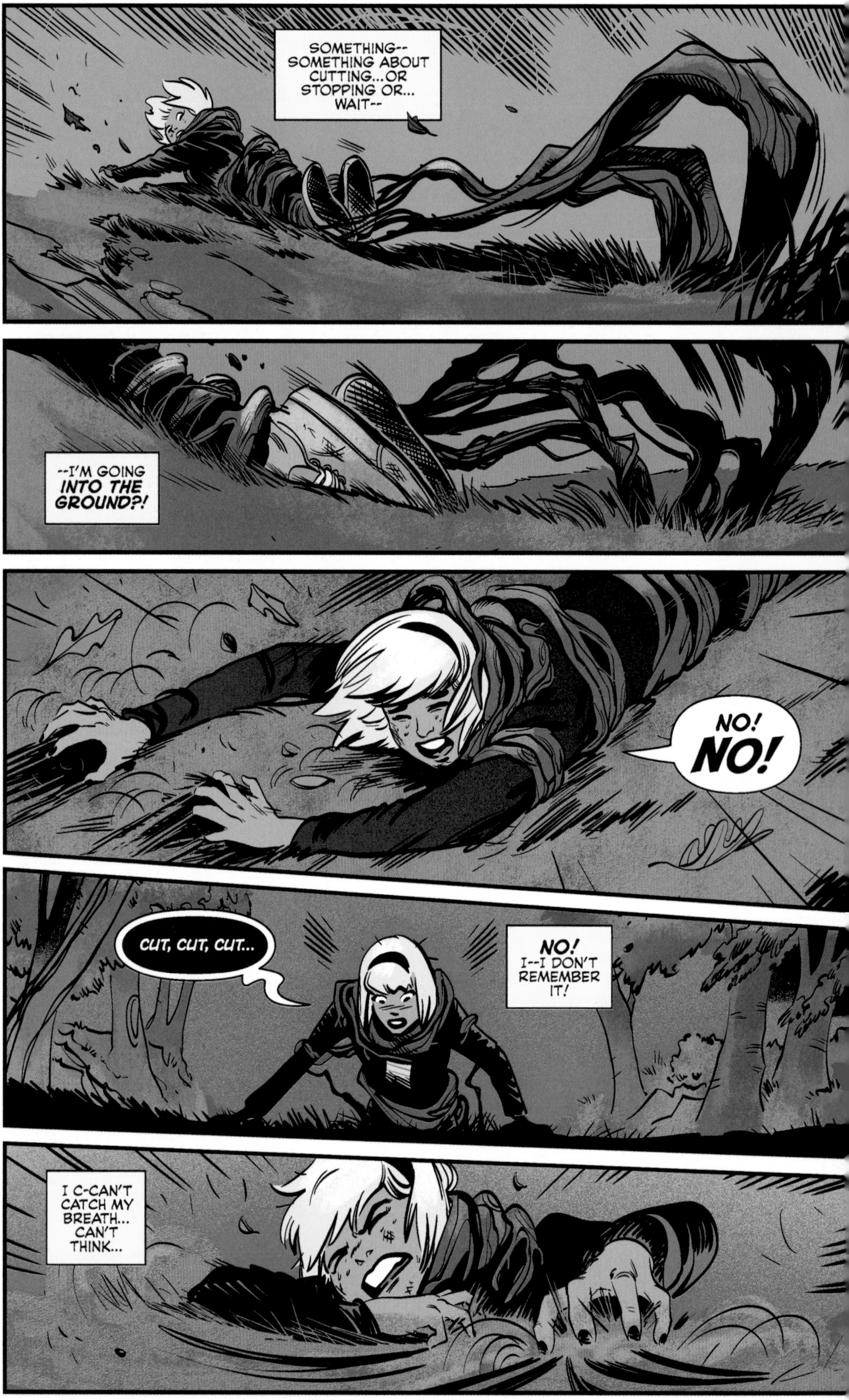
SOMETHING--
SOMETHING ABOUT
CUTTING...OR
STOPPING OR...
WAIT--
--I'M GOING
INTO THE
GROUND?!
NO!
NO!
CUT, CUT, CUT...
NO!
I--I DON'T
REMEMBER
IT!
I C-CAN'T
CATCH MY
BREATH...
CAN'T
THINK...

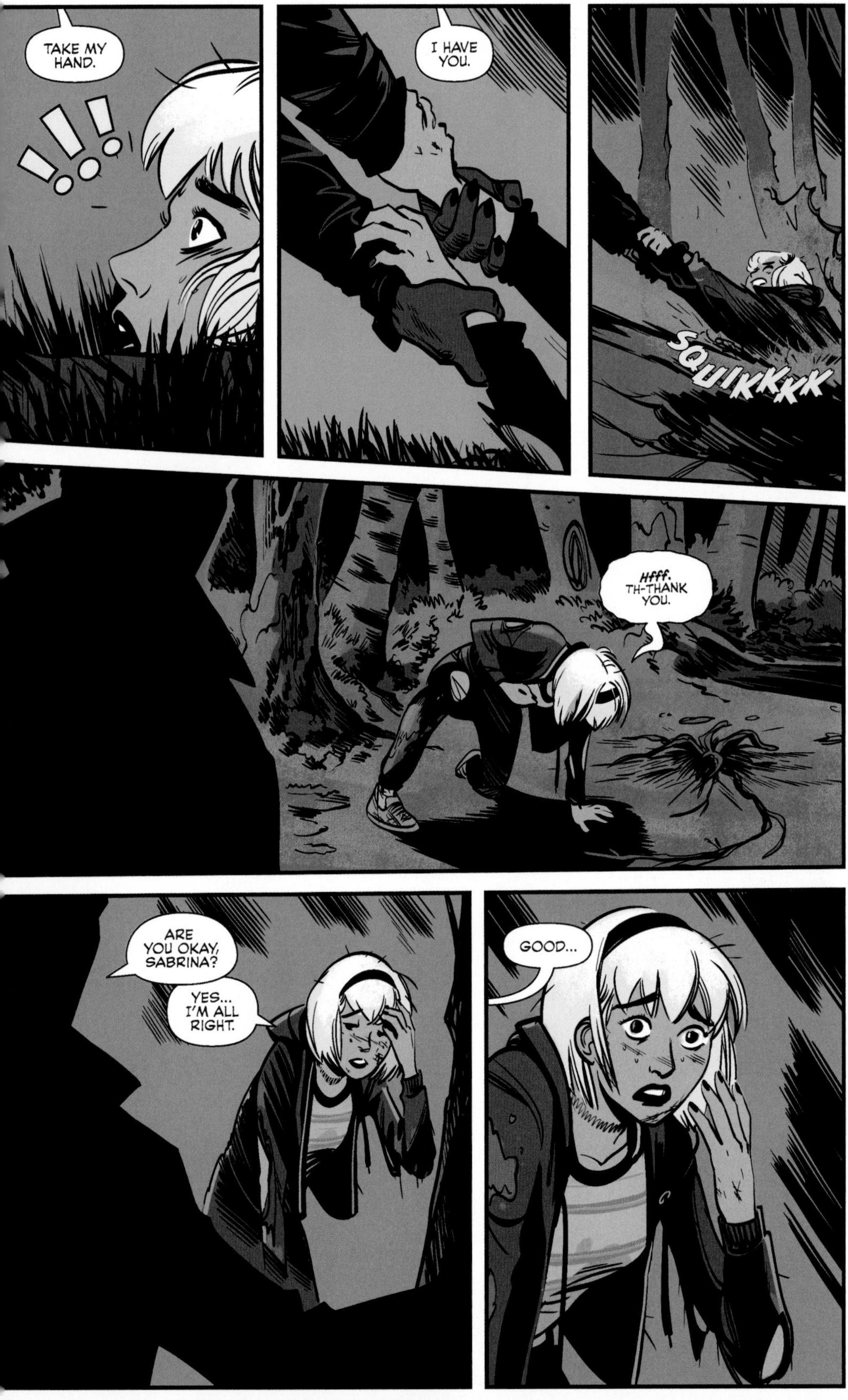
TAKE MY HAND.
!!!
I HAVE YOU.
SQUIKKKK
Hfff. TH-THANK YOU.
ARE YOU OKAY, SABRINA?
YES... I'M ALL RIGHT.
GOOD...

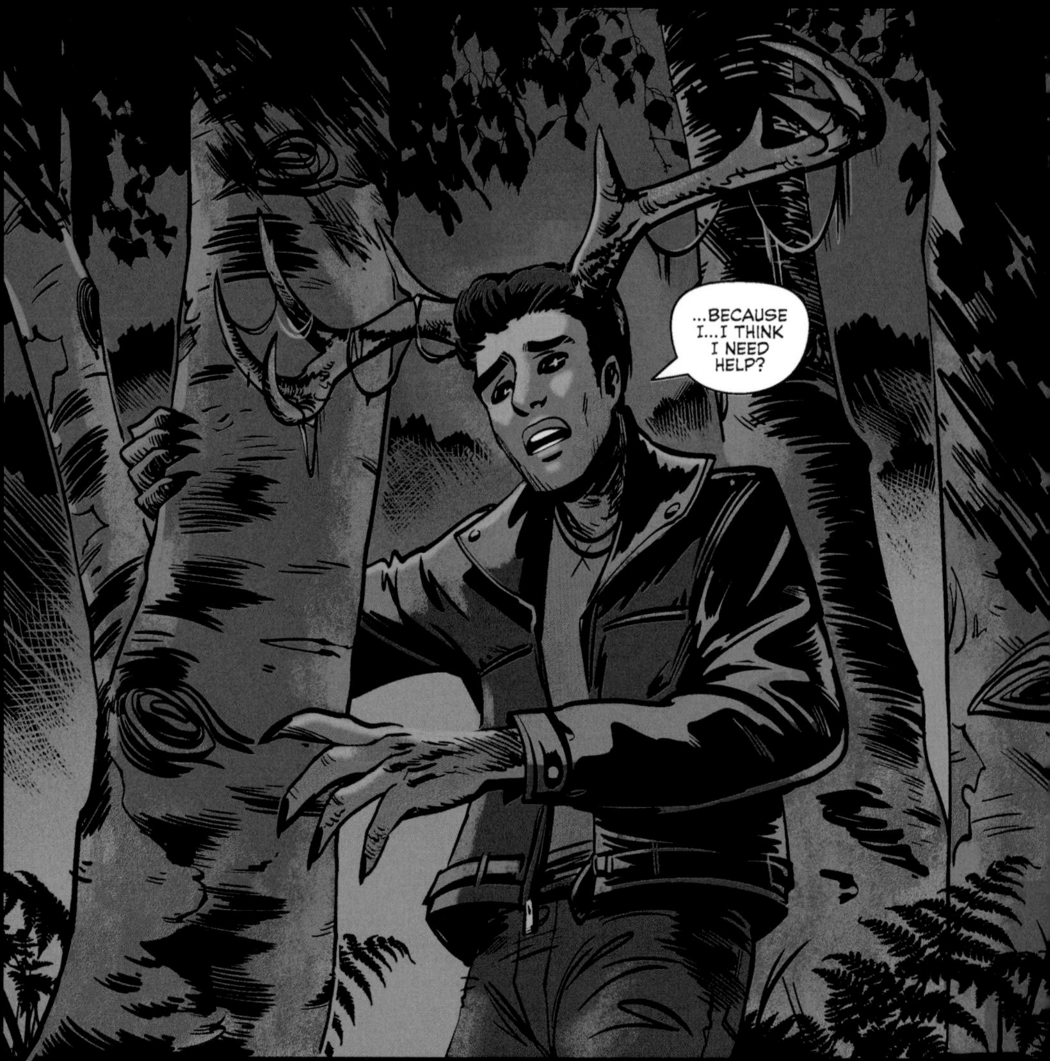
...BECAUSE I...I THINK I NEED HELP?

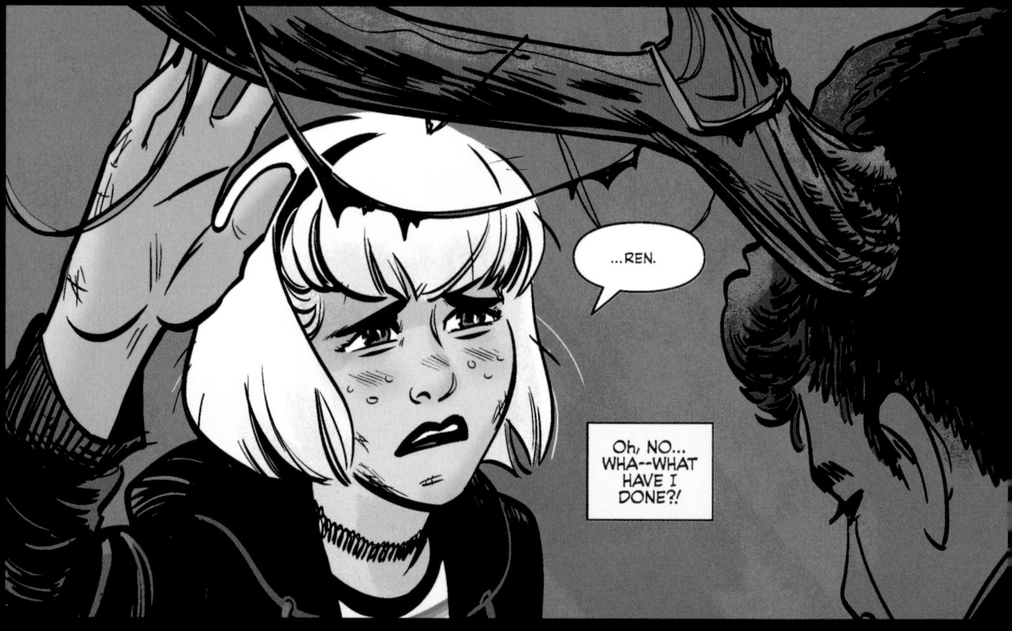
...REN.
Oh, NO... WHA--WHAT HAVE I DONE?!

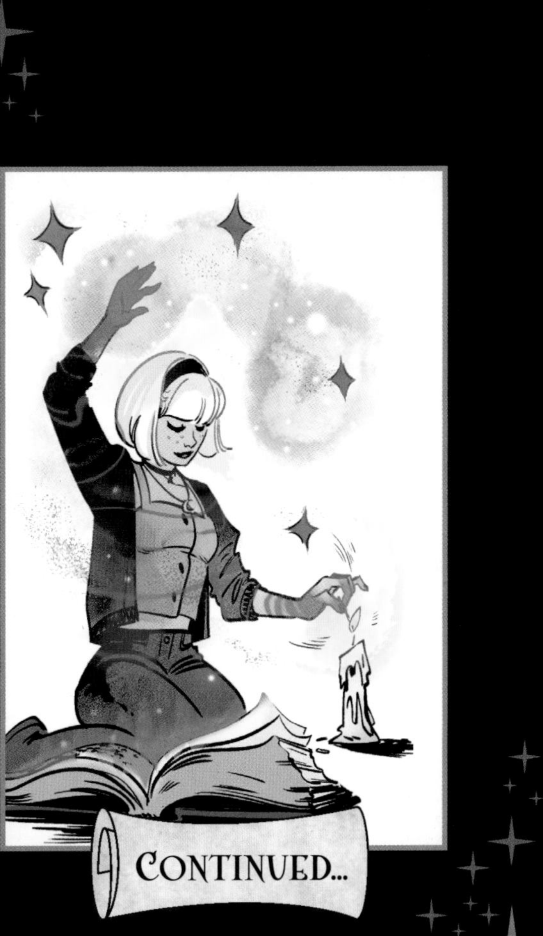
CONTINUED...

04

STORY BY
KELLY THOMPSON

ART BY
VERONICA FISH
AND ANDY FISH

LETTERING BY
JACK MORELLI

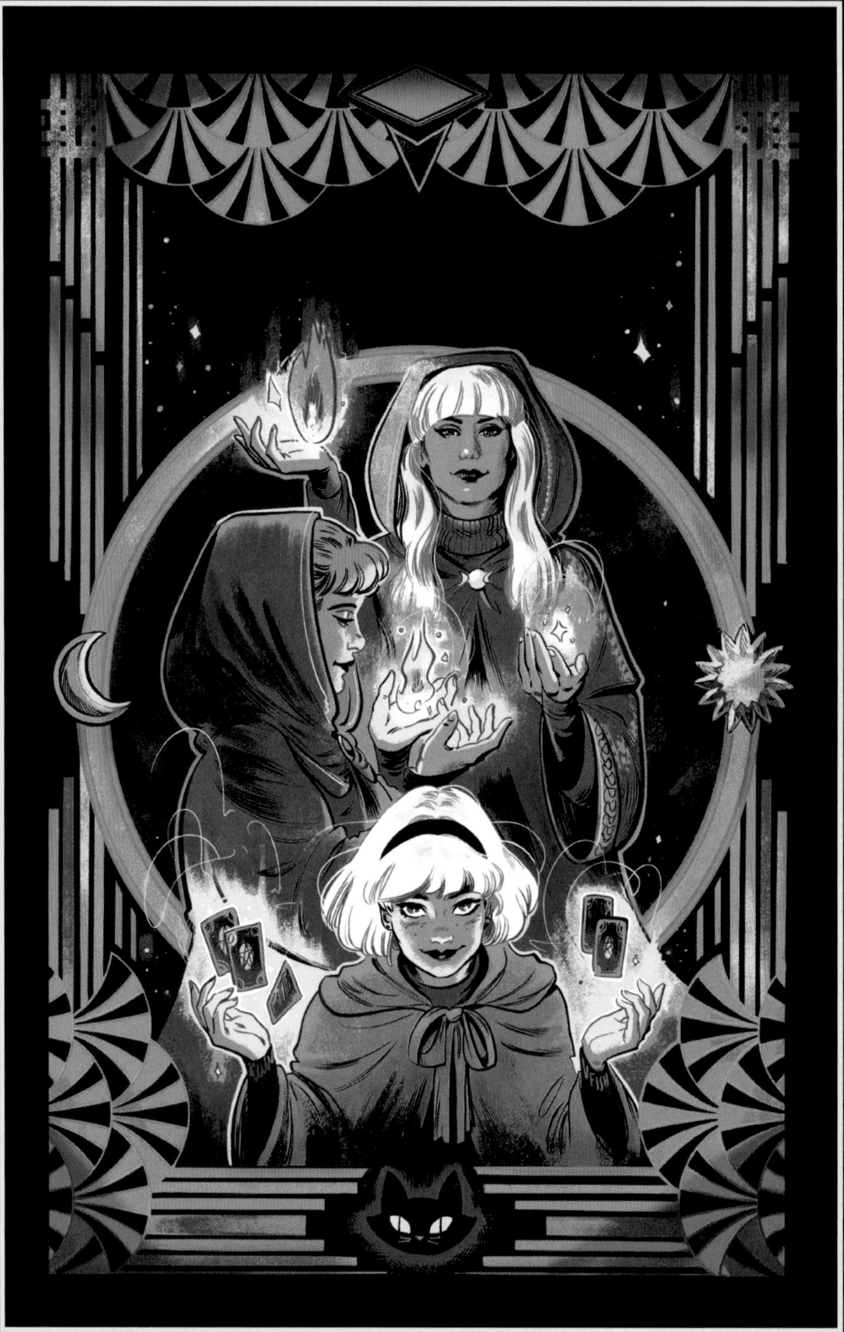

COVER ART: VERONICA FISH

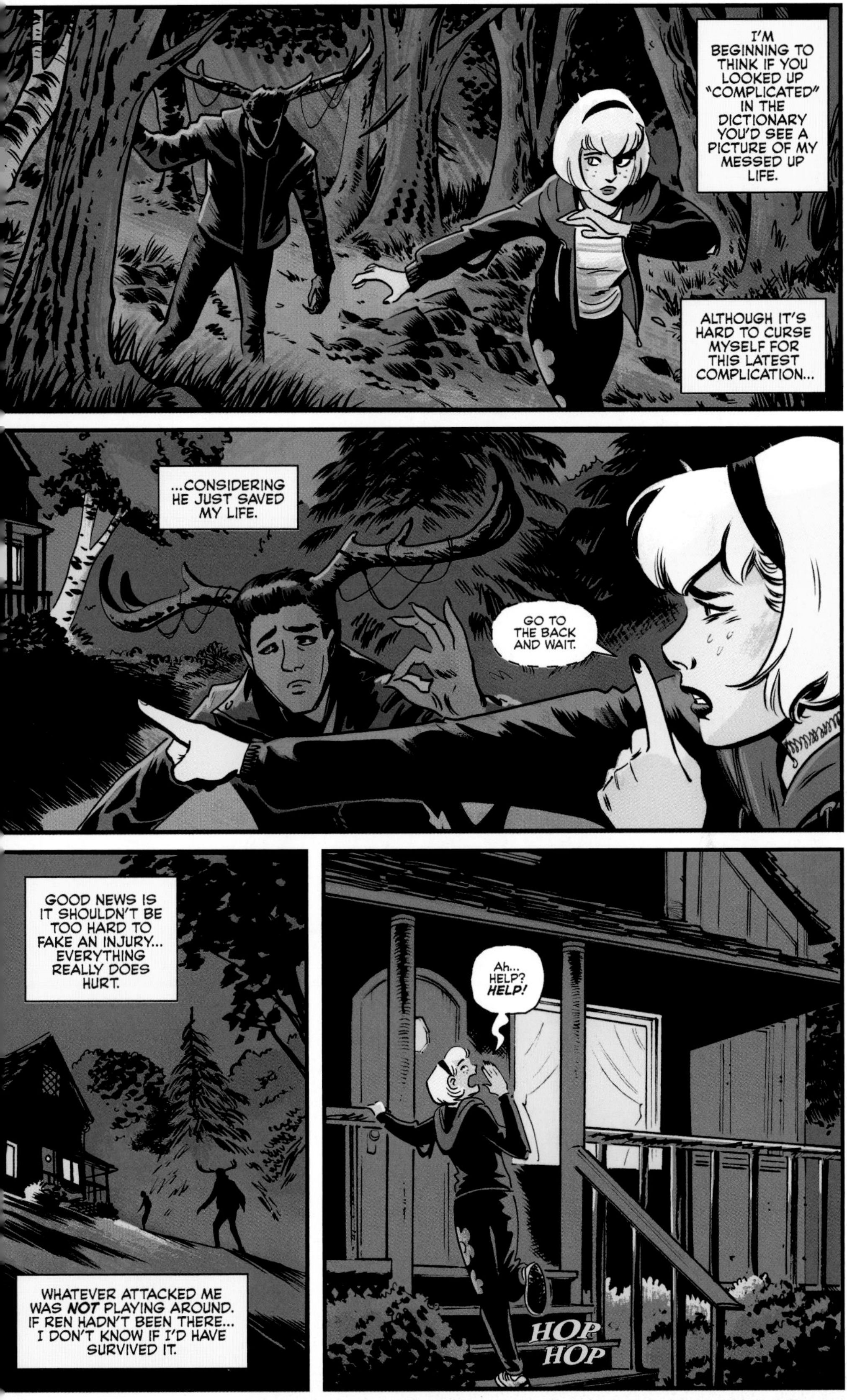
I'M BEGINNING TO THINK IF YOU LOOKED UP "COMPLICATED" IN THE DICTIONARY YOU'D SEE A PICTURE OF MY MESSED UP LIFE.
ALTHOUGH IT'S HARD TO CURSE MYSELF FOR THIS LATEST COMPLICATION...
...CONSIDERING HE JUST SAVED MY LIFE.
GO TO THE BACK AND WAIT.
GOOD NEWS IS IT SHOULDN'T BE TOO HARD TO FAKE AN INJURY... EVERYTHING REALLY DOES HURT.
WHATEVER ATTACKED ME WAS **NOT** PLAYING AROUND. IF REN HADN'T BEEN THERE... I DON'T KNOW IF I'D HAVE SURVIVED IT.
Ah... HELP? ***HELP!***
HOP
HOP

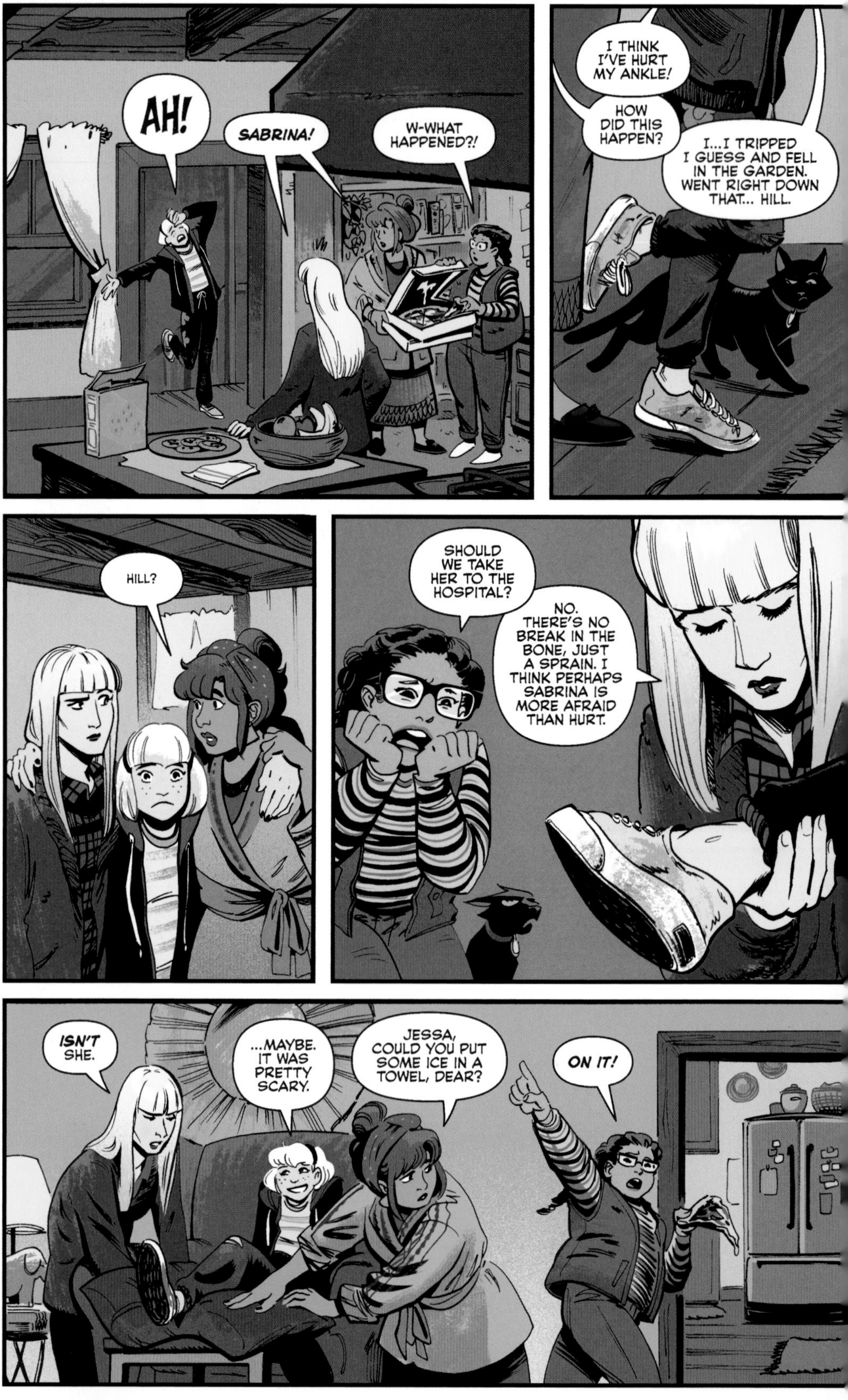
AH!
SABRINA!
W-WHAT HAPPENED?!
I THINK I'VE HURT MY ANKLE!
HOW DID THIS HAPPEN?
I...I TRIPPED I GUESS AND FELL IN THE GARDEN. WENT RIGHT DOWN THAT... HILL.
HILL?
SHOULD WE TAKE HER TO THE HOSPITAL?
NO. THERE'S NO BREAK IN THE BONE, JUST A SPRAIN. I THINK PERHAPS SABRINA IS MORE AFRAID THAN HURT.
ISN'T SHE.
...MAYBE. IT WAS PRETTY SCARY.
JESSA, COULD YOU PUT SOME ICE IN A TOWEL, DEAR?
ON IT!

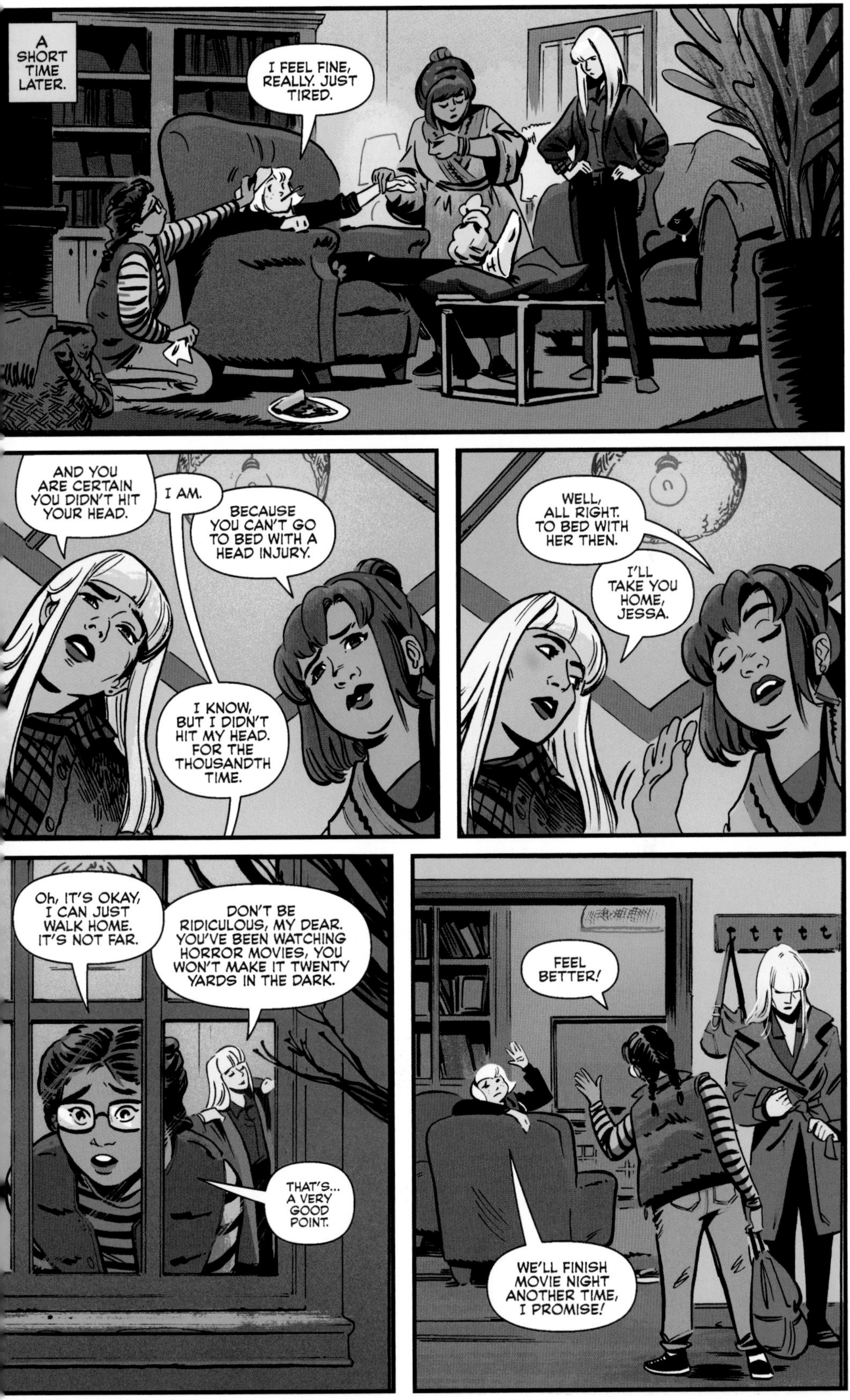
A SHORT TIME LATER.
I FEEL FINE, REALLY. JUST TIRED.
AND YOU ARE CERTAIN YOU DIDN'T HIT YOUR HEAD.
I AM.
BECAUSE YOU CAN'T GO TO BED WITH A HEAD INJURY.
I KNOW, BUT I DIDN'T HIT MY HEAD. FOR THE THOUSANDTH TIME.
WELL, ALL RIGHT. TO BED WITH HER THEN.
I'LL TAKE YOU HOME, JESSA.
Oh, IT'S OKAY, I CAN JUST WALK HOME. IT'S NOT FAR.
DON'T BE RIDICULOUS, MY DEAR. YOU'VE BEEN WATCHING HORROR MOVIES, YOU WON'T MAKE IT TWENTY YARDS IN THE DARK.
THAT'S... A VERY GOOD POINT.
FEEL BETTER!
WE'LL FINISH MOVIE NIGHT ANOTHER TIME, I PROMISE!

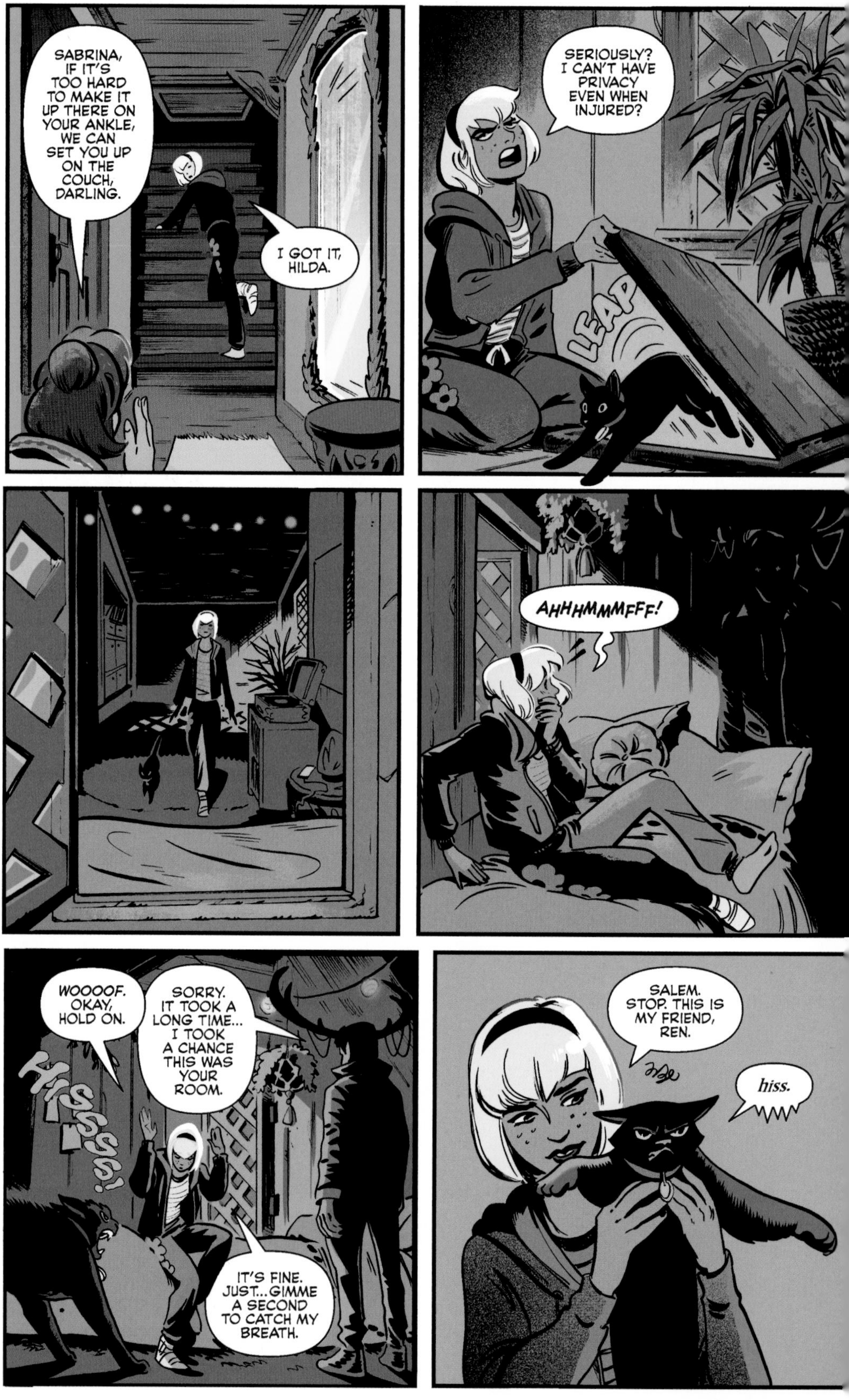
SABRINA, IF IT'S TOO HARD TO MAKE IT UP THERE ON YOUR ANKLE, WE CAN SET YOU UP ON THE COUCH, DARLING.
I GOT IT, HILDA.
SERIOUSLY? I CAN'T HAVE PRIVACY EVEN WHEN INJURED?
LEAP
AHHHMMMFFF!
WOOOOF. OKAY, HOLD ON.
SORRY. IT TOOK A LONG TIME... I TOOK A CHANCE THIS WAS YOUR ROOM.
HISSSS!
IT'S FINE. JUST...GIMME A SECOND TO CATCH MY BREATH.
SALEM. STOP. THIS IS MY FRIEND, REN.
hiss.

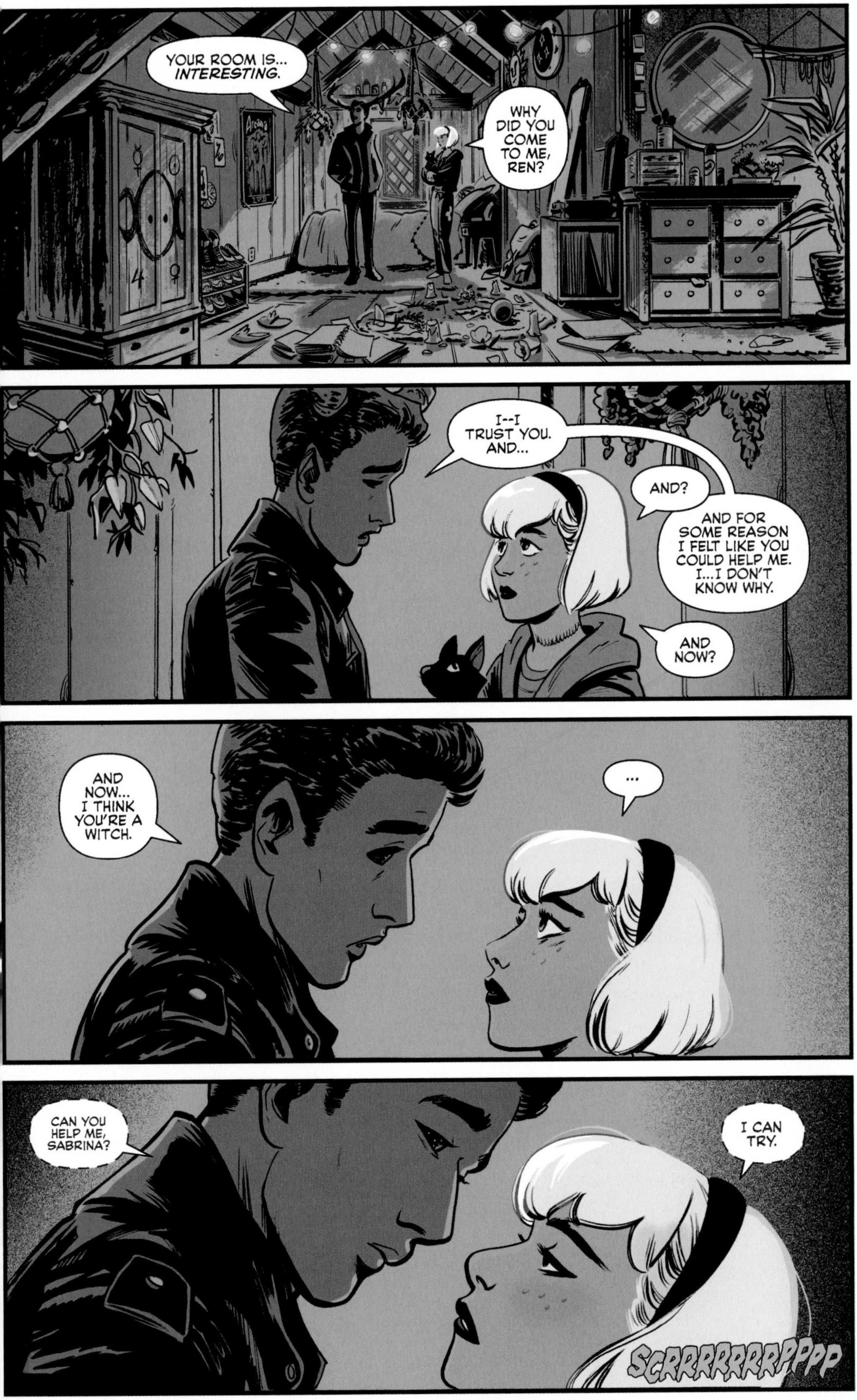
YOUR ROOM IS... INTERESTING.
WHY DID YOU COME TO ME, REN?
I--I TRUST YOU. AND...
AND?
AND FOR SOME REASON I FELT LIKE YOU COULD HELP ME. I...I DON'T KNOW WHY.
AND NOW?
AND NOW... I THINK YOU'RE A WITCH.
...
CAN YOU HELP ME, SABRINA?
I CAN TRY.
SCRRRRRRRPPPP

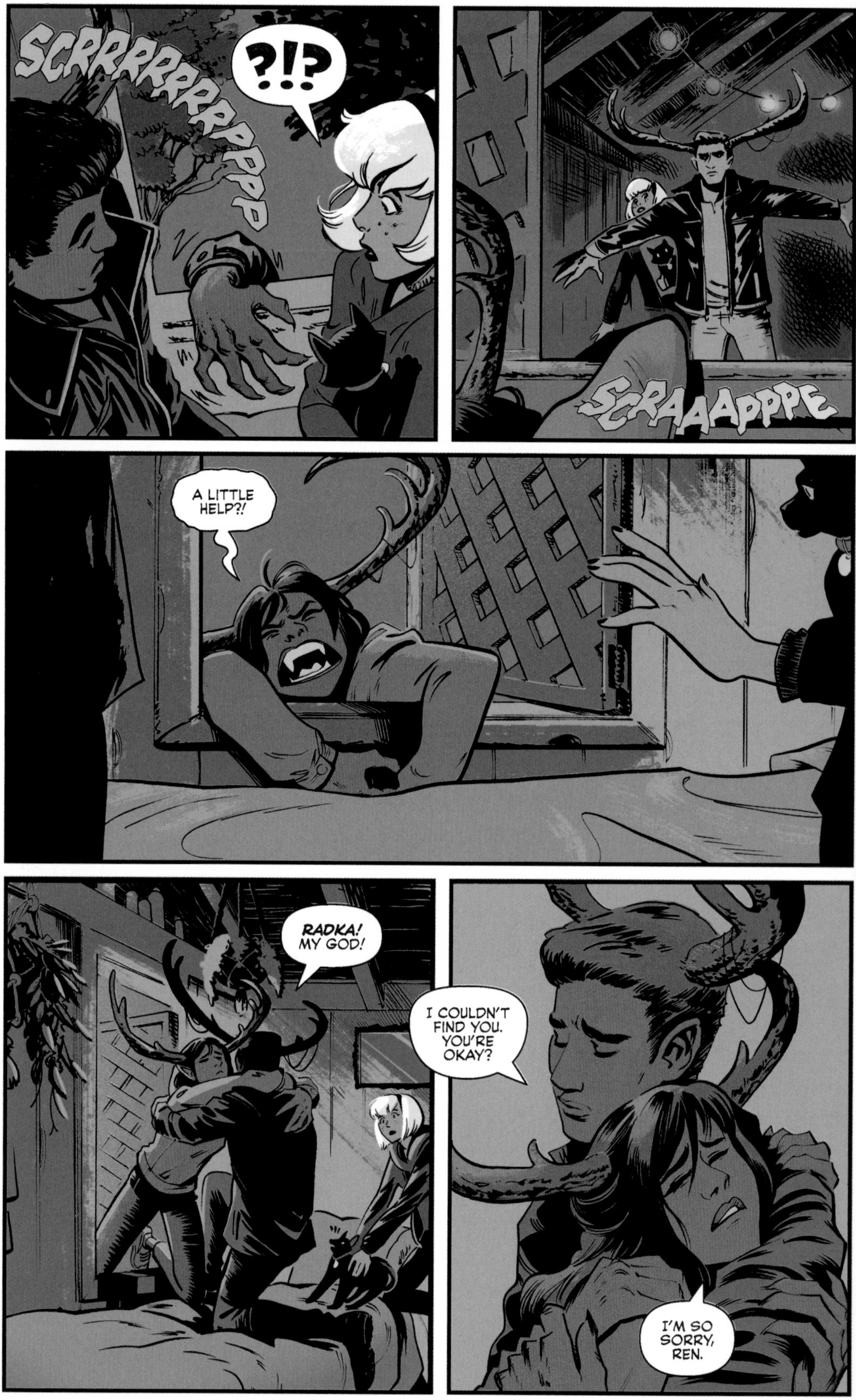
SCRRRRRRRRPPPP
?!?
SCRAAAPPPE
A LITTLE HELP?!
RADKA! MY GOD!
I COULDN'T FIND YOU. YOU'RE OKAY?
I'M SO SORRY, REN.

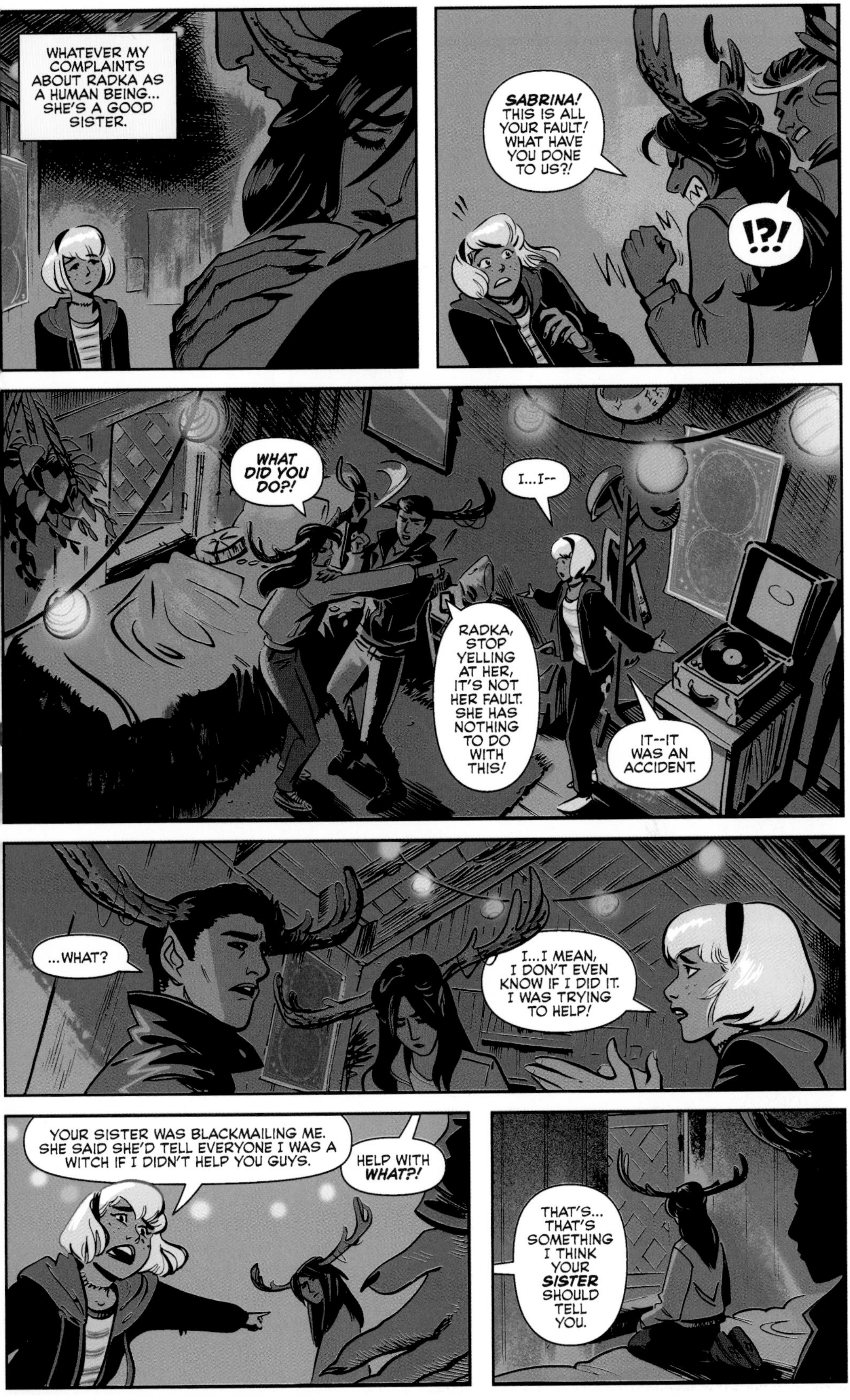
WHATEVER MY COMPLAINTS ABOUT RADKA AS A HUMAN BEING... SHE'S A GOOD SISTER.
SABRINA! THIS IS ALL YOUR FAULT! WHAT HAVE YOU DONE TO US?!
!?!
WHAT DID YOU DO?!
I...I--
RADKA, STOP YELLING AT HER, IT'S NOT HER FAULT. SHE HAS NOTHING TO DO WITH THIS!
IT--IT WAS AN ACCIDENT.
...WHAT?
I...I MEAN, I DON'T EVEN KNOW IF I DID IT. I WAS TRYING TO HELP!
YOUR SISTER WAS BLACKMAILING ME. SHE SAID SHE'D TELL EVERYONE I WAS A WITCH IF I DIDN'T HELP YOU GUYS.
HELP WITH WHAT?!
THAT'S... THAT'S SOMETHING I THINK YOUR SISTER SHOULD TELL YOU.

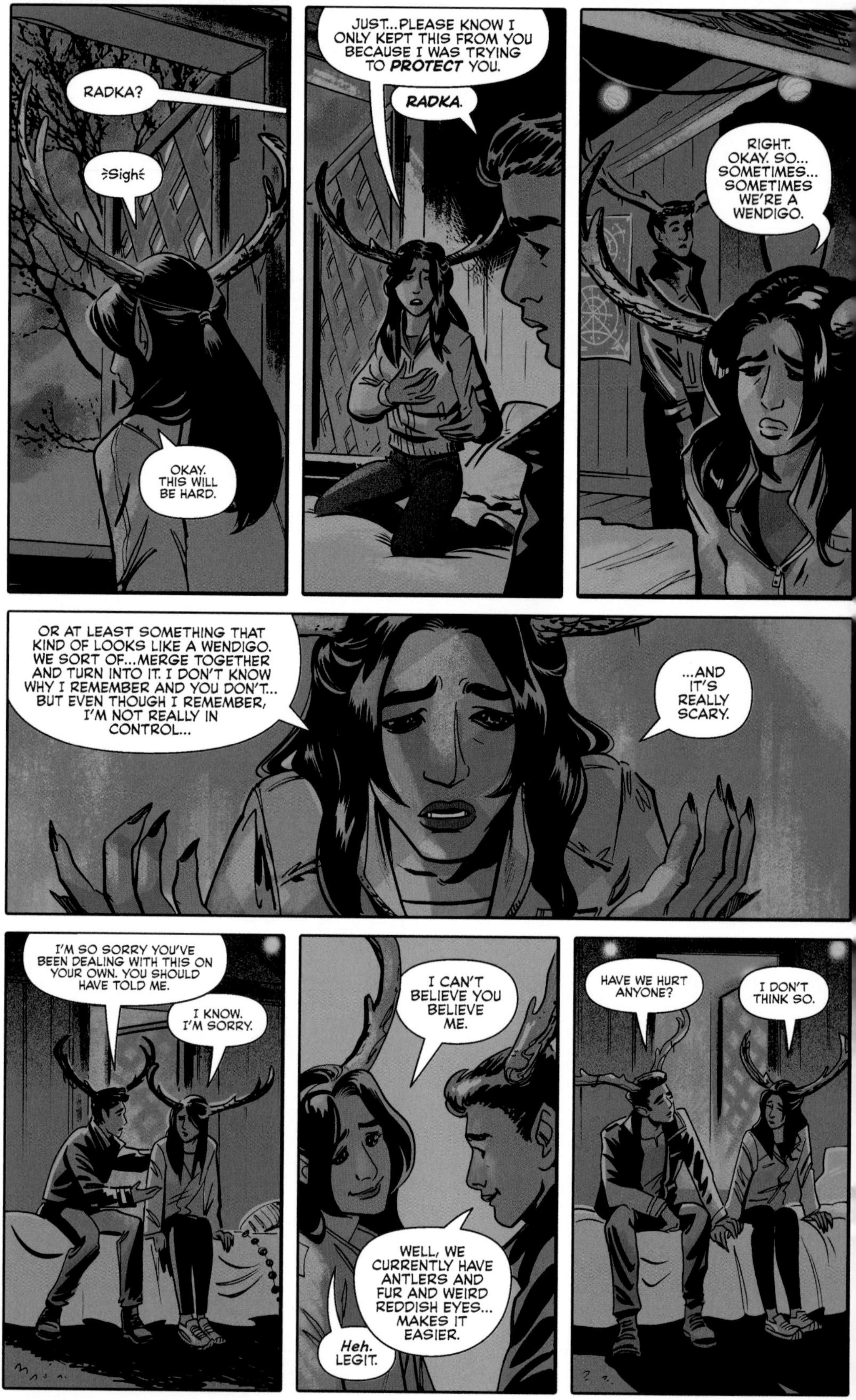
RADKA?
Sigh
OKAY. THIS WILL BE HARD.
JUST...PLEASE KNOW I ONLY KEPT THIS FROM YOU BECAUSE I WAS TRYING TO *PROTECT* YOU.
RADKA.
RIGHT. OKAY. SO... SOMETIMES... SOMETIMES WE'RE A WENDIGO.
OR AT LEAST SOMETHING THAT KIND OF LOOKS LIKE A WENDIGO. WE SORT OF...MERGE TOGETHER AND TURN INTO IT. I DON'T KNOW WHY I REMEMBER AND YOU DON'T... BUT EVEN THOUGH I REMEMBER, I'M NOT REALLY IN CONTROL...
...AND IT'S REALLY SCARY.
I'M SO SORRY YOU'VE BEEN DEALING WITH THIS ON YOUR OWN. YOU SHOULD HAVE TOLD ME.
I KNOW. I'M SORRY.
I CAN'T BELIEVE YOU BELIEVE ME.
WELL, WE CURRENTLY HAVE ANTLERS AND FUR AND WEIRD REDDISH EYES... MAKES IT EASIER.
Heh. LEGIT.
HAVE WE HURT ANYONE?
I DON'T THINK SO.

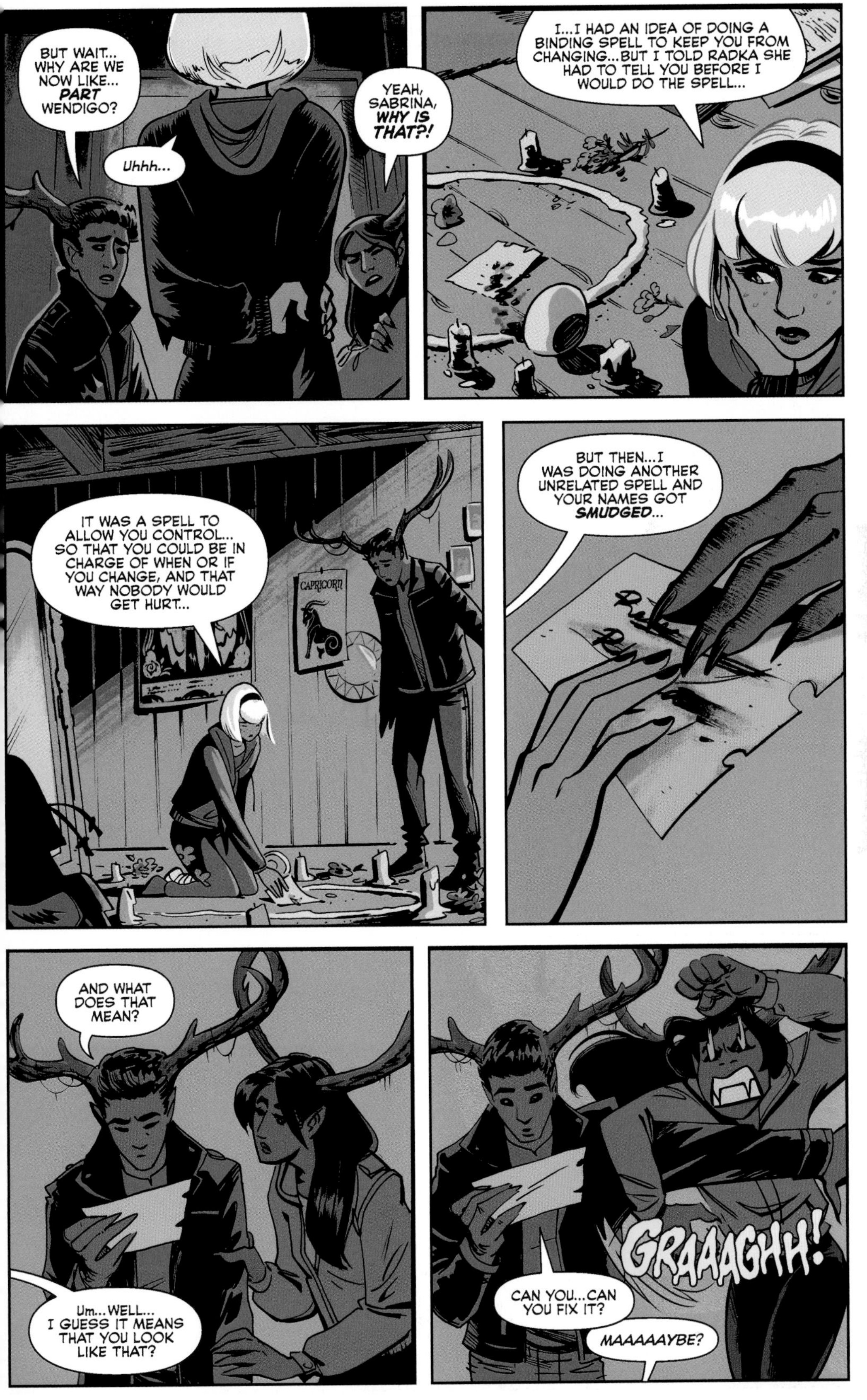
BUT WAIT... WHY ARE WE NOW LIKE... ***PART*** WENDIGO?
Uhhh...
YEAH, SABRINA, ***WHY IS THAT?!***
I...I HAD AN IDEA OF DOING A BINDING SPELL TO KEEP YOU FROM CHANGING...BUT I TOLD RADKA SHE HAD TO TELL YOU BEFORE I WOULD DO THE SPELL...
IT WAS A SPELL TO ALLOW YOU CONTROL... SO THAT YOU COULD BE IN CHARGE OF WHEN OR IF YOU CHANGE, AND THAT WAY NOBODY WOULD GET HURT...
CAPRICORN
BUT THEN...I WAS DOING ANOTHER UNRELATED SPELL AND YOUR NAMES GOT ***SMUDGED***...
AND WHAT DOES THAT MEAN?
Um...WELL... I GUESS IT MEANS THAT YOU LOOK LIKE THAT?
GRAAAGHH!
CAN YOU...CAN YOU FIX IT?
MAAAAAYBE?

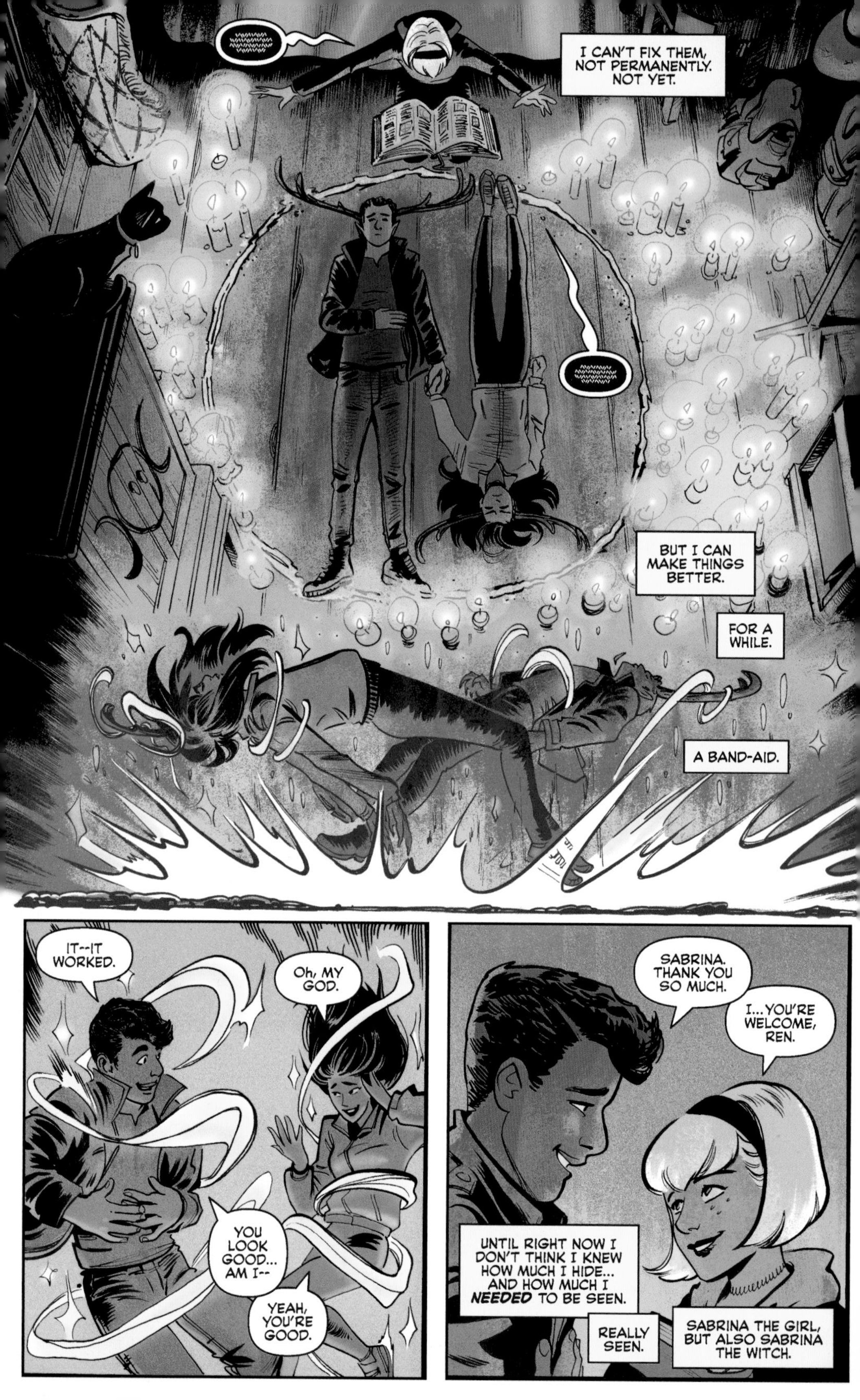

I CAN'T FIX THEM, NOT PERMANENTLY. NOT YET.
BUT I CAN MAKE THINGS BETTER.
FOR A WHILE.
A BAND-AID.
IT--IT WORKED.
Oh, MY GOD.
YOU LOOK GOOD... AM I--
YEAH, YOU'RE GOOD.
SABRINA. THANK YOU SO MUCH.
I... YOU'RE WELCOME, REN.
UNTIL RIGHT NOW I DON'T THINK I KNEW HOW MUCH I HIDE... AND HOW MUCH I NEEDED TO BE SEEN.
REALLY SEEN.
SABRINA THE GIRL, BUT ALSO SABRINA THE WITCH.

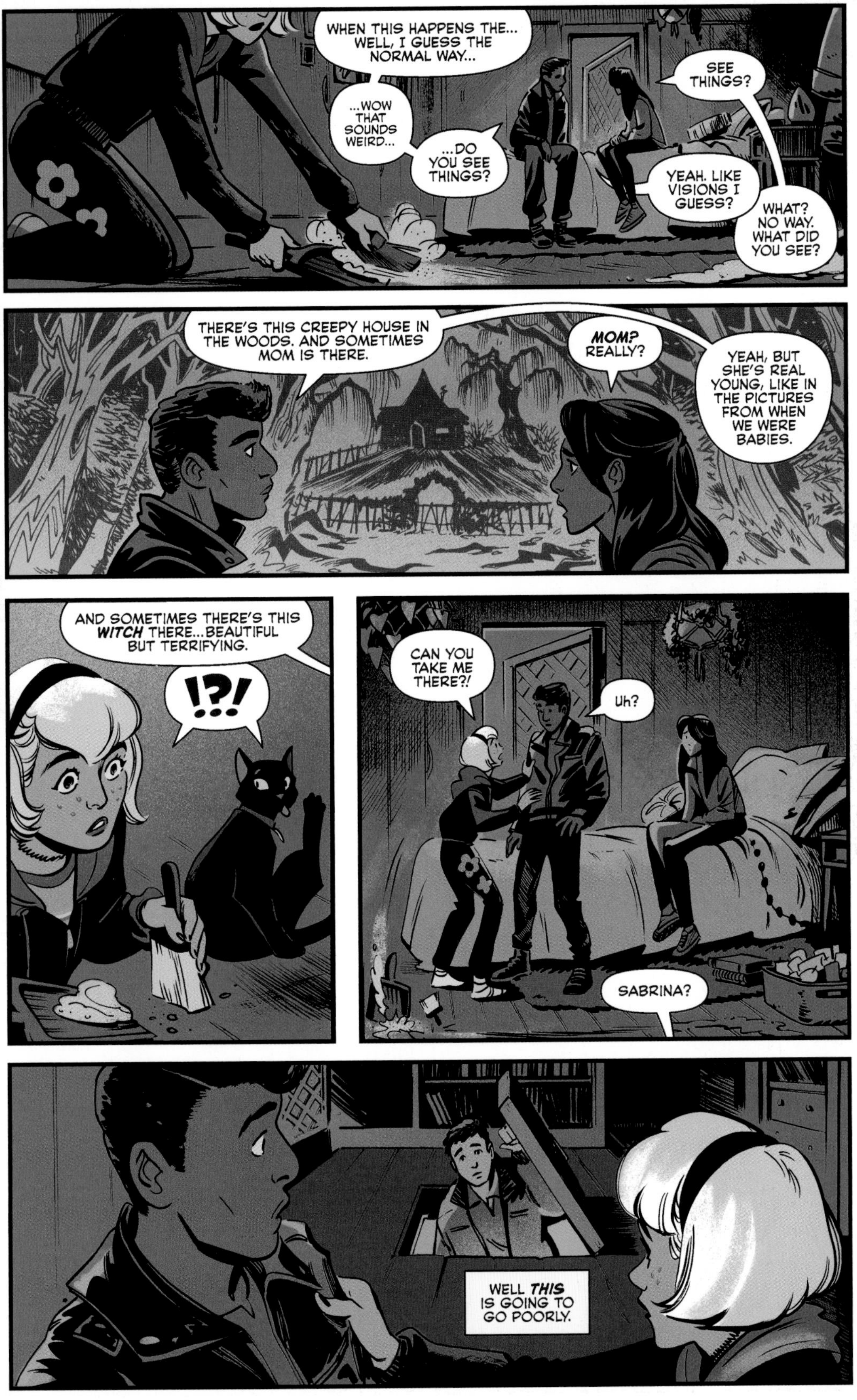
WHEN THIS HAPPENS THE... WELL, I GUESS THE NORMAL WAY...
...WOW THAT SOUNDS WEIRD...
...DO YOU SEE THINGS?
SEE THINGS?
YEAH. LIKE VISIONS I GUESS?
WHAT? NO WAY. WHAT DID YOU SEE?
THERE'S THIS CREEPY HOUSE IN THE WOODS. AND SOMETIMES MOM IS THERE.
MOM? REALLY?
YEAH, BUT SHE'S REAL YOUNG, LIKE IN THE PICTURES FROM WHEN WE WERE BABIES.
AND SOMETIMES THERE'S THIS *WITCH* THERE...BEAUTIFUL BUT TERRIFYING.
!?!
CAN YOU TAKE ME THERE?!
Uh?
SABRINA?
WELL *THIS* IS GOING TO GO POORLY.

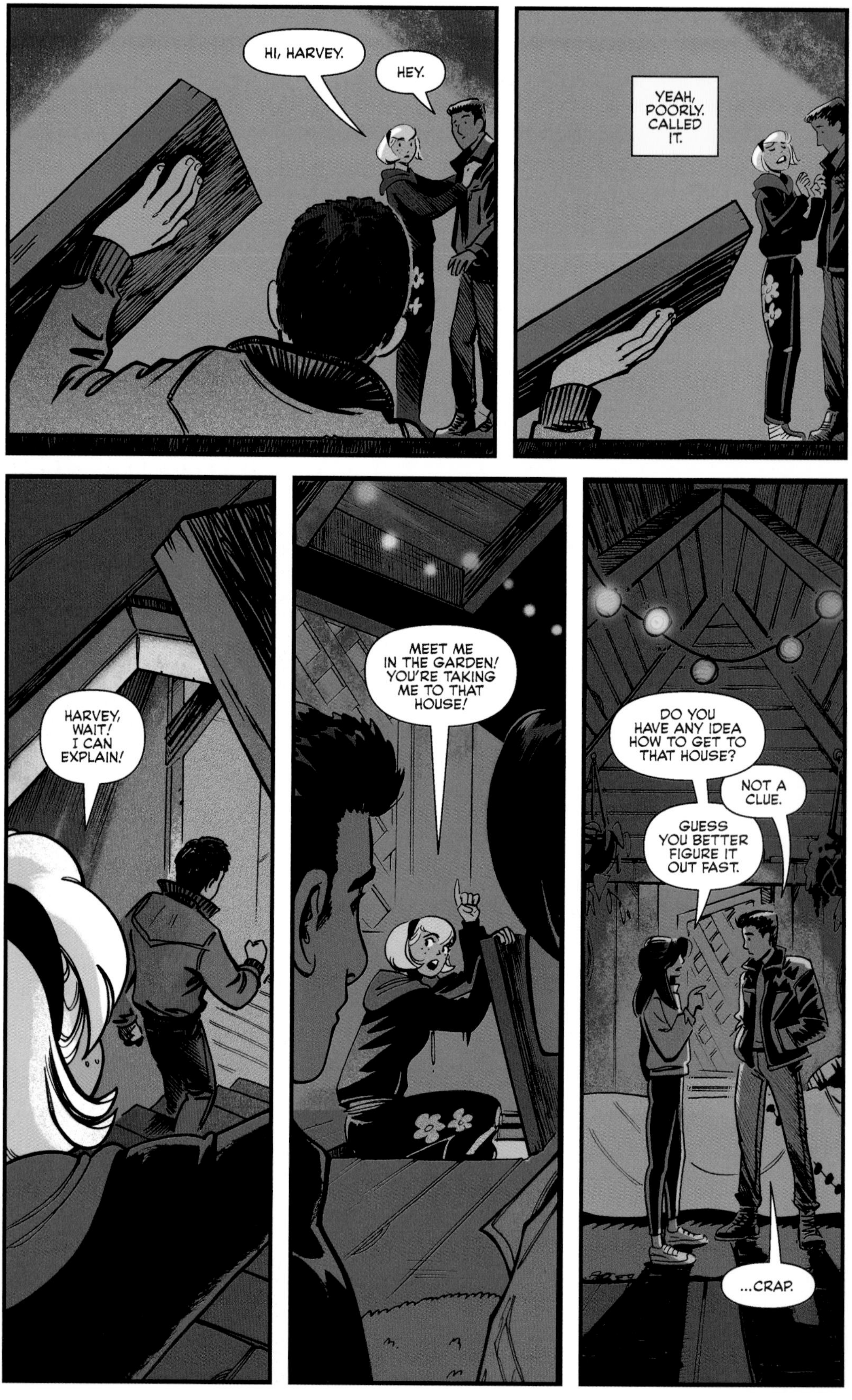
HI, HARVEY.
HEY.
YEAH, POORLY. CALLED IT.
HARVEY, WAIT! I CAN EXPLAIN!
MEET ME IN THE GARDEN! YOU'RE TAKING ME TO THAT HOUSE!
DO YOU HAVE ANY IDEA HOW TO GET TO THAT HOUSE?
NOT A CLUE.
GUESS YOU BETTER FIGURE IT OUT FAST.
...CRAP.

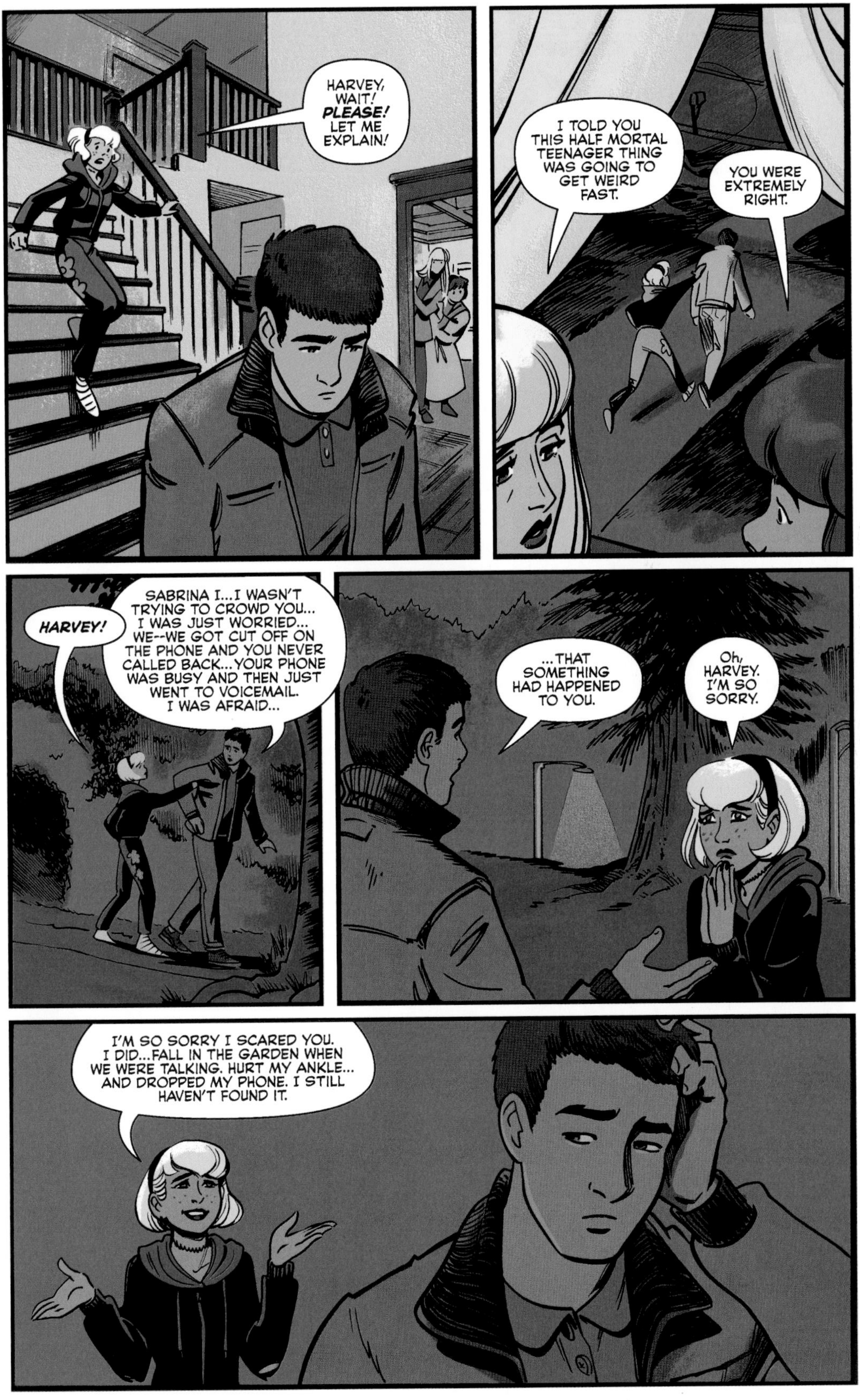
HARVEY, WAIT! **PLEASE!** LET ME EXPLAIN!
I TOLD YOU THIS HALF MORTAL TEENAGER THING WAS GOING TO GET WEIRD FAST.
YOU WERE EXTREMELY RIGHT.
HARVEY!
SABRINA I...I WASN'T TRYING TO CROWD YOU... I WAS JUST WORRIED... WE--WE GOT CUT OFF ON THE PHONE AND YOU NEVER CALLED BACK...YOUR PHONE WAS BUSY AND THEN JUST WENT TO VOICEMAIL. I WAS AFRAID...
...THAT SOMETHING HAD HAPPENED TO YOU.
Oh, HARVEY. I'M SO SORRY.
I'M SO SORRY I SCARED YOU. I DID...FALL IN THE GARDEN WHEN WE WERE TALKING. HURT MY ANKLE... AND DROPPED MY PHONE. I STILL HAVEN'T FOUND IT.

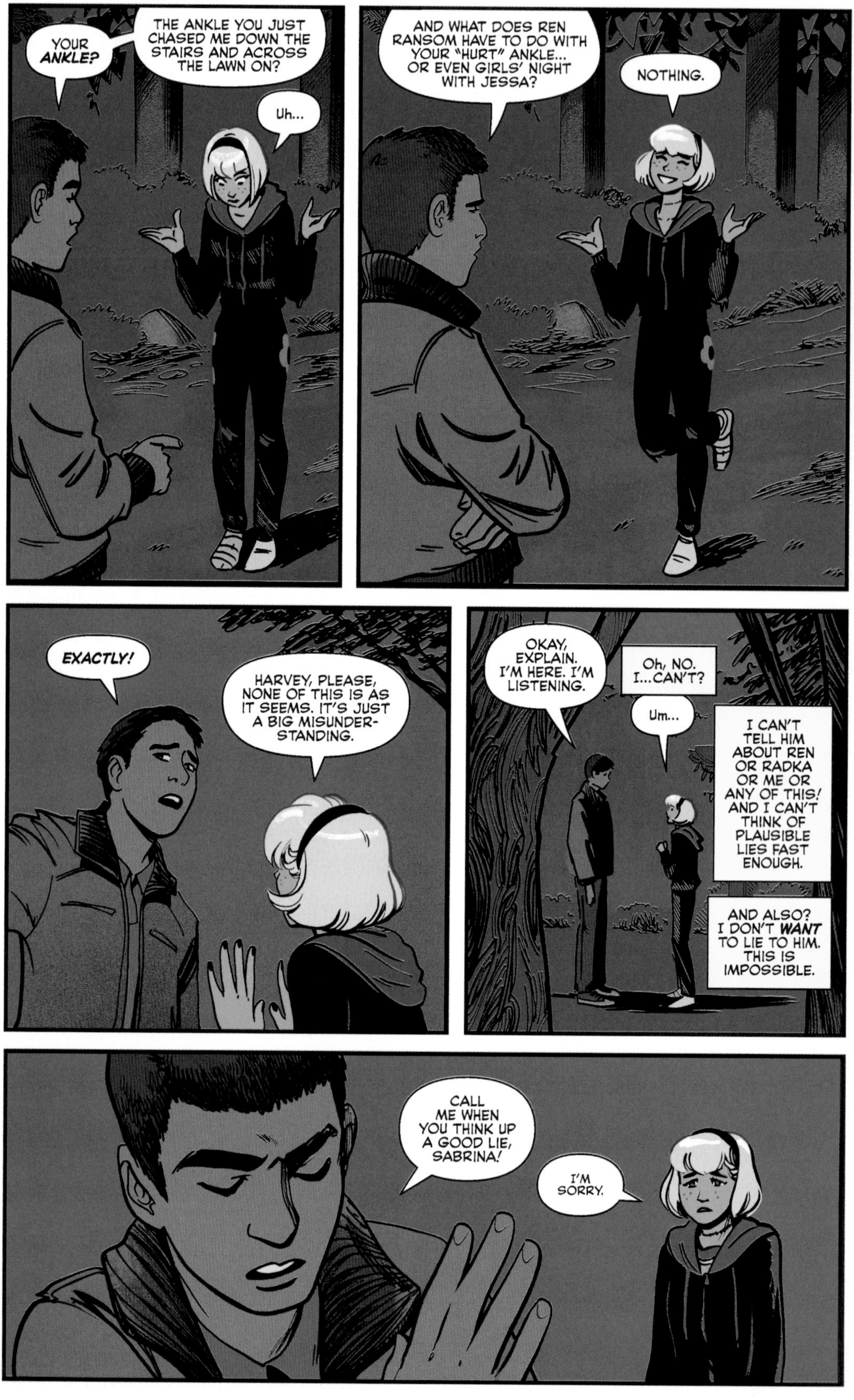

YOUR ANKLE?
THE ANKLE YOU JUST CHASED ME DOWN THE STAIRS AND ACROSS THE LAWN ON?
Uh...
AND WHAT DOES REN RANSOM HAVE TO DO WITH YOUR "HURT" ANKLE... OR EVEN GIRLS' NIGHT WITH JESSA?
NOTHING.
EXACTLY!
HARVEY, PLEASE, NONE OF THIS IS AS IT SEEMS. IT'S JUST A BIG MISUNDER-STANDING.
OKAY, EXPLAIN. I'M HERE. I'M LISTENING.
Oh, NO. I...CAN'T?
Um...
I CAN'T TELL HIM ABOUT REN OR RADKA OR ME OR ANY OF THIS! AND I CAN'T THINK OF PLAUSIBLE LIES FAST ENOUGH.
AND ALSO? I DON'T WANT TO LIE TO HIM. THIS IS IMPOSSIBLE.
CALL ME WHEN YOU THINK UP A GOOD LIE, SABRINA!
I'M SORRY.

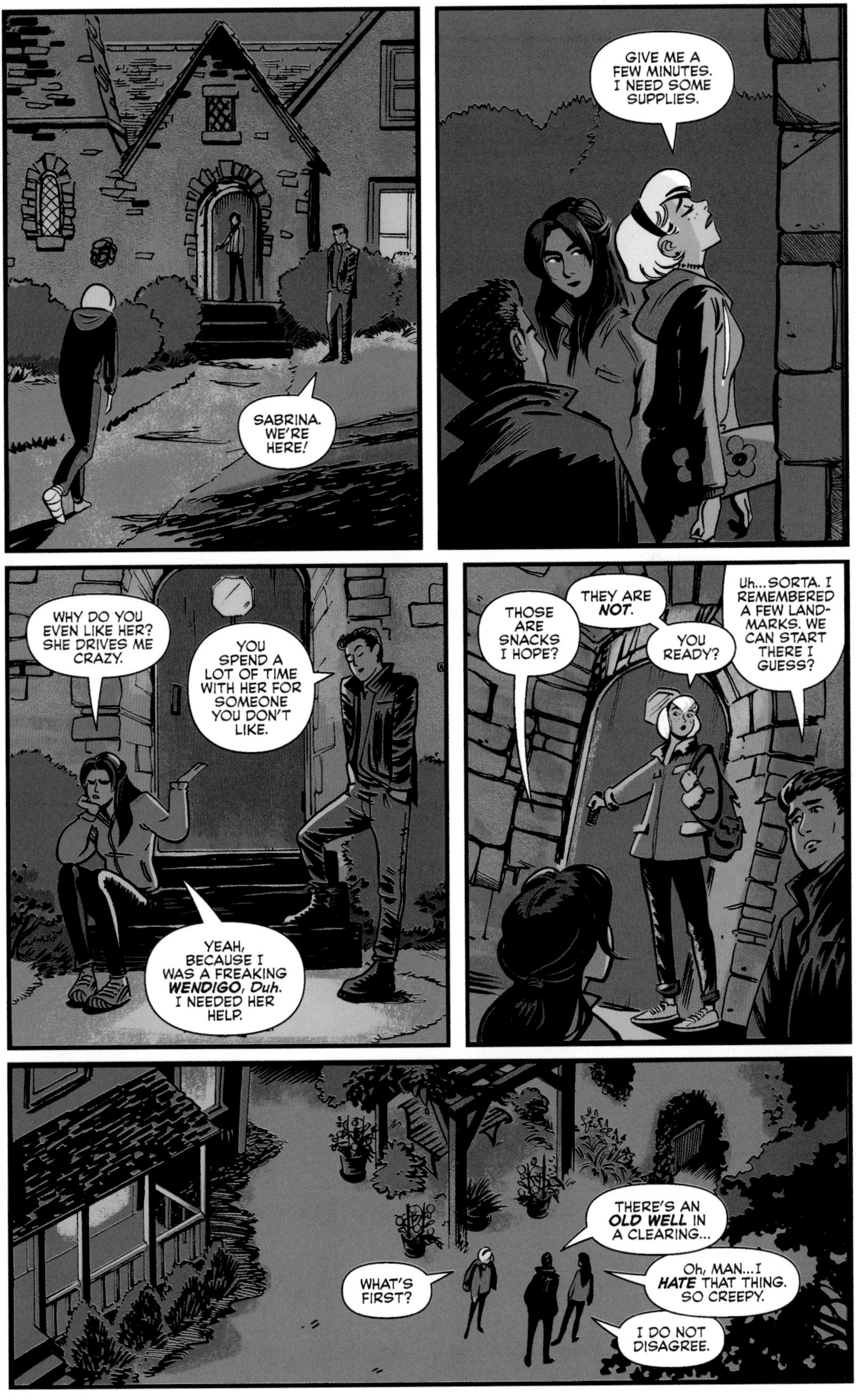
SABRINA. WE'RE HERE!
GIVE ME A FEW MINUTES. I NEED SOME SUPPLIES.
WHY DO YOU EVEN LIKE HER? SHE DRIVES ME CRAZY.
YOU SPEND A LOT OF TIME WITH HER FOR SOMEONE YOU DON'T LIKE.
YEAH, BECAUSE I WAS A FREAKING *WENDIGO*, Duh. I NEEDED HER HELP.
THOSE ARE SNACKS I HOPE?
THEY ARE *NOT*.
YOU READY?
Uh...SORTA. I REMEMBERED A FEW LAND-MARKS. WE CAN START THERE I GUESS?
WHAT'S FIRST?
THERE'S AN *OLD WELL* IN A CLEARING...
Oh, MAN...I *HATE* THAT THING. SO CREEPY.
I DO NOT DISAGREE.

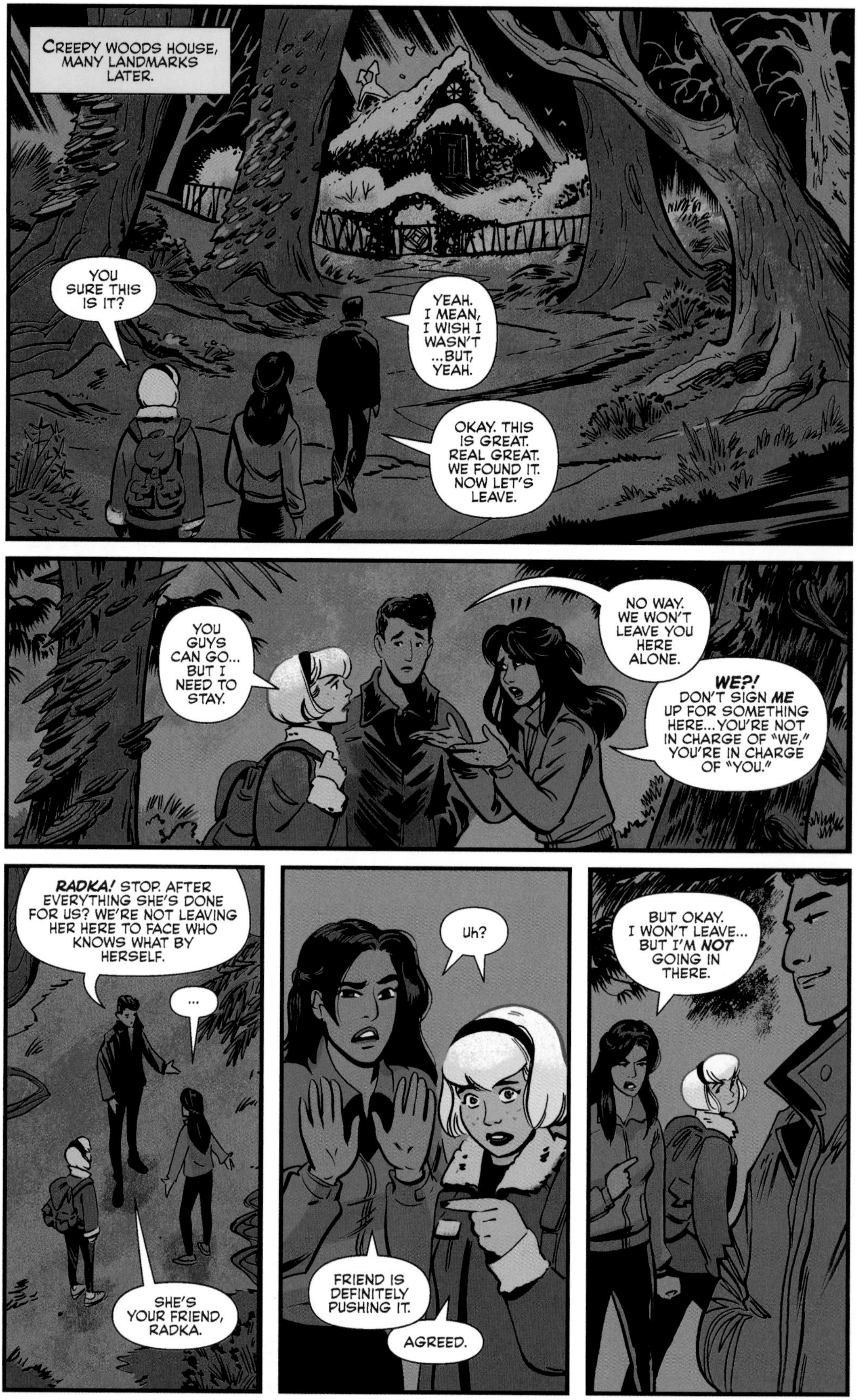
CREEPY WOODS HOUSE, MANY LANDMARKS LATER.
YOU SURE THIS IS IT?
YEAH. I MEAN, I WISH I WASN'T ...BUT, YEAH.
OKAY. THIS IS GREAT. REAL GREAT. WE FOUND IT. NOW LET'S LEAVE.
YOU GUYS CAN GO... BUT I NEED TO STAY.
NO WAY. WE WON'T LEAVE YOU HERE ALONE.
WE?! DON'T SIGN ME UP FOR SOMETHING HERE...YOU'RE NOT IN CHARGE OF "WE," YOU'RE IN CHARGE OF "YOU."
RADKA! STOP. AFTER EVERYTHING SHE'S DONE FOR US? WE'RE NOT LEAVING HER HERE TO FACE WHO KNOWS WHAT BY HERSELF.
...
SHE'S YOUR FRIEND, RADKA.
Uh?
FRIEND IS DEFINITELY PUSHING IT.
AGREED.
BUT OKAY. I WON'T LEAVE... BUT I'M NOT GOING IN THERE.

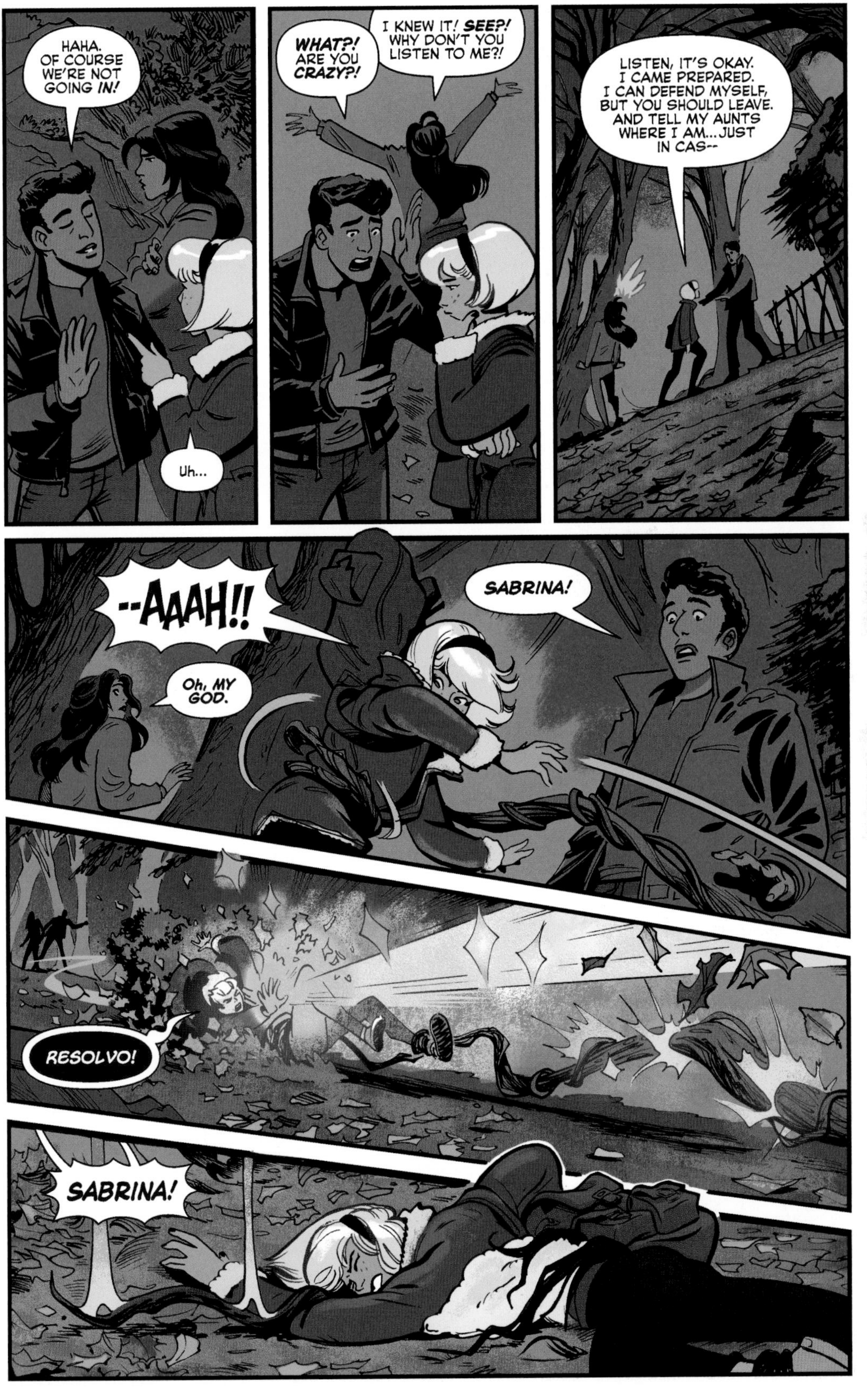
HAHA. OF COURSE WE'RE NOT GOING IN!
Uh...
WHAT?! ARE YOU CRAZY?!
I KNEW IT! SEE?! WHY DON'T YOU LISTEN TO ME?!
LISTEN, IT'S OKAY. I CAME PREPARED. I CAN DEFEND MYSELF, BUT YOU SHOULD LEAVE. AND TELL MY AUNTS WHERE I AM...JUST IN CAS--
--AAAH!!
SABRINA!
Oh, MY GOD.
RESOLVO!
SABRINA!

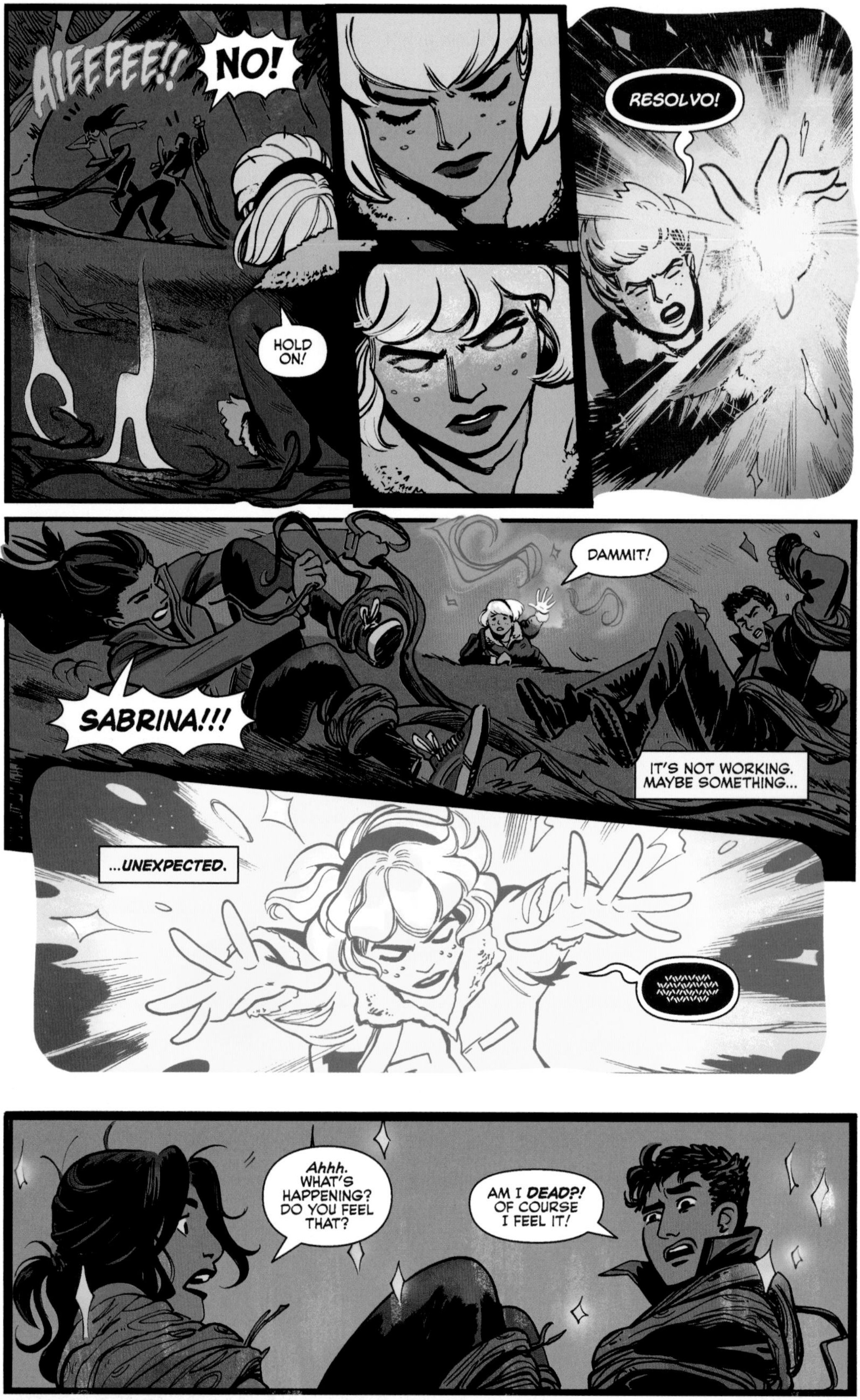
AIEEEEE!!
NO!
HOLD ON!
RESOLVO!
SABRINA!!!
DAMMIT!
IT'S NOT WORKING. MAYBE SOMETHING...
...UNEXPECTED.
Ahhh. WHAT'S HAPPENING? DO YOU FEEL THAT?
AM I DEAD?! OF COURSE I FEEL IT!

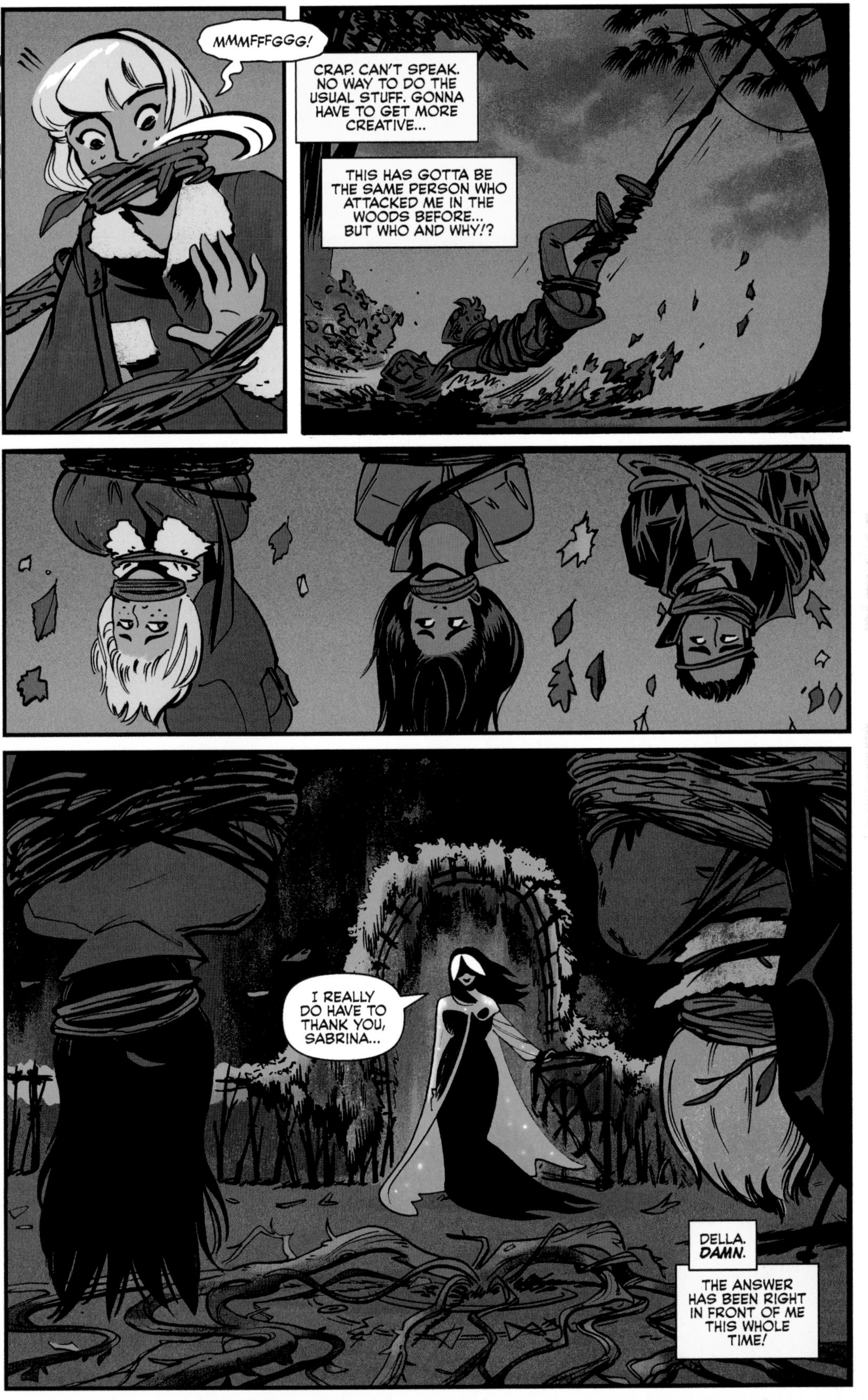
MMMFFFGGG!
CRAP. CAN'T SPEAK. NO WAY TO DO THE USUAL STUFF. GONNA HAVE TO GET MORE CREATIVE...
THIS HAS GOTTA BE THE SAME PERSON WHO ATTACKED ME IN THE WOODS BEFORE... BUT WHO AND WHY!?
I REALLY DO HAVE TO THANK YOU, SABRINA...
DELLA. ***DAMN***.
THE ANSWER HAS BEEN RIGHT IN FRONT OF ME THIS WHOLE TIME!

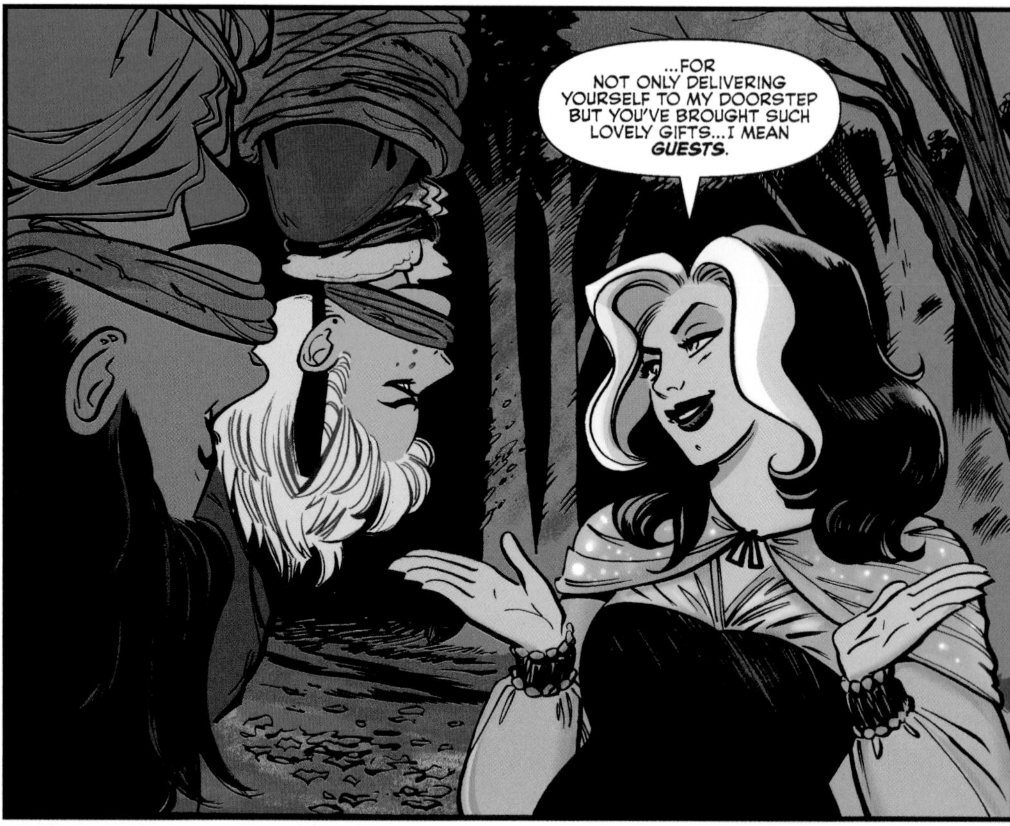
...FOR NOT ONLY DELIVERING YOURSELF TO MY DOORSTEP BUT YOU'VE BROUGHT SUCH LOVELY GIFTS...I MEAN *GUESTS*.

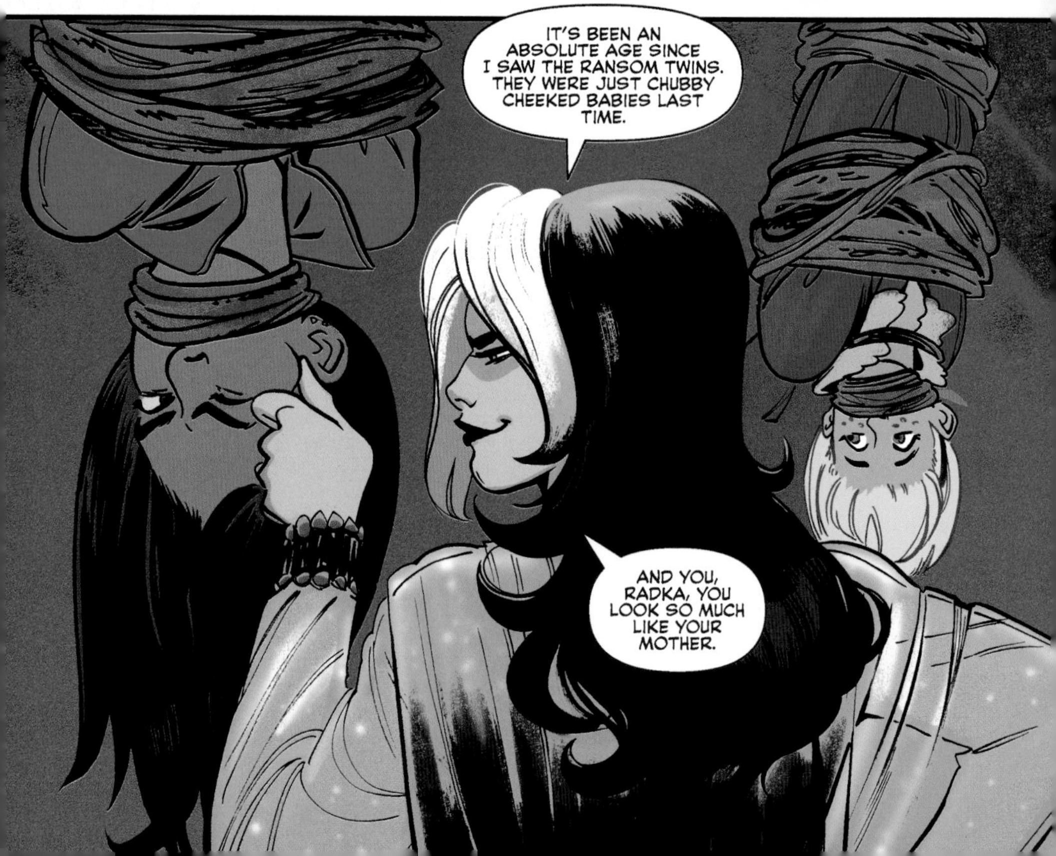
IT'S BEEN AN ABSOLUTE AGE SINCE I SAW THE RANSOM TWINS. THEY WERE JUST CHUBBY CHEEKED BABIES LAST TIME.
AND YOU, RADKA, YOU LOOK SO MUCH LIKE YOUR MOTHER.

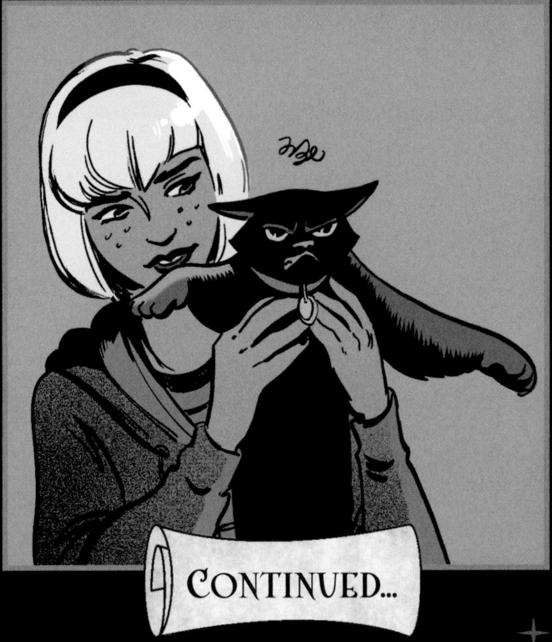
CONTINUED...

05

STORY BY
KELLY THOMPSON

ART BY
VERONICA FISH
AND ANDY FISH

LETTERING BY
JACK MORELLI

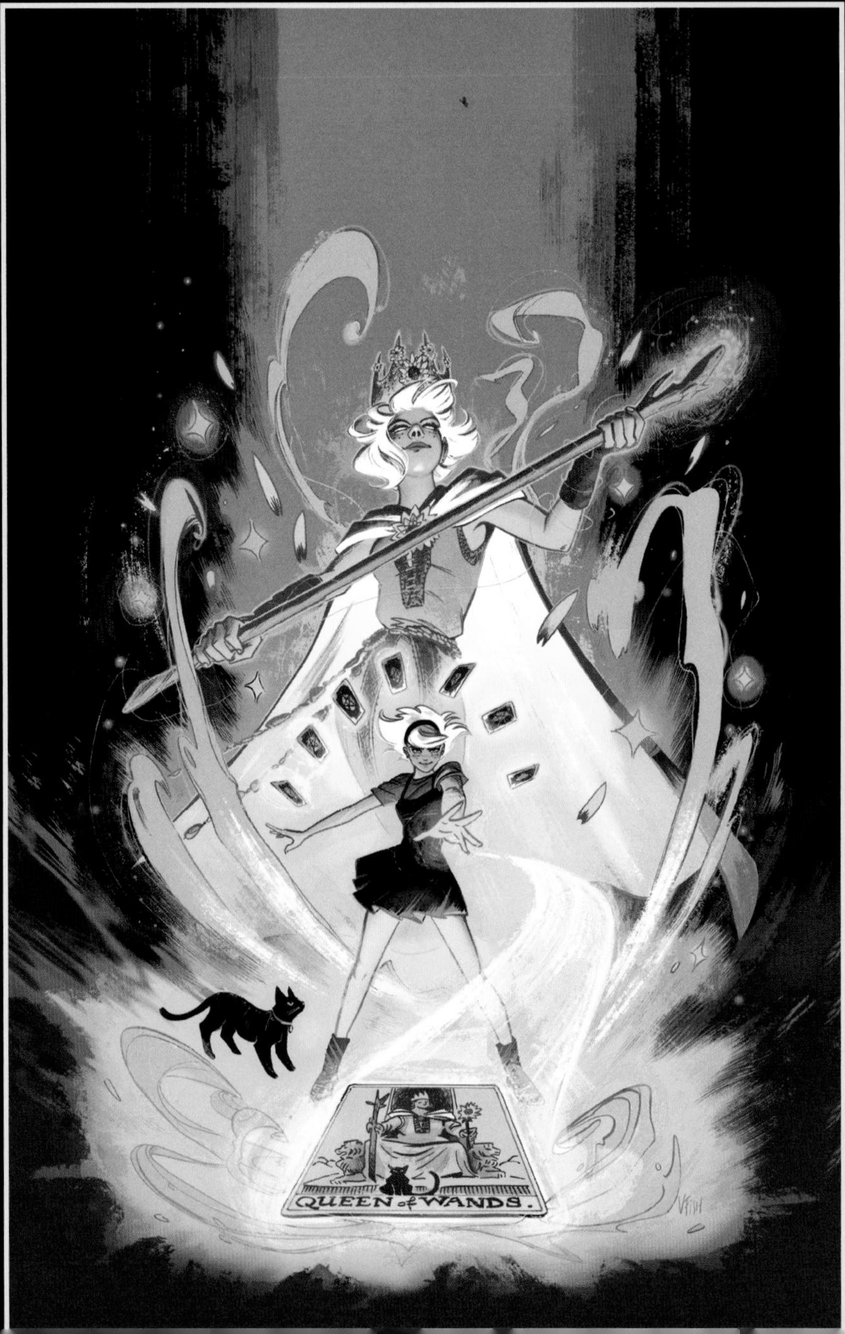
QUEEN of WANDS.

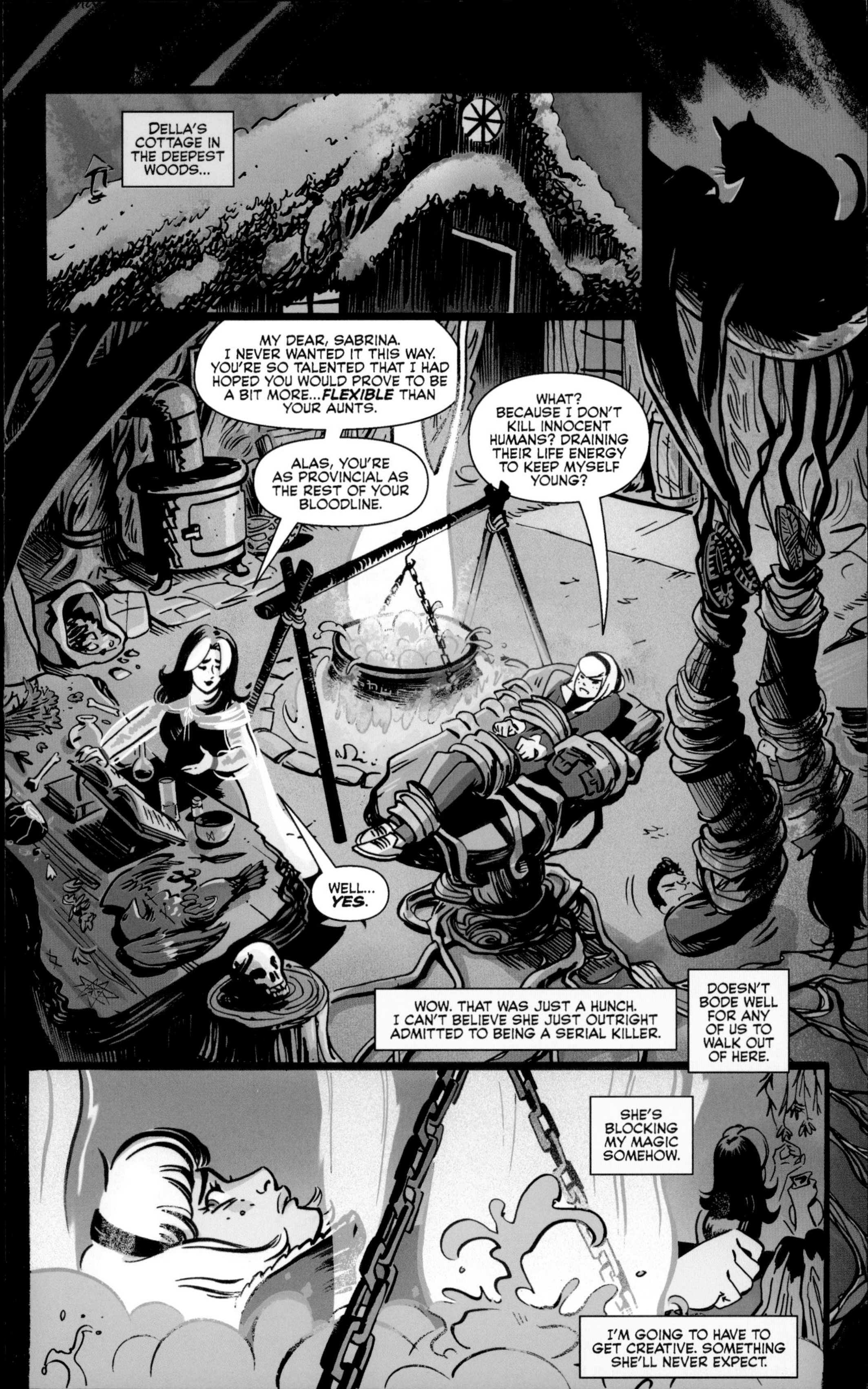
DELLA'S COTTAGE IN THE DEEPEST WOODS...
MY DEAR, SABRINA. I NEVER WANTED IT THIS WAY. YOU'RE SO TALENTED THAT I HAD HOPED YOU WOULD PROVE TO BE A BIT MORE...*FLEXIBLE* THAN YOUR AUNTS.
ALAS, YOU'RE AS PROVINCIAL AS THE REST OF YOUR BLOODLINE.
WHAT? BECAUSE I DON'T KILL INNOCENT HUMANS? DRAINING THEIR LIFE ENERGY TO KEEP MYSELF YOUNG?
WELL... ***YES***.
WOW. THAT WAS JUST A HUNCH. I CAN'T BELIEVE SHE JUST OUTRIGHT ADMITTED TO BEING A SERIAL KILLER.
DOESN'T BODE WELL FOR ANY OF US TO WALK OUT OF HERE.
SHE'S BLOCKING MY MAGIC SOMEHOW.
I'M GOING TO HAVE TO GET CREATIVE. SOMETHING SHE'LL NEVER EXPECT.

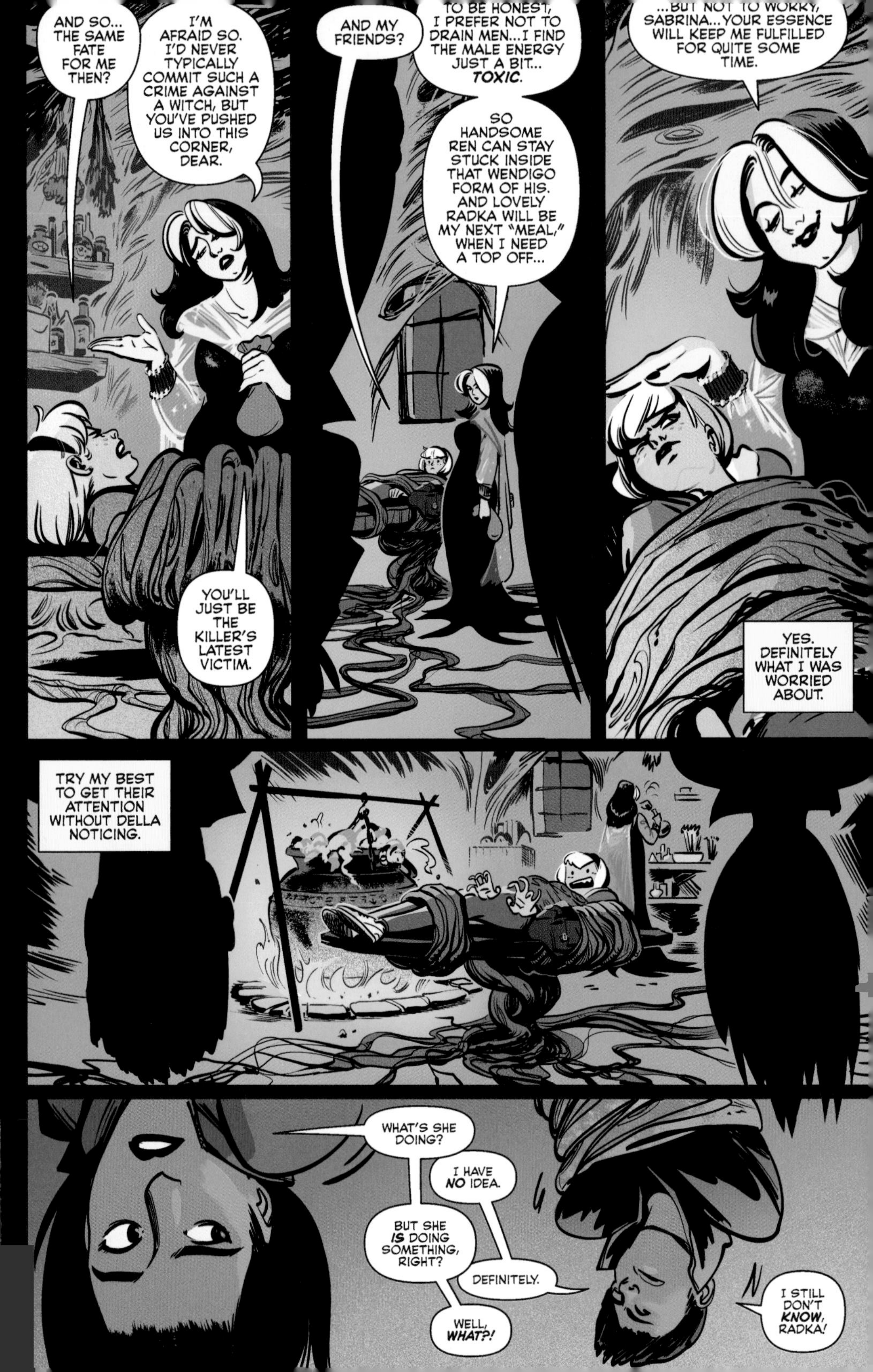
AND SO... THE SAME FATE FOR ME THEN?
I'M AFRAID SO. I'D NEVER TYPICALLY COMMIT SUCH A CRIME AGAINST A WITCH, BUT YOU'VE PUSHED US INTO THIS CORNER, DEAR.
YOU'LL JUST BE THE KILLER'S LATEST VICTIM.
AND MY FRIENDS?
TO BE HONEST, I PREFER NOT TO DRAIN MEN...I FIND THE MALE ENERGY JUST A BIT... ***TOXIC***.
SO HANDSOME REN CAN STAY STUCK INSIDE THAT WENDIGO FORM OF HIS. AND LOVELY RADKA WILL BE MY NEXT "MEAL," WHEN I NEED A TOP OFF...
...BUT NOT TO WORRY, SABRINA...YOUR ESSENCE WILL KEEP ME FULFILLED FOR QUITE SOME TIME.
YES. DEFINITELY WHAT I WAS WORRIED ABOUT.
TRY MY BEST TO GET THEIR ATTENTION WITHOUT DELLA NOTICING.
WHAT'S SHE DOING?
I HAVE **NO** IDEA.
BUT SHE ***IS*** DOING SOMETHING, RIGHT?
DEFINITELY.
WELL, ***WHAT?!***
I STILL DON'T ***KNOW***, RADKA!

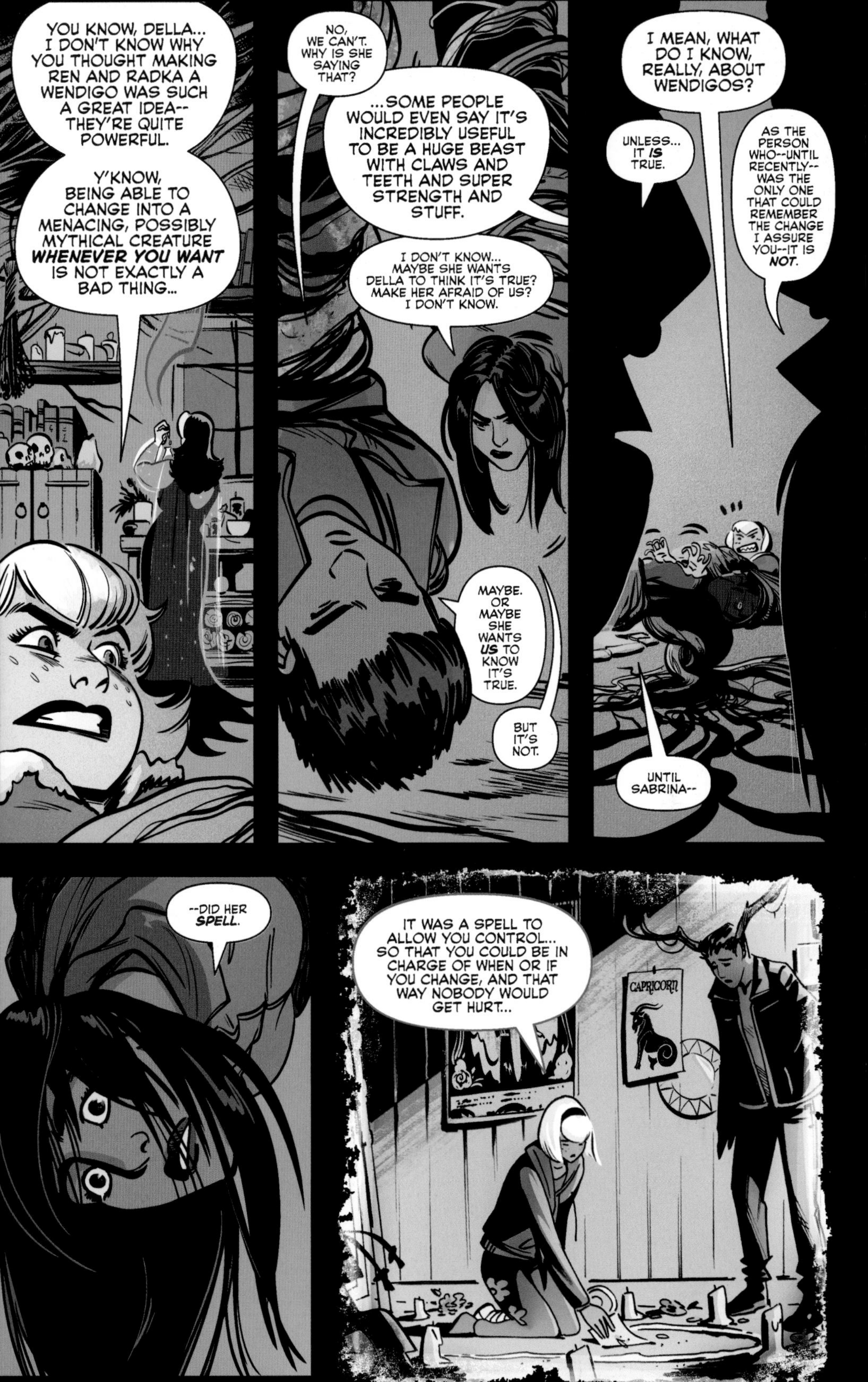
YOU KNOW, DELLA... I DON'T KNOW WHY YOU THOUGHT MAKING REN AND RADKA A WENDIGO WAS SUCH A GREAT IDEA-- THEY'RE QUITE POWERFUL.
Y'KNOW, BEING ABLE TO CHANGE INTO A MENACING, POSSIBLY MYTHICAL CREATURE WHENEVER YOU WANT IS NOT EXACTLY A BAD THING...
NO, WE CAN'T. WHY IS SHE SAYING THAT?
...SOME PEOPLE WOULD EVEN SAY IT'S INCREDIBLY USEFUL TO BE A HUGE BEAST WITH CLAWS AND TEETH AND SUPER STRENGTH AND STUFF.
I DON'T KNOW... MAYBE SHE WANTS DELLA TO THINK IT'S TRUE? MAKE HER AFRAID OF US? I DON'T KNOW.
MAYBE. OR MAYBE SHE WANTS US TO KNOW IT'S TRUE.
BUT IT'S NOT.
I MEAN, WHAT DO I KNOW, REALLY, ABOUT WENDIGOS?
UNLESS... IT IS TRUE.
AS THE PERSON WHO--UNTIL RECENTLY--WAS THE ONLY ONE THAT COULD REMEMBER THE CHANGE I ASSURE YOU--IT IS NOT.
UNTIL SABRINA--
--DID HER SPELL.
IT WAS A SPELL TO ALLOW YOU CONTROL... SO THAT YOU COULD BE IN CHARGE OF WHEN OR IF YOU CHANGE, AND THAT WAY NOBODY WOULD GET HURT...
CAPRICORN

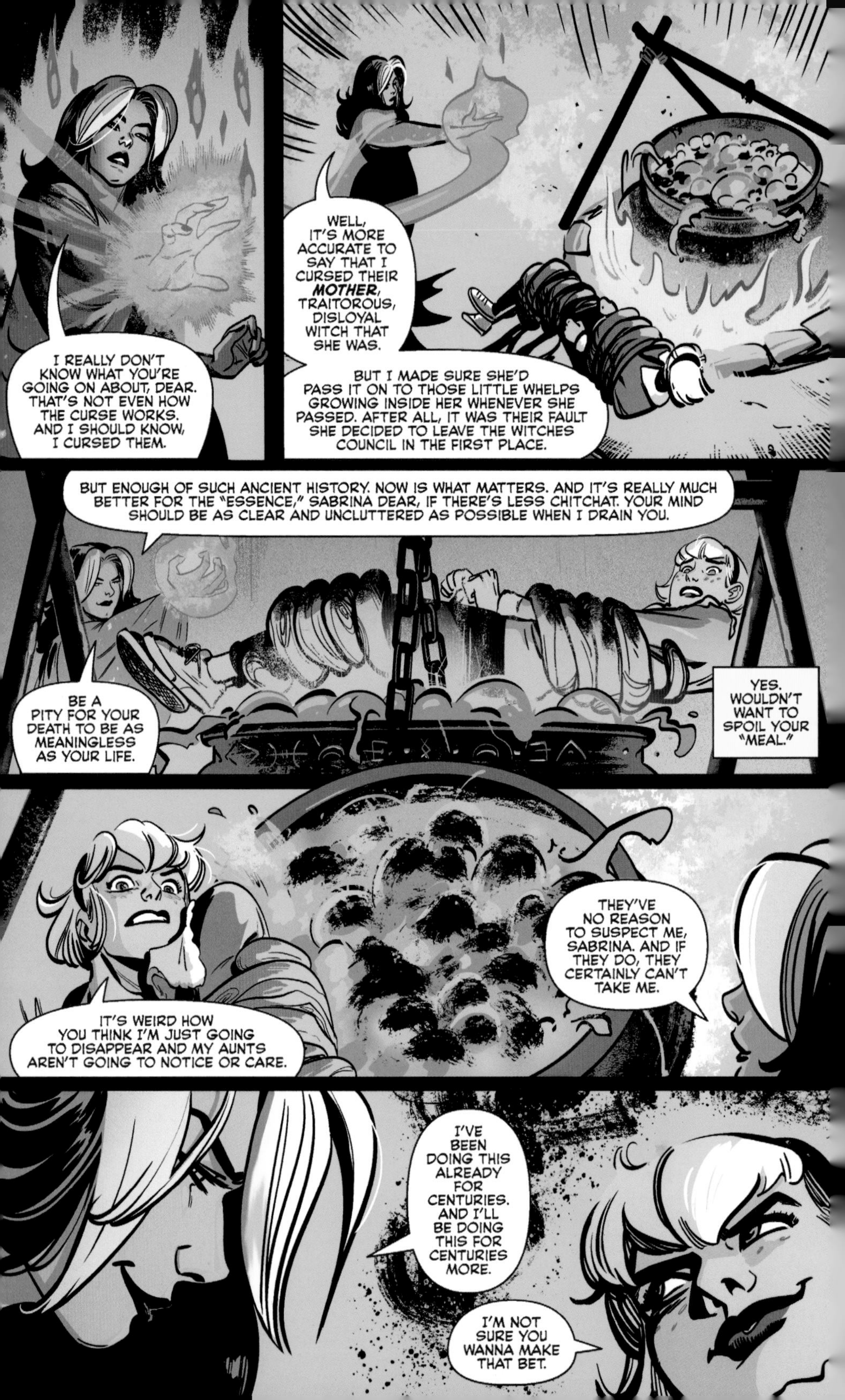

I REALLY DON'T KNOW WHAT YOU'RE GOING ON ABOUT, DEAR. THAT'S NOT EVEN HOW THE CURSE WORKS. AND I SHOULD KNOW, I CURSED THEM.
WELL, IT'S MORE ACCURATE TO SAY THAT I CURSED THEIR ***MOTHER***, TRAITOROUS, DISLOYAL WITCH THAT SHE WAS.
BUT I MADE SURE SHE'D PASS IT ON TO THOSE LITTLE WHELPS GROWING INSIDE HER WHENEVER SHE PASSED. AFTER ALL, IT WAS THEIR FAULT SHE DECIDED TO LEAVE THE WITCHES COUNCIL IN THE FIRST PLACE.
BUT ENOUGH OF SUCH ANCIENT HISTORY. NOW IS WHAT MATTERS. AND IT'S REALLY MUCH BETTER FOR THE "ESSENCE," SABRINA DEAR, IF THERE'S LESS CHITCHAT. YOUR MIND SHOULD BE AS CLEAR AND UNCLUTTERED AS POSSIBLE WHEN I DRAIN YOU.
BE A PITY FOR YOUR DEATH TO BE AS MEANINGLESS AS YOUR LIFE.
YES. WOULDN'T WANT TO SPOIL YOUR "MEAL."
IT'S WEIRD HOW YOU THINK I'M JUST GOING TO DISAPPEAR AND MY AUNTS AREN'T GOING TO NOTICE OR CARE.
THEY'VE NO REASON TO SUSPECT ME, SABRINA. AND IF THEY DO, THEY CERTAINLY CAN'T TAKE ME.
I'VE BEEN DOING THIS ALREADY FOR CENTURIES. AND I'LL BE DOING THIS FOR CENTURIES MORE.
I'M NOT SURE YOU WANNA MAKE THAT BET.

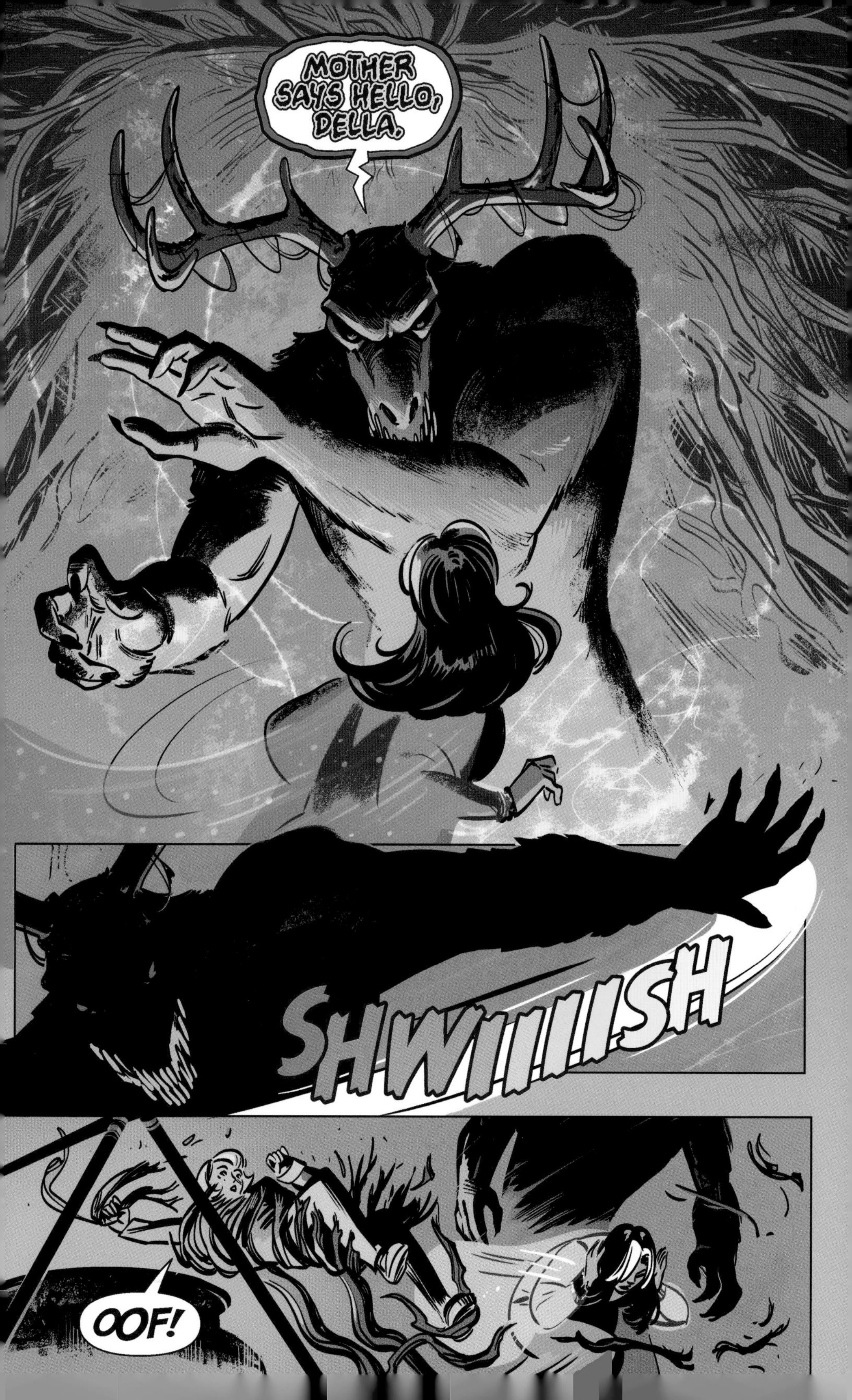
MOTHER SAYS HELLO, DELLA.
SHWIIIIISH
OOF!

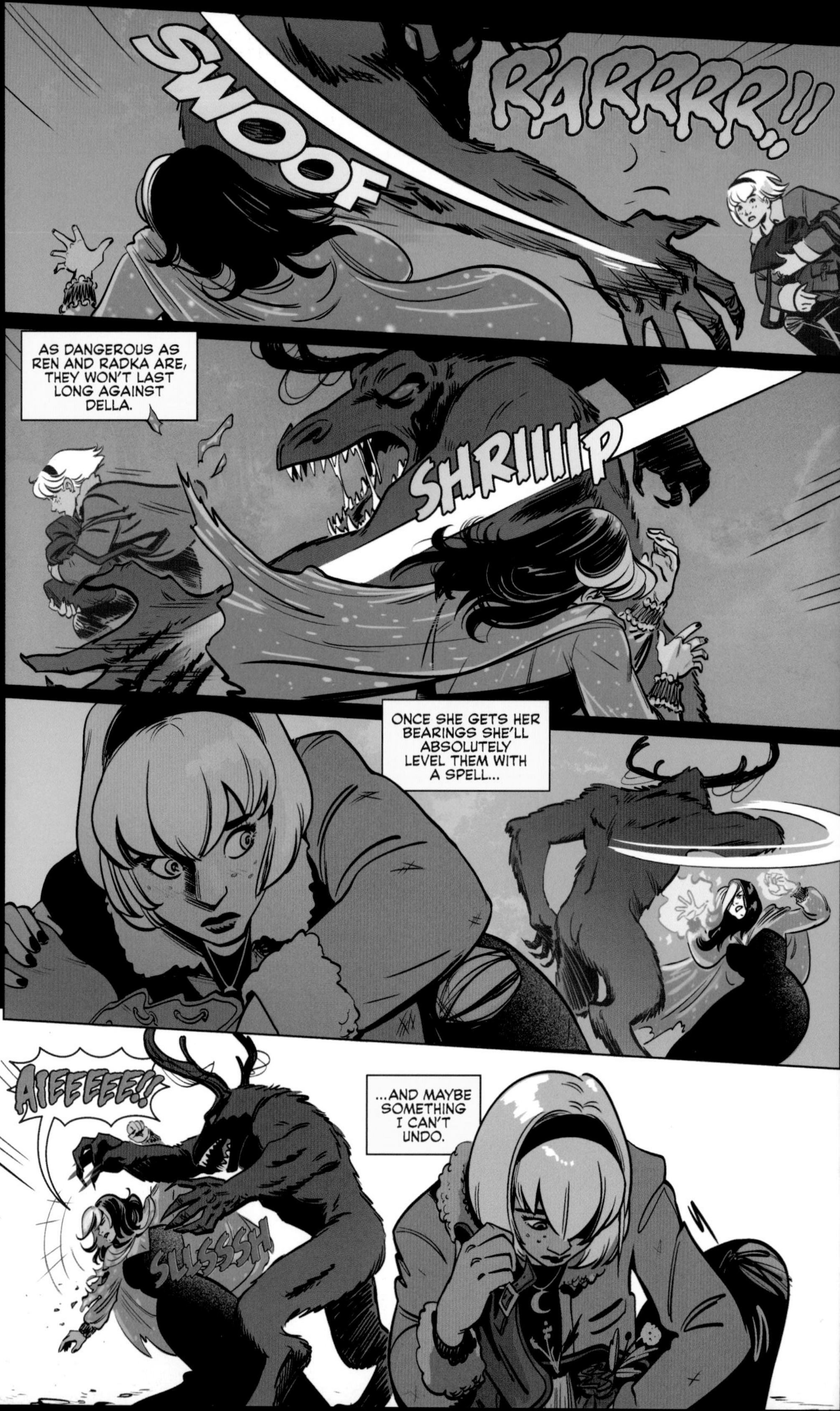

SWOOF
RARRRR!!
AS DANGEROUS AS REN AND RADKA ARE, THEY WON'T LAST LONG AGAINST DELLA.
SHRIIIIP
ONCE SHE GETS HER BEARINGS SHE'LL ABSOLUTELY LEVEL THEM WITH A SPELL...
AIEEEEEE!!
...AND MAYBE SOMETHING I CAN'T UNDO.
SLLSSSH

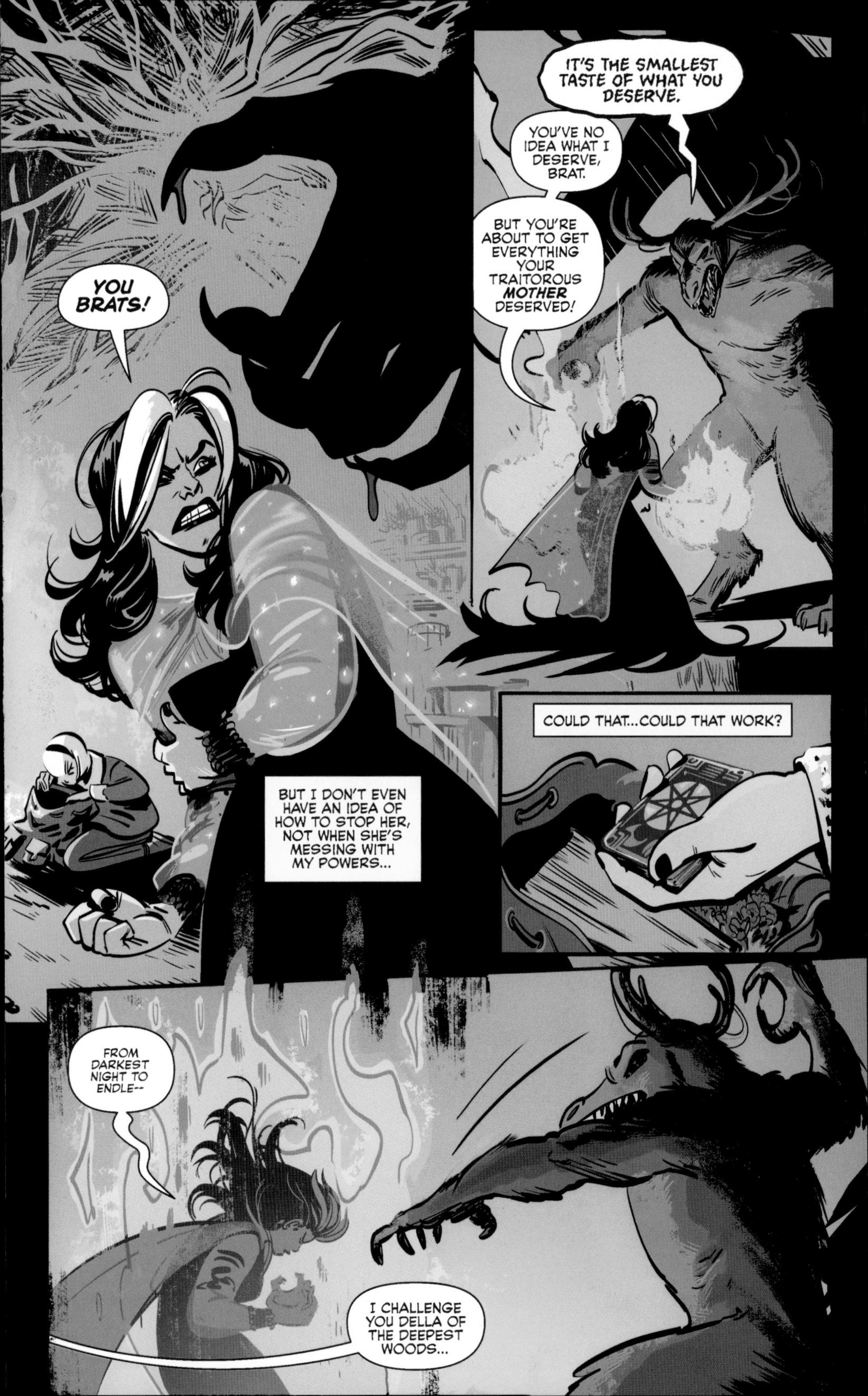
YOU BRATS!
IT'S THE SMALLEST TASTE OF WHAT YOU DESERVE.
YOU'VE NO IDEA WHAT I DESERVE, BRAT.
BUT YOU'RE ABOUT TO GET EVERYTHING YOUR TRAITOROUS MOTHER DESERVED!
BUT I DON'T EVEN HAVE AN IDEA OF HOW TO STOP HER, NOT WHEN SHE'S MESSING WITH MY POWERS...
COULD THAT...COULD THAT WORK?
FROM DARKEST NIGHT TO ENDLE--
I CHALLENGE YOU DELLA OF THE DEEPEST WOODS...

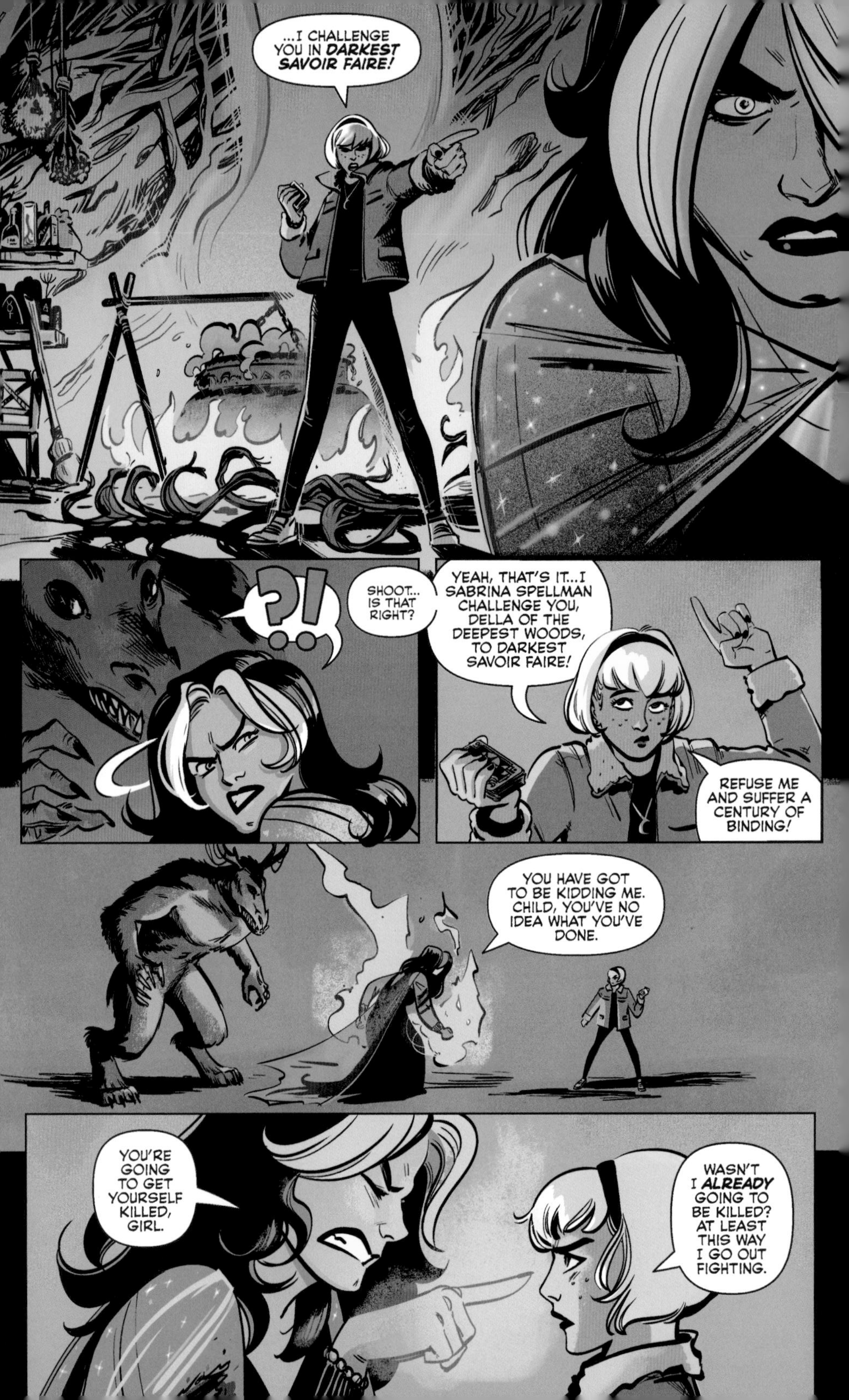

...I CHALLENGE YOU IN *DARKEST SAVOIR FAIRE!*
?!
SHOOT... IS THAT RIGHT?
YEAH, THAT'S IT...I SABRINA SPELLMAN CHALLENGE YOU, DELLA OF THE DEEPEST WOODS, TO DARKEST SAVOIR FAIRE!
REFUSE ME AND SUFFER A CENTURY OF BINDING!
YOU HAVE GOT TO BE KIDDING ME. CHILD, YOU'VE NO IDEA WHAT YOU'VE DONE.
YOU'RE GOING TO GET YOURSELF KILLED, GIRL.
WASN'T I *ALREADY* GOING TO BE KILLED? AT LEAST THIS WAY I GO OUT FIGHTING.

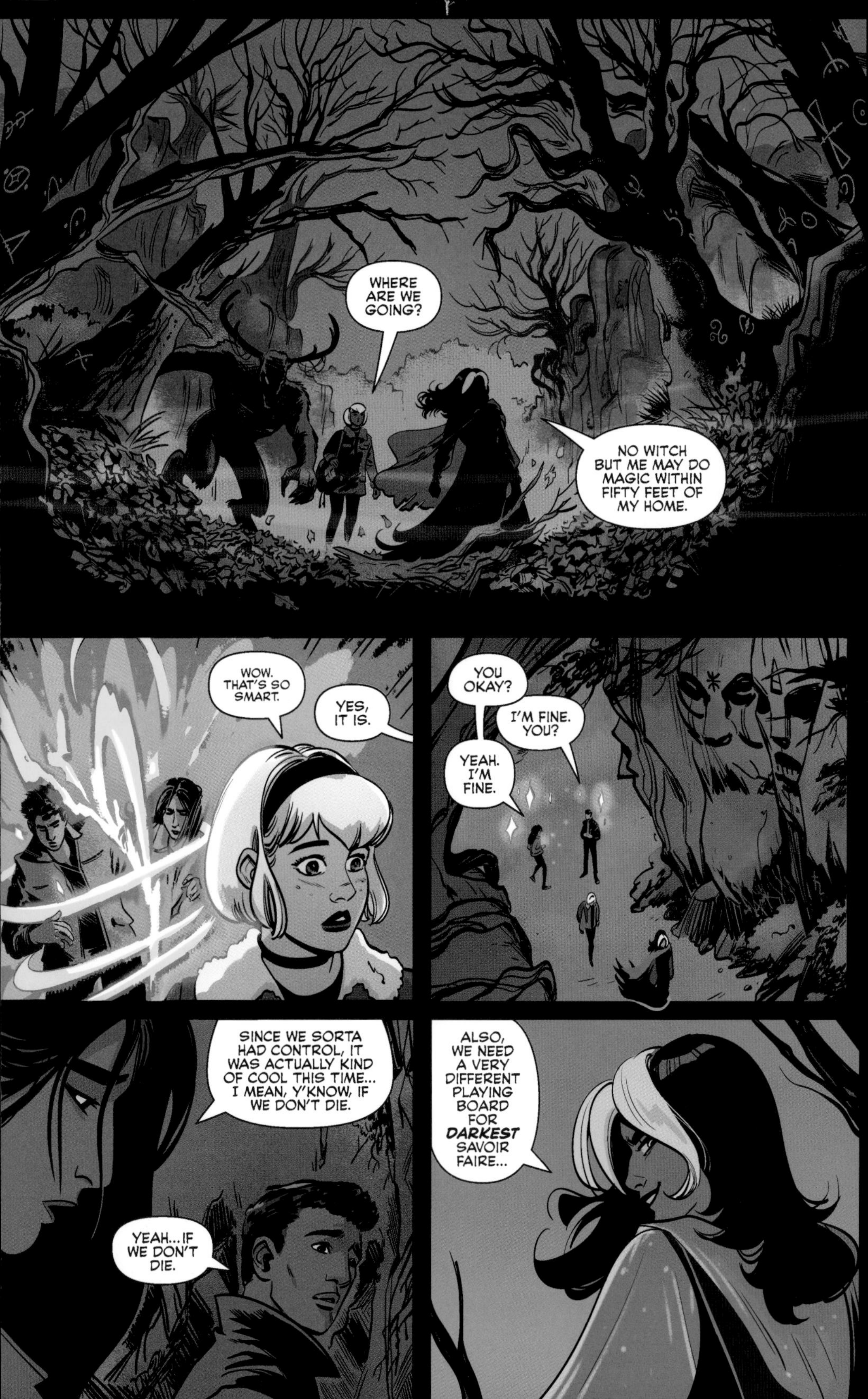

WHERE ARE WE GOING?
NO WITCH BUT ME MAY DO MAGIC WITHIN FIFTY FEET OF MY HOME.
WOW. THAT'S SO SMART.
YES, IT IS.
YOU OKAY?
I'M FINE. YOU?
YEAH. I'M FINE.
SINCE WE SORTA HAD CONTROL, IT WAS ACTUALLY KIND OF COOL THIS TIME... I MEAN, Y'KNOW, IF WE DON'T DIE.
YEAH...IF WE DON'T DIE.
ALSO, WE NEED A VERY DIFFERENT PLAYING BOARD FOR ***DARKEST*** SAVOIR FAIRE...

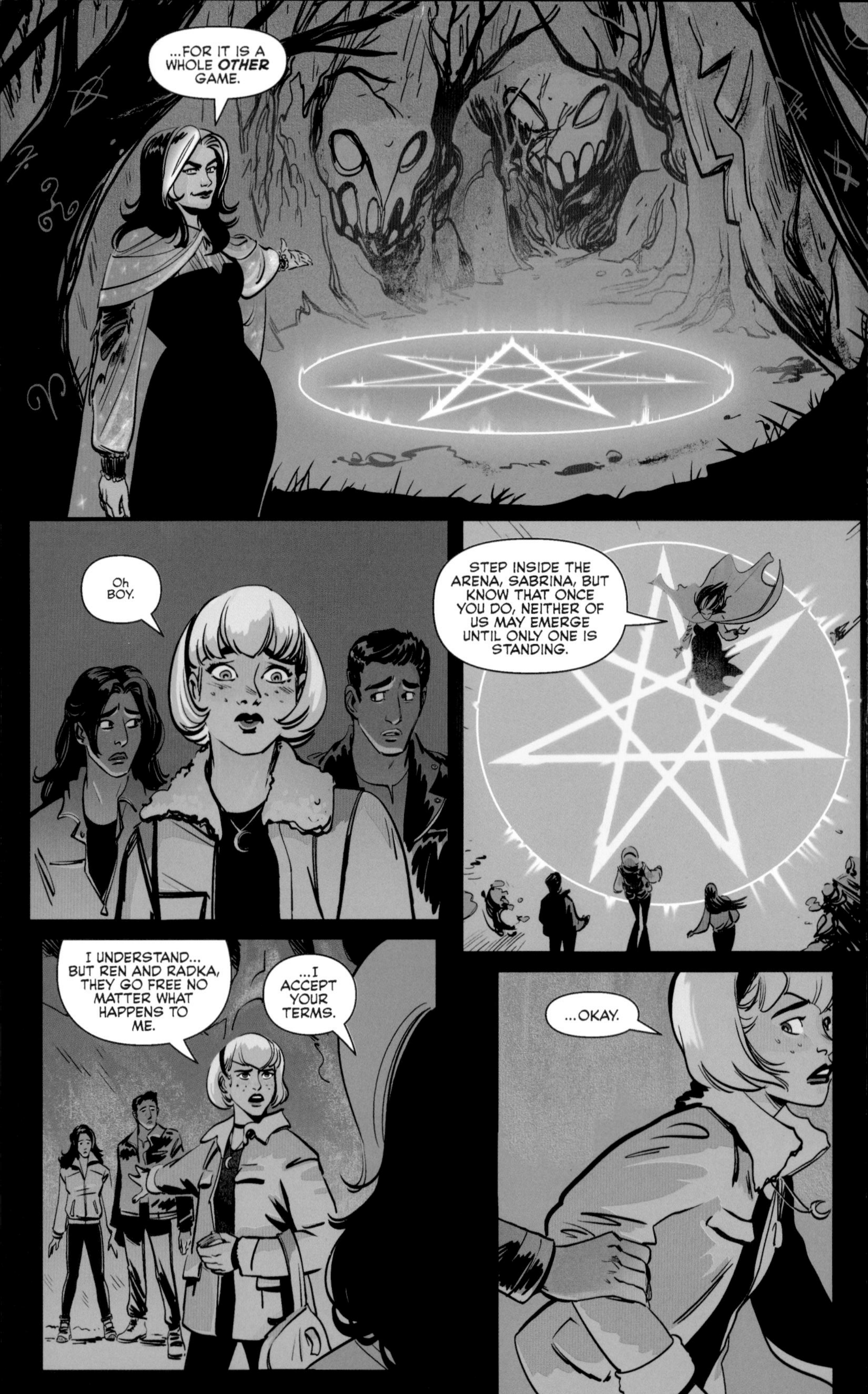
...FOR IT IS A WHOLE *OTHER* GAME.
Oh BOY.
STEP INSIDE THE ARENA, SABRINA, BUT KNOW THAT ONCE YOU DO, NEITHER OF US MAY EMERGE UNTIL ONLY ONE IS STANDING.
I UNDERSTAND... BUT REN AND RADKA, THEY GO FREE NO MATTER WHAT HAPPENS TO ME.
...I ACCEPT YOUR TERMS.
...OKAY.

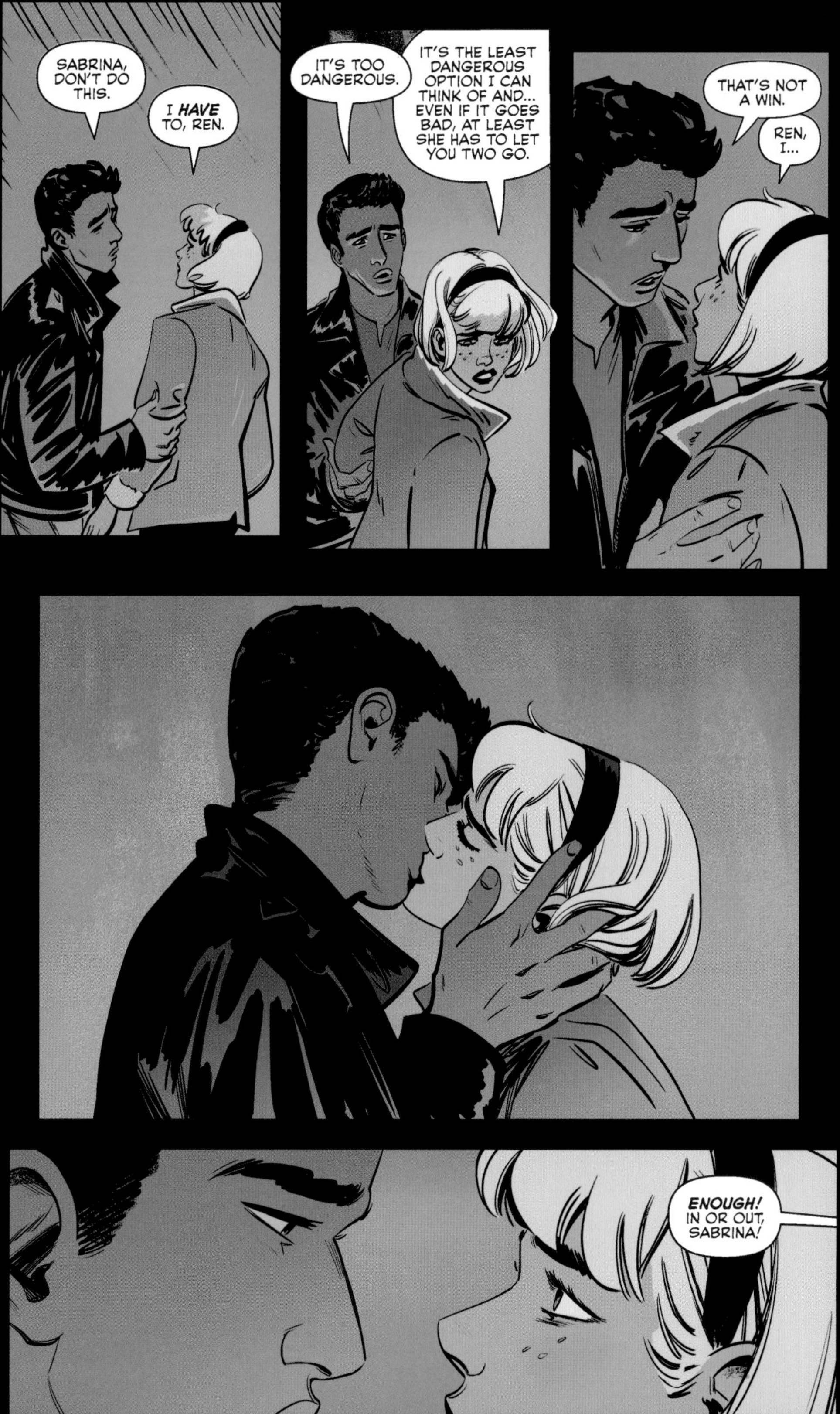
SABRINA, DON'T DO THIS.
I **HAVE** TO, REN.
IT'S TOO DANGEROUS.
IT'S THE LEAST DANGEROUS OPTION I CAN THINK OF AND... EVEN IF IT GOES BAD, AT LEAST SHE HAS TO LET YOU TWO GO.
THAT'S NOT A WIN.
REN, I...
ENOUGH! IN OR OUT, SABRINA!

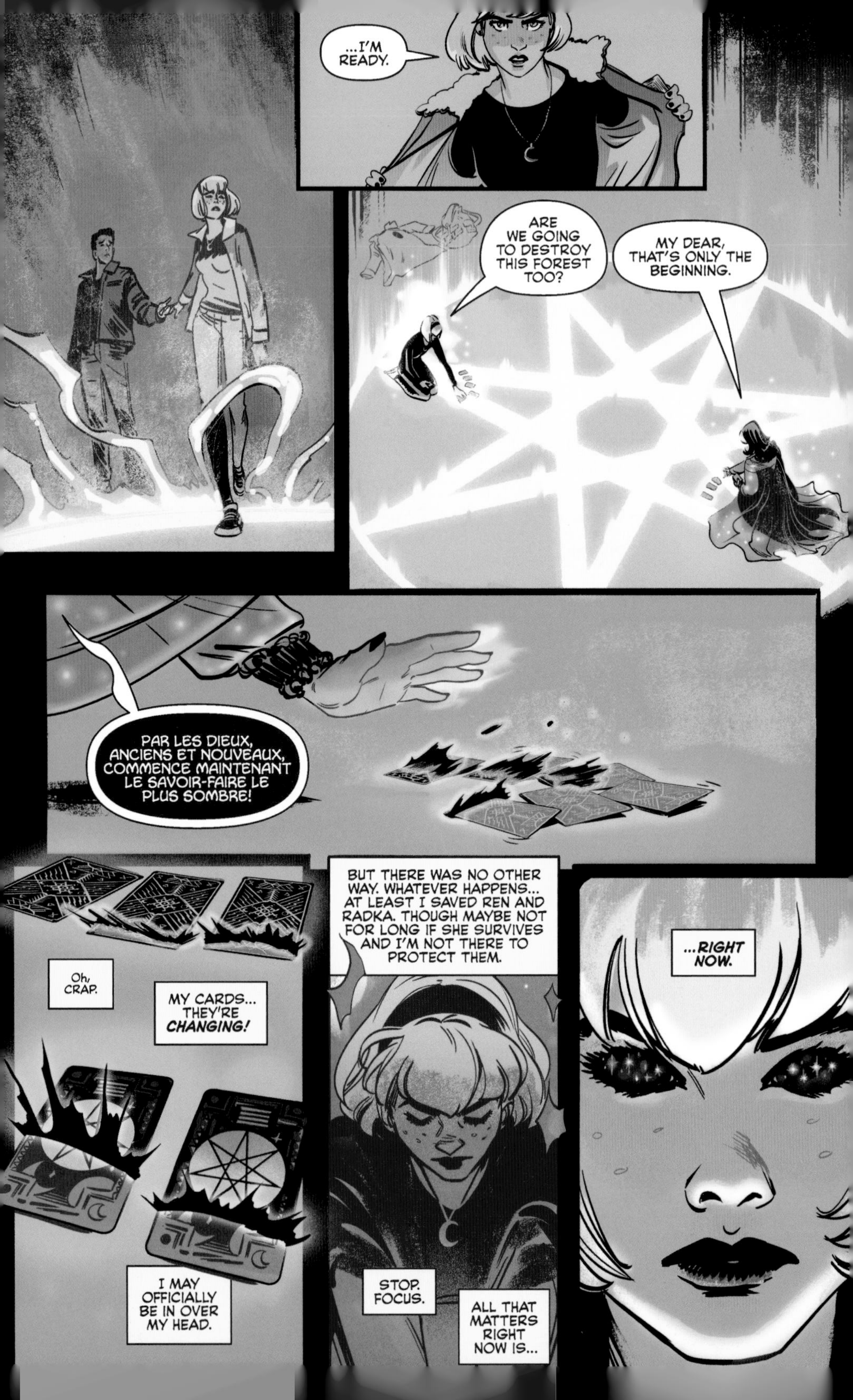
...I'M READY.
ARE WE GOING TO DESTROY THIS FOREST TOO?
MY DEAR, THAT'S ONLY THE BEGINNING.
PAR LES DIEUX, ANCIENS ET NOUVEAUX, COMMENCE MAINTENANT LE SAVOIR-FAIRE LE PLUS SOMBRE!
Oh, CRAP.
MY CARDS... THEY'RE *CHANGING!*
I MAY OFFICIALLY BE IN OVER MY HEAD.
BUT THERE WAS NO OTHER WAY. WHATEVER HAPPENS... AT LEAST I SAVED REN AND RADKA. THOUGH MAYBE NOT FOR LONG IF SHE SURVIVES AND I'M NOT THERE TO PROTECT THEM.
STOP. FOCUS.
ALL THAT MATTERS RIGHT NOW IS...
...RIGHT NOW.

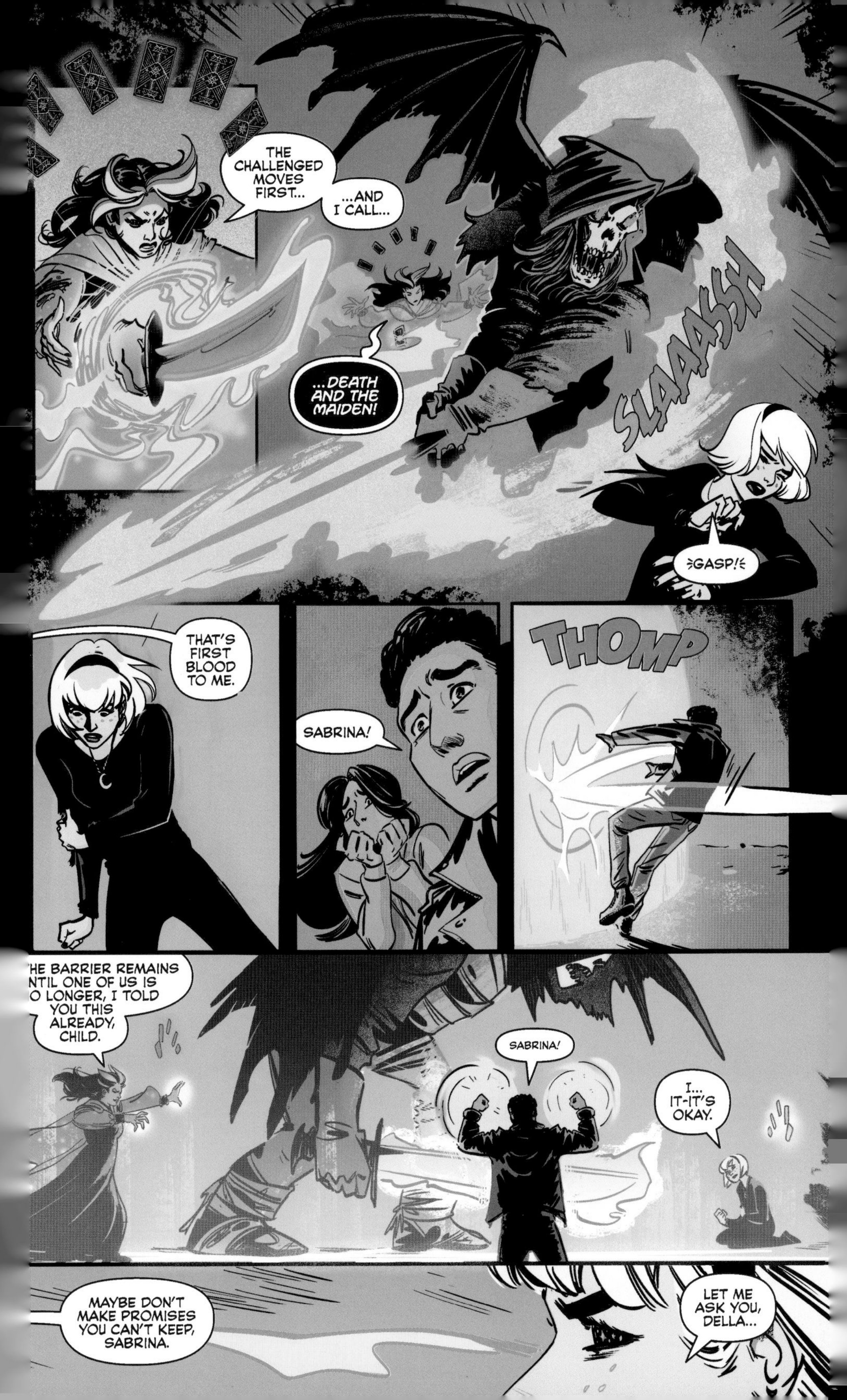
THE CHALLENGED MOVES FIRST...
...AND I CALL...
...DEATH AND THE MAIDEN!
SLAAASSH
GASP!
THAT'S FIRST BLOOD TO ME.
SABRINA!
THOMP
THE BARRIER REMAINS UNTIL ONE OF US IS NO LONGER, I TOLD YOU THIS ALREADY, CHILD.
SABRINA!
I... IT-IT'S OKAY.
MAYBE DON'T MAKE PROMISES YOU CAN'T KEEP, SABRINA.
LET ME ASK YOU, DELLA...

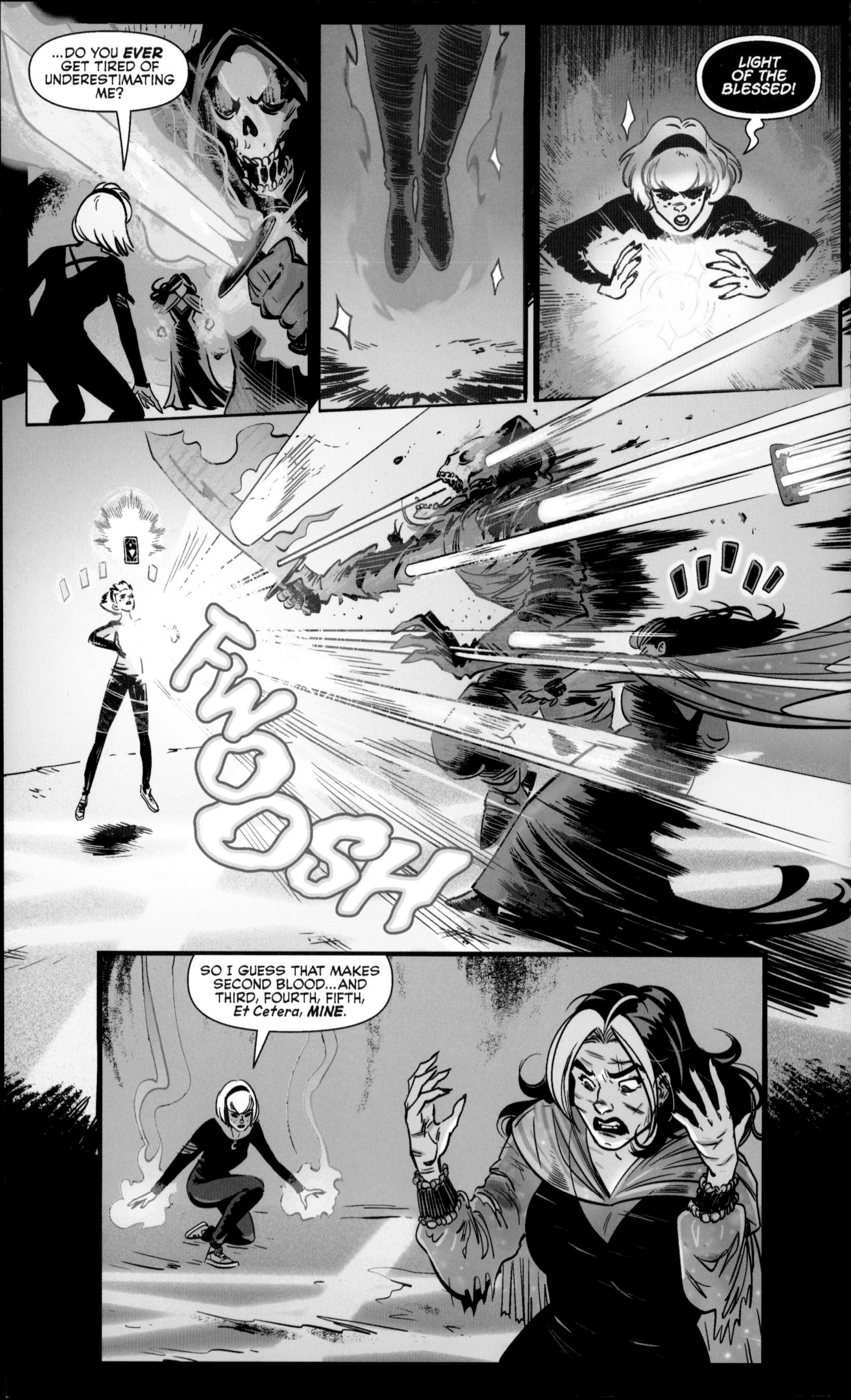
...DO YOU EVER GET TIRED OF UNDERESTIMATING ME?
LIGHT OF THE BLESSED!
FWOOSH
SO I GUESS THAT MAKES SECOND BLOOD...AND THIRD, FOURTH, FIFTH, Et Cetera, MINE.

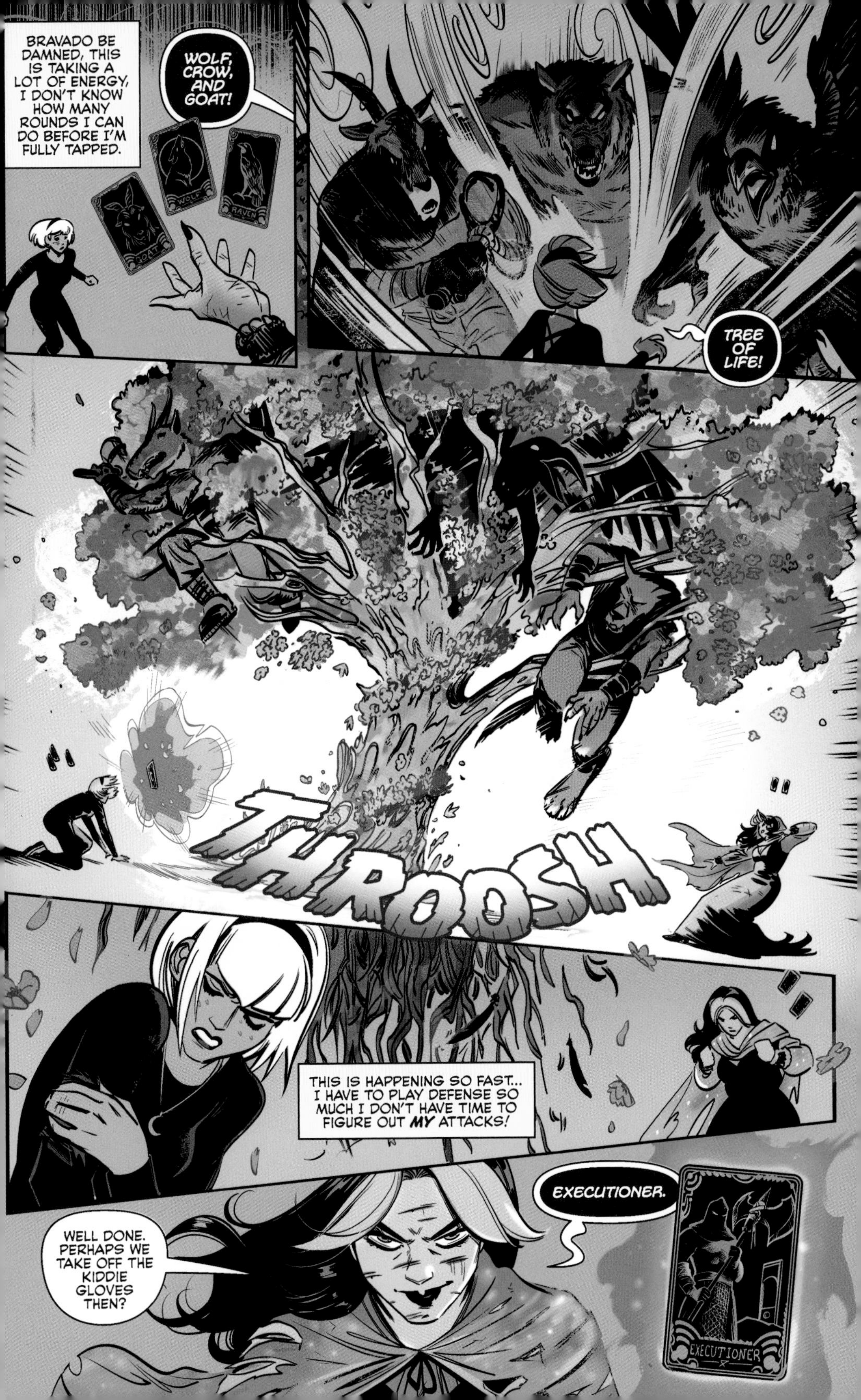
BRAVADO BE DAMNED, THIS IS TAKING A LOT OF ENERGY, I DON'T KNOW HOW MANY ROUNDS I CAN DO BEFORE I'M FULLY TAPPED.
WOLF, CROW, AND GOAT!
GOAT
WOLF
RAVEN
TREE OF LIFE!
THROOSH
THIS IS HAPPENING SO FAST... I HAVE TO PLAY DEFENSE SO MUCH I DON'T HAVE TIME TO FIGURE OUT MY ATTACKS!
WELL DONE. PERHAPS WE TAKE OFF THE KIDDIE GLOVES THEN?
EXECUTIONER.
EXECUTIONER

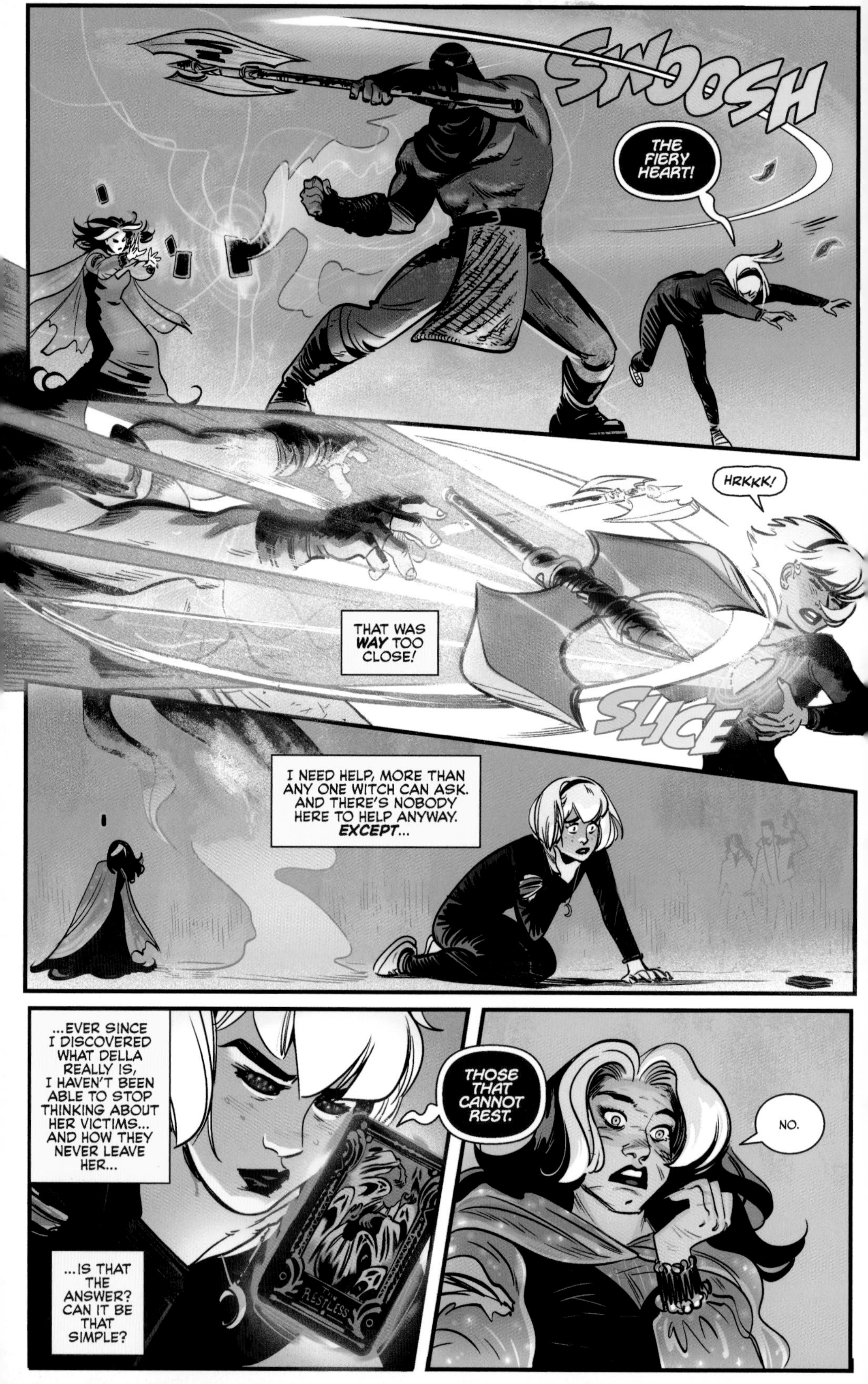
SNOOSH
THE FIERY HEART!
HRKKK!
THAT WAS **WAY** TOO CLOSE!
SLICE
I NEED HELP, MORE THAN ANY ONE WITCH CAN ASK. AND THERE'S NOBODY HERE TO HELP ANYWAY. **EXCEPT**...
...EVER SINCE I DISCOVERED WHAT DELLA REALLY IS, I HAVEN'T BEEN ABLE TO STOP THINKING ABOUT HER VICTIMS... AND HOW THEY NEVER LEAVE HER...
...IS THAT THE ANSWER? CAN IT BE THAT SIMPLE?
THE RESTLESS
THOSE THAT CANNOT REST.
NO.

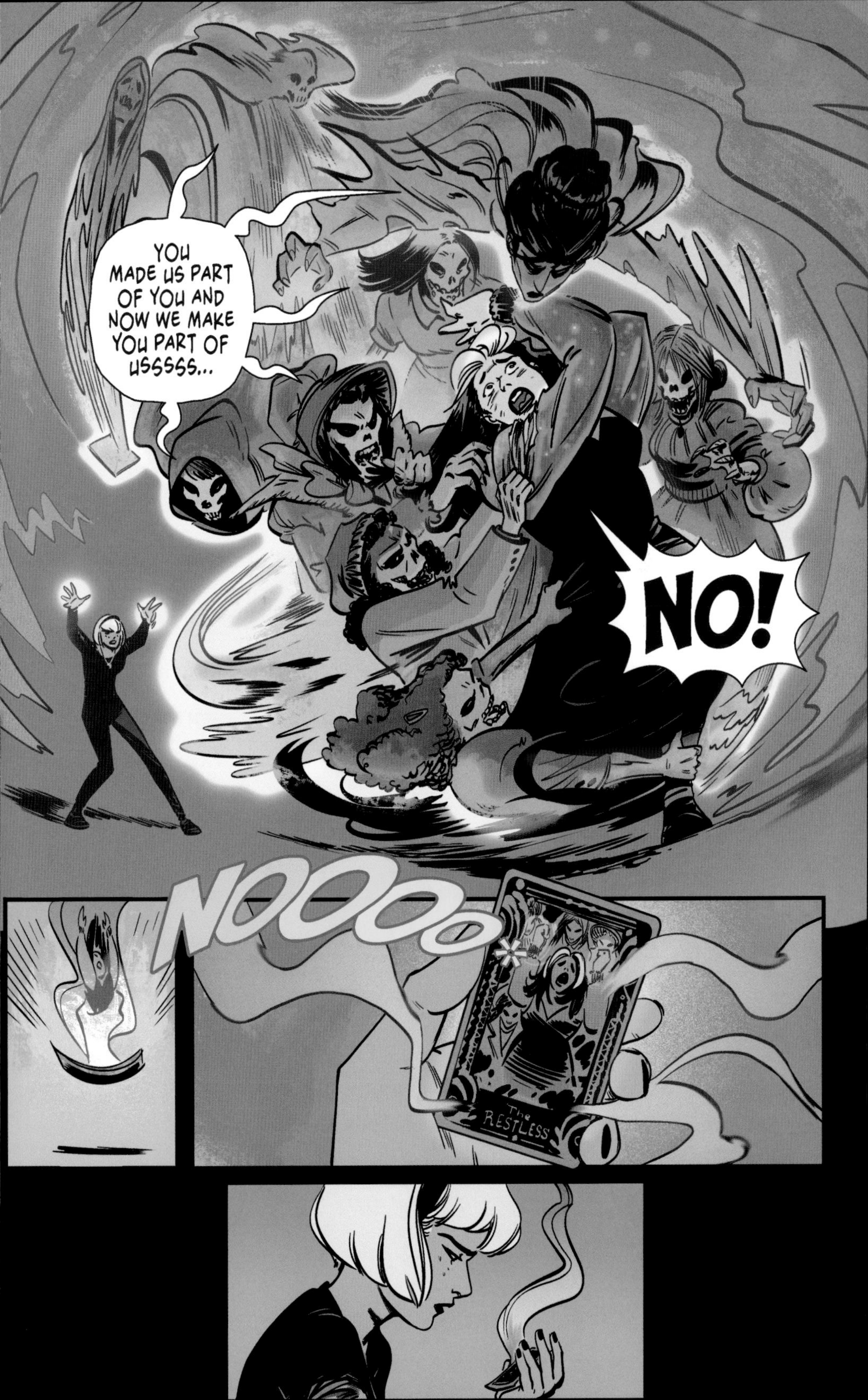
YOU MADE US PART OF YOU AND NOW WE MAKE YOU PART OF USSSSS...
NO!
NOOOO
The RESTLESS

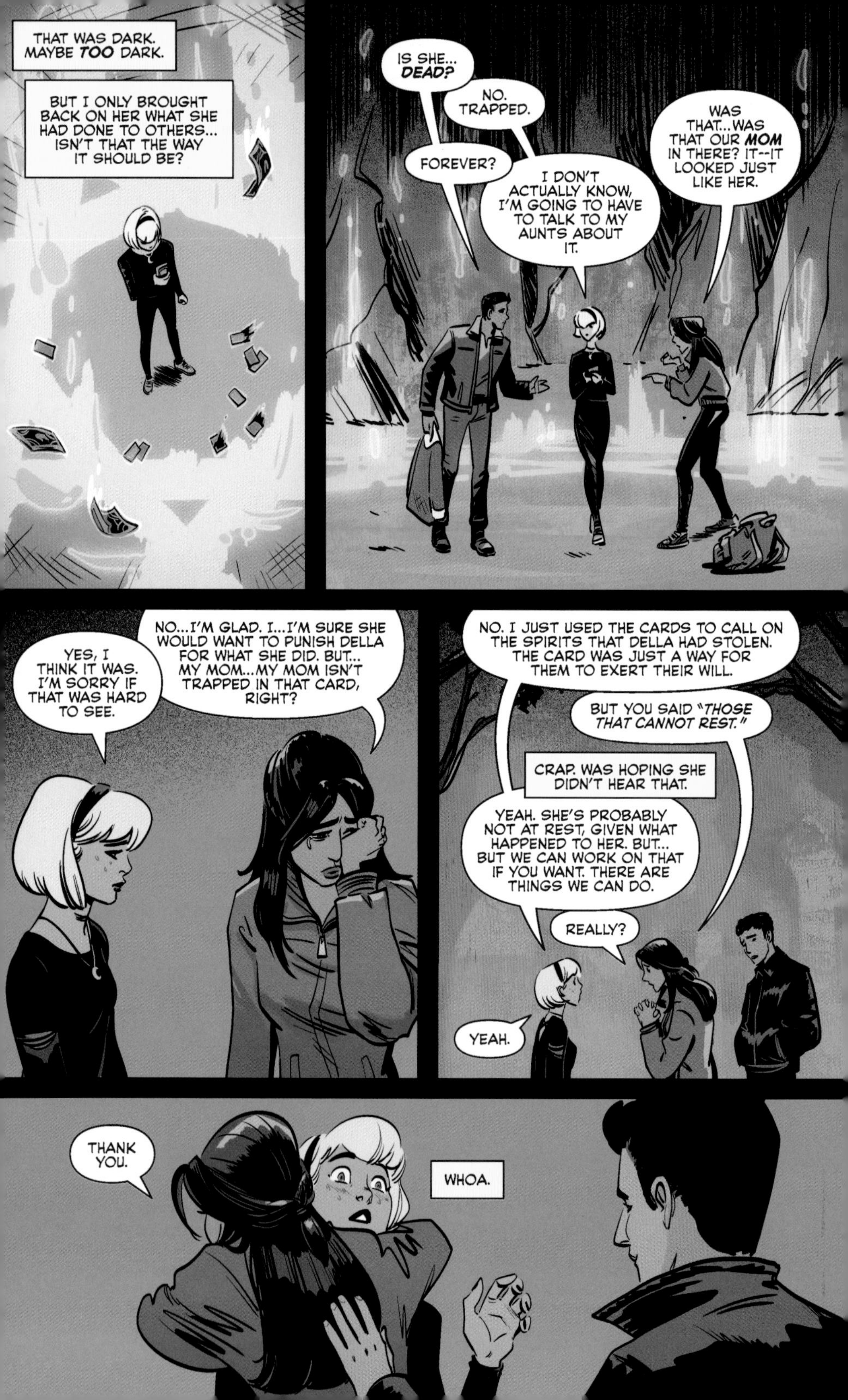
THAT WAS DARK. MAYBE *TOO* DARK.
BUT I ONLY BROUGHT BACK ON HER WHAT SHE HAD DONE TO OTHERS... ISN'T THAT THE WAY IT SHOULD BE?
IS SHE... *DEAD?*
NO. TRAPPED.
FOREVER?
I DON'T ACTUALLY KNOW, I'M GOING TO HAVE TO TALK TO MY AUNTS ABOUT IT.
WAS THAT...WAS THAT OUR *MOM* IN THERE? IT--IT LOOKED JUST LIKE HER.
YES, I THINK IT WAS. I'M SORRY IF THAT WAS HARD TO SEE.
NO...I'M GLAD. I...I'M SURE SHE WOULD WANT TO PUNISH DELLA FOR WHAT SHE DID. BUT... MY MOM...MY MOM ISN'T TRAPPED IN THAT CARD, RIGHT?
NO. I JUST USED THE CARDS TO CALL ON THE SPIRITS THAT DELLA HAD STOLEN. THE CARD WAS JUST A WAY FOR THEM TO EXERT THEIR WILL.
BUT YOU SAID *"THOSE THAT CANNOT REST."*
CRAP. WAS HOPING SHE DIDN'T HEAR THAT.
YEAH. SHE'S PROBABLY NOT AT REST, GIVEN WHAT HAPPENED TO HER. BUT... BUT WE CAN WORK ON THAT IF YOU WANT. THERE ARE THINGS WE CAN DO.
REALLY?
YEAH.
THANK YOU.
WHOA.

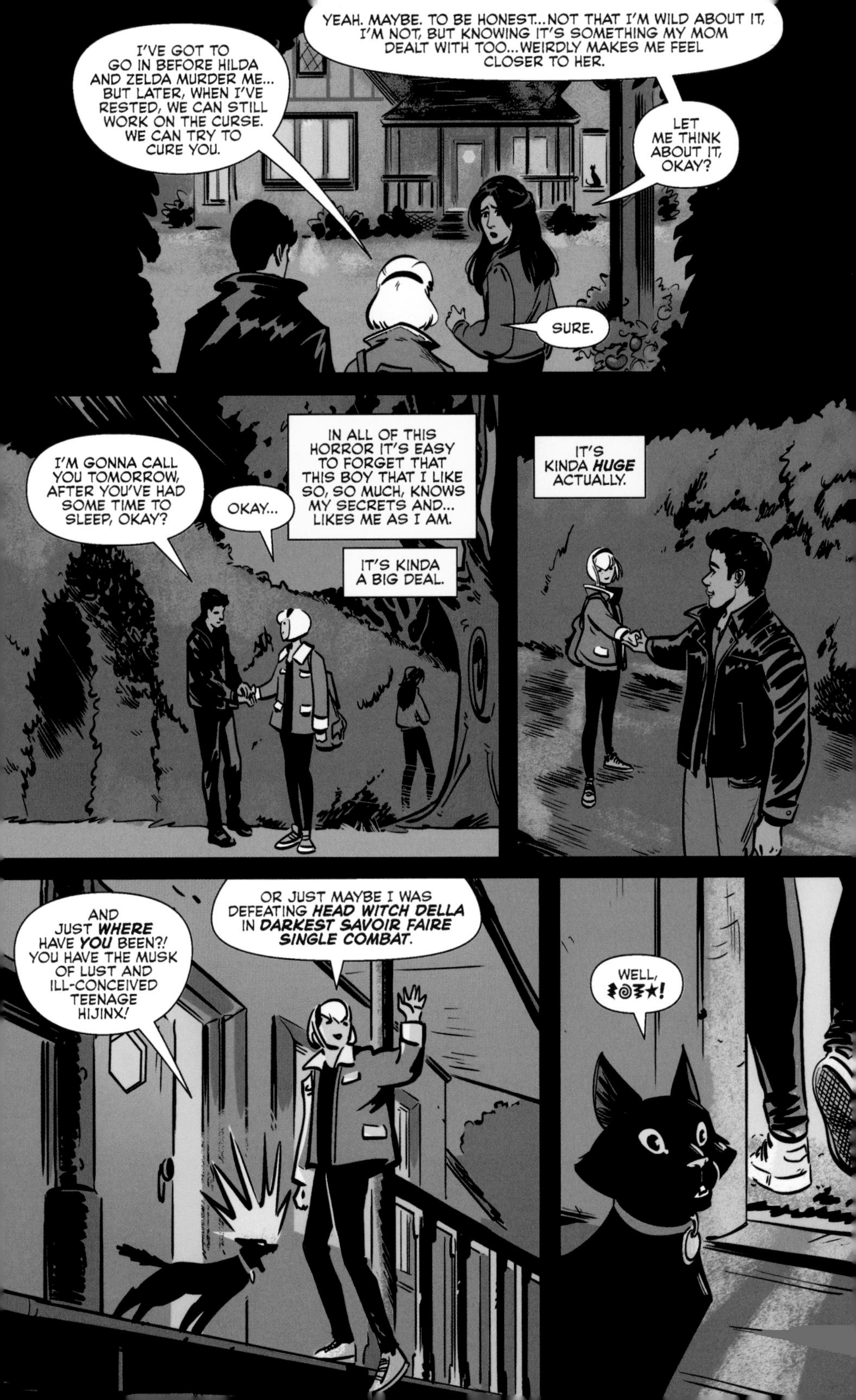
YEAH. MAYBE. TO BE HONEST...NOT THAT I'M WILD ABOUT IT, I'M NOT, BUT KNOWING IT'S SOMETHING MY MOM DEALT WITH TOO...WEIRDLY MAKES ME FEEL CLOSER TO HER.
I'VE GOT TO GO IN BEFORE HILDA AND ZELDA MURDER ME... BUT LATER, WHEN I'VE RESTED, WE CAN STILL WORK ON THE CURSE. WE CAN TRY TO CURE YOU.
LET ME THINK ABOUT IT, OKAY?
SURE.
I'M GONNA CALL YOU TOMORROW, AFTER YOU'VE HAD SOME TIME TO SLEEP, OKAY?
OKAY...
IN ALL OF THIS HORROR IT'S EASY TO FORGET THAT THIS BOY THAT I LIKE SO, SO MUCH, KNOWS MY SECRETS AND... LIKES ME AS I AM.
IT'S KINDA A BIG DEAL.
IT'S KINDA ***HUGE*** ACTUALLY.
AND JUST ***WHERE*** HAVE ***YOU*** BEEN?! YOU HAVE THE MUSK OF LUST AND ILL-CONCEIVED TEENAGE HIJINX!
OR JUST MAYBE I WAS DEFEATING ***HEAD WITCH DELLA*** IN ***DARKEST SAVOIR FAIRE SINGLE COMBAT***.
WELL,

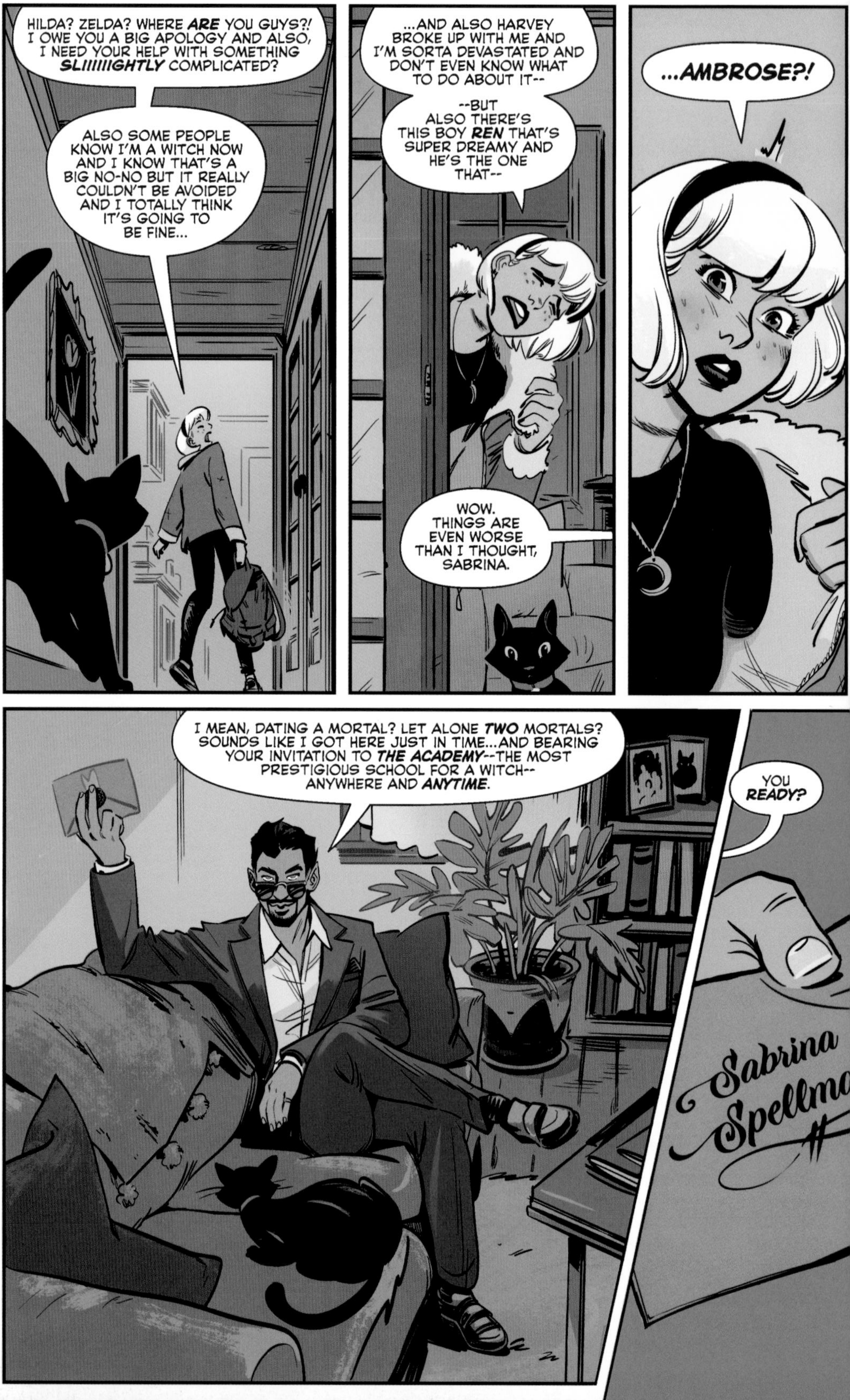

HILDA? ZELDA? WHERE ARE YOU GUYS?! I OWE YOU A BIG APOLOGY AND ALSO, I NEED YOUR HELP WITH SOMETHING SLIIIIIIGHTLY COMPLICATED?
ALSO SOME PEOPLE KNOW I'M A WITCH NOW AND I KNOW THAT'S A BIG NO-NO BUT IT REALLY COULDN'T BE AVOIDED AND I TOTALLY THINK IT'S GOING TO BE FINE...
...AND ALSO HARVEY BROKE UP WITH ME AND I'M SORTA DEVASTATED AND DON'T EVEN KNOW WHAT TO DO ABOUT IT--
--BUT ALSO THERE'S THIS BOY REN THAT'S SUPER DREAMY AND HE'S THE ONE THAT--
WOW. THINGS ARE EVEN WORSE THAN I THOUGHT, SABRINA.
...AMBROSE?!
I MEAN, DATING A MORTAL? LET ALONE TWO MORTALS? SOUNDS LIKE I GOT HERE JUST IN TIME...AND BEARING YOUR INVITATION TO THE ACADEMY--THE MOST PRESTIGIOUS SCHOOL FOR A WITCH--ANYWHERE AND ANYTIME.
YOU READY?
Sabrina Spellm

SPECIAL
FEATURES

SABRINA
the teenage witch ™

**VARIANT
COVER
GALLERY**

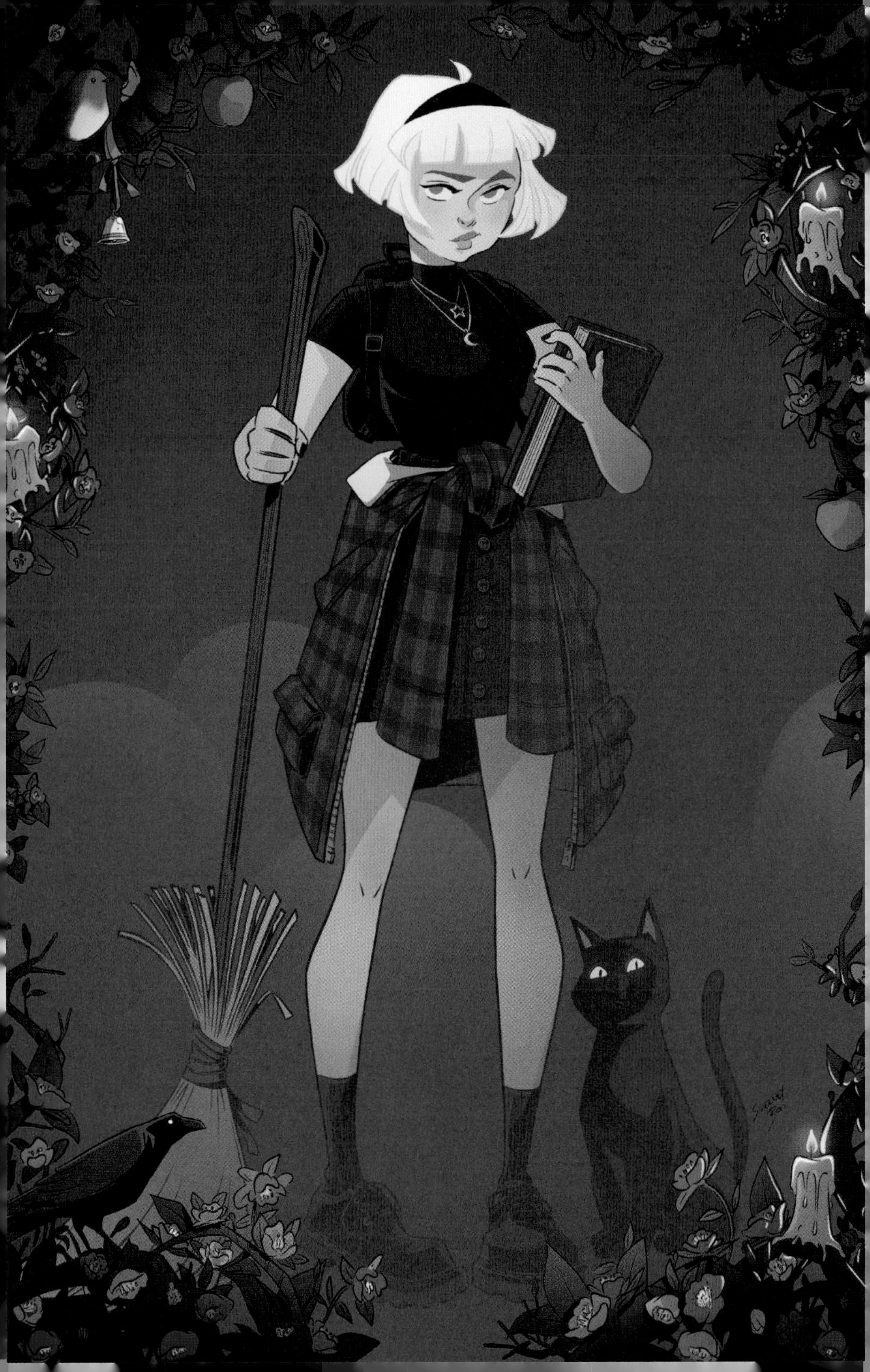

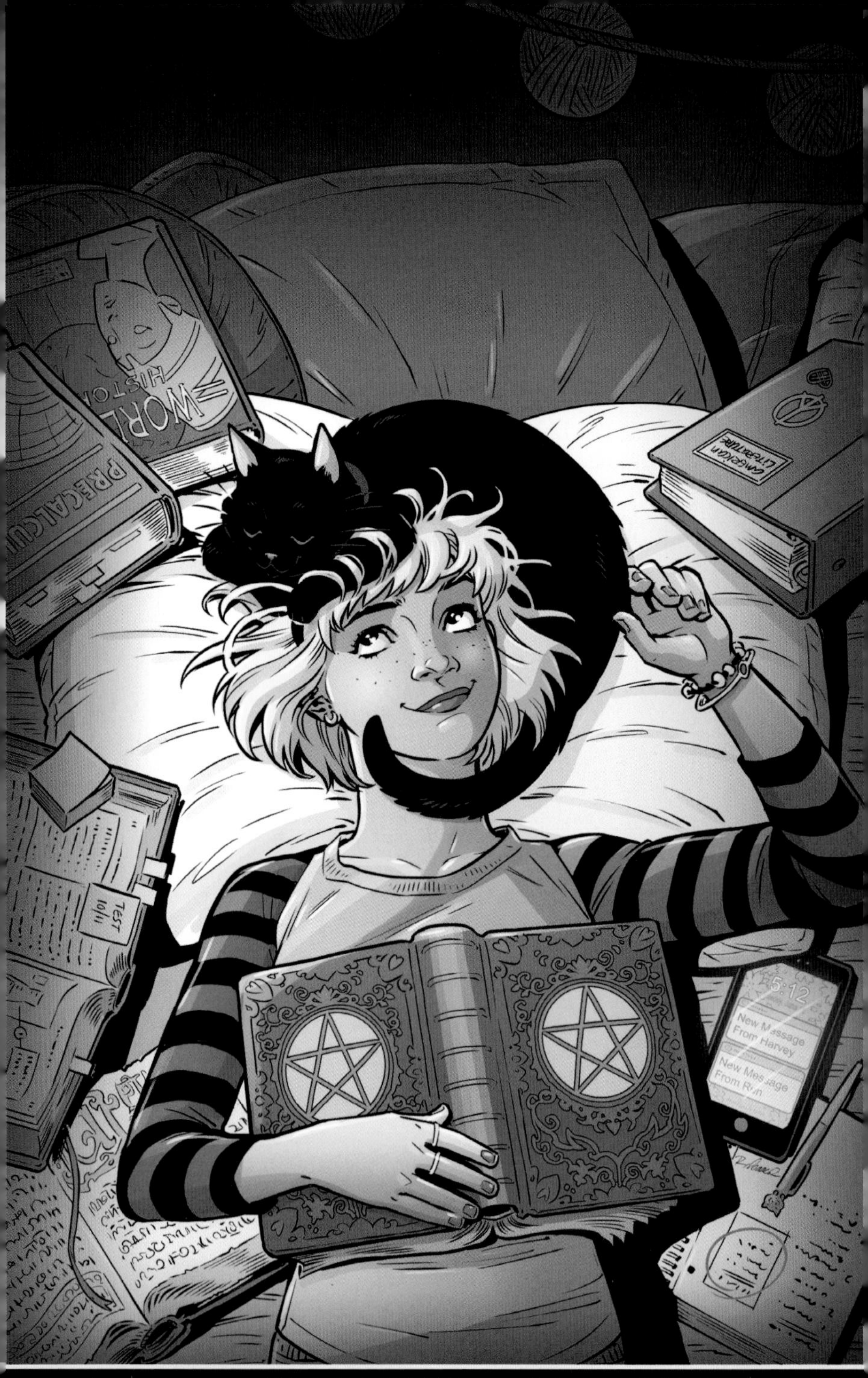
WORL
HISTO
PRECALCU
American Literature
TEST 10/11
5:12
New Message From Harvey
New Message

COVER ART: REBEKAH ISAACS WITH LEE LOUGHRIDGE

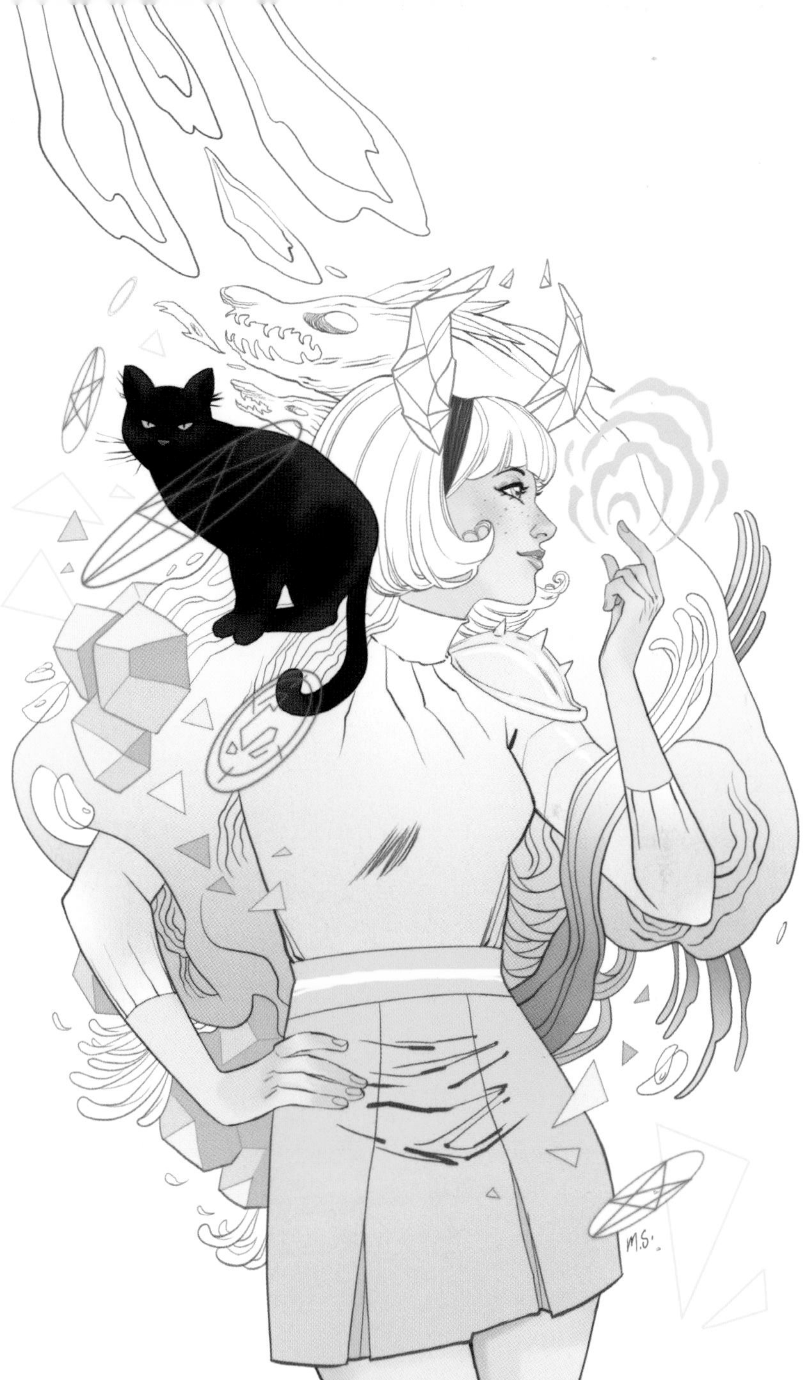
M.S.

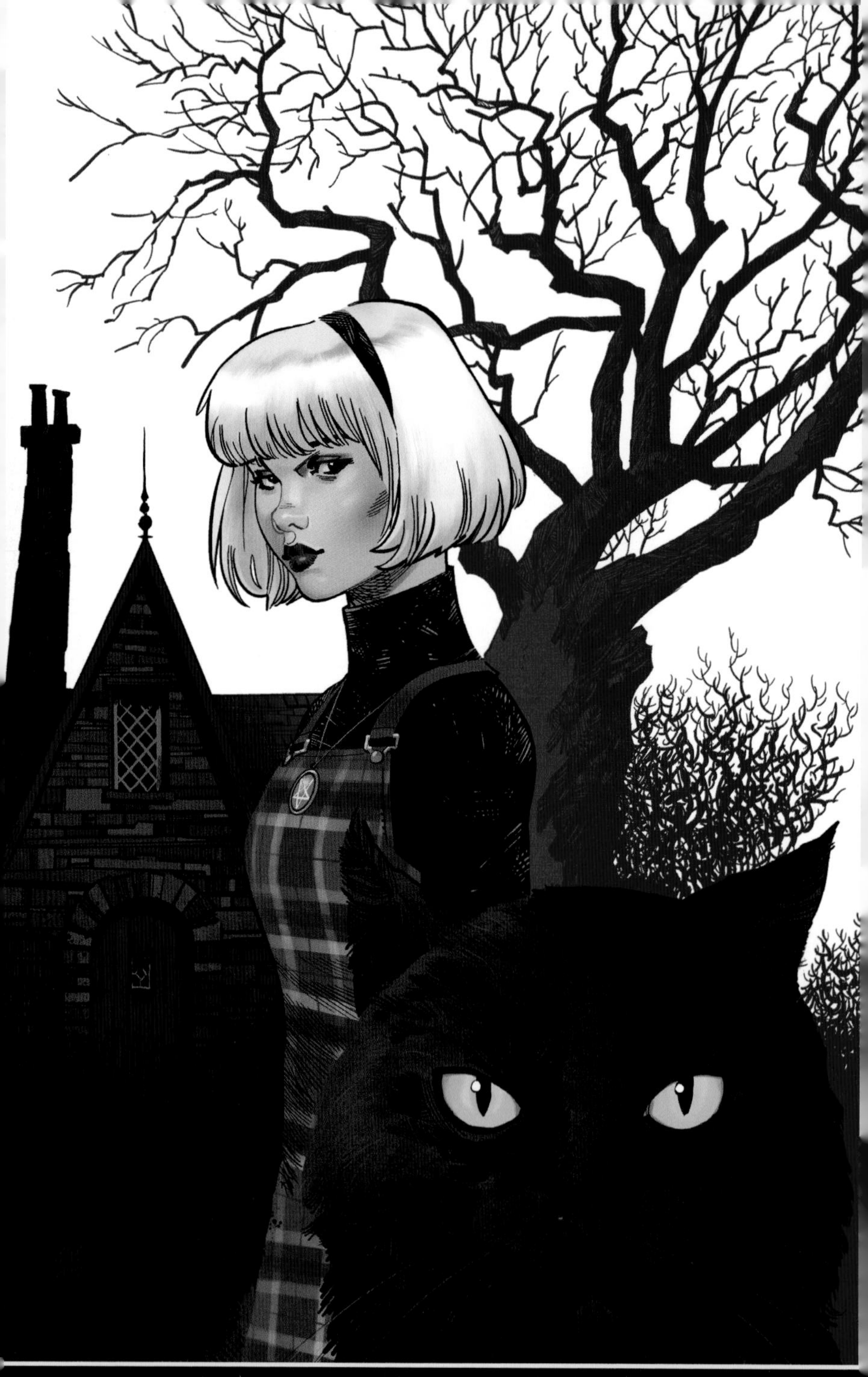

COVER ART CAMERON STEWART

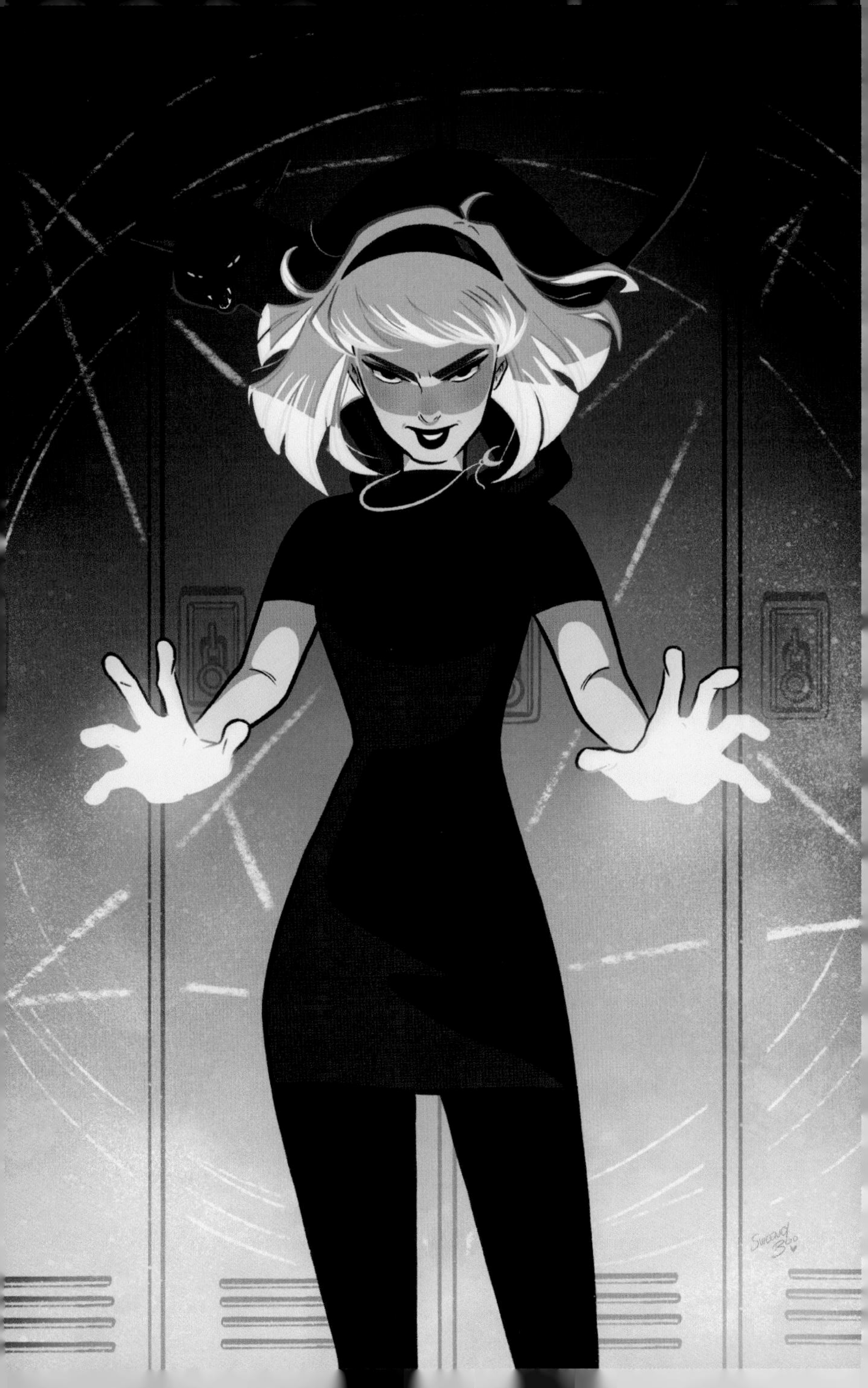

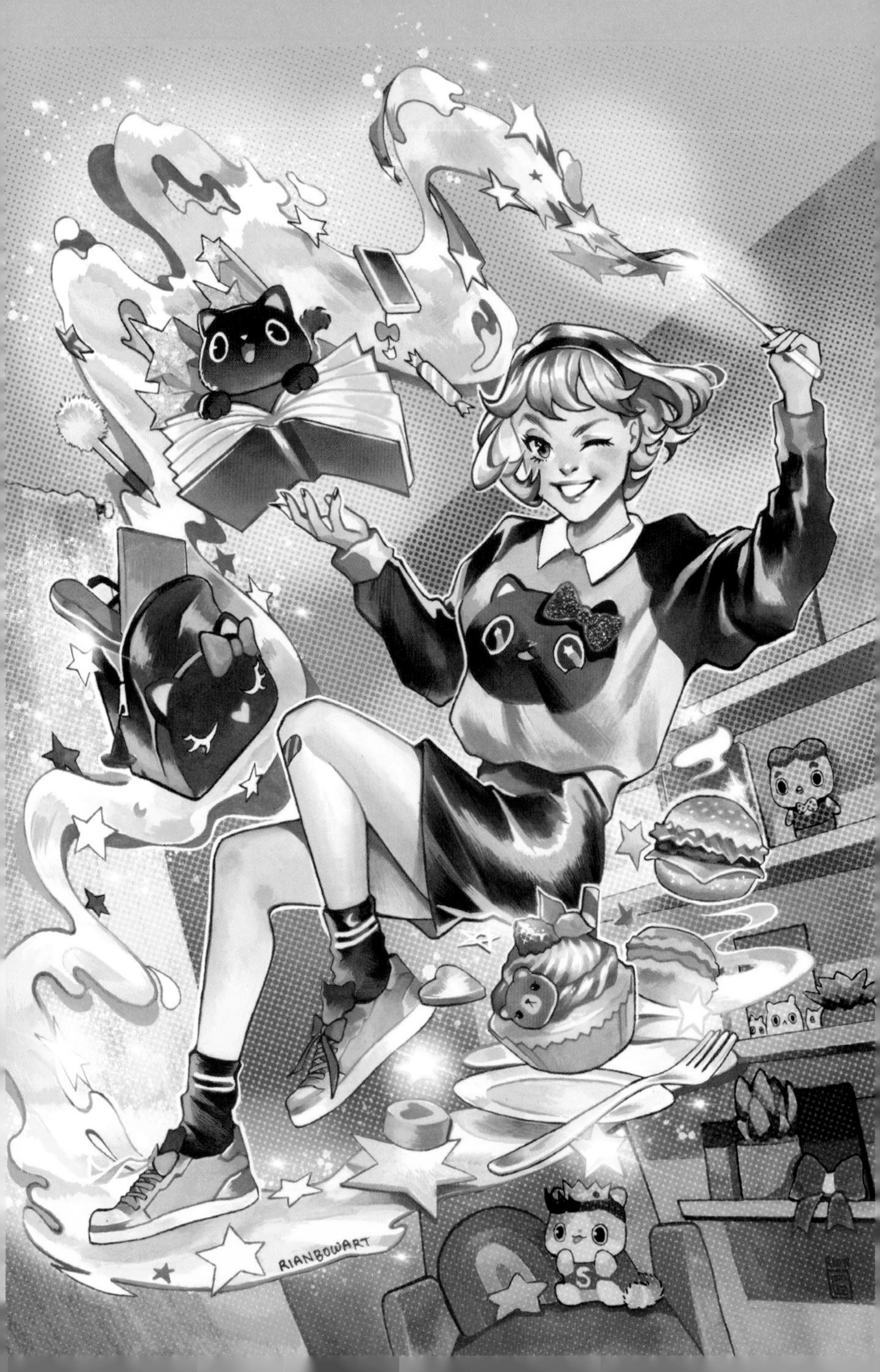
RIANBOWART

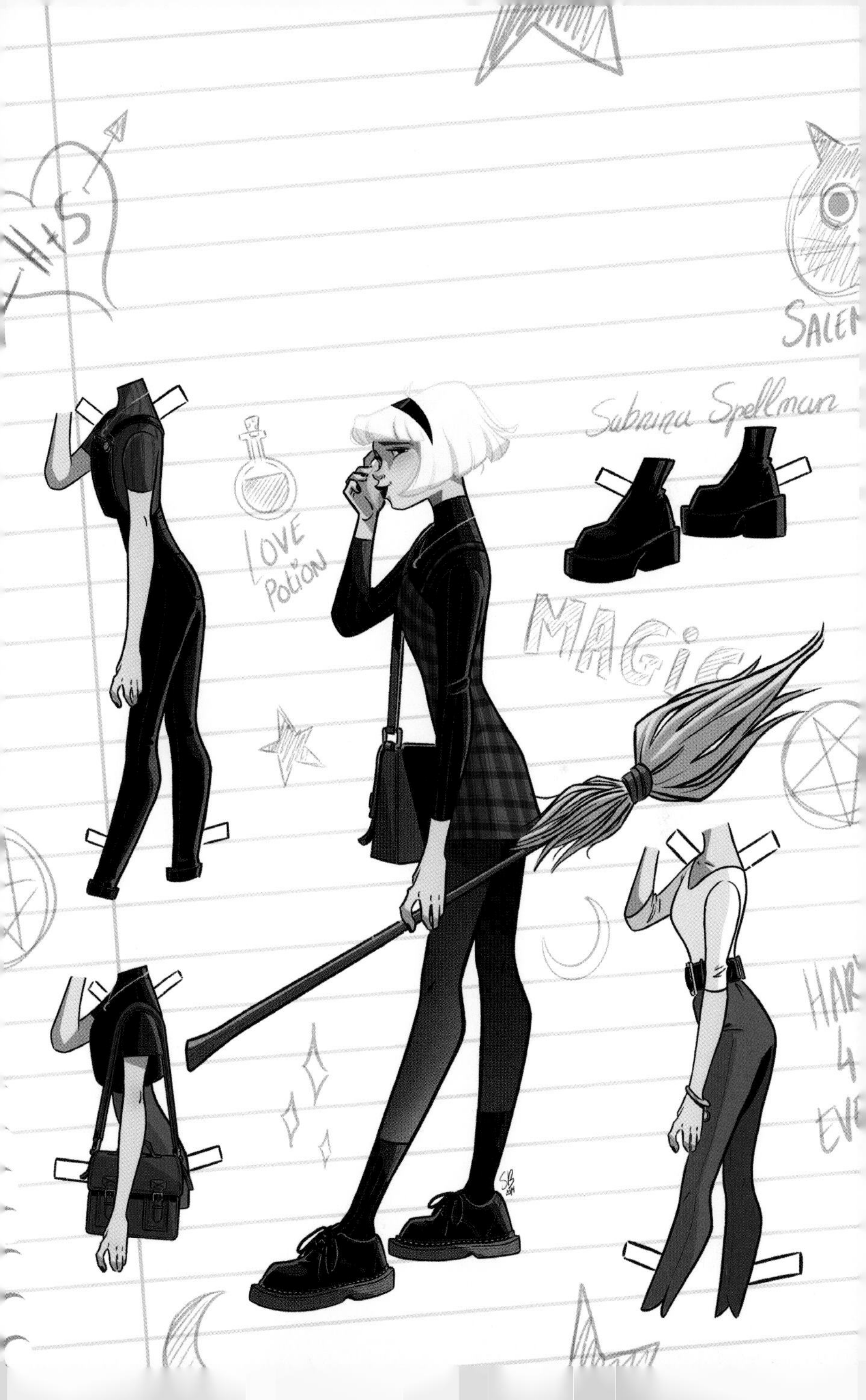
H+S
SALEM
Sabrina Spellman
LOVE Potion
MAGIC
SB 2019

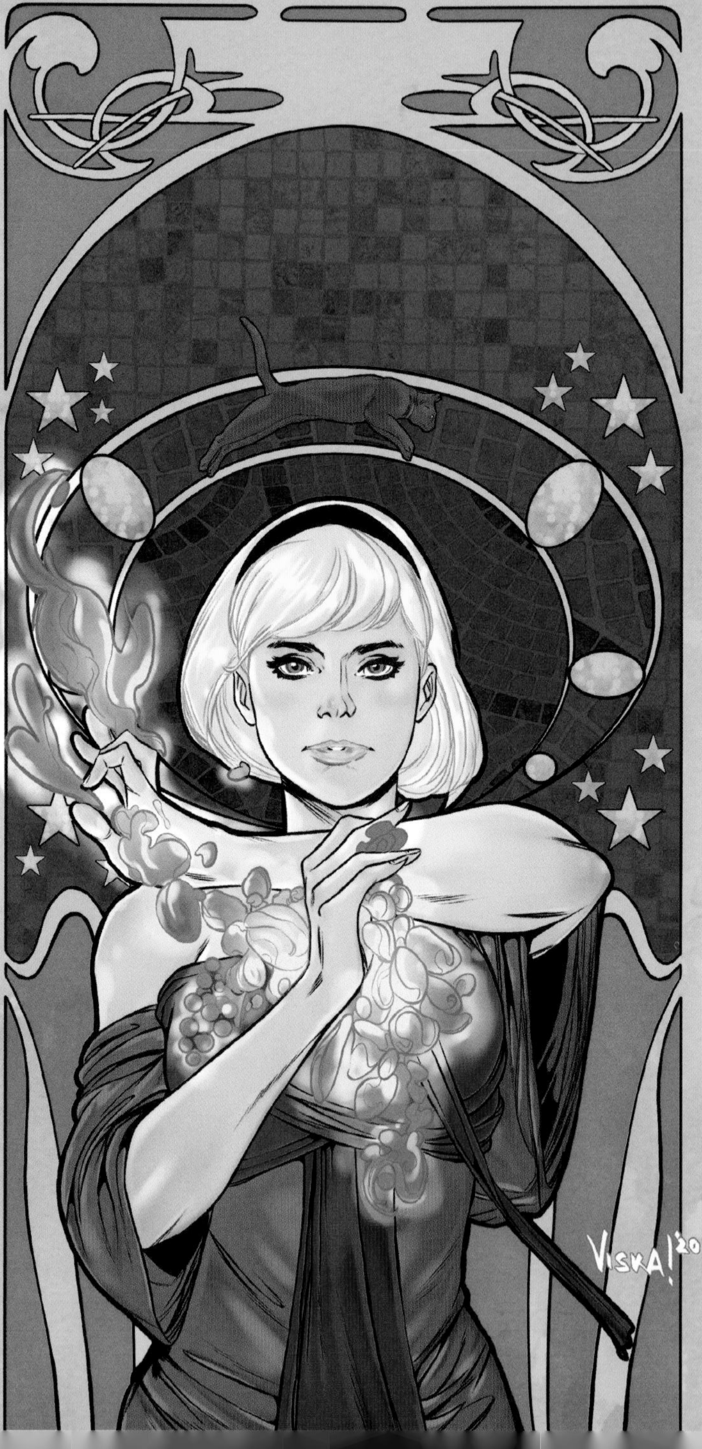
VISKA! '20

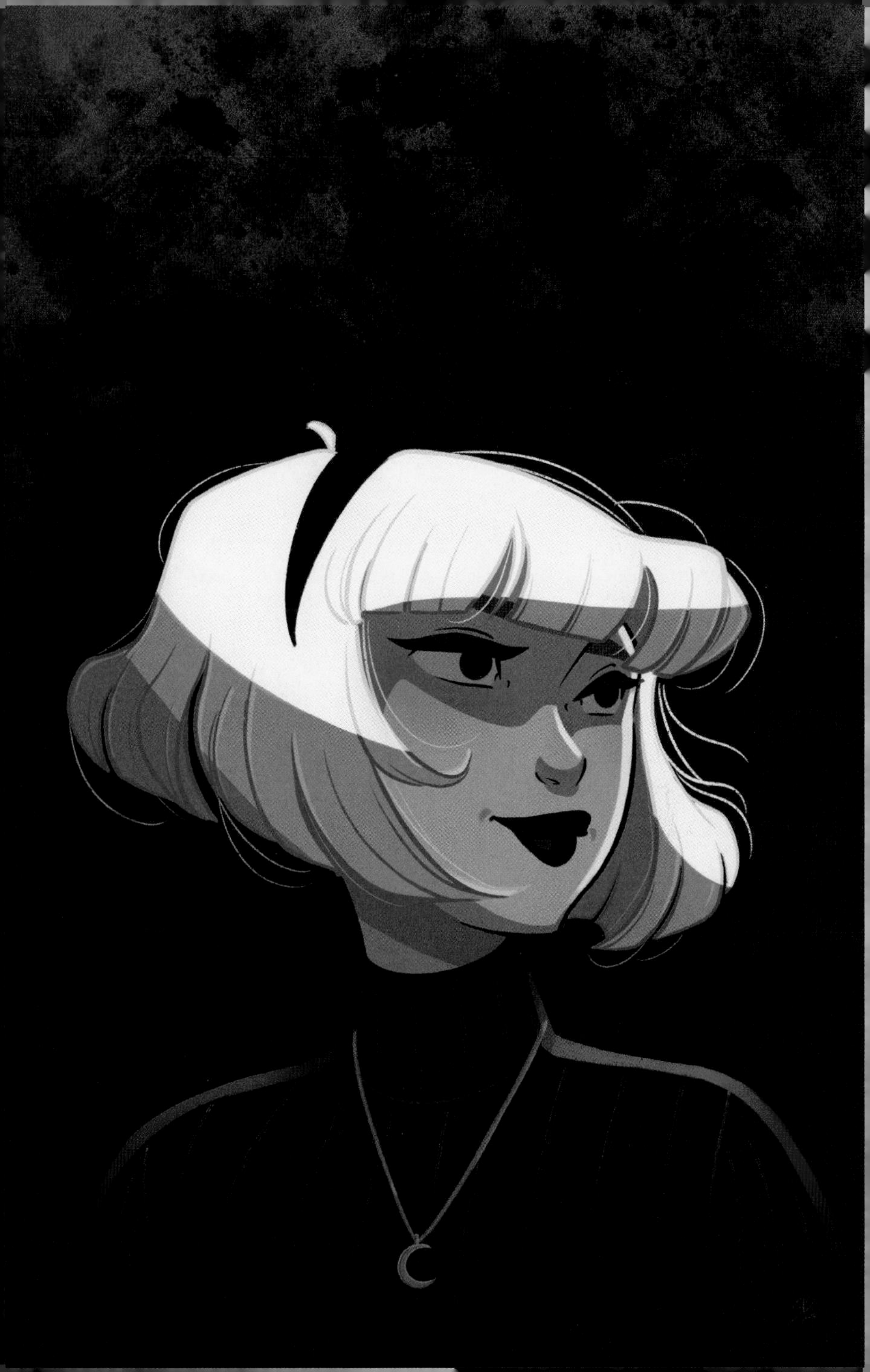

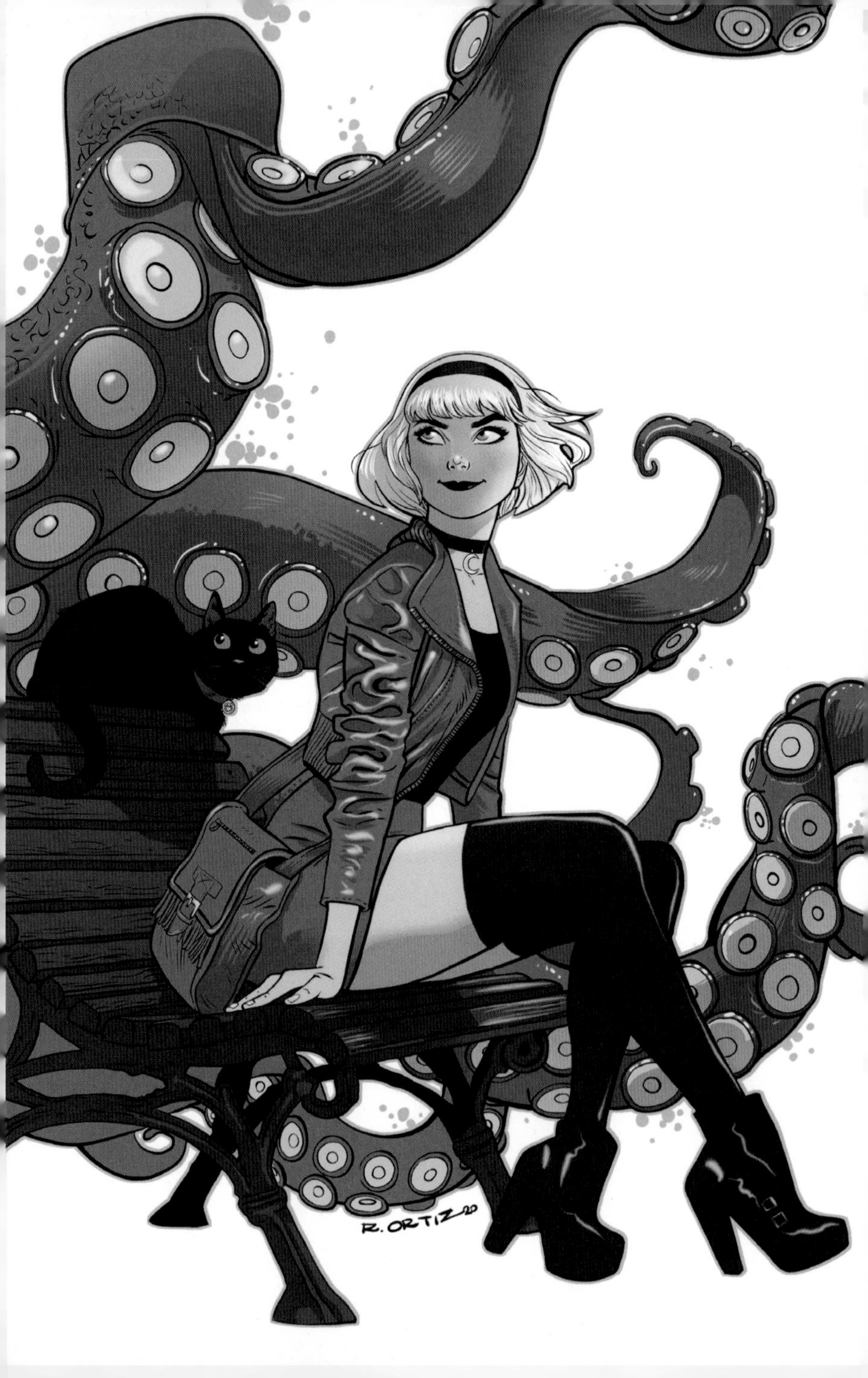
R. ORTIZ 20

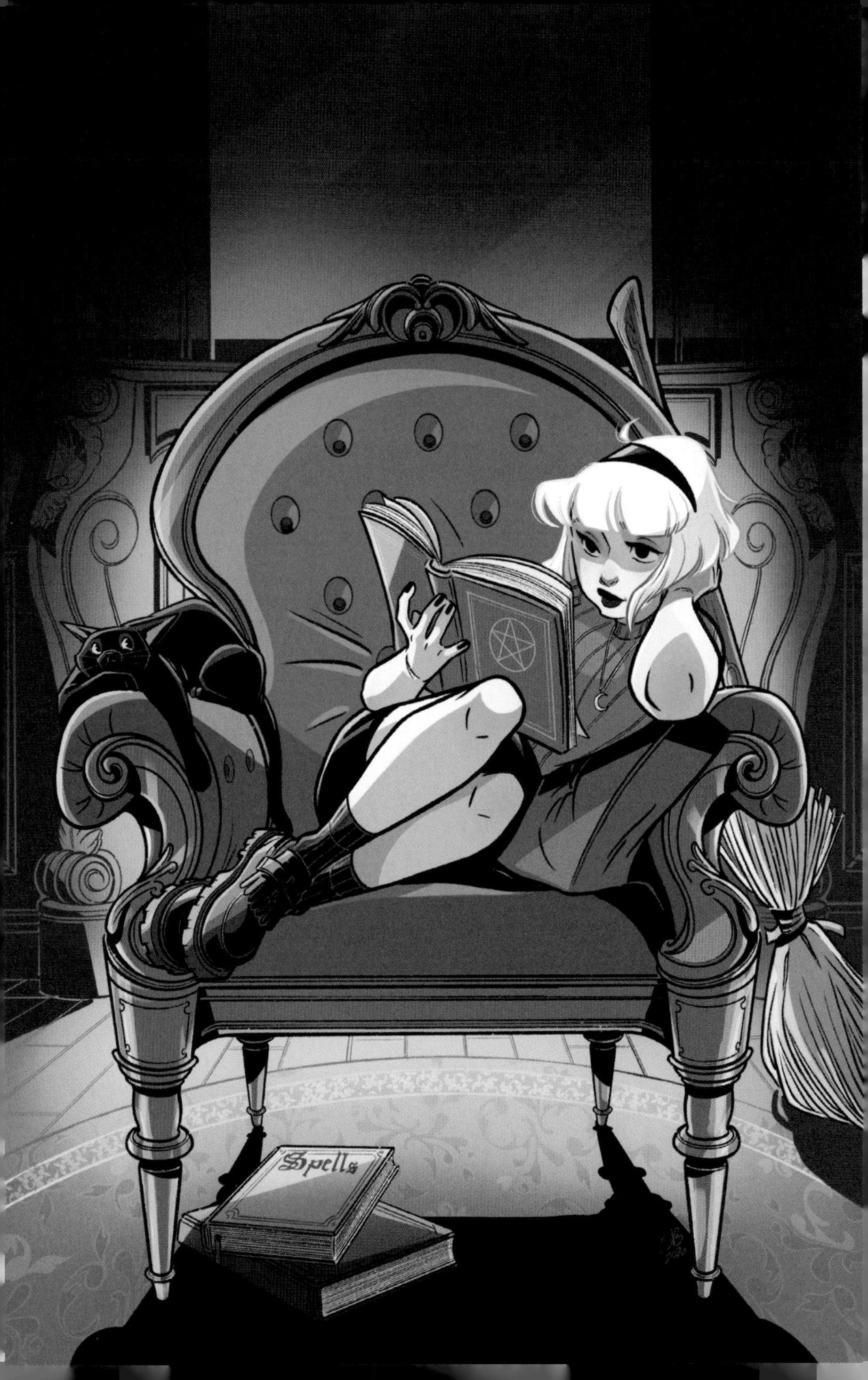
Spells

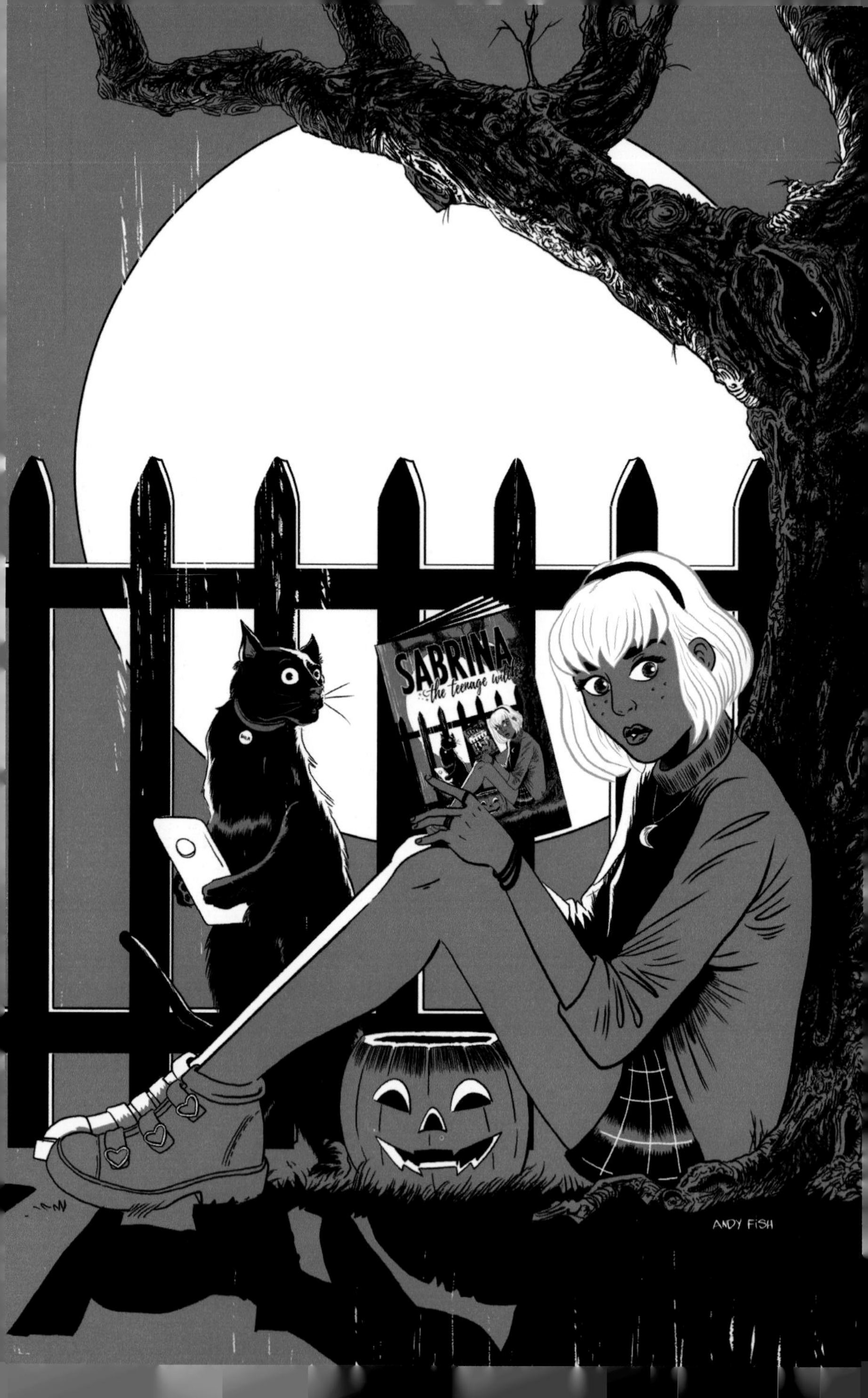
SABRINA
ANDY FISH

SABRINA the teenage witch™

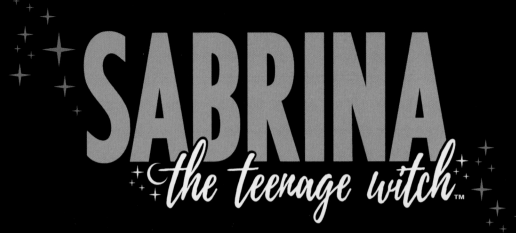

SKETCH GALLERY

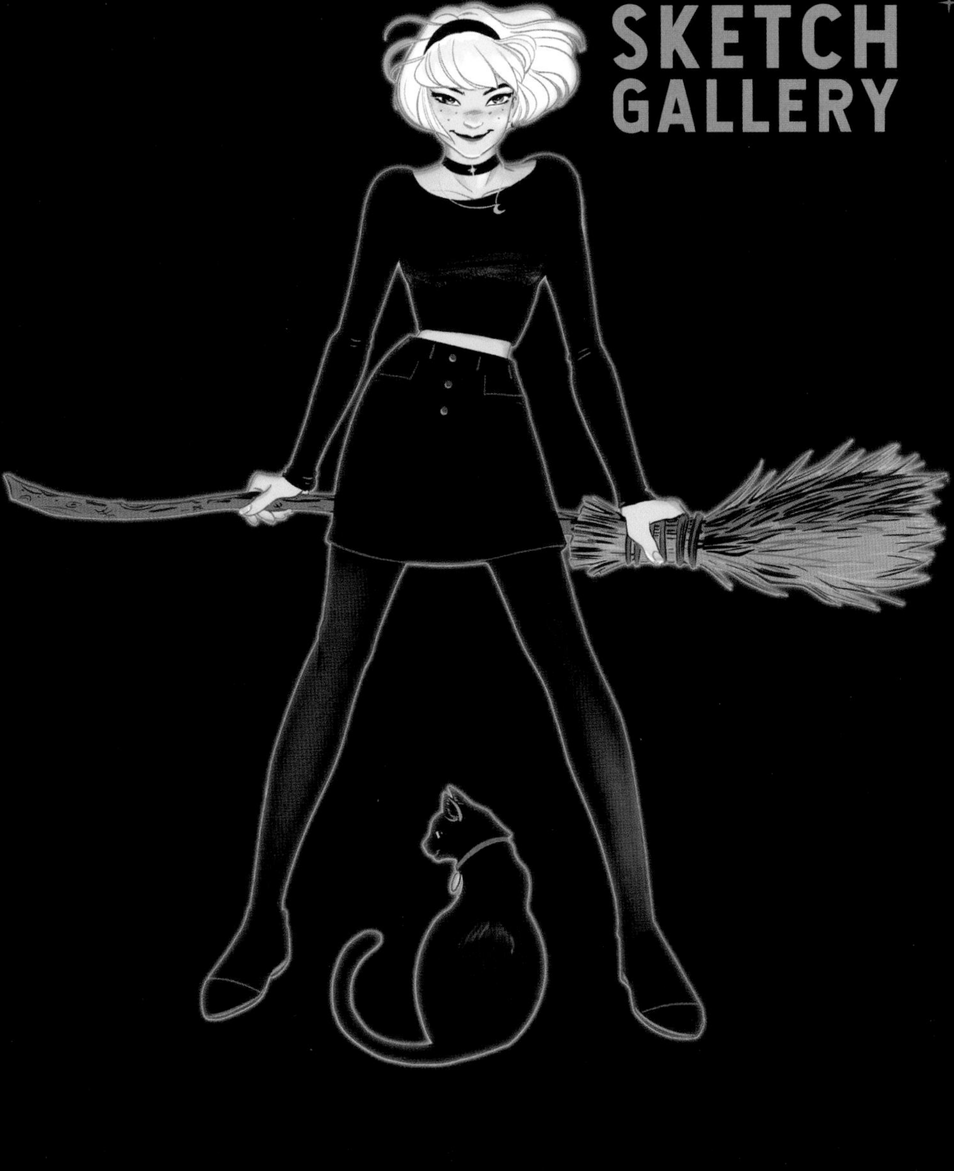

VERONICA FISH
COVER OPTIONS

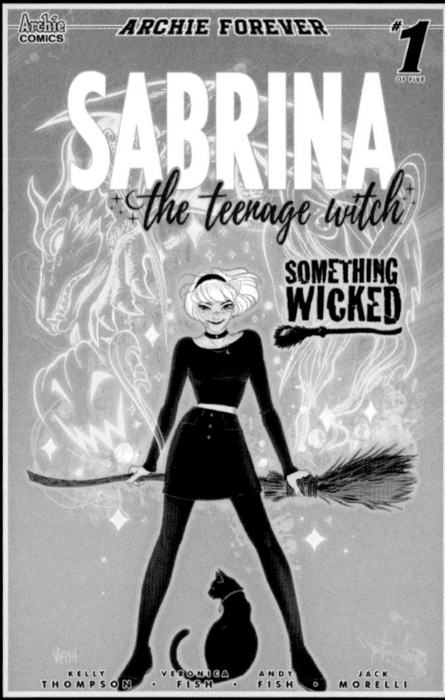
Archie COMICS
ARCHIE FOREVER
#1 OF FIVE
SABRINA
the teenage witch
SOMETHING WICKED
KELLY THOMPSON • VERONICA FISH • ANDY FISH • JACK MORELLI

FINAL COVER

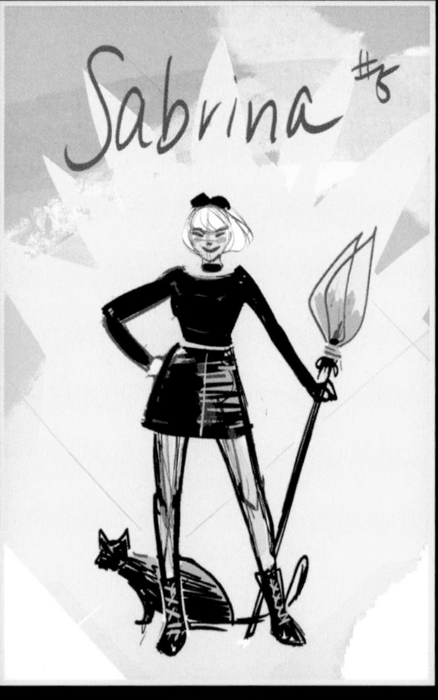
Sabrina #5

OPTION 1

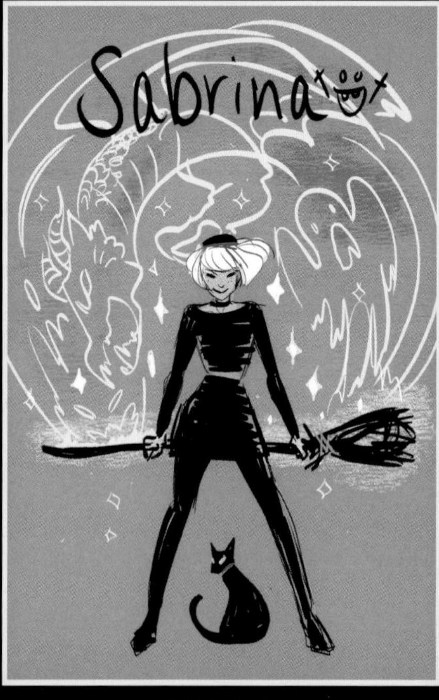
Sabrina

OPTION 2

SWEENEY BOO
COVER OPTIONS

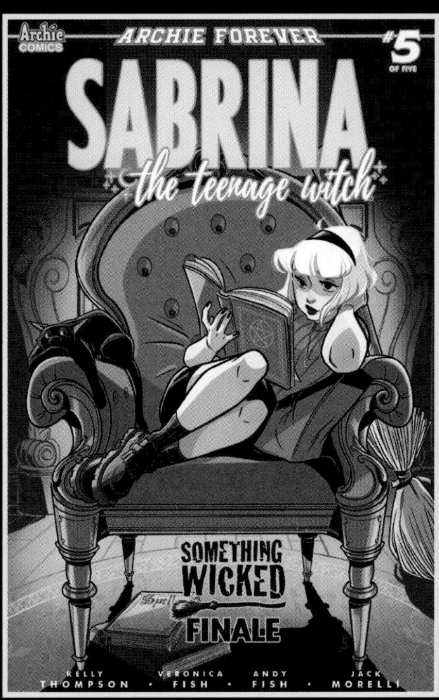
Archie COMICS
ARCHIE FOREVER
#5 OF FIVE
SABRINA
the teenage witch
SOMETHING WICKED
FINALE
Spells
KELLY THOMPSON • VERONICA FISH • ANDY FISH • JACK MORELLI

FINAL COVER

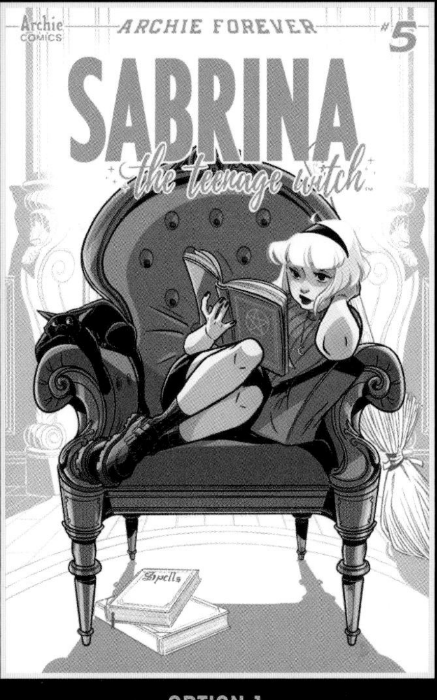
Archie COMICS
ARCHIE FOREVER
#5
SABRINA
the teenage witch
Spells

OPTION 1

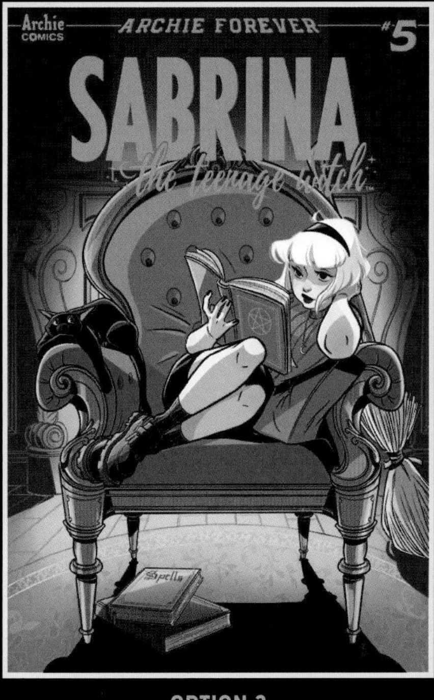
Archie COMICS
ARCHIE FOREVER
#5
SABRINA
the teenage witch
Spells

OPTION 2

AMBROSE CHARACTER SKETCHES

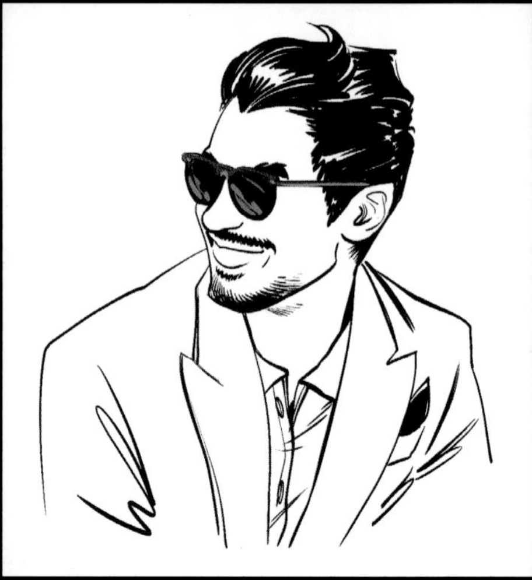

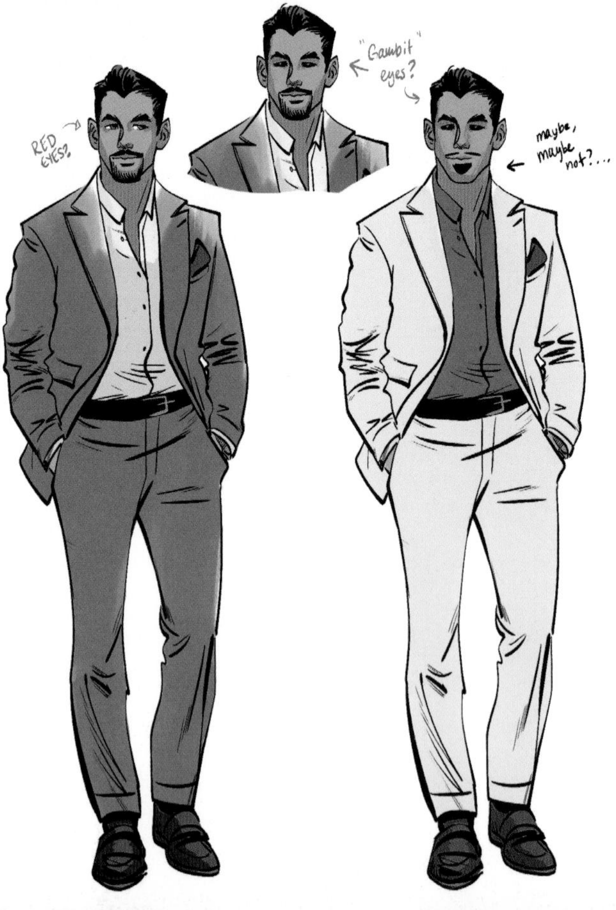

RED EYES?
"Gambit" eyes?
maybe, maybe not?...

BONUS COMIC

This original graphic novel, written by Micol Ostow and illustratec by Thomas Pitilli, features the world of The CW's *Riverdale*! Fou interconnected stories trap each of our main characters in c unique high-stakes conflict over the course of a few pressure cooker hours! Will Archie and company even make it to sunrise? f they do, will they ever be the same again?

ART BY	ART BY	LETTERING BY	COLORS BY
MICOL OSTOW	THOMAS PITILLI	JOHN WORKMAN	ANDRE SZYMANOWICZ

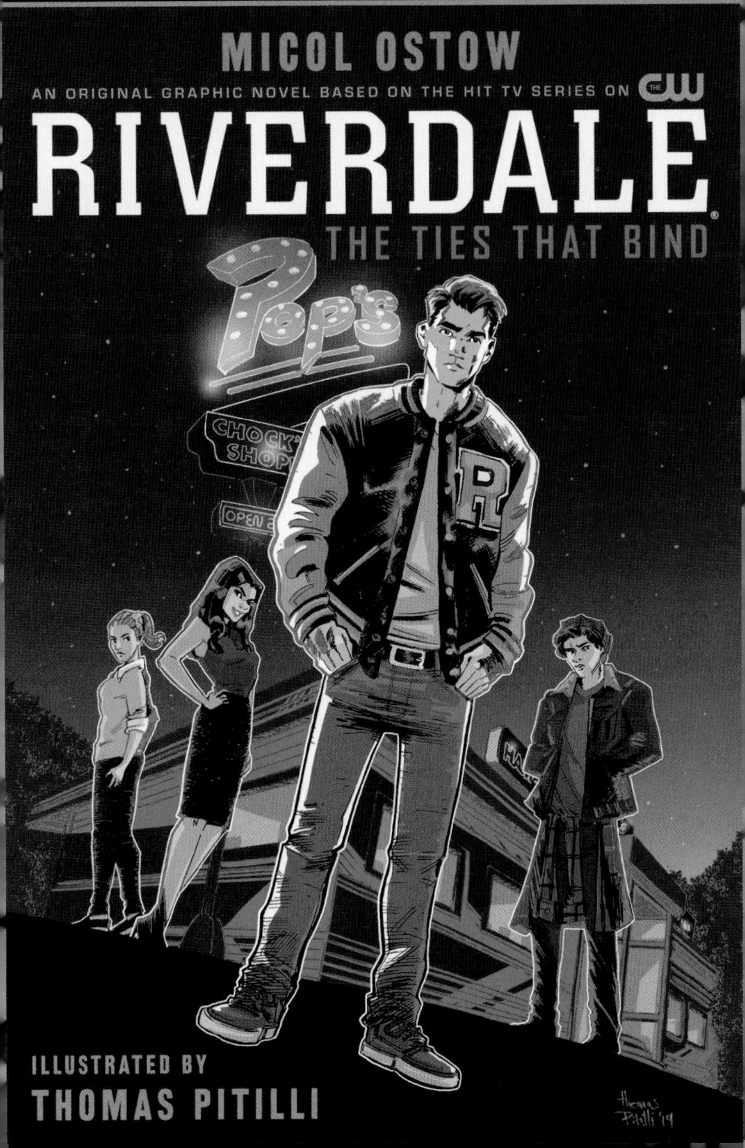
MICOL OSTOW
AN ORIGINAL GRAPHIC NOVEL BASED ON THE HIT TV SERIES ON THE CW
RIVERDALE®
THE TIES THAT BIND
Pop's
ILLUSTRATED BY
THOMAS PITILLI

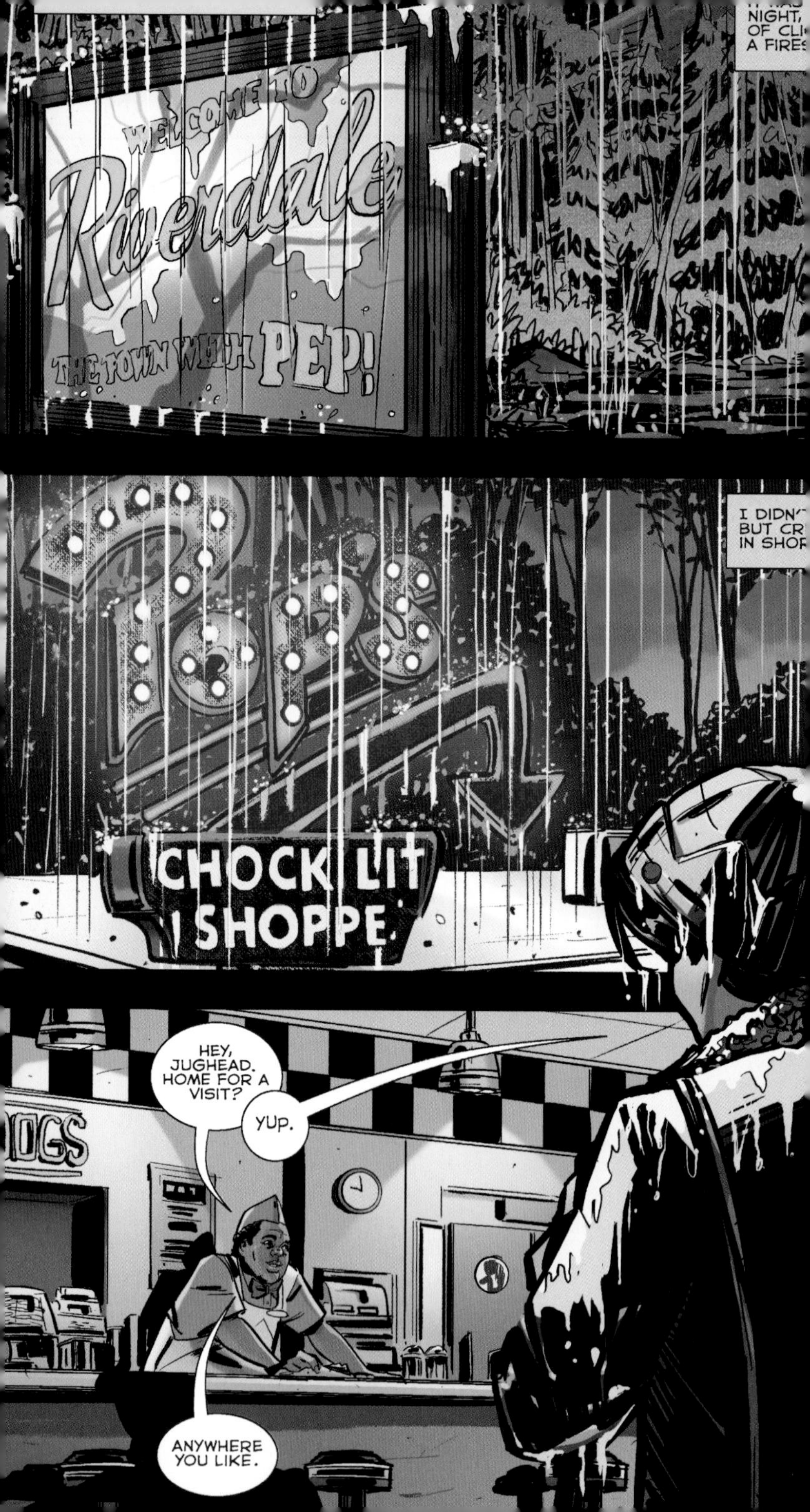

WELCOME TO
Riverdale
THE TOWN WITH PEP!
CHOCK LIT
SHOPPE
HEY, JUGHEAD. HOME FOR A VISIT?
YUP.
ANYWHERE YOU LIKE.

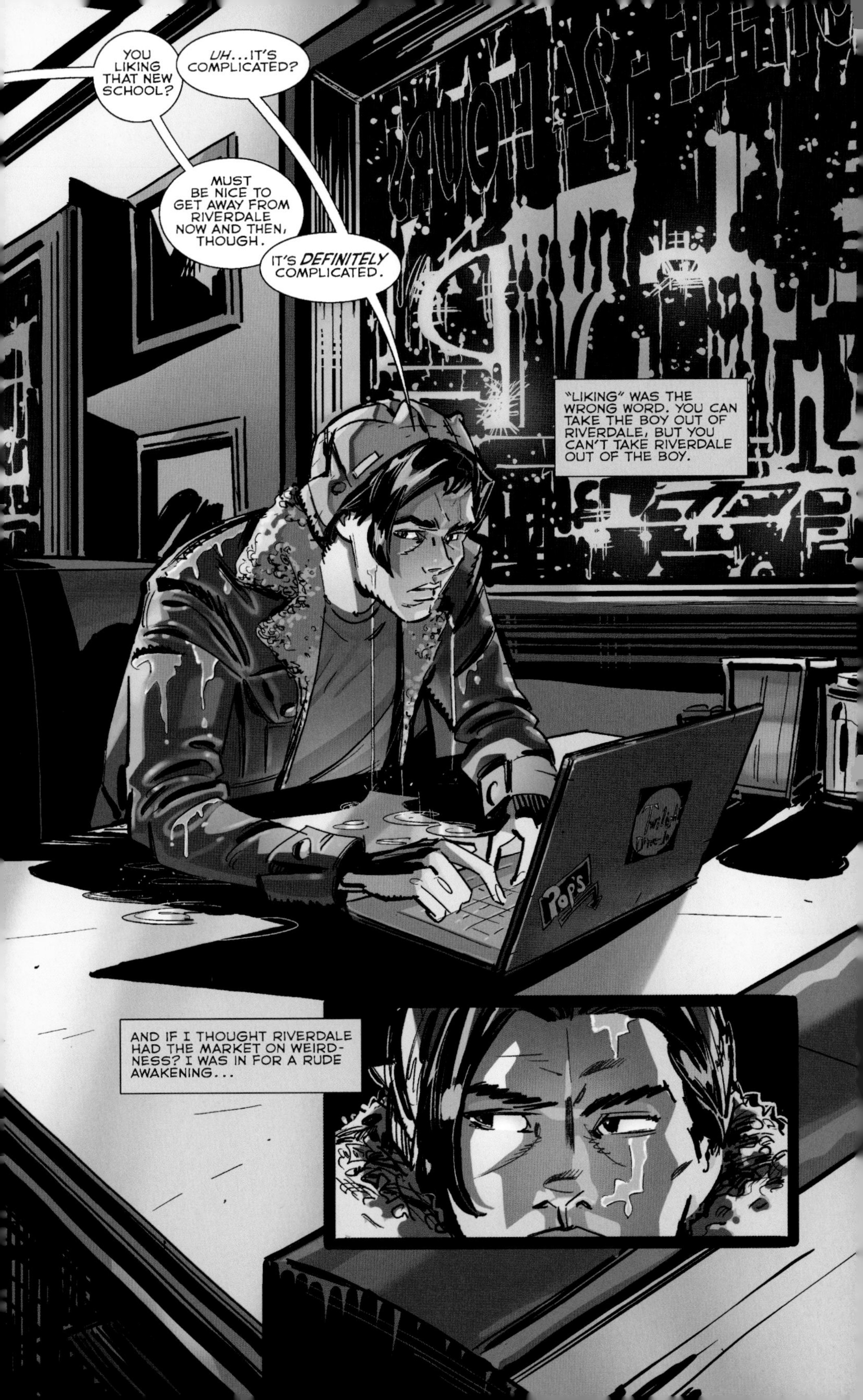
YOU LIKING THAT NEW SCHOOL?
UH...IT'S COMPLICATED?
MUST BE NICE TO GET AWAY FROM RIVERDALE NOW AND THEN, THOUGH.
IT'S *DEFINITELY* COMPLICATED.
"LIKING" WAS THE WRONG WORD. YOU CAN TAKE THE BOY OUT OF RIVERDALE, BUT YOU CAN'T TAKE RIVERDALE OUT OF THE BOY.
Pop's
AND IF I THOUGHT RIVERDALE HAD THE MARKET ON WEIRD-NESS? I WAS IN FOR A RUDE AWAKENING...

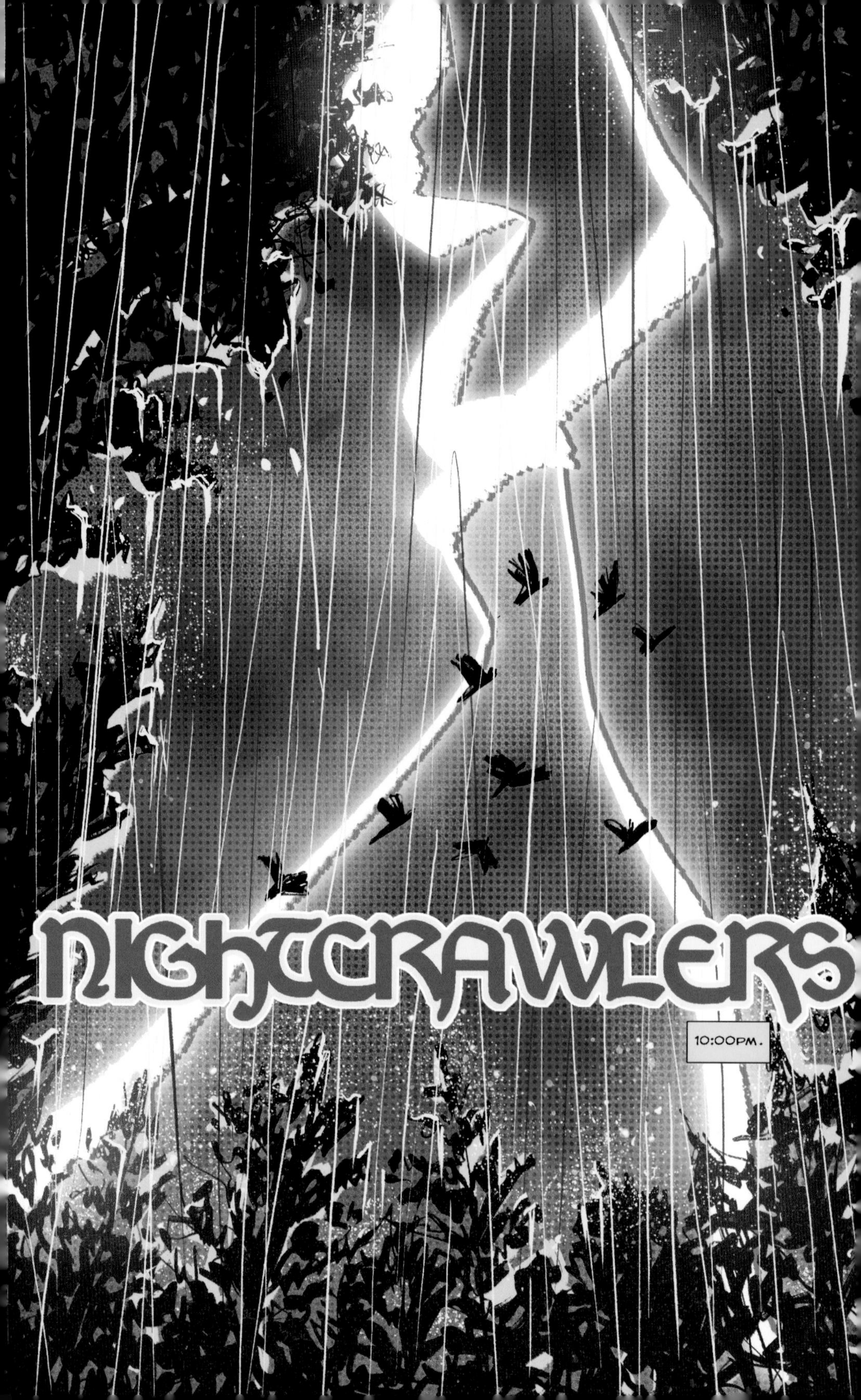
NIGHTCRAWLERS
10:00PM.

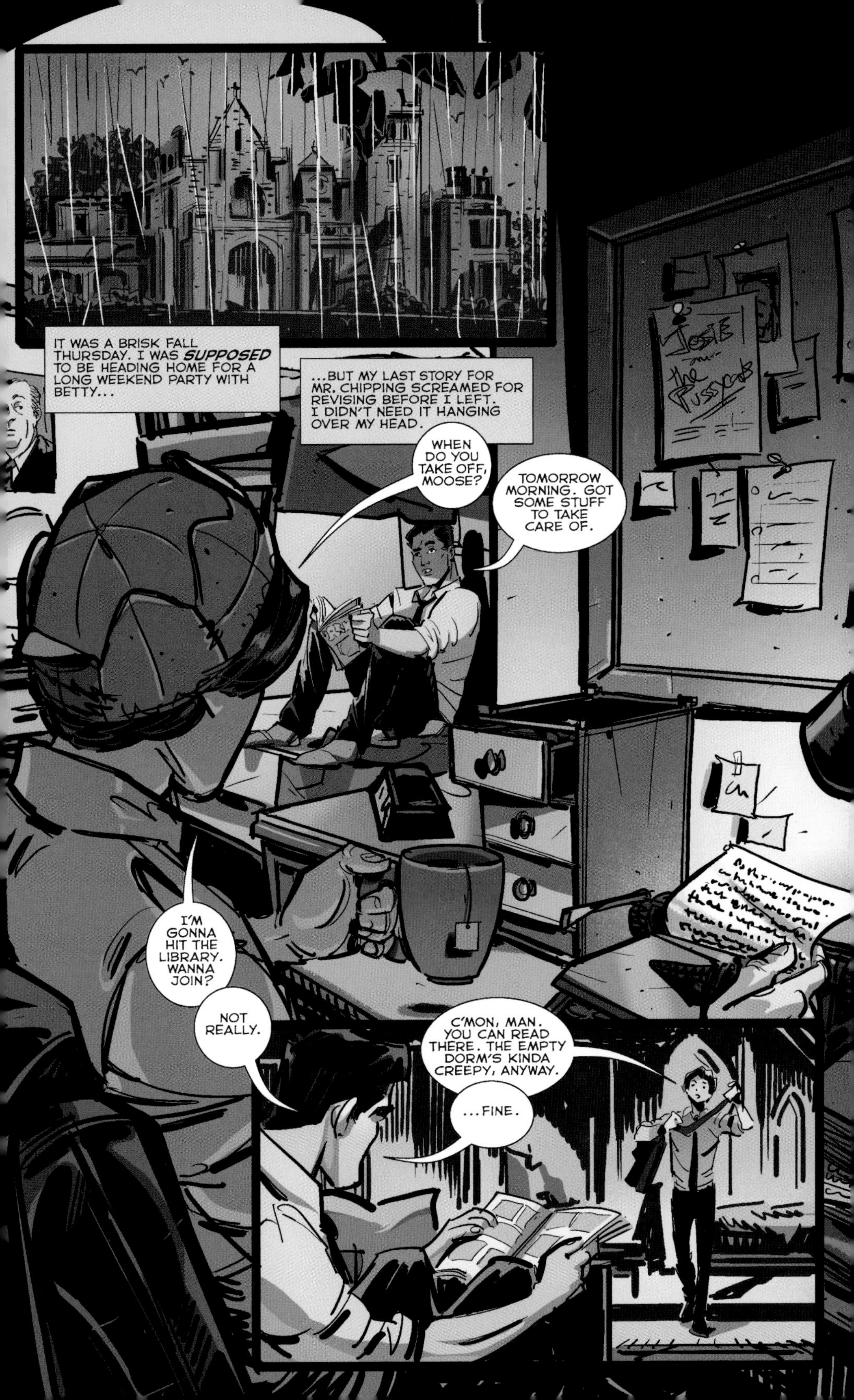
IT WAS A BRISK FALL THURSDAY. I WAS SUPPOSED TO BE HEADING HOME FOR A LONG WEEKEND PARTY WITH BETTY...
...BUT MY LAST STORY FOR MR. CHIPPING SCREAMED FOR REVISING BEFORE I LEFT. I DIDN'T NEED IT HANGING OVER MY HEAD.
WHEN DO YOU TAKE OFF, MOOSE?
TOMORROW MORNING. GOT SOME STUFF TO TAKE CARE OF.
I'M GONNA HIT THE LIBRARY. WANNA JOIN?
NOT REALLY.
C'MON, MAN. YOU CAN READ THERE. THE EMPTY DORM'S KINDA CREEPY, ANYWAY.
...FINE.

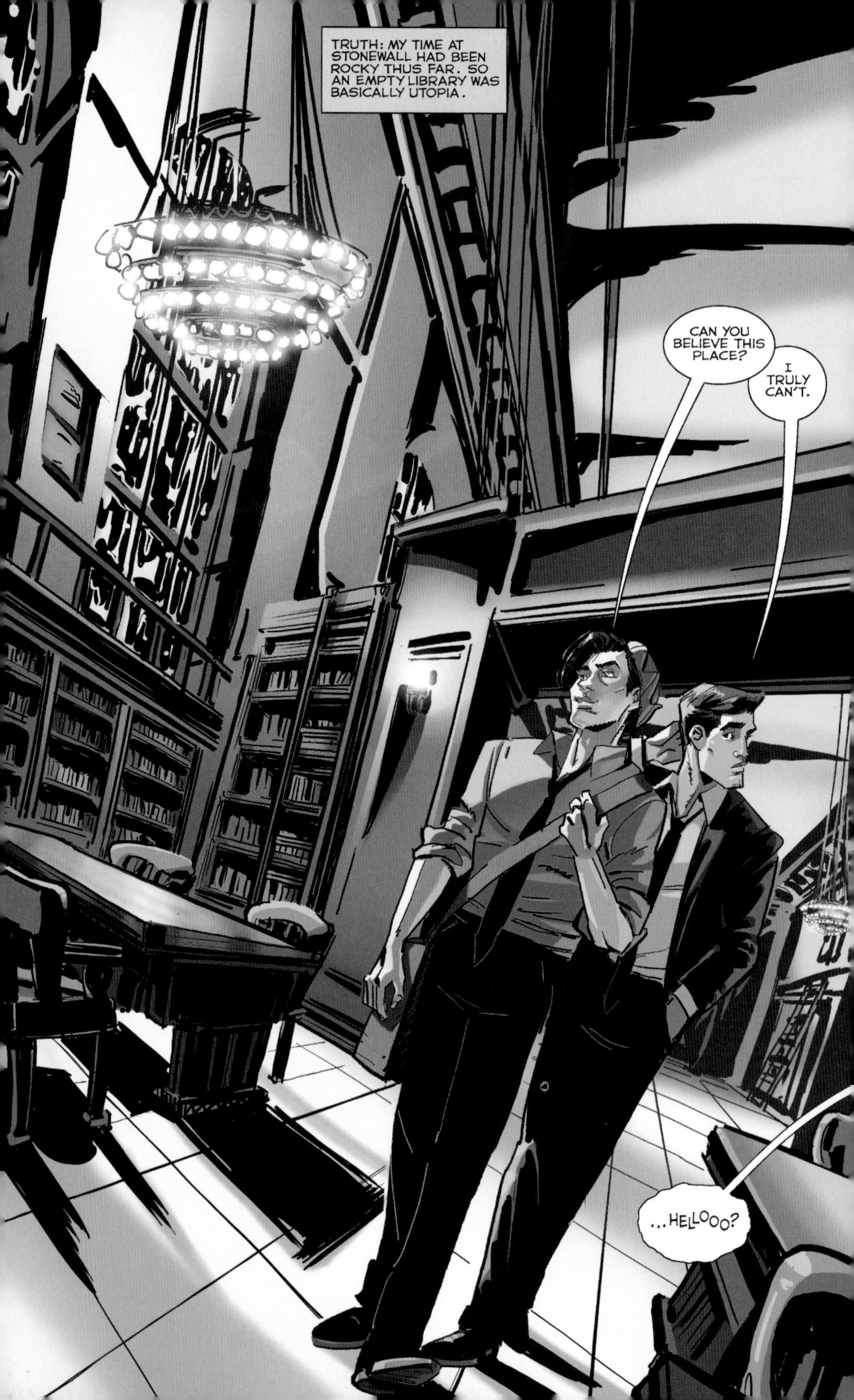
TRUTH: MY TIME AT STONEWALL HAD BEEN ROCKY THUS FAR. SO AN EMPTY LIBRARY WAS BASICALLY UTOPIA.
CAN YOU BELIEVE THIS PLACE?
I TRULY CAN'T.
...HELLOOO?

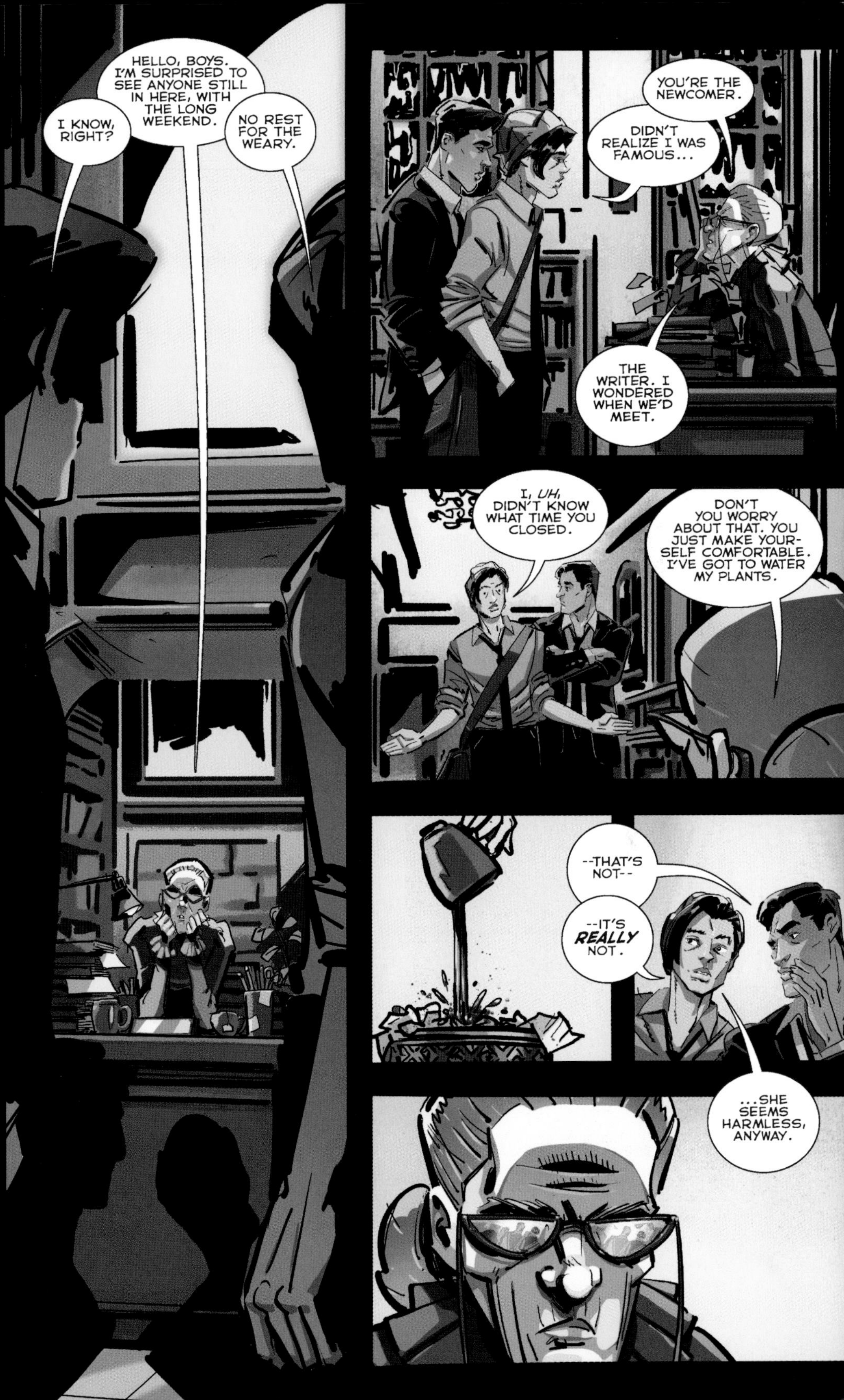
HELLO, BOYS. I'M SURPRISED TO SEE ANYONE STILL IN HERE, WITH THE LONG WEEKEND.
I KNOW, RIGHT?
NO REST FOR THE WEARY.
YOU'RE THE NEWCOMER.
DIDN'T REALIZE I WAS FAMOUS...
THE WRITER. I WONDERED WHEN WE'D MEET.
I, *UH*, DIDN'T KNOW WHAT TIME YOU CLOSED.
DON'T YOU WORRY ABOUT THAT. YOU JUST MAKE YOUR-SELF COMFORTABLE. I'VE GOT TO WATER MY PLANTS.
--THAT'S NOT--
--IT'S ***REALLY*** NOT.
...SHE SEEMS HARMLESS, ANYWAY.

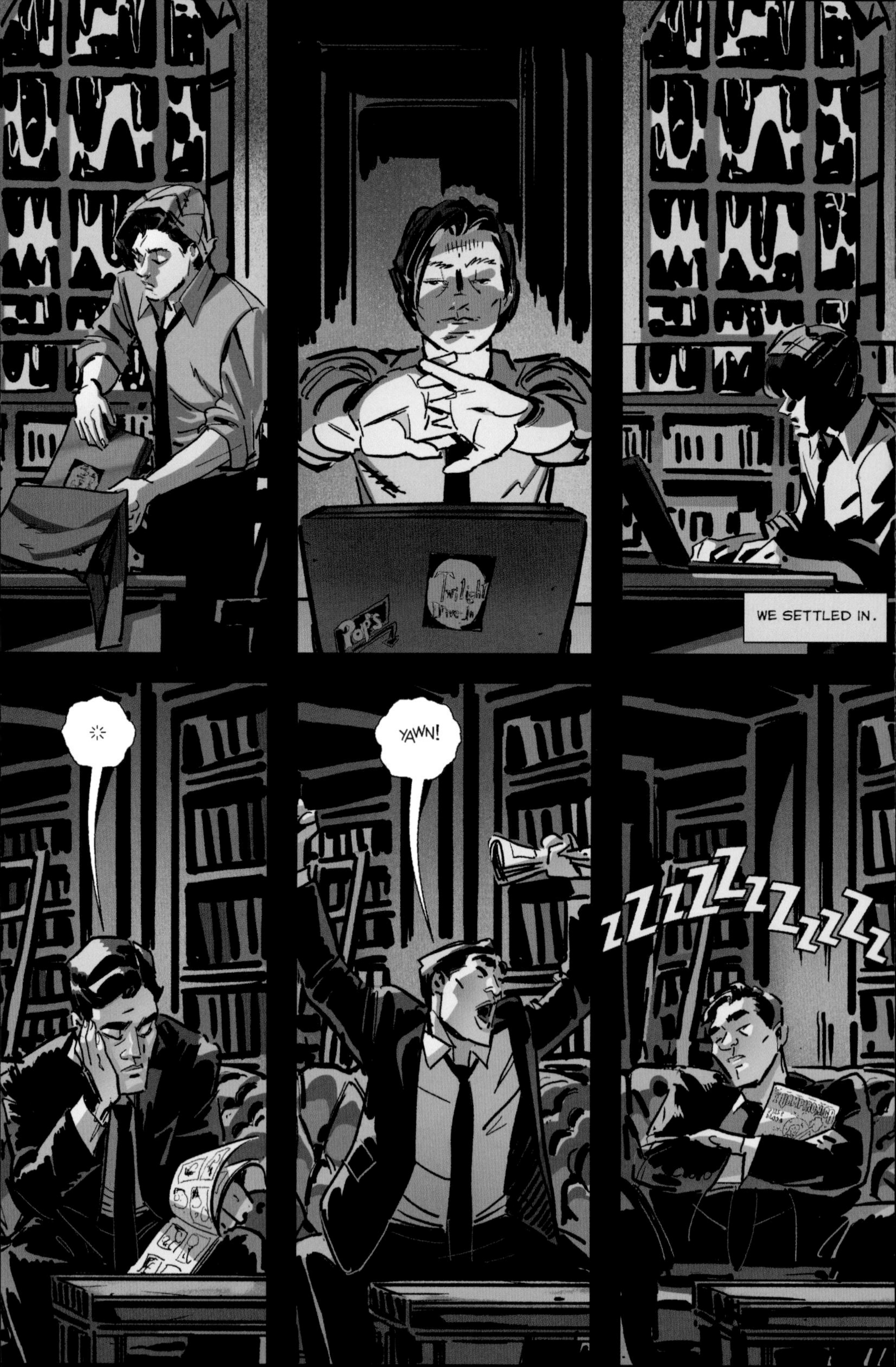
WE SETTLED IN.
YAWN!
ZZZZZZZZZZZZ

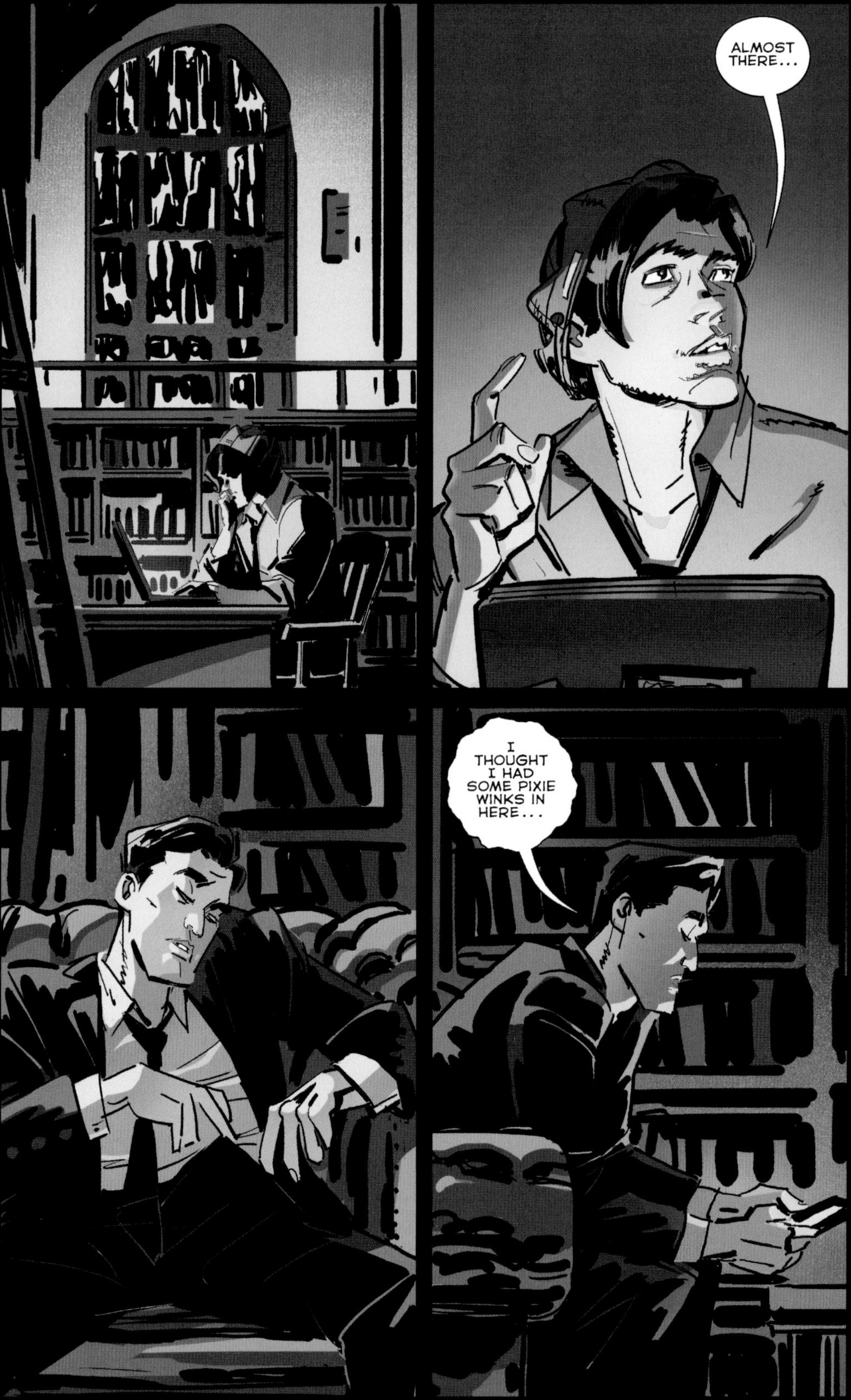
ALMOST THERE...
I THOUGHT I HAD SOME PIXIE WINKS IN HERE...

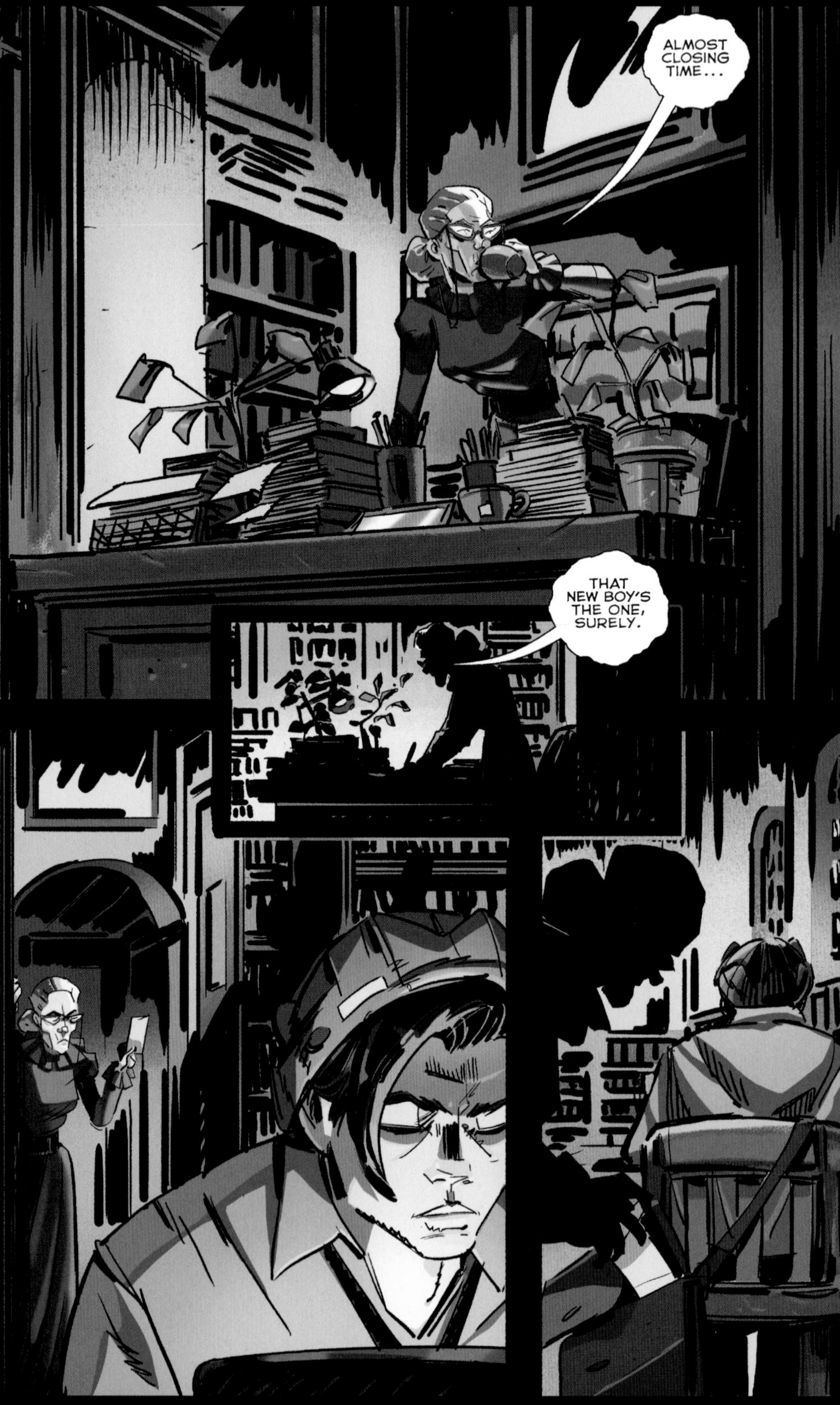
ALMOST CLOSING TIME...
THAT NEW BOY'S THE ONE, SURELY.

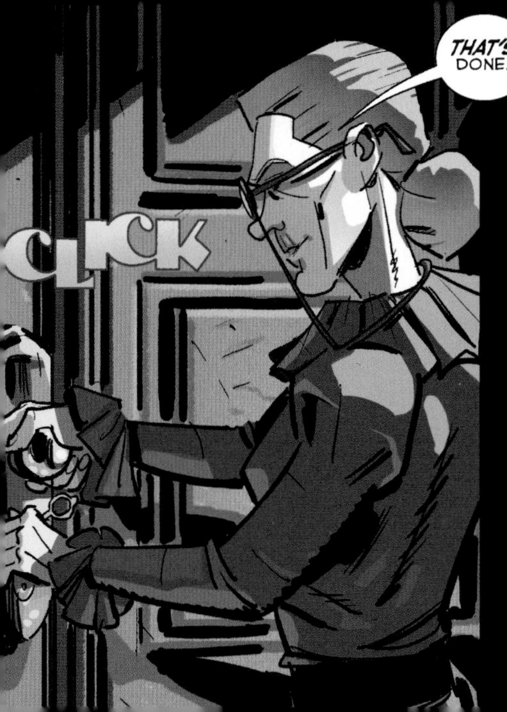
THAT'S DONE!
CLICK

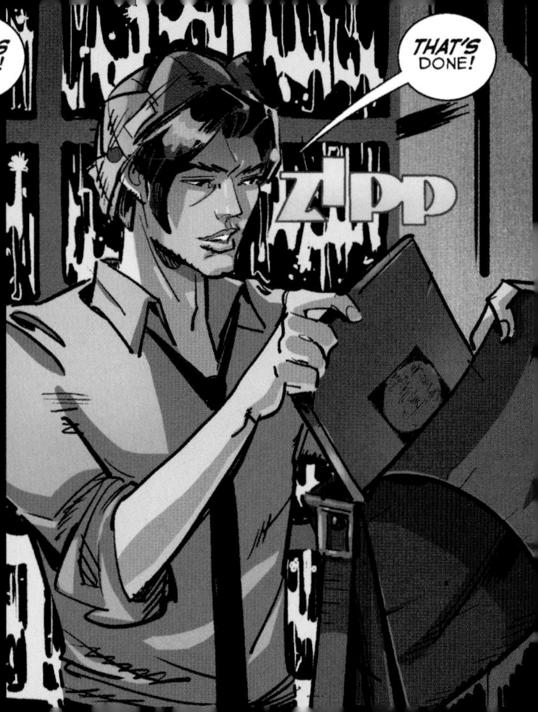
THAT'S DONE!
ZIPP

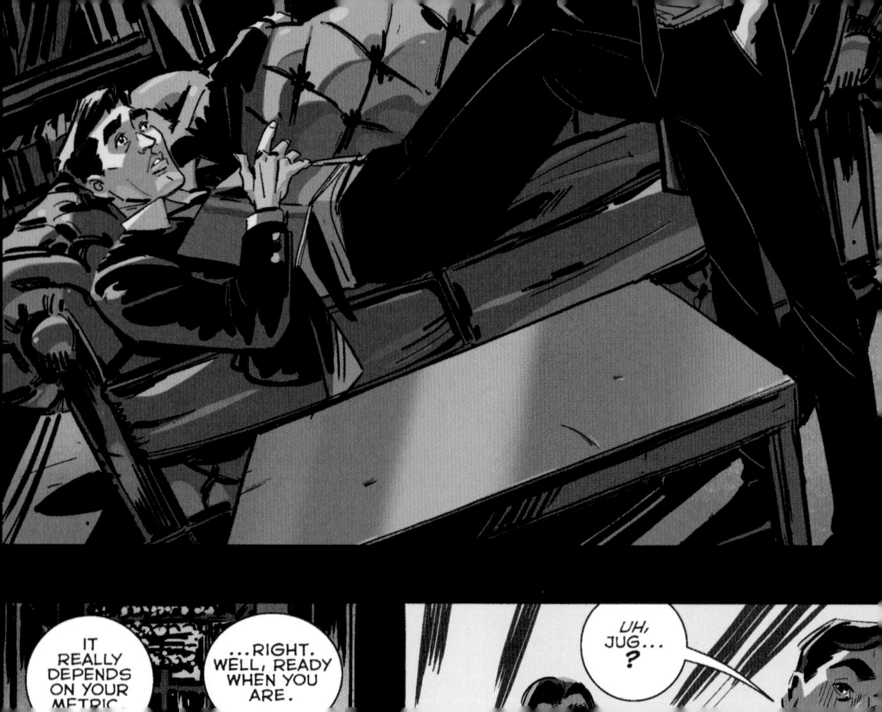
IT REALLY DEPENDS ON YOUR
...RIGHT. WELL, READY WHEN YOU ARE.
UH, JUG...?

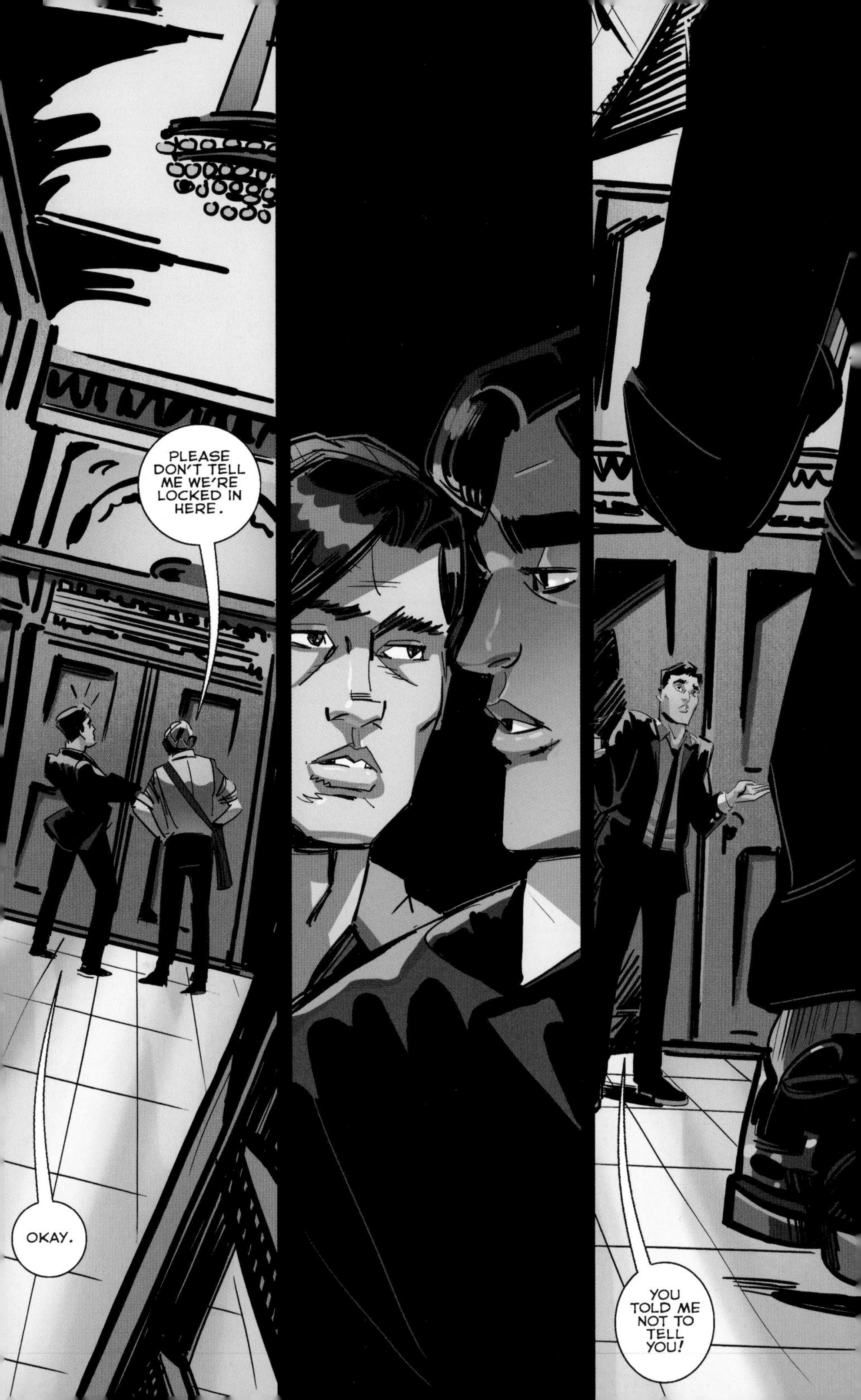
PLEASE DON'T TELL ME WE'RE LOCKED IN HERE.
OKAY.
YOU TOLD ME NOT TO TELL YOU!

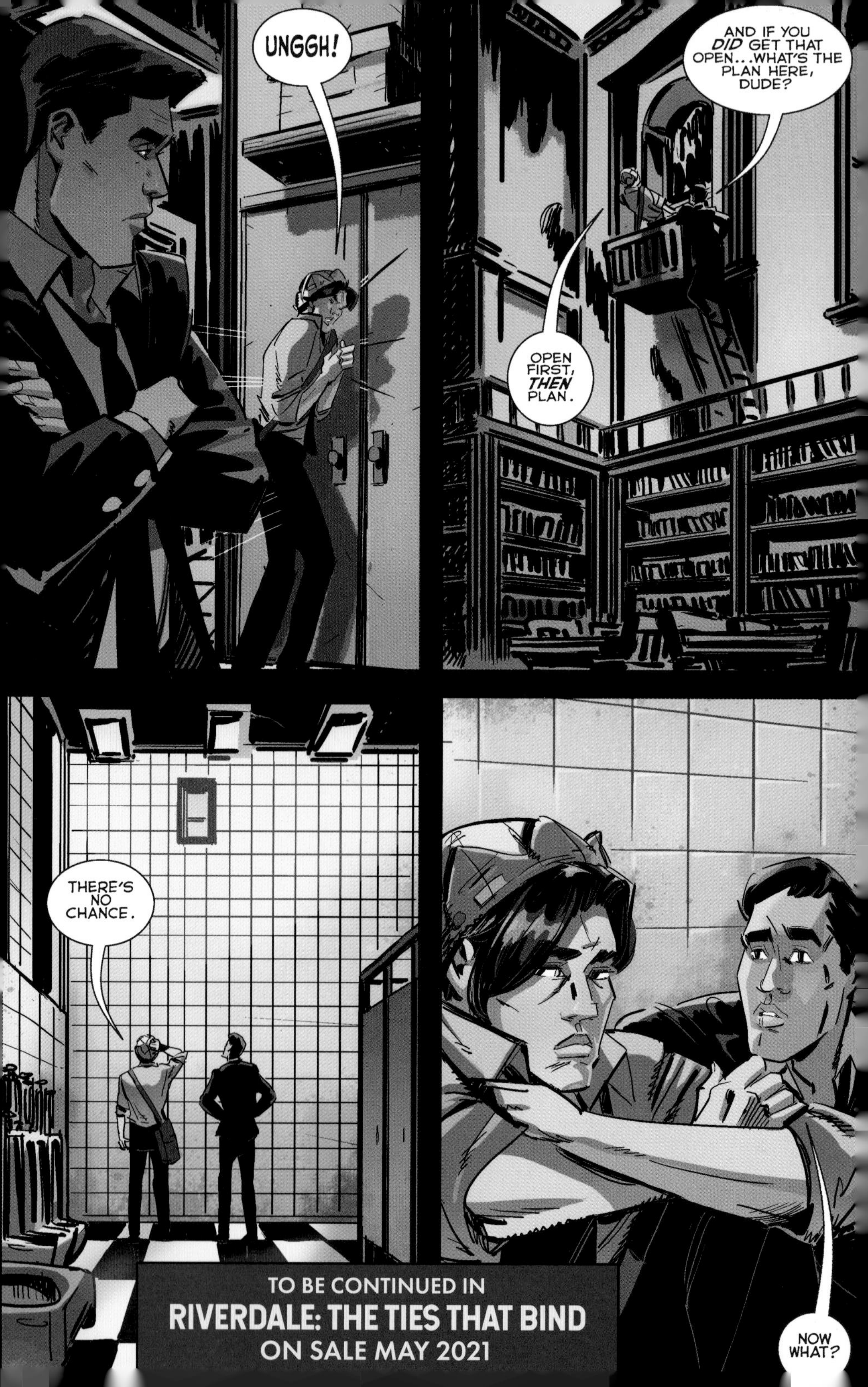
UNGGH!
AND IF YOU *DID* GET THAT OPEN...WHAT'S THE PLAN HERE, DUDE?
OPEN FIRST, *THEN* PLAN.
THERE'S NO CHANCE.
NOW WHAT?
TO BE CONTINUED IN
RIVERDALE: THE TIES THAT BIND
ON SALE MAY 2021